OF A STRANGER

A large hand suddenly clamped over Anne's mouth and a strong arm banded around her waist. He drew her into a dark corner and leaned against the wall, keeping her flush against him. She could feel his hard chest against her back, his muscled thigh against her buttocks. He was warm and smelled of brandy and smoking tobacco.

"Your spirit tells you to fight, but your mind and heart tell you that I won't hurt you. *N'est-ce pas*, mademoiselle?"

Anne nodded.

"*Bon*. You are a sensible girl. But still I cannot release you till I know for sure that my friends have gotten away safely. I have the best task of all, keeping you busy while my compatriots do the work, eh? *Mon Dieu*, you feel good in my arms!"

He loomed above her, a tall, broad-shouldered man dressed entirely in black. He was like a shadow, blending into the darkness.

"Who are you?" she whispered.

He didn't answer, but his mouth curved in a small, wry, tender smile—and then he kissed her . . .

ARMS OF A STRANGER

DANICE ALLEN

AVON BOOKS ◆ NEW YORK

ARMS OF A STRANGER is an original publication of Avon Books. This work has never before appeared in book form. This work is a novel. Any similarity to actual persons or events is purely coincidental.

AVON BOOKS
A division of
The Hearst Corporation
1350 Avenue of the Americas
New York, New York 10019

Copyright © 1995 by Danice Allen
Inside cover author photo by Steve Ducher
Published by arrangement with the author
Library of Congress Catalog Card Number: 94-94476
ISBN: 0-380-77726-6

First Avon Books Printing: January 1995

AVON TRADEMARK REG U.S. PAT. OFF. AND IN OTHER COUNTRIES, MARCA REGISTRADA, HECHO EN U.S.A.

Printed in the U.S.A.

RA 10 9 8 7 6 5 4 3 2

With warmest affection to my mom-in-law, Simone Allen.
Thanks for paying off my first computer.
And thanks for being brave enough to
come to America forty years ago.
Bons Baisers

Chapter 1

September 1841

"Isn't this heaven, Uncle Reggie?" Anne crossed her arms and leaned on the brass rail of the steamboat, gazing at the passing scenery of the Mississippi state coast as they glided through the calm waters of Mobile Bay. Just around the bend was Biloxi, and by tomorrow morning they'd land at New Orleans. Dusk was tracing the distant island forests in vivid pink, the reflection in the water cooled to a softer golden-mauve. The steamboat's giant paddle wheel churned a soothing rhythm, filling the air with a fine mist. A cool breeze ruffled through the blond curls that escaped Anne's bonnet.

It had been several weeks since she, Uncle Reggie, Aunt Katherine, and a handful of servants had set sail from Dover, England. After leaving the harbor at New York, they'd changed vessels three times. At Charleston, they'd boarded the *Belvedere*, an ornate three-deck riverboat with huge golden-crowned smokestacks. It was like a luxury hotel on water, with ever-changing scenery to take your breath away.

"I admit, Anne, 'tis pleasant to look upon from a distance," Reggie conceded reluctantly. "However, I shudder to think what wild beasts and

1

reptiles may make their nests in that lush greenery."

"Don't be a milquetoast, Reggie," chided Katherine in her deep, no-nonsense voice. "Every Eden must have its serpent."

Anne's two chaperones stood, like formidable bookends, on either side of her. Though of slightly more than medium height herself, she had to look up to observe their faces. At sixty-two, Reggie was lean, dapper, and dignified. He had iron-gray hair, a large nose, and a drooping walruslike mustache, and he wore small, round-rimmed spectacles. He was her father's bachelor brother, and he had lived at Weston Hall in Surrey with her family for as long as Anne could remember. She and her four older sisters loved the old fusspot dearly, as he took a lively interest in all their concerns.

With her plain bonnet on, Katherine was nearly as tall as Reggie. Of an angular build, except for her imposing bosom, she could best be described as handsome. She had a broad forehead, piercing gray eyes, and straight, resolute features. She stood rigidly linear at all times, usually gripping in her left hand a cherrywood cane that she didn't need in the least, except for the purpose of none-too-subtle intimidation.

Katherine was Anne's mother's sister, and the family considered her to be quite eccentric. She'd outlived three husbands already—all of them American—the last one the New Orleans banker Samuel Grimms, whom she had met while they were both on safari in Africa. She dressed with elegant, severe simplicity, disdaining feathers and ribbons as unseemly decoration for a woman on the shady side of fifty.

Katherine was well-educated, innately intelligent, and extremely opinionated. She and Reggie had been at daggers-drawn since the moment the steamer had set sail from England, and, in truth, since the moment they'd first met. Every few years or so, Katherine traveled from America to visit her relatives in England, and each time she and Reggie were compelled to spend time together, their mutual animosity blossomed.

"And every Eden must have its tart-tongued Eve, I suppose," Reggie retorted, "forever tempting one to eat the forbidden fruit." Reggie gave his mustache an agitated tug.

Katherine rapped her cane against the polished wood floor of the deck. "Simpleton! Eve was only doing what was necessary! She couldn't live forever in a state of ignorance with that sniveling, unquestioning Adam! They'd never have populated the earth if they hadn't finally observed that they were naked as jaybirds and got on with the . . . the . . ." She waved her cane in the air. ". . . conception thing! She was opening Adam's eyes to the real world, Reginald, much as I'm doing for Anne."

"I was raised to believe that women should be protected from the 'real world'!" Reggie declared with another tug.

"I know you consider *me* the Eve of this particular Eden," Katherine continued, as if Reggie hadn't said a word, "and that I'm taking Anne—as you so like to say—'out of the garden and into Babylon.' But, ye Gods, Reginald, she's twenty-three years old! Hardly a babe!"

"Thank you, Aunt," Anne murmured dryly.

" 'Twas time Anne saw something beyond the gates of Weston Hall and London during the Season, where she was surrounded by fops who called themselves men, but who did nothing more manly than preen and pose in front of a looking glass. I dareswear I don't know how she stood it for five years."

Anne saw Reggie stiffen. He considered Katherine's frequent swipes at British manhood downright unpatriotic.

"Please, Aunt Katherine," Anne implored, "you know Reggie doesn't like it when you malign our fellow countrymen."

"Damned good men, too," muttered Reggie. "Pluck to the backbone. Fops don't beat monsters like Napoleon, y'know."

"Anne said it herself—and don't contradict me, niece! She said she wanted to go to a country where men were *men*, not sycophants living off their fathers' money or their wives' dowry. Men who have a purpose in life, with something more important to do than wager, womanize, gossip, and dance."

When Reggie gave his niece a hurt look from beneath his bushy, protruding eyebrows, Anne hastily explained, "I did not mean to imply that *all* English men were made of such frippery stuff, Uncle, but most of the men I met during the London Season *were* a trifle shallow. They seemed much more concerned with the cut of their coat than the cast of their character."

"You can't fault a man for endeavoring to look his best, niece. I daresay you'd shun a man who didn't take pains with his appearance. You wouldn't want to be seen with the fellow!"

"I'm not talking about neatness and good grooming," Anne said seriously. "I'd expect that of anyone, male or female. But it seems to me that there's a direct correlation between how many frills, fobs, and furbelows a man wears on his person and how many serious, original thoughts pass through his brain. The more fuss there is to a man's dress, the less real substance there is to the man himself. In my experience, it is a theory which has proven true time and again."

"Then I wonder that you choose New Orleans to find a husband," Reggie persisted. " 'Tis my understanding that most Creole men fairly dote on the pastimes of wagering, womanizing, gossiping, and dancing."

"She chose New Orleans because *I* live there, and I'm her only relative in America," said Katherine, looking at Reggie as if he were a nitwit. "Her reasoning is self-evident. And what better place is there to find a husband than New Orleans? I will admit that the Creole society does have its share of frippery fellows, and Anne will be obliged to meet and converse with several, but the city is brimming with *real* men, as well. I should know ... having had three m'self. The best thing I ever did was leave England."

If Reggie was of a mind to made a sarcastic retort to Katherine's last statement, he stifled it. He stared straight ahead, his lips clamped tightly together. Anne was grateful for his restraint. She knew from past experience that an argument between her two guardians could last for hours.

Anne wrapped her hands around Reggie's arm and leaned close to him. "Uncle, here's a diverting thought for you. To continue the biblical analogies, let's just say you're my guardian angel, sent to keep me safe from the sins and snakes of Louisiana!"

"There's truth to that," Reggie informed her in a softened tone. "Your parents would never have allowed you to come if *I* hadn't agreed to accompany you."

Sharp-eared and always listening, Katherine said, "Anne didn't need her parents' permission. She's a grown woman. She controls her own money—a fortune, I might add. She doesn't need a guardian, either. She has me."

Reggie sighed heavily, trying manfully to disregard yet another of Katherine's interruptions. "I'm happy to be of service to you, Anne, as you know. And always glad to show my affection and respect for your parents by helping out where I can. But, I daresay, this shall be the longest year of my life. Heaven, you say? *Hell*, rather."

Anne squeezed his arm and clicked her tongue consolingly. "No, don't say that. It's truly beautiful here, and everything is so exciting and new. It's nothing like we're used to."

"Precisely," sulked Reggie.

"Things will improve. We've been too much together on this long trip. You and Aunt Katherine needn't spend so much time together once we've arrived." Anne felt the strained muscles in his arm loosen a little. "And remember, while 'tis true that I didn't need my parents' permission to come to America, and I could have refused your chaperonage, your coming along has made them much easier about me. For that I'm very grateful."

Reggie's furrowed brow relaxed. She had managed to soothe his nettled nerves for perhaps the hundredth time that week alone. Silently she added, *Yes, your presence has made my parents easier, Uncle, but I still intend to do exactly as I please.*

Hoping the respite from arguing would last, Anne turned her attention back to the landscape. "Look at those beautiful trees, Uncle Reggie. The captain identified some of them for me. That's a sycamore, there's a pecan, and those flowered ones—"

"Magnolias," Katherine instructed.

"And the Spanish moss looks like the long, soft beards of old men, doesn't it? Those vines climbing up the trees, are they—?"

Reggie said, "Yes, it's wild honeysuckle, which accounts, in part, for the incredible sweetness of the air, I suppose."

"I love honeysuckle!" Anne said with enthusiasm, winning a genuine smile from Reggie. Relieved to see Reggie's equanimity restored, Anne turned to her aunt and gave her a remonstrative look, as if to say, *Why do you make me work so hard to keep the peace?* Katherine merely shrugged and laid her hands, one on top of the other, over the large golden globe at the top of her cane.

The waters were becoming more congested now as they approached the landing at Biloxi, Mississippi. There the *Belvedere* would restock firewood to fuel the engines, enough to get them to New Orleans by morning.

Anne would be glad to finally reach their destination. Though she'd taken to life on the ship and the ungainly steamboat like a born sailor, she'd had enough water travel to last her for a while. The landing was in view now, and the boat gave three mighty blasts from its smokestacks. Anne felt a thrill go through her. Every landing was exciting. She smiled to herself, for no other reason than the pure joy of living. She'd never been happier.

Lucien Delacroix watched the *Belvedere* pull alongside the dock, his eyelids drooping in appar-

ent boredom. In reality he was anything but bored.
He'd been visiting a horse farm in Biloxi, shopping for a new team of high-steppers for his town
carriage, when, by mere chance, he'd overheard
that Charles Bodine was transporting by steamboat a family of slaves he'd bought at auction that
day.

Lucien quickly rearranged his plans for returning to New Orleans, sending his carriage back by
land and purchasing himself a ticket on the *Belvedere*. If asked, he'd explain his change of plans by
confessing a hankering for the steamboat chef's
specialty of *pompano en creme*. No one would
doubt that the pleasure-loving, impetuous Lucien
Delacroix allowed his tastebuds to dictate his
travel plans.

Yes, there they were. In his peripheral vision,
Lucien saw Bodine and two of his most trusted
slaves herding a group of Negroes toward the
dock. He would not look directly at them; after all,
he shouldn't be expecting to see them, nor should
he exhibit any interest in something so common-
place as another plantation owner and his latest
purchases. But Lucien was determined that this
particular plantation owner would not get home
with his new slaves. That is, Renard, the Fox,
would see to it that he did not.

He concentrated on the steamboat, keeping his
posture as loose and casual as possible under the
circumstances, since every time he got near Bodine
his whole body tensed. Charles Bodine was a close
friend of his father's, but Lucien loathed the man.
As a boy, Lucien had learned through a deeply
painful personal experience just how cruel and li-
centious Bodine could be.

Most people were generally ignorant of the ex-
tent of Bodine's mistreatment of his slaves, but,

because of his underground connections, Lucien had heard every sordid story of murder and rape. These stories only added fuel to the consuming hatred that Lucien had felt ever since that devastating boyhood experience. He would do anything to keep another family of slaves from falling into Bodine's hands. This family had nothing to lose, everything to gain. The risks of escape were minuscule compared to the risk of permanent incarceration at Belle Fleur.

His gaze drifted lazily over the smattering of passengers lining the steamboat railing. Suddenly his eyes widened, his interest piqued. Virtually penned in by two tall elders—one a man he didn't know, and the other Katherine Grimms, returning from a visit to her sister's in England—stood a very fetching female.

Used to the waxen "magnolia" paleness of Creole women and the varying shades of brown in the Negro population, Lucien was attracted to the honey-gold complexion of this slim young woman in a scoop-shaped straw bonnet with yellow ribbons. He could tell she'd not minded her elders' admonitions to stay out of the sun, for though she wasn't unattractively sunburned, she had the delicate blush of a sun-kissed peach. Her hair, as pale and shiny as an English sovereign, was arranged in short ringlets at the sides and presumably bundled in a knot at the back.

She was wearing a straw-colored silk traveling gown with a long, pointed waist, dome skirt, high neckline with a lace collar, and long, tight sleeves. Her waist was tiny, making Lucien extremely curious about how much she depended on a corset to achieve such a result.

Fashion-wise, she was up-to-date but conservative. Thank God she did not appear to embrace the present popular philosophy of English femininity, the idea that quiet, anemic helplessness was appealing to the male sex. She fairly glowed with awareness of her surroundings, her very posture suggesting barely contained energy and passion. Just looking at her stirred Lucien. She was a firecracker waiting for a spark. Lucky would be the man to ignite that little explosive.

Unfortunately, since she was apparently a guest of Katherine's, and he did not dare to advertise his very real friendship with such a reformist type of female as Katherine Grimms, there would be no social interaction beyond brief public encounters. He would much rather get to know the new arrival in front of a cozy fire in Katherine's drawing room. Such an intimate setting might put him in the way of a flirtation or a friendship. But friendship required a sharing of ideas and confidences. For Lucien that was impossible. He had too much to hide. If he expressed his true thoughts and feelings, revealed his true self, he'd jeopardize the cause, as well as his own life.

For the first time in a long while, Lucien felt strong regret that he could not at least explore the possibility of a relationship with a lovely woman. However, for all he knew, this woman—this stranger who was engendering regrets without even speaking a word to him—could be as spiritually pallid and intellectually insipid as most of the unmarried women of his acquaintance.

On the boat, he would secure an introduction through Katherine and discover for himself if the girl was worth regretting. Getting to know her would, as always, be a bit encumbered by the fact that he must not abandon his public persona of the decadent, devil-may-care aristocrat nicknamed Dandy Delacroix. After all, what girl

worth her salt would encourage a scoundrel like
him?

Anne always managed to be on deck when the
steamboat pulled along shore. She loved to watch
the teeming activity at the docks: boxes and crates
being hefted from carriage to ground, then loaded
on various types of boats to be floated to market
somewhere; pushcarts filled with luggage; families
bidding farewell to one another; musicians playing
for free, hoping for benevolent music lovers to toss
them a coin.

Sometimes what she saw on the landings, and
had also seen on the steamboat, troubled her.
Slaves. She'd always known they existed, of
course. She'd learned about them in her history
and geography lessons with Miss Bishop, her
governess. But, like most people who are not
directly impacted by slavery, she'd thought it
very immoral, then put it out of her mind. Seeing the practice in action, in front of her horrified eyes, was very different from deploring
it in theory.

Most of the time the slaves seemed happy enough. They sang as they worked, moving about without the restraint of chains and
shackles, but Anne would never forget the sad
refrain of a song she'd heard a group of them
singing on the dock the night the *Belvedere* left
Charleston.

> *De night is dark, de day is long*
> *And we are far from home*
> *Weep, my brodders, weep.*

Over and over again, they'd sung it till Anne
felt like weeping herself. On the landing, right

now, was a group of slaves tied together by a rope, neck to neck. They appeared to be a family. There were a tall man and woman, both bone-thin, three teenaged boys, and a girl who looked to be just past childhood. The girl's small breasts pushed against the thin fabric of her ragged gown.

The girl was pretty, and, despite her tangled hair and disreputable clothes, she seemed fresh and untouched. Men were looking at her, walking slowly past, leering. The girl stood with her shoulders hunched forward, her eyes downcast, obviously frightened. It made Anne so angry she unconsciously bit the inside of her mouth till she drew blood. She tasted the salt of it on her tongue.

"Despicable!" said Katherine with a hard pound of her cane. "From a bankrupt estate, it seems, or else they'd be dressed better."

Anne turned to her aunt. "They're a family?"

"So it appears."

Anne grasped for an optimistic point. "At least they can stay together. It must be hard to be separated from your family with no hope of seeing them again."

"Bodine likes to keep them together, but he's not motivated by sympathy. It's more expensive to buy whole families, but they're less apt to run away, and since it costs money to recapture them, Bodine sees it as a wise investment."

Anne fixed her gaze on the white man who was sitting on a bench near the slaves. He looked to be in his forties, tall, powerfully built, balding, already dressed for the evening in a black jacket and trousers and a shiny, pale blue waistcoat. "You know him, Aunt Katherine?"

Katherine snorted. "Yes, more's the pity. We'll

have to exchange polite how-do-you-do's when he boards the boat. Mr. Grimms was obliged to do business with Mr. Bodine once or twice, a rare happenstance of a Creole crossing Canal Street to bank with an American. It was an opportunity Mr. Grimms could not pass up, since it might lend courage to other Creoles to mix more in the American business world. Mr. Grimms, like myself, abhorred the social segregation practiced by so many narrow-minded Creoles and Americans alike. Bodine, however, is not one of those Creole with whom I would care to nurture an acquaintance, business or otherwise. He's—" She stopped, her eyes narrowing. "He's not very nice."

"I don't like the looks of him, either, Anne," said Reggie, frowningly observing Bodine. "You'll stay away from him."

"Of course I will," Anne readily agreed.

Katherine strayed a few feet away, apparently to greet an acquaintance who'd just boarded, and Reggie added in an emphatic whisper, "I want you to associate with the best of New Orleans society, not just the opportunistic ragtags your aunt might introduce you to!"

Anne smiled and shook her head. "Uncle Reggie, you know Aunt Katherine is quite wealthy herself. What makes you think her friends are ragtags?"

"I understand that your aunt had a rather meager dowry," he confided out of the side of his mouth, like a conspirator. "She is only wealthy now because she ensured a generous bequeathal to herself in each of her husbands' wills"—he snatched a glance over his shoulder—"then drove them to their graves!"

Anne laughed. "How can you be so unfair! Each

of Katherine's husbands was self-made," she argued. "She *helped* them become rich and successful. She deserves her money. I've a mind to model
myself after my aunt, you know. I think it would
be exciting and romantic to help one's mate carve
a niche for himself in the world, as she did, instead of simply helping support him with your
dowry while he fritters his time away at White's
and Boodle's!"

"Struggle and penury are not romantic,"
Reggie said stubbornly. "They are deuced uncomfortable. And as for Katherine, I can think of any
number of women I'd rather see you emulate
than *her*. So unladylike! Her voice so abrasive it
reminds one of porcupines tumbling in the bri-
ars! And that stick of hers, forever poking it in
people's faces—"

"What? Did I hear my name being bandied
about, and to no good report, I suppose?" said
Katherine, bouncing her cane several times on the
deck behind them. Anne and Reggie did a quick
about-face. "I want to introduce you to Mr. Lucien
Delacroix. My niece, Mr. Delacroix, the Honorable
Miss Anne Weston. And this gentleman"—
Katherine waved the globed end of her cane under
Reggie's nose—"is her uncle on her father's side.
No blood relation to *me*, you understand. Mr. Wes-
ton, Mr. Delacroix."

Before Anne had time to take a good look at
the man before her, he swept into a low bow, then
took her hand and lightly kissed her fingertips.
She stared at the bent head, the black, wavy hair
so thick one could positively lose her fingers in
it . . .

Anne was jolted out of her bemused contempla-
tion when the gentleman slid her a sly look from
under eyelashes as thick and black as his hair.

They had barely met, and he was already flirting with her! She stared as he straightened up and shook hands with Reggie, murmuring a polite greeting. She discovered her mouth hanging open and hastily closed it. She had never seen a man so divinely handsome.

Mr. Delacroix wore a well-tailored ensemble of a black jacket and narrow trousers that fit his tall, athletic figure to a nicety. At his throat and wrists were a modicum of snowy-white ruffles, just enough to lend him the continental flair for which Creole men were known. He wore a little more jewelry than the typical English gentleman, with two large rings on each hand and several chains and fobs crisscrossing his vest like glittery corset ribbons. He was somewhat showy, but still very tasteful. His slight excess in dress did not detract from his masculinity, either. Rather, a bit of ruffle and glitter served as a wonderful foil to his obvious male charms.

The dashing fellow bent his gaze on her now, his finely arched, ebony eyebrows raised in supercilious inspection. His chocolate-brown eyes were long and almond-shaped. His mouth was the inexplicable combination of firm and soft, the corners just now an unprincipled, sly curve.

That smile, and his jaded appraisal of her from beneath drooping eyelids, announced Delacroix's arrogance and conceit. It seemed Anne's theory about dandyism was about to be proved once more. She slid an amused, incredulous glance at Reggie. His returning look was smug; it said, *I told you so.*

Chapter 2

"Mon Dieu! You say this ravishing young woman is your niece, madame?" Delacroix had a deep voice and a pronounced French accent, which was charming. The bored drawl he affected was not. It reminded Anne of the dandies in London.

"I did," Katherine agreed, her own expression carefully neutral.

One brow arched, the beautiful eyes widened with artificial surprise, the sly smile curved a little higher. "I do not remark a resemblance in the least. Are you quite sure you're related?"

Katherine pounded her cane against the floor. "If you are trying to flummery the girl with a compliment, Delacroix, kindly refrain from insulting me in the same breath, if you please!"

Delacroix chuckled softly. "Dear madame," he scolded in a teasing voice, "how could you ever think I meant to insult you? You and your niece are simply different. She is slender and delicate, like an exquisite flower, while you"—he cocked his head to the side and studied Katherine—"are tall and sturdy, like an elegant, majestic oak. Both of you are very beautiful, but in different ways, *n'est-ce pas?*"

Katherine's only reply was another pound of

her cane, perhaps aimed at the highly polished toe
of Delacroix's boot. However, he moved just then,
shifting his attention back to Anne and his foot
out of harm's way. "Forgive my impertinence, Mademoiselle Weston, but which of your fortunate
relatives *do* you resemble?"

Anne answered archly, "I shan't forgive your
impertinence, Mr. Delacroix. Forgiveness can only
be granted when there is true repentance. *You're*
not repentant. You positively enjoy being impertinent."

Delacroix's look of genuine surprise was ample
reward against the risk of a lecture from Reggie on
vulgar manners. He collected his wits quickly,
then waggled a finger at her, saying ever so softly,
"Ah! I see I'm not the only one who enjoys being
impertinent."

"Does it offend you, sir? I hope not," Anne said
breezily. "I want to make a good first impression
here in America."

"Mademoiselle, you are most charming," said
Delacroix with a courtly nod of his head, his eyes
gleaming. "And you've made quite a first impression already. At least you've made quite an impression on *me*." He spread long, beautiful fingers
over his waistcoat, reluctantly drawing Anne's attention to the broad expanse of his chest. His voice
lowered seductively. "Can't you see how my heart
beats wildly against my waistcoat?"

Anne's gaze lifted to Delacroix's. There was a
flirtatious twinkle in his eyes that Anne was sure
flattered and fascinated most women. Although
she could feel a flush creeping up her neck in response to the scoundrel's lavish and probably
completely insincere compliments, she repressed
her traitorous reaction and tilted her chin at a defiant angle. "Well, then, if I can be impertinent and

still be charming, I shall remain impertinent. One's curiosity is satisfied so much faster that way, don't you think? Tell me, Mr. Delacroix, whom do *you* resemble?"

"People say I'm the image of my father," Delacroix readily replied. "He was rather a dashing rogue in his youth, but now, sadly, he's allowed himself to lag behind the current fashion trends." He paused to straighten a ruffle that had caught on one of his numerous watch fobs. "He works too hard, plays far too seldom. But in all other respects, we are very much cut from the same cloth, as the Americans say." Delacroix's mouth twisted in a patronizing smirk. "They have so many quaint phrases, the Americans."

Anne felt her temper stir at Delacroix's attitude of superiority, but she kept her smile firmly in place. "I don't know about that. But I do know that I admire American people very much. They are so open and unaffected, so industrious and enterprising."

Delacroix shuddered slightly, then lifted a hand in mock surrender. A quasi-apologetic smile tilted his lips. "Pray stop, Mademoiselle Weston. You're making a useless fellow like myself feel quite ashamed. The Americans are a busy lot, I'll admit. It sometimes fatigues me simply to converse with them."

Anne's brows lifted. "I understand there's a great distinction made in New Orleans between the Creole culture and what is called the American culture. Surely you're *all* Americans, Mr. Delacroix? Surely you consider yourself an American as well as a Creole?"

Delacroix dispatched a fly from his sleeve with a fillip of slim fingers. The bored drawl was pronounced as he said, "Not at all, mademoiselle. But must we discuss such an uninteresting topic? After all, neither of us is an American. It doesn't apply." His face brightened. He bent and took her hand, kissing it again. "I've never met an American woman half as beautiful as you are, mademoiselle. Your hair is as bright as an English sovereign."

Anne drew back her hand, ashamed at the very pleasant thrill that ran up her arm in response to his brief kiss. Couldn't this fellow be serious for even one minute? She would force him to talk sense. "Surely, Mr. Delacroix, you have some sort of occupation?"

He grinned slyly. "I do keep occupied. My services are much in demand these days."

Anne cleared her throat, not able to believe he'd truly meant a double entendre in such a public and mixed-sex conversation. "Er ... your services? What do you do?"

"Many things, *ma petite*." His smile broadened. He seemed to enjoy her discomfort. "Perhaps it would clarify things if I told you I am heir to Bocage, a sugar plantation just outside of New Orleans."

"So you do ... ?"

"I do nothing." He made an elegant shrug. "What is there to do?"

Anne recognized in Lucien Delacroix the same sort of lazy fellow she'd met a hundred times in London, content to live off his inheritance, contributing nothing, doing nothing constructive. "Management of the plantation does not keep you busy?"

He replied, "No, of course not. It keeps my father busy."

Yet even that was an exaggeration. Anne knew Delacroix's father must own dozens of slaves. The slaves were the truly busy ones, the ones who did all the real work on the estate.

Delacroix studied her for a moment, as if he were penetrating her thoughts. For such a shallow person, this seemed unlikely, but his next words were surprisingly astute. "Ah, now I remark the resemblance between you and your aunt! It goes much further than skin-deep. You, too, have the tender heart of an abolitionist, *n'est-ce pas?* You do not think any of us plantation owners keep busy, except in the exploitation of slaves? You do not approve?" He watched her closely, waiting, a slight mocking smile on his lips.

He had implied that she was being presumptuous, that as a foreigner and someone who had not as yet even set foot in New Orleans, she shouldn't be passing judgment on their lifestyle. But Anne had seen enough to feel that she was entitled to her opinions without being treated condescendingly. She did not trust herself to reply.

Finally Delacroix inquired with gentle sarcasm, "You don't believe in idle chitchat, do you, mademoiselle? You do not speak unless you can cut straight to the heart of things." He smiled brilliantly then, and Anne couldn't help the way her pulse skittered. She told herself he was all charm and no substance. She willed her heart to resume a more normal pace.

"She's like me, Delacroix," Katherine declared proudly. "Nothing mealymouthed about her!"

Delacroix acknowledged this with a tiny sardonic nod of his head. "I see. Charming, I'm sure. I myself prefer chitchat. But just for the sake of finishing this rather unlucky turn in conversation, Mademoiselle Weston must understand that my family roots go back to the first French settlers ... before the Spanish, before the Americans. Delacroix is a venerated Catholic Creole name, and Bocage is one of the largest plantations in the state. Could she really expect me to hold opinions of a different nature than those I've just expressed?"

"Indeed," said Anne, finally finding her voice. "I shouldn't expect anything from you but the truth. And if you believe differently than I do, then that is certainly your choice."

"In many other matters, mademoiselle," said Delacroix, "I hope we will agree."

Anne gave a tiny shrug, implying that that was unlikely. By the answering spark of interest in his eyes, Delacroix apparently took her indifference as a challenge. That he would continue to pursue her with flirtatious advances ought to have annoyed her, but she was filled with a strange and thrilling sense of anticipation. It was just her luck, though, that the first handsome man she'd met in America was the very type she'd left England to avoid!

"Ah! But how I rattle on," he said at last, spreading one hand wide in a helpless gesture. He had beautiful hands—strong, tapered, capable-looking. It seemed grossly incongruent that they belonged to such a wastrel. "You must excuse me. Someone I particularly wish to talk to has just boarded."

He glanced over his shoulder, then turned back to Anne. "But one last word of advice, mademoiselle." While Reggie glared disapprovingly, Delacroix leaned close so that only she could hear. His breath fanned across her cheek. "Your lips look like an angel's. Soft as clouds, and moist as morning dew. Don't press them so tightly together like the knees of an old maid aunt. They were not made for such a disapproving frown. They were made to be kissed."

Anne was caught in the throes of very conflicting feelings. She was indignant at the fellow's bold flirting—conducted right in front of her two guardians, no less!—and unwillingly flattered by his poetic description of her lips. She caught herself just as she was about to lift her hand and touch her lips, just to see if they were as soft as he suggested.

By now he'd turned back to the others, speaking in far less intimate tones. "Lovely to see you, Madame Grimms. So pleased to make your acquaintance, Monsieur Weston. I hope we meet again." Then he made another flourishing bow and strode away to greet their newest passenger, Mr. Bodine.

"I should have known he'd be friends with that man," Anne remarked disapprovingly. The two of them were talking and smiling as if they were long-lost chums. It was repugnant to watch the display of easy, privileged camaraderie while in the background the family of slaves, their expressions dejected and tired, moved to the stairs that led below-deck.

Bodine made a gesture at the young black girl and winked at Delacroix, his intentions obvious. Anne knew Bodine would bed the girl that very night. She felt bile burn her throat. Men of Bodine's nature sickened her. How she wished there was some way to extricate that poor child from her fate.

Katherine greeted another acquaintance, and Anne moved through the gathering crowd of people to the side of the steamboat that faced away from the dock, looking out toward the last remnants of the sunset over a distant island. She heard Reggie's footsteps behind her, felt his sleeve brush hers as he, too, leaned against the railing.

"Uncle Reggie, please don't say, 'I told you so!'" Anne pleaded. "Obviously not all American men are the type I was hoping to meet here. And America has as many problems with snobbishness as England does. The Creoles and the Americans both think they're better than the other."

Reggie sighed. "Yes, I'm sure that's true." He paused, then said, "I can't believe I'm saying this ... But to be fair, you mustn't judge all American men by Delacroix and Bodine."

"I should hope not," Anne returned with a grim smile. "What a conceited care-for-nobody Delacroix is! He's very full of himself and thinks he can entertain a woman simply by flashing that smile of his and flattering her excessively. I should hope I'm not so addle-brained that my head can be so easily turned by a few pretty words."

Reggie snorted. "Indeed!"

"But this slavery issue ..." Anne's smile fell away. "I never expected to feel so strongly about it. It's so wrong, Uncle Reggie. But men like Delacroix and Bodine don't seem to think there's anything wrong with it."

Reggie pushed back a stray wisp of hair from Anne's eyes. "I know, dear. But there's not a blessed thing you can do about it. Now give your old uncle a kiss, and let's put our minds on something more pleasant, shall we?"

Anne kissed Reggie, then took his advice and tried to think of something more pleasant, but out of the corner of her eye she could see Delacroix. He was standing with Bodine, their conversation interrupted by some late arrivals. A cluster of women had boarded the boat and headed straight for Delacroix. Peals of feminine laughter rang out, fans waved coquettishly, and many lashes fluttered over blushing cheeks as Delacroix wielded his charm.

Anne's own cheeks blazed with color, too. How

could those women be so silly? she thought indignantly. What could that scoundrel possibly be saying that could be so entertaining? She strained to
listen but, regrettably, could make out nothing.
There was just the deep, pleasant rumble of his
voice across the deck.

She lifted a hand and briefly, shyly touched her
lips. Were they as soft as an angel's?

Lucien watched enviously as Anne Weston
stretched on her tiptoes to kiss her uncle on the
cheek. He lifted his hand to his own face, imagining the light pressure of her lips against his skin.
Having finally warded off the onslaught of female
acquaintances as they'd boarded the boat, he was
listening with half an ear to Bodine's meaningless
babble, inserting comments when necessary, but,
for the most part, allowing himself the indulgence
of regret.

Anne Weston was everything he admired in a
woman. Normally he'd never allow an exchange
with a beautiful woman to get so serious, but
Anne had seemed determined to take his measure
by his conversation. The resulting bout of seriousness had been brief, but it had certainly shown
Lucien *her* measure. He'd learned that she was
spirited, full of convictions, and as open and unaffected as she claimed the Americans were. She
was idealistic and passionate. All this, and pack-
aged so fetchingly in golden perfection. He was
intrigued, caught up in a wild infatuation the likes
of which he'd never felt before.

Sharp and tearing, the regret persisted, intensified. To her, he was a flirtatious wastrel, a conceited cad, and so he must remain in her
estimation. He'd no business even wanting her to
know his true self, the part of him that echoed ev-

ery sentiment she'd expressed, felt every bit of re-
pulsion she did for the institution of slavery. He
watched her rest her head against Reggie's shoulder and wished it was his own shoulder she used
as a prop for those fair curls.

"Delacroix, what do you say to a game of cards
tonight?"

Lucien bowed, relegating his regrets to the back
of his mind. It simply wasn't meant to be. "You
know I can never resist a bit of gambling on a riverboat."

"Or anywhere else." Bodine gave a bark of
laughter.

"You know me too well, Bodine. Directly after
supper, I suppose?"

"I'll be looking forward to it."

"Shall we dine together?"

"If you like."

"Directly, then. *J'ai faim.* Save the girl for later,
Bodine, when you've got the leisure to enjoy her.
Besides, it's too damned hot for rutting."

Bodine had fully intended to deflower the girl
before dinner, but money was money, and he
didn't want to lose out on winning a few dollars
by refusing to take supper earlier than usual. "I'll
only be a moment."

Bodine tipped his hat and walked away. Lucien
watched him strut toward the stairs, so pleased
with his latest purchases, and no doubt anticipating an evening of pleasure: good food, gambling,
and rape.

I look forward to the evening as well, you swine,
Lucien thought. *By the time you leave the card table,
you'll be lucky to make it to bed before you pass out. Unconscious from the sleeping herbs Armande mixed up for
me, you won't be able to lay a hand on the girl, or do a*

*damned thing about it when I send your family of slaves
down the river to their freedom.*

He turned away, his eyes returning of their own
volition to where Anne Weston stood at the rail,
her slim figure outlined against the Mississippi
sunset, the cool breeze lifting her ringlets and
bouncing them against her cheek as she looked
out over the water.

God, how he hated this masquerade.

Anne woke up suddenly. Because her abigail insisted on closing the only small window to the
tiny cabin they shared on the top deck of the *Belvedere*, the room was hot. All was silent except for
the soft huffing of the smokestacks.

Anne threw off her covers and pushed aside the
mosquito netting that fell in a canopy over her
bed. She picked up her watch locket from the bedside table, then swung her legs over the side of the
bed and walked to the window, shifting back the
curtain. Squinting and holding the watch to catch
the faint glow of moonlight, she could just make
out the time: ten minutes past four. In another
hour dawn would break. She had just enough time
for a cooling walk on deck before the daily activities resumed and the crew began preparations for
landing at New Orleans.

Three or four of the crew would be on duty in
the pilot's cabin, navigating the boat and watching
for river pirates, but otherwise the decks would be
virtually deserted. The gamblers and revelers usually retired around two or three in the morning
and would be sleeping off their booze by now, so
predawn was probably the quietest time on the
boat and the best opportunity Anne would have to
be alone. She hadn't been entirely alone since

she'd left England, and it was making her feel a bit barmy.

Anne turned to observe the dark form of her sleeping abigail, Sarah. The girl was sprawled on the small cot set against the opposite wall. Anne couldn't detect any movement under the tent of mosquito netting, and Sarah's breathing sounded quite deep. Normally Sarah was a heavy sleeper, and tonight didn't seem to be an exception to the rule.

For the sake of modesty, lest she accidentally run into someone on the deck, Anne threw a light pale blue evening cloak over her shoulders, completely covering the white, ankle-length muslin nightdress she wore. Her hair was pulled back in a braid, and she flipped its long length out of her way as she stooped and slid her feet into soft kid slippers. Then she carefully unlocked and opened the door that led into a narrow gallery, and crept out.

The minute Anne stepped into the fresh night air, cooled by the movement of the boat and the water, she took deep, cleansing breaths. Instantly exhilarated, she hurried along the gallery to the short flight of stairs that led down to the second deck. She descended into a fairyland of swirling predawn mist. She walked to the rail and looked down, black water showing in snatches through the mist, the ripples shimmering with a silver gilding of moonlight. They were gliding through a channel that brought the *Belvedere* close to a ghostly-looking shore.

The air was heavy with scent. Musky, sweet, earthy. Soon the birds would begin their morning serenades. Anne lifted her face to the sky. The three-quarter moon was nearly set. The stars still twinkled like diamonds through the hazy gray

light of approaching daybreak. Like diamonds.
Like the diamonds in Delacroix's rings.

Delacroix ... She'd watched him and Bodine in
the saloon at supper. The meal had been served
banquet-style, and people sat at small tables arranged randomly in the large, rather gaudily orna-
mented room. Anne had a good view of the table
where Delacroix and Bodine sat together eating
and drinking. They were drinking quite a lot, actually. She hoped Bodine had drunk so much that
he'd been incapable of bedding the slave girl last
night. If that occurred, at least Delacroix would
have served some useful purpose, though he
would have done it without intending to be useful. Anne supposed he was never useful intentionally.

It was fascinating to observe the differences between the two men. Bodine was, by most stand-
ards, a gentleman, but next to Delacroix he
appeared coarse and graceless. Delacroix was a par-
adox, too. While he radiated grace and refinement,
he still exuded a vitality that seemed incongruent
with his lazy way of life.

As he sat at the table with Bodine, she'd noticed
his legs. Yes, she blushed now to recall her preoc-
cupation with looking at those long supple limbs
of his, stretched out as they were beneath the table. His trousers fit closely, and every sinewy calf
and thigh muscle had been outlined against the
expensive black material. How did such a wastrel
get so strong? In the pursuit of pleasure, no doubt,
not in anything productive.

And his hands ... They were beautiful. Once he
smiled and saluted her across the room, catching
her off-guard, making her feel acutely embarrassed to be discovered staring. But when he and
Bodine had left the table and retired to the smok-

ing room upstairs, she'd actually been rather disappointed to see him go.

Anne shook her head, trying to clear them of thoughts of Delacroix. She moved along the rail toward the stern of the boat, through the mist toward the huge revolving paddle wheel and its glistening fall of water. She heard a cow lowing below-deck, down where the animals and the cargo and the slaves were kept.

The slaves were human beings, yet they were ranked as having the same value—and received the same consideration—as animals and inanimate crates of merchandise and food. It reminded her of all the reasons that she loathed Delacroix. Any man who sanctioned the bondage of other people to maintain his own extravagant lifestyle wasn't worth thinking about. And he certainly wasn't worth lusting after, either.

Anne nearly laughed out loud. *Lust?* Where had that thought come from?

She had stopped and was leaning against the rail. She had been looking down at the mist-shrouded water when she suddenly realized that on the bottom deck dark figures were leaving the boat and climbing aboard a raftlike conveyance that was being maneuvered by two men with long poles. Someone was helping them, steadying them as they scrambled over the rail.

Slaves were escaping! Anne squinted hard. Oh, how she hoped that among them was the family Bodine had brought on the boat last night, tied together like common criminals! To lose them before he'd had time to deflower the girl would really serve the old lech right!

Anne's delight in the scene before her came to an abrupt end when a large hand suddenly clamped over her mouth and a strong arm banded

around her waist, pulling her away from the rail.
She was terrified and completely helpless. Her
arms were caught against her sides, held motion-
less by the strength of her captor. She wasn't
dragged across the deck, but instead was slowly
maneuvered backward at a pace that allowed her
to walk. Was this a *considerate* criminal?

Her mind and heart were racing. Where was
this stranger taking her? What did he want? She
could feel the man's hard chest against her back,
his muscled thighs against her buttocks as he held
her firmly against him. Beneath her thin cloak and
nightdress, she wore only a chemise, and without
her layers of undergarments, she was especially
aware of the intimate contact of their bodies.

He drew her into a dark corner under an overhanging projection from the upper deck and
leaned against the wall, keeping her flush against
him. She could feel his breath in her hair, feel the
back and forth motion of his chest against her
shoulders. He was warm and smelled of brandy
and smoking tobacco. Now that the initial shock
was over and she could think more clearly, she realized that she hadn't been seized for the purpose
of robbery or rape. She was being detained so that
she couldn't alert the crew about the escape.

Anne felt a surge of relief and excitement. She
wanted to tell this man that she had no intention
of alerting anyone, that she was glad he and his
friends were doing something so noble and brave.
She struggled, but he held her tightly and kept his
hand over her mouth.

"Don't squirm so, *cher*," he murmured, bending
close to her ear. "I'm not going to hurt you." He
spoke in a whisper. His voice was deep and clear,
with a very slight French inflection to his words.

Anne nodded yes to tell him she wouldn't

squirm. How could she let this man know she was completely in sympathy with his scheme to free the slaves?

He chuckled, and she could feel the vibration ripple through his chest. Hearing and feeling his laughter gave Anne a shivery feeling deep inside. "Your spirit tells you to fight, but your mind and heart tell you that I won't hurt you. *N'est-ce pas*, mademoiselle?"

After a slight pause, Anne nodded again.

"*Bon.* You are a sensible girl. But still I cannot release you till I know for sure that they have gotten away safely. I have the best task of all, keeping you busy while my compatriots do the work, eh? *Mon Dieu*, you feel good in my arms!"

Anne was thrilled by the outlaw's words. Did he really mean what he was saying, or did he sweet-talk every girl who happened to stumble onto one of his slave escapes? She turned her head toward the voice, straining to see his face. She saw nothing but black melding into black. He pressed closer, till his lips were nearly touching her cheek. "Still you squirm! From boredom, *ma petite?* But I can fix that."

When she stiffened a little after his last remark, the man chuckled again. Anne loved how the sound rumbled up from deep inside him.

"Don't worry. If I distract you, I will end up distracting myself from everything outside the circle of your arms. Do you know how distracting you are to me, *cher?* Do you know how easy it would be for me to forget everything, including my duty?" He sighed. "Do not be nervous, *cher.* Soon I will release you. But while we wait for my friends to disappear into the mist, lean back in my arms, close your eyes, listen to the paddle wheel, and breathe the sweet perfume that is Louisiana. I will not hurt you."

She thought perhaps she was crazy to do so, but Anne believed him. His voice was soothing, almost hypnotic. She took a deep breath through her nose and closed her eyes. There really wasn't anything else she could do but wait till he was ready to release her. She couldn't speak, and it was useless to struggle, so she allowed herself to relax against him. The hard planes of his body fit perfectly against her soft curves.

Too perfectly . . . Whom was she kidding? It was impossible to relax while she was so intimately connected to such an attractive man. Without seeing him, Anne knew he was attractive. His voice, the feel of him, the things he said, all came together to make this stranger the most appealing man she'd ever met. He believed in equality and freedom; he was brave and exciting. He was certainly not an arrogant wastrel!

Now that she'd encountered a *real* man, her examination in the saloon of Delacroix's physical attributes hidden beneath the expensive clothing seemed silly and self-deceiving. What really made a man attractive had nothing to do with his good looks, or the way he dressed, or where he'd been born, or how old and established his family was. What made a man attractive was what he believed in and lived for.

His hand fell away from her mouth, and now both arms circled her waist. In the earlier struggle, her cloak had fallen from her shoulders and was wedged loosely between them. He moved slightly, and the cloak fell to the ground. The strong, long fingers of both his hands splayed over her midsection just below her uncorseted breasts. He must have known she wouldn't scream or cry out to alert the crew. She couldn't speak if she'd wanted to. She could hardly breathe. It no longer seemed necessary to explain how she felt about the escape. Obviously he already knew.

The mist swirled in the semidark; the paddle wheel churned and splashed rhythmically. The warmth from the stranger who was holding her permeated Anne's clothes and seemed to seep into her very blood. A sweet tension vibrated between them. Did he feel it, too? she wondered. She felt as though she could stand there in his arms till the sun rose, the bright morning rays dispelling the darkness to reveal the man she'd been fantasizing about through five dreadful Seasons in London.

Was she imagining it, or had his restraining hold on her turned into an embrace? He was holding her as if he were her lover, not her captor. Was he as attracted to her as she was to him? Anne felt her nipples harden against the thin muslin of her nightdress. Her breathing was shallow and erratic. So was his.

Suddenly his hands loosened their grip, and Anne was struck with a different kind of terror. He was letting her go! He was leaving! But no . . . not yet. She held her breath as, slowly, slowly, his hands slid up and around her ribs—the pads of his thumbs skimming the underside of her breasts—then up along the outside of her arms. Finally his hands cupped her shoulders and turned her around to face him.

She opened her eyes and released her held breath in a gasp. In the reflected moonlight off the misty deck and at such close range, she could just barely see him. He loomed above her, a tall, broad-shouldered man dressed entirely in black. A scarf was tied around his head, covering his hair completely. He wore a black mask with slits just large enough to see through. His plain long-sleeved shirt was tucked into trim-fitting trousers. He wore tall boots. He was like a shadow, blending into the darkness.

"Who are you?" she whispered, feeling disoriented, as if she were stumbling through a strange, thrilling dream.

He didn't answer, but his mouth curved in a smile—a small, wry, tender smile that made Anne's heart bound like a rabbit in spring grass. She stared at that beautiful mouth till a memory stirred, something deep in her consciousness that couldn't quite surface . . .

Then he kissed her, and every thought and memory flew from Anne's mind like birds scattered by a thrown stone.

His hands slid down her arms and around to her back, pulling her close as his lips settled over hers, then parted. Anne had been kissed before, but never had she felt the smooth, silken textures of tongue and teeth. She'd never felt the disturbing sensation of a hard male chest against her breasts, either. Nor had she ever felt the urge to throw her arms around someone's neck and press herself closer and closer . . .

A bird's call, low but distinct, splintered the silence. He pulled away. Dazed, distressed, she gave a small whimper of protest. "I must go, *cher,*" he told her, his voice grown husky. "Truly you have distracted me too well."

"I wish I could help you," she whispered.

He touched her lips with his fingers, tracing the soft swollen shape where he'd kissed her. "Just remember me, *cher.* Remember Renard. Till we meet again, eh?"

Then he was gone, through the mist and into the night.

Till they met again? Anne trembled at the thought. Was there a woman on earth lucky enough to encounter such a man twice in a lifetime?

Chapter 3

The saloon buzzed with excited conversations, all focused on the slave escape. At Anne's table, Aunt Katherine unfolded her serviette and placed it on her lap, where it would certainly be useless against dribbles and fallen crumbs that couldn't possibly make it past her shelflike bosom. She leveled her sharp gaze on the steamboat's captain, who had joined them for breakfast. "It was the Fox, then?"

Captain Duval nodded his head. "There can be no doubt, madame, that it was the work of Renard. No one else dares to undertake such dangerous missions. Silent and quick as the cunning fox, he and his comrades boarded the boat last night and got away with ten slaves."

"And Mr. Bodine's latest purchases ... were they among the slaves who escaped?" asked Anne, with assumed idle interest as she stirred a third spoonful of sugar into her morning cup of *café au lait*.

The captain took a sip from his mug, then nodded again—gravely. "Yes, they were."

"And how did he ... er ... receive the news?"

"I don't know yet. He's still abed."

"Gracious!" remarked Katherine, briskly buttering her toast. "Not yet up, and the time already a

36

quarter past eight! The day is practically half-spent."

"I believe he may have imbibed a little too freely last night," the captain speculated. "Delacroix has offered to break the bad news to him when he wakes up, though there really isn't much to tell. There were no witnesses to the escape."

No witnesses except me, thought Anne, reaching for a beignet. She found the sugar-coated pastries very delicious and addictive. Too bad they were so messy. "But surely the other slaves below-deck must have been aware of something going on, Captain? After all, they're crammed into such close quarters. Why didn't they all escape when they had the chance?"

The captain looked indulgently at Anne down the length of the breakfast table, past Aunt Katherine as she busily and lavishly peppered her boiled egg, past Uncle Reggie as he twisted his mustache and disapprovingly watched as pepper sprinkled the white damask tablecloth. The captain had been very kind to Anne on the trip, seeming amused by her intense curiosity and the forthright way she asked questions.

"If there were Negro witnesses, Mademoiselle Weston," he said now, "none of them is speaking up. This fact supports our theory that the escape was accomplished by Renard. There appears to be a conspiracy among the slave population to protect the outlaw. Even the slaves who have no desire to be 'emancipated' and make no attempt to escape become deaf, dumb, and blind when Renard helps other slaves to their freedom."

"But what I don't understand," Anne persisted, her hands spread palms up on the tabletop, her fingertips coated with powdery sugar, "is why *all* the slaves don't want their freedom? Who *wouldn't* want to be emancipated?"

Captain Duval replied, "The life of slavery is the only life these Negroes have ever known. In most cases, they are treated kindly by their owners, fed well, and given necessary medical attention. They are attached to their homes and wouldn't know what to do if thrust suddenly into the world to make their own living and set up their own households. Most of them are terrified at the idea of freedom."

"But if they were given the same opportunities as the white man—"

"Anne," Reggie broke in with a pained look on his face, "perhaps there are things you don't understand—"

"Why do you suppose she's asking questions, Reginald?" Katherine asked tartly. "How's she supposed to know how to think about a subject if she's ignorant of it? Ah, but I'm forgetting. You Englishmen think ignorance is a blessing in your womenfolk."

"I never said any such thing," spluttered Reggie, indignant.

"I'm sure you don't wish me to be ignorant, Uncle Reggie, though you may certainly wish me to be silent," said Anne, cutting to the truth. "But sometimes it's important to understand something no matter how upsetting the facts are. Well-treated or not, who could be truly happy without freedom? If the slaves were allowed to be taught to read and to be educated, I can't but think they'd all want their freedom eventually."

"I daresay it would be a monumental undertaking to responsibly free the slaves," said Reggie. "And the attempt would, no doubt, horribly disrupt the entire economic foundation of the South."

"The South could make the changes slowly. But it would have to be a joint effort, since no man can make the changes by himself." She was thinking of Renard, of course. She'd been thinking of him constantly since last night. Remembering the conflicting feelings of excitement and safety she'd felt in the notorious outlaw's embrace was like reliving a wonderful dream. She still couldn't believe she'd been kissed by a local legend.

"My dear Mademoiselle Weston," said the captain, rising from his seat and smiling down at her from his great height. "What makes you think the South wants to make any changes at all? I assure you, most people don't give the matter a moment's thought."

He reached down and gave her arm an affectionate pat. "I must prepare for landing, as we will arrive at port within the hour. But my parting advice to you, mademoiselle, is this. Enjoy your life. As pretty and bright and passionate as you are, you will be the object of many men's desires as you are launched into the gay society of New Orleans." Then he bowed and was gone.

"How dare he!" exclaimed Reggie, reddening to the color of a ripe tomato. "How dare that coarse man speak so loose and free within hearing of such innocent ears! *Passionate*, indeed! The object of men's *desires*! His terms of expression are straight out of a boudoir scene from a French penny novel. What can he be thinking to talk like that in front of Anne?"

"I see prudery rearing its ugly head again," Katherine remarked dryly as she brushed the crumbs off her bodice. "Captain Duval was simply speaking the truth, Reginald, only in more colorful terminology than you're used to hearing. I wonder whose ears are really the more innocent—Anne's or yours? *Yours* are the shade pinker."

"Mine are pink, Aunt Katherine," said Anne, "not because I objected to the captain's terminology, but because he spoke so condescendingly. Oh, is there no one who takes these matters seriously, or who might take *me* seriously? What this country needs are more men like Renard!"

"Like Renard?" croaked Reggie. "He's an outlaw!"

"But he's doing what he believes in. Inside the law, he can do nothing. Don't tell me, Uncle Reggie, that you agree with the captain!"

"Anne, of course I don't. But in England, where people are civilized, such unpleasant matters need not be thought about, much less discussed at such great length."

"Well, I'd rather be dead than simpering and silent," Anne announced, licking the powdered sugar off her fingers one at a time.

"Anne, 'tis unbecoming in a young lady to speak so violently, and *do* use your serviette, my dear!" admonished Reggie, at the end of his tether; but too late. With a thumb knuckle-deep in her mouth, Anne looked up to see Delacroix staring at her from the doorway of the saloon, Bodine at his side. And the dratted man was smiling.

With all the people in the saloon—many of whom had lingered over their meal in hopes of witnessing the entrance of the unfortunate Bodine—Anne found it rather unlucky that Delacroix's lazy, mocking gaze had happened to fix on her just as she was sucking sugar off her thumb.

She quickly looked away from Delacroix's amusement and removed the offending digit, wiping it dry on the serviette in her lap.

Anne was embarrassed and reluctant to look back toward the saloon entrance again, but she was just as curious as the other passengers to see how Bodine fared after receiving his bad news. Anne hoped he was wretched. By the quick look she'd had of him, she suspected he was nursing a hangover headache as well as a self-pitying conviction of ill usage at the hand of the Fox. *Bravo, Renard!* thought Anne. *Bodine got no less than he deserved.*

She slid a glance their way, sideways and surreptitious, out of the corner of her eye. Delacroix and Bodine were moving toward an empty table just next to theirs. Like everyone else in the room, she watched their progress. Delacroix walked with haughty nonchalance, as if he hadn't a care in the world. Anne noticed again that he had wonderful legs. She sighed and looked away. No rogue should have legs like that. He'd only use them to further his nefarious designs on women's hearts. Thank goodness, she was immune!

Anne Weston sat in a pool of sunshine, dressed in a butter-yellow dress and with a frothy, feathered bonnet sprigged with daisies perched atop her fair curls. She was sucking on her fingers, avidly enjoying every slick, sugary mouthful. Even from across the room, Lucien could see the white confectioner's powder from the beignet outlining the curve of her upper lip. One swipe of the tongue—preferably his—and she'd be as clean as a whistle and ready for kissing.

Kissing. It was not his usual habit to intersperse his undercover activities with romance, but last night he'd been unable to resist such an enchanting armful as Anne Weston had been. When he'd first seen her standing at the railing of the steamboat as it eased against the levee at Biloxi, he'd wondered how much she owed to her corset for that tiny waist. Now he knew that the nipped-in waist and just-right swell of hips and breasts were perfect without the benefit of undergarments; actually more perfect.

He vividly recalled the feel of her as she'd leaned against his chest and thighs. He'd felt the pulsing warmth of her skin through the fine muslin material of her nightdress. Her lips had been as sweet and eager as a besotted bride's. But more disrupting to Lucien's peace of mind than all these luscious physical delights was the unbelievable fact that Anne Weston supported Renard's cause with the sort of dedicated fervor most females saved for picking out a new bonnet or parasol. She'd been quivering with excitement last night because she was glad the slaves were escaping. Anne had fire and substance. She was an idealist. So far, she was damned near perfect.

And he must leave her alone. Lucien had no time for such foolishness. He had a masquerade to play out, and he didn't need such a tempting wench distracting him from his purpose.

She was watching him as he walked across the saloon toward the unoccupied table near theirs. For a panicked instant Lucien imagined she recognized something about him that might connect him to Renard. He gave her a sly smile and winked. She looked annoyed and turned away. Success, but at a price.

Before Anne Weston came on the scene, Lucien had actually taken a certain wicked enjoyment in his masquerade, amused by how easily he controlled people's opinions of him with a little playacting, a few careless, selfish remarks, and prideful allusions to wenching and gambling. But fooling

Anne was a bittersweet triumph indeed. With her, Lucien wanted desperately to be himself.

"Will this do, Bodine?" Lucien gestured toward the empty table.

Bodine squinted and snarled, "There's too much sun, but I suppose it shall have to do since it's the only available place to sit."

Lucien knew they were the center of the room's attention, but he only cared about the presence of the young woman who watched from the nearest table, and the scrutiny of the bluest and most clear-sighted pair of eyes. Bodine plopped into a chair without glancing around him, propped his elbows on the table, and cradled his head in his hands.

Before sitting down himself, Lucien took the time to briefly visit the surrounding tables. He kissed several hands and got several saucy looks and coy smiles in return. One young girl blushed to the roots of her hair and ducked shyly behind her fan. Having done his roguish duty, he at last approached Anne's table and bowed low.

"Bonjour, ladies, Monsieur Weston. I trust you are all well and happy this fine day?" He bared his teeth in the most insouciant smile he could manage. But Anne was watching, and it was hard to appear as unconcerned and carefree as he wanted to. He felt a tic in his jaw.

"Certainly happier than your friend, Mr. Bodine," said Katherine, tilting her chin in Bodine's general direction.

Lucien spread one hand in front of him to inspect his nails. Between his slightly splayed fingers, he saw Anne's upper lip—still dusted with sugar—lift in a barely perceptible sneer. He had doubtless irritated her by flirting with all the women within hand-kissing range. How very satisfying.

"*Oui*, last night's incident was most regrettable, *n'est-ce pas*? I understand he paid a pretty penny for the family of slaves. No matter how rich one gets, you know, it's never easy to part with one's property in such a manner. I'm sure it irks Bodine all the more because it was the doing of the outlaw Renard."

"Yes, Mr. Bodine does look dreadfully drawn this morning," said Anne with sweet rancor. She sighed and looked mournful. "How I pity him. But perhaps he'll improve once he's eaten breakfast."

"With a thundering headache and a queasy stomach, he probably won't order more than a cup of strong coffee," Lucien said in a voice of mild concern. "But as his friend, it is my duty to persuade him to eat at least a little something. How *are* the beignets this morning, Mademoiselle Weston? I was going to kiss your hand, but once I got a taste of that sugar on your fingers, I might embarrass us both by lingering overly long . . . Sugar is so divinely sweet, like a woman's lips."

He watched her blush. It was like watching a rose open, all dewy freshness and color. He stood there most rudely and smiled his enjoyment. Her uncle threw him a fretful glance, then leaned close to Anne's ear and whispered something. She quickly wiped the sugar off her lip with a serviette, then briskly wiped her fingers, too. Recovering her composure, she lifted haughty eyes to Lucien's mocking ones and said, "The beignets are especially light and delicious today, Mr. Delacroix, and perhaps even sweet enough to charm away Mr. Bodine's sour mood. Perhaps you ought to advise him to order some before he sends the server away."

Lucien recognized a broad hint when he heard one. She was dismissing him. But it was time he got on with the business of pretending to soothe Bodine's battered pride, anyway, and proving himself an excellent friend to the blackguard. His false friendship with Bodine was the most repugnant of his deceptions in the masquerade he played.

"How right you are, mademoiselle," conceded Lucien with a courtly bow. "I will advise Monsieur Bodine to order a plate of beignets immediately. *Au revoir*, ladies. *Au revoir*, Monsieur Weston. I hope we meet frequently in town."

Anne's responding look assured him that she'd probably much prefer meeting the devil to meeting a wretch like him. He ought to be pleased that his wastrel act was convincing enough to make her dislike him so intensely. But instead he found it damned irritating. He returned to the table and Bodine, determined to put the saucy baggage out of his mind and keep his thoughts on the pressing matters at hand.

As Lucien sat down, Bodine lifted his head from his hands. "Doing the pretty, Delacroix?"

Lucien dispassionately observed Bodine's bloated face. He looked as though he'd just walked through a sandstorm. His eyes were red and runny, his face unnaturally flushed. No one would think he was suffering from anything worse than a hangover, but Lucien knew differently. The sleeping herbs Armande had given him had done the job wonderfully. "Chirped a little too merry last night, eh, Bodine?"

"No merrier than I have done on numerous other occasions," he rasped. "You drank as much as I did, and I'd like to think I can throw down as many goblets of Madeira as the next man. I don't know why I feel worse than usual after a little brew tipping." Bodine rubbed his eyes with the heels of his hands. "My head is throbbing."

"I had the sorry task of waking you this morning with that damnable news. Learning you were robbed by Renard again must surely contribute to your feelings of misery, *n'est-ce pas?*"

Bodine dropped his hands to the tabletop, where they formed into fists. A look of hatred radiated from his bleary, bloodshot eyes. "If I ever manage to get hold of that bastard, I'll strangle him with my bare hands!"

Lucien pretended to look slightly awestruck by Bodine's vehemence. "*Mon Dieu,* I can only thank the saints that I'm not the man who inspires so much anger in you, Bodine." Lucien casually crossed his legs. "Pray tell me, just how many times *has* the Fox crept into your henhouse?"

Bodine looked truculent and did not reply. Smoothly, mercilessly, Lucien rubbed salt into the adeptly inflicted wound. "I think the henhouse a most apt metaphor, don't you? He frequently absconds with females you're interested in. Too bad you weren't able to have your way with that fetching little wench before Renard took her."

Bodine bristled. "What makes you think I didn't?"

Lucien shook his head. "Ah, *mon ami,* you forget. I helped you to your cabin last night. I assisted your manservant in pulling off your boots and tucking you snugly into bed. You are a large man, and last night you were—how shall I say?— less than graceful? You were snoring long before your head hit the pillow."

Bodine hadn't the energy to dispute what was

indisputable. His head sunk into his hands again. Lucien pretended to be instantly contrite. He reached over and clasped Bodine's hulking shoulder, ignoring the revulsion he felt at merely touching the man. "But what kind of friend am I to remind you of such frustrations? I wonder that you do not take a mistress and save yourself the trouble of seeking your ... er ... comfort in the inexpert arms of child slaves. Settle some beauty in her own *petite maison* on Rampart Street and come and go at your leisure."

Bodine shrugged out of Lucien's light hold and started rubbing his eyes again. "I won't buy a whore her own house. Once I'd grown tired of her—as I surely would before a year was out—she'd expect me to leave the place to her, just as our damned chivalrous custom demands. That doesn't sound very money-wise to me. The slaves I already own cost me nothing when I bed them. Besides, I like variety, and I like them young and virginal, if possible."

"I see. Your tastes run to the pure and innocent," Lucien remarked agreeably, hiding his disgust, strangling his urge to spit in Bodine's face. "You must eat. Mademoiselle Weston assures me that the beignets are divine today."

"Coffee. All I want is black coffee," Bodine mumbled, laying his balding head on his folded arms on the table.

Lucien waved for the server. When the uniformed black man hurried over, Lucien ordered coffee for Bodine and a substantial breakfast for himself. Last night's escapade had left him ravenous. If the smell of eggs made Bodine nauseous, well, that was regrettable.

"Oh, one more thing, boy," said Lucien, purposely using the denigrating form of address, "send a plate of beignets to that table, with my compliments." He gestured toward Anne's table and in so doing, caught her eye. Her look was scathing. He smiled and winked. She turned away, pretending not to have noticed him at all. He chuckled to himself. Pretending. Everyone was always pretending.

Compared to the reserved elegance of London, New Orleans was an eclectic paradise, Anne thought. From the bustling port to Katherine's house across Canal Street, they traveled by carriage through the Vieux Carre, the oldest section of New Orleans, which had been rebuilt after a fire in 1788. The pastel stucco houses were generally two and a half stories high with flat roofs, built flush with the sidewalks, or banquettes.

Ornamental iron surrounded the balconies overlooking streets that were fluid with masses of people of every imaginable variation in skin color. There were Creole women protecting their delicate white skin under parasols, amber-skinned quadroons in bright scarves called tignons, and ebony slaves who looked as though they'd just been imported from Guinea.

Women on the streetcorners sold candy and fruit and flowers. Some had even set up copper charcoal heaters and cooked rice cakes called calas and sold mugs of frothy *café au lait* to eager customers. The rich aroma of coffee, along with the stench of gutters, wafted through the open carriage windows. It was late September, but the heat was stifling. Anne could feel the perspiration trickle down her neck from beneath her bonnet.

Reggie, sitting next to Anne and facing forward, took out his handkerchief and held it to his nose. "Do you still think we're in heaven, Anne?"

"As a matter of fact, I was just mentally comparing all this to a sort of hodgepodge paradise." She waved a hand outside the window, indicating with one sweeping gesture all of New Orleans.

Reggie sniffed, then—judging by his grimace— wished he hadn't. "I never imagined heaven having such a pungent odor about it. I don't know how people can tolerate living here. Do you ... er ... live *near* here?" Reggie ventured to ask Katherine.

"No, I live in an area predominately inhabited by Americans. It's called the Faubourg St. Mary. The houses stand much farther back from the road there. I've all sorts of trees in my yard, too. Oaks, magnolias, palm, and even a banana tree. It makes it cooler in the house, you know. I can't wait to get there! I hope Theresa has everything ready for us." She suddenly clutched Anne's wrist. "Look there, Anne, it's St. Louis Cathedral."

Anne looked. And looked. And looked. She was enthralled with everything she saw, eager to know all she could about the history and culture of her temporary home.

Eventually they passed Canal Street and into the so-called American part of town. Here was where the non-Creole society built their own churches, theaters, hotels, and elegant homes. The Americans spurned the simple lines of the Creole homes and built large houses with more elaborate facades in the Greek Revival mode. Bougainvillaea, rosa-de-montana, wisteria, and roses adorned the yards with color. The houses were brick and painted pale muted tones. Everything was neat and lovely.

Katherine's house was on a street called Prytania. As they turned onto the gravel lane that led to the carriage house in the back, Anne stared up at an ivory-brick mansion that was as impressive as anything she'd seen thus far in New Orleans. She thought perhaps she'd underestimated her aunt's wealth. Even Reggie looked a bit awed. At least it kept him from talking, and that kept him and Katherine from arguing.

Once inside the house, Reggie was still silent. Anne supposed he had never expected to be so comfortable in any house that belonged to Katherine Grimms. But despite the grandeur of the place, with its plaster ceiling medallions, cornices, and carved marble mantels, it had a homey feeling about it, as well as an exotic atmosphere.

Katherine had managed this mix of welcoming impressions by combining artifacts and items from her many travels with plush cushioned sofas and ottomans and convenient tables covered with books. And there were flowers everywhere. Anne loved it. And she suspected that Reggie, though he didn't say so, loved it, too.

Theresa, the housekeeper, was a free black. Although many Americans had slaves, Katherine was not one of them. Theresa was a tall, large-boned woman of indeterminate age. Her mahogany skin looked as smooth as the inside of a kitten's ear, but her springy hair beneath the white tignon she wore was gray.

She showed Anne to her room, which was decorated in cabbage roses from the bed canopy, to the silk wallpaper, to the Aubusson rug on the gleaming wood floor. Gauzy curtains hung at the windows, shuttered now against the bright noon sun, and mosquito netting draped the large bed. Just off Anne's room was a huge dressing "closet" with a deep porcelain tub Anne immediately made use of.

After her bath, Anne decided to rest and acclimate to the hot weather before attempting to eat lunch. Lying on the bed, luxuriating in a slight breeze that blew in through the louvered shutters, Anne thought about the year ahead. What would happen to her in New Orleans? Would she see Renard again? Of all her hopes for the future, that one—silly though it seemed—dominated her scattered, presleep images. She drifted off, remembering how wonderful and safe and excited she'd felt in the embrace of a dangerous outlaw.

Chapter 4

⟨⟨∽∾⟩⟩

Like an unhinged gate, the three-quarter moon hung crooked on the horizon of a black, cloudless sky. Standing on the balcony attached to his apartments at the Hotel St. Louis, Lucien loosely gripped the top rail of the wrought-iron balustrade and looked out over Royal Street below. A low-creeping fog hovered over the gutters, and steam hazed the few closed windows of the adjacent building where the Blue Ribbon Ball was in full swing.

A steady stream of Creole gentlemen trod back and forth along the wooden walkway between the two buildings, judiciously allocating their time between their quadroon mistresses at the Blue Ribbon Ball and their wives, who sat in regal martyrdom at the King's Ball, taking place inside the Hotel St. Louis's grandest ballroom. On the periphery of the dancing, the deserted wives gossiped in little groups—like coveys of chattering fowl—and waited for their husbands to return from a "smoking break."

Cheroots smoldered bright orange in the dark as the men passed between the buildings, the pinpoint of burning embers brightening, then fading like indecisive fireflies. But everyone knew that saving their wives the annoyance of a little smell and smoke from a cheroot was only an excuse for the men to absent themselves from the King's Ball for the more titillating companionship of their mistresses.

It was a sultry night for early October, and the muddy tang of the Mississippi, mixed with the smell of aromatic tobacco and gutter swill, permeated the turbid atmosphere, making Lucien's attempt to fill his lungs with fresh air an exercise in futility. A raucous laugh drifted up from a nearby alley, followed by scuffling feet and muted exclamations—another fight.

The social season was in full swing, and everyone from aristocrat to demirep was in high gig. Almost all the "best" families had returned to town from the outlying plantations, where they routinely escaped from the sweltering, disease-infested summer months in the city. Lucien's family had taken up residence in the Delacroix mansion on Esplanade Avenue just that morning, and he'd received a curtly phrased summons from his father to pay a courtesy call on his mother. Lucien had begged off, promising to meet his mother at the opera that night for the season-opening performance of *The Barber of Seville.*

It wasn't that he didn't want to see his mother. He loved her, despite her blind devotion to Lucien's dictatorial father. He loved his father, too, but with reservations.

As a child, Lucien had not readily grasped his importance as heir to Bocage, an honor Jean-Luc Delacroix considered above everything else. Lucien had been an active, sociable child and had a wide circle of playmates, but his best friend was a slave child named Roy.

Up to the age of ten or so, sons of white plantation owners were allowed to play with the slave children when the slaves weren't busy in the fields or doing some other chore about the estate. Then, when the plantation owner's son went away to school, the friendships diminished naturally and were eventually forgotten or, if not forgotten, relegated to the past.

Lucien, a fiercely loyal young man, did not forget his friendship with Roy, even when they were both in their early teens and obviously destined for very different futures. His father disapproved of this continuing relationship, although Lucien thought it rather ironic that his father wouldn't have minded if he were bedding down with some of the female slaves. It was an odd set of rules that Lucien never really understood.

Lucien wasn't sure he wanted the lifestyle his father was proud to pass on to his eldest son. He questioned Creole tradition and the social protocol of the South. He couldn't understand why things had to continue being the way they were simply because they'd always been that way.

Infuriated by Lucien's rebellion against all he held near and dear, Jean-Luc decided to teach his son a lesson. He gave Lucien a final warning to stay away from Roy at the risk of punishment, knowing full well the two young men would disobey him. They went fishing, were caught, then were brought, unrepentant, before Jean-Luc to receive their punishment.

Jean-Luc ordered his son to give Roy twenty lashes with a whip. Horrified, Lucien refused. Jean-Luc explained to his son that if he didn't mete out the punishment, his friend, Charles Bodine, who happened to be visiting that afternoon, would be glad to do it for him.

Knowing Bodine's taste for blood, Lucien was forced to whip his friend. When Lucien didn't put enough twist in his wrist to execute the most painful blow, Bodine stepped in and showed him how to do it right. Lucien was in agony throughout the ordeal, trying to hurt his friend as little as possible, but knowing if he didn't hurt him quite enough, Bodine would take up the slack with relish.

That afternoon was a turning point for Lucien. He and Roy never spoke to each other again. Lucien learned to hate Bodine and to pity and despise his father. He also learned that he could never be a slave owner.

He stayed away at school, even on holidays, then went to Europe when he graduated and remained till he was thirty. Two years ago, Lucien had returned to New Orleans a changed man. But now he was another kind of embarrassment to his father. True, he no longer questioned slavery and other firmly entrenched ideas Jean-Luc held near and dear to his old-fashioned heart, but his son had turned into a worthless cad. He had no interest in the estate he was going to inherit, and no ambitions beyond wenching and gambling.

Lucien had planned the masquerade months before returning to the States. He knew that nothing had changed in the South, and he knew he couldn't go back home without trying to make some sort of a difference when he got there. His travels abroad hadn't changed his views about slavery; they reinforced what he already believed and had learned most painfully that summer day nearly twenty years before. Slavery was wrong. Thus Dandy Delacroix and Le Renard came into being.

Visiting his mother frequently put Lucien in his father's company as well, and that was always painful. And there was another disadvantage to his mother's return to town. Now that the frenetic social season had begun, Madame Delacroix would once again belabor the point that he'd let another year pass without selecting a wife from the cream of Creole aristocracy. This year Lucien's mother was hinting that the virtuous sixteen-year-old Liliane Chevalier would suit her perfectly as a daughter-in-law.

Lucien thought of the doe-eyed, raven-haired Mademoiselle Chevalier, seventeen years his junior—so proper, so passive, her untainted French bloodlines so well-documented in the ancient records kept safe and sound in the guarded vaults of St. Louis Cathedral.

Mademoiselle Chevalier, like so many well-born Creole girls, had been educated by the Ursuline nuns in the morally correct, tight-kneed frigidity of all marriageable women. And it would be her husband's singular honor to pry apart those maidenly knees to expose his properly unresponsive bride to the shocking sounds and movements attached to matrimonial consummation, all done in the modesty-preserving pitch-black of an unlit bedchamber. Almost never motivated by love, these awkward alliances seemed necessary to produce the requisite pure-blooded heir to a Creole dynasty.

Lucien refused to compromise his life's happiness by shackling himself in such a sham union. As well, marriage to him would not be fair to any woman—whether or not she was Creole. His subversive activities were far too dangerous to allow him the freedom to commit to a long-term relationship.

He thought of Anne Weston. He hadn't seen her since the *Belvedere* docked in New Orleans, but he'd thought about her every day, every night. He'd tried to obliterate her golden image from his mind by paying more frequent visits to his mistress, Micaela, trying to lose himself in an orgy of undiluted sex. But it hadn't worked. He only wanted Anne more and more.

Sometimes he whiled away an hour or two making up excuses to visit Katherine Grimms. Common sense always prevailed, and the visits were never paid; at least no acknowledged visits. But late at night he sometimes drove his carriage down the street where she lived, pausing across the way and watching Anne's bedroom window.

Twice he was lucky enough to see her lean out of the opened window, her hair loose and falling over her shoulders. A tree near her window looked as though it could be easily climbed. As each day passed, that tree seemed more and more tempting. Someday he would climb it and enter Anne's bedroom while she slept. And then . . .

He dared not imagine further. It would be enough just to look at her. Or perhaps just to kiss her once . . .

Unexpectedly a cool breeze blew softly against Lucien's heated skin. He arched his neck and closed his eyes, relishing the freshness, the crispness of it. It reminded him of the mountain wind that blew through Switzerland's snowy vales into northern France, and of the bracing river wind on the banks of the Thames. It was a taunting whisper of another time, another place.

How he wished he could be himself, as he had been in Europe! How he longed to talk to Anne with nothing between them but the truth! This masquerade was crushing his soul . . .

There was a knock at the door. Lucien had dismissed his small staff of servants for the night, and he wasn't expecting anyone. He moved across the shadowy room with the confidence of familiarity and the soundless grace of an athletic man used to maneuvering in the dark. He opened the door a crack.

"Lucien, I know I shouldn't be here, but—"

Lucien grabbed the man and pulled him into the room, darting his head through the doorway to scan the hall before shutting the door behind him and locking it.

"Christ, Armande, you're damned right you shouldn't be here!"

"No one saw me."

"Are you sure?"

Armande nodded his head. "I was very careful." He swallowed hard and threw Lucien a beseeching look. "I had to come."

Lucien observed his friend by the weak light of a single-candle wall sconce just inside the door. Tall and lean with copper-brown skin, dark hair, and hazel eyes, Armande was a free black of mixed blood. He was dressed in a neatly tailored gray suit, as if he'd just come from one of the ticketed balls being held in the public rooms. Sweat trickled down his temples, more from agitation than from the heat, Lucien surmised.

Armande was obviously very upset. Lucien was ready to believe whatever he told him, because Armande was the best spy and, more importantly, the most trusted friend a man could hope for. They'd met in the intellectual society that orbited the university in Paris, where Armande had studied to be a physician. Armande was the son of a quadroon and a wealthy American banker in New Orleans.

In Paris, he and Lucien had become instant comrades, finding their views on slavery to be identical. When Lucien confided his plan to begin underground abolitionist activities when he re-

turned to the United States, Armande wanted to
be included.

Armande's several years in Paris made him
seem more French than American, and his accent
and the sometimes poetic brevity of his English
reflected this Parisian influence.

"What has happened?"

"Bodine. He's done it again."

Lucien's jaw clenched. "What? Rape?"

"Worse. He's killed all three of the men we'd arranged to transport next week. One of them confided in another slave—trying to convince her to
come along, I suspect—a mulatto girl Bodine gives
special privileges for tattling on the others."

Lucien kneaded the tight cords at the back of his
neck. "The fool! He knew the terms of our agreement! Didn't he know the risk he was taking, the
danger he was placing himself and the other two
men in?"

"He may have been a fool, but he was a brave
fool. They all were. Our connection at Belle Fleur
saw it all and reported this bad news to me not
more than an hour ago. Bodine beat them. He
wanted them to tell him where you were planning
to rendezvous. He was going to surprise you with
a posse of hangmen in place of the slaves. Ever
since we took the family of slaves from the Belvedere he has a vendetta against you, Lucien. They
wouldn't tell him where the meeting place was."
Armande's voice quivered with suppressed anger
and emotion. "We can be grateful for that."

"Gratitude is the least of what I'm feeling right
now! I'd like to take Bodine's whip and layer a
few welts on his worthless hide, then string him
up with it! Now there will be rampant fear at Belle
Fleur. There won't be another man or woman
who'll dare try for freedom, though that planta-

tion of Bodine's is the worst hellhole for slaves in the South, I'd wager."

Armande wiped his brow with a handkerchief he'd pulled from a waistcoat pocket. "Time will dull some of the fear. Because of the cruelty at Belle Fleur, there will be others brave enough to take the chance of escape. So far, you've been amazingly adept at moving them out of the state. This is the first . . . mishap."

"One too many, Armande." Lucien sighed deeply and moved to the French doors leading to the balcony, wishing again for the whisper of cool air on his face. Armande stayed behind in the shadows. Silent, pain-filled moments passed.

"Maybe it was a premonition," Lucien said at last, more to himself than to Armande.

"What, *mon ami?*"

Lucien turned slightly, throwing Armande a self-derisive and grim smile. "The weather has been hotter than usual for this time of year. I've felt smothered all day. I was thinking about . . . things, when suddenly I imagined I felt a cool breeze. I could smell the mountain air of Switzerland, Armande. I could feel the brisk wind from the Thames. It was eerie. Now I begin to think it was a premonition, a chilling precursor to your grisly news."

"The Creole, the blacks, we are all superstitious. Probably it was a premonition, but maybe not a bad one."

Lucien made a scornful noise at the back of his throat. "It sure as hell appears that way to me!"

"No, Lucien. The beatings, they were done yesterday. Maybe this cool breeze—this spiritual transportation to a place where you were happy and serene—maybe it was a good omen. Maybe something good is coming to you, something from the continent."

Lucien immediately thought of Anne, and his heart lifted, but he ruthlessly dismissed the wistful, foolish surge of hope and made a wry face. "A broad interpretation for the whimsy of river breezes, my friend."

Armande shrugged and smiled, a purely Gallic gesture. "Perhaps. I'm no fortune-teller. If you want your fortune told, you must visit the voodoo queen."

Lucien shook his head with resignation. "All I see in the future for me and the South is strife and danger."

"It will change, *mon ami*. You will help to bring the changes—slow and sure, like the Mississippi swelling in the spring to overflow the banks. Once they build in power, in momentum, nothing will stop the changes. But until that time comes, you must still keep the secret, you must still wear the mask, you must still play the masquerade."

Lucien sighed and turned away, staring into the dark night.

"It's lovely, Anne, but it's not white." Reggie peered critically through his spectacles at Anne's midnight-blue gown.

"You didn't really expect me to bedeck myself in white like some debutante straight out of the schoolroom, did you, Uncle Reggie? Goodness, I'm twenty-three years old!"

"I only thought it might be more traditional if you first presented yourself to New Orleans society in a coming-out color. I understand all the young ladies make their first social appearance at the opening night of the opera. There will be a veritable sea of white, and probably one little dab of midnight-blue."

"Good," said Anne, fastening a gold bracelet over the long white glove that came to the middle of her upper arms. "I shouldn't wish to be just another fleck of foam in a sea of white. I like being different. And if there are going to be so many young women there, it's best I wear something that makes me stand out in a crowd. An old spinster like myself must use every possible trick!"

"What nincompoopery!" Katherine's voice preceded her as she entered the drawing room. "You will always stand out in a crowd, my dear, no matter what you wear. You're beautiful. You take after *my* side of the family."

"You look splendid, Aunt Katherine," said Anne, eyeing her aunt appreciatively. "You look absolutely regal in purple."

"It's the height and the bosom, I suppose," agreed Katherine, patting her upswept hair, simply styled as usual to match the austere elegance of her town and opera cape.

"Ahem," said Reggie, pinkening.

"What is it, Reginald?" said Katherine, turning to observe him as he stood uncomfortably by the mantel, tugging on his mustache. "Oh, yes, of course. You look very nice, too. All men look best in black."

"Good God, you don't imagine I was fishing for a compliment, do you?" He shifted from foot to foot, obviously flustered.

"Well, if you weren't wishing to be noticed and flattered, why were you clearing your throat in that odious manner?"

"If you must be told, I was discreetly objecting to your use of the word bosom in so casual and coarse a fashion, and in *mixed* company!"

"Lord, you're a prude, Reginald. Did you think Anne had never heard the word before? Sheltered though you are, you can't be objecting for *your* sake, I hope. If you've never heard the word bosom spoken in the company of females at your advanced age, Reginald, I pity you."

"Save your pity, madame," he said stiffly, thrusting up his nose in a pose of offended dignity. "I cherish and honor the purity of my past no matter how dull you might deem it to be in comparison to your own. Now, shall we go the opera? I trust I won't be humiliated by your conduct in so public and revered a place as the opera house, will I, ladies?"

Reggie slid a meaningful glance at Anne. He obviously felt he had no influence with Katherine, and, besides, her behavior was probably tolerated by a society who knew her well after twenty years of exposure. But he cared what they thought of Anne, and he believed her debut tonight could determine her acceptance into the more preferable circles.

Anne wasn't sure just how much she and Reggie agreed on who and what were "preferable," but she had no desire to cause him undue distress by debating the point as they were about to leave for an evening on the town. She smiled sweetly and answered just as she ought. "I will be as good as an angel, Uncle."

Relieved, Reggie smiled and offered his arm to Anne. "Shall we go, then? The carriage has been waiting this quarter-hour."

Anne slid her gloved hand into the crook of Reggie's elbow. As he was about to lead her into the hall, she squeezed his arm and smiled up at him. "Aren't you forgetting something, Uncle?"

Reggie's brow furrowed. "I've a gardenia for my

lapel, my opera glasses, money, and a clean hand-kerchief. What could I have possibly forgotten?"

"Ahem!"

They turned at Katherine's exaggerated imita-tion of Reggie's habitual throat clearing. Her lips were pursed, her arms were crossed, one slipper-shod toe was tapping the Persian rug beneath her feet, and her gaze was directed at the ceiling. There could be no clearer message to Reggie of ex-actly what—or whom—he'd forgotten.

Before any other vanity the modest man might own, Reggie prided himself on his gentleman's manners. Turning the rosy shade that was fast be-coming his usual complexion, Reggie offered Katherine his other arm. He cleared his throat, caught himself, then blushed more deeply. "Yes . . . er . . . Katherine, why don't we . . . er . . . go?"

Katherine's teeth gleamed in a benign smile, much in the manner of a potentate forgiving an underling. She floated majestically across the short distance that separated them and rested her fin-gers lightly on Reggie's forearm, holding her ever-present cane in the opposite hand. Anne squeezed his arm gratefully, and the three of them sashayed into the hall with a rustle of silk and satin, and the infinitesimal squeak of new patent-leather pumps.

Lucien arrived late at the opera. Dandy Dela-croix considered punctuality a fashion faux pas. He headed straight for his parents' box, intending to stay through the first act, then slip away to an elegant little house on Rampart Street and into the voluptuous embrace of his mistress. After the news of Bodine's most recent deplorable crimes, he was in no mood for the trivial gossip and smug self-importance of society's "best."

Lucien's four jeweled rings winked in the bright

candlelight spilling from the large chandeliers in
the hall as he strode to his parents' box. Just outside the curtained entrance, he shook down the
cuff of his white silk shirt and adjusted his cravat.
A single white rose adorned the lapel of his black
evening jacket. One last deep breath, and he was
ready to face his family.

He slipped inside and quietly took stock of the
situation before making his presence known. Just
his mother and father, his younger brother,
Etienne, and one of his numerous sisters, Renee,
were present. Renee, who had turned sixteen last
month, was making her come-out. Just like all his
other sisters, Renee was beautiful—tall, slender,
and raven-haired.

During first intermission, the box would be
bombarded with would-be beaux, vying for her attention. Champagne would flow, and compliments
would be thrown around like so much confetti.
Within the fortnight, there would be offers for her
hand. After weighing each competitor's wealth
and family genealogy, Jean-Luc Delacroix would
make a choice for Renee. A betrothal would be announced, and she would be duly married after a
decent interval of engagement. Unless Renee was
very different from his other sisters, she would acquiesce to this method of courtship without the
slightest complaint. It was the way things were
done.

Just then his mother turned and motioned to
him. Lucien stepped forward, kissed his sister on
the cheek, and bowed to Etienne—who returned
the bow with a curt nod—before sitting down beside his mother in the front row. Etienne was
highly critical of Lucien's wastrel pastimes and,
just like their father, he took every available opportunity to manifest his disapproval.

Lucien's father was scrutinizing the audience through a pair of opera glasses, paying not the least attention to the beautiful aria being performed or even bothering to acknowledge his son's presence.

"Maman, you look charming as usual."

"Lucien, *mon fils*, how delicious to see you." She tapped his knee with her pearl-seeded fan and smiled warmly. Even after bearing twelve children, only seven of which had lived beyond infancy, Marie Delacroix was still an attractive woman. Her black hair was streaked rather strikingly with silver, and her waist, with the help of a corset, was only a couple of inches thicker than it had been on her wedding day thirty-five years before.

"Are you all settled in, Maman?"

"After so many years of setting up housekeeping in the city each autumn, Lucien, I have perfected a system. That is why your father insists we stay at Bocage till the very day the opera begins. He feels there is no need to come sooner, and you know how he loves the country."

Lucien glanced at his father's stern profile, his thick silver hair combed in a smooth pompadour above his high brow, his mouth a thin, straight, unequivocal line. "How is Papa?"

Lucien's mother leaned close to him and whispered. "Not as well as he pretends to be. He's short of breath sometimes. I worry for his heart."

"I'm sorry to hear that."

"Oh, Lucien, you come so seldom to Bocage!"

"I come as often as business dictates."

"Your father would enjoy it if you came just to see him, you know."

"You're mistaken, Maman, if you think I'm a comfort to my father. Once we've talked about the crops, we've nothing to say to each other. He won't discuss his health, and I've learned not to inquire after it unless I want my head bitten off."

"It would make him so happy ..." She paused and took Lucien's hand, squeezing it till the facets of his rings cut into his fingers. "It would make us both very happy if you married this year, Lucien."

Lucien smiled wanly. "Must we argue, Maman?"

"Lucien, have you seen Liliane Chevalier since their visit to Bocage last spring? She is enchanting, so grown-up now. Here, take my glasses and look at her. Next to Renee, I believe she's the handsomest girl in the house."

Grudgingly, Lucien accepted the opera glasses his mother handed him. Then he remembered that Katherine Grimms had a box at the opera and made it a point to attend opening night. In his depression over the murders at Belle Fleur, Lucien had forgotten that he might catch a glimpse of Anne Weston tonight. That sudden realization caused his spirits to soar to the domed ceiling of the Orleans Opera House. He looked through the glasses with a boyish eagerness that frightened him.

Dutifully, impatiently, he panned the room first to locate the Chevalier box. Finding it quickly by the coordinates whispered in his ear by his mother, he gave Mademoiselle Chevalier a cursory inspection. She was good-looking enough, even-featured, plump in all the right places, ruddy-lipped, dusky-haired, and dressed in the usual white. But she radiated about as much liveliness as a marble statue.

"Well, aren't I right, Lucien? Don't you think she's lovely?"

By now Lucien had turned his head slightly to

the right and up a tier, and was looking at a vision
in midnight-blue; a vivid, animated female with
smiling lips and sparkling eyes. Among the several guests Katherine Grimms had already attracted to her box, Anne Weston stood out like a
full-blown wild rose in a patch of field daisies.

She was just as he remembered her. No, she was
more than he remembered. More lovely, more
alive, more desirable than ever. And she was sitting by a man Lucien knew well by reputation. Jeffrey Wycliff was an editorial journalist and
reporter for the American newspaper, the *Picayune*.
They were whispering to each other, smiling and
laughing as if they were old friends.

"Lucien . . . What do you think of her?" his
mother prompted.

"I think she's lovely," he replied truthfully, his
eyes still trained on Anne.

"*Bon*. I knew she would be just to your liking.
Will you visit her at intermission?"

"Who, Maman?"

"Why, whom do you think? Will you pay a call
to the Chevalier box?"

Lucien slowly lowered the opera glasses and
handed them to his mother. "I won't have time."

"Why not?"

"Because I've business to attend to."

"But surely, Lucien, you have time to say *bonsoir*?"

"There will be hordes of men clambering to say
bonsoir to Liliane Chevalier. I'm sure I won't be
missed in such a crush."

"All the more reason why you should go. Do
you want to lose your lovely lady to someone
else?"

Lucien paused and pondered his mother's question. He didn't suppose he had any hope at all of

preventing Anne Weston from getting romantically involved with any one of the numerous men who might pursue her. He had no right, no business even wishing he could pursue her for himself. But that didn't stop him from wanting to be near her. And now that he'd seen her again, he didn't think he could help himself from spending just a few precious moments in her presence. Even if she hated him for it.

The ponderous velvet curtain fell at the end of the first act. He got up, kissed his mother good-bye, exchanged brief stilted pleasantries with his father and siblings, then excused himself just as Renee's first admirers stepped through the curtained entryway. He walked quickly around the opera house and up the stairs till he found Katherine Grimms's box. Muttering "Caution be damned" under his breath, he stepped inside.

Chapter 5

"**M**r. Wycliff, I believe you've managed to make me talk about myself through the entire first act!" Anne said gaily. "I'm embarrassed, and Uncle Reggie is looking very disapproving."

"I hope he doesn't lecture you on my account. I don't believe I've ever enjoyed the *Barber of Seville* quite so much."

Anne smiled. "Do you always know exactly what to say?"

Jeffrey Wycliff smiled back, his brown eyes crinkling at the corners. "I'm a writer, you know. I'm never at a loss for words. At the opera I'd always rather converse with someone than watch the dramatics on stage, but I've never been fortunate enough before to sit next to a good-looking female who goes after a subject with the same relish that you do, Miss Weston."

Anne laughed. "What? Don't you like the opera, Mr. Wycliff? How gauche of you to admit it! And how very much I like you for being so unfashionably honest. But if you don't enjoy the drama and the music, why do you come?"

Anne was aware that behind her someone had entered the box, but she was enjoying her talk with Mr. Wycliff so much, she was determined to avoid the inevitable callers as long as politely possible. Since Katherine had been away several months, Anne hoped that her aunt would be the center of their attention for a few more moments while she enjoyed a rather stimulating conversation.

"I come to the opera because everyone comes, and it amuses me to watch society all tricked out in their finery and playing their circumscribed parts. I have the natural curiosity of a journalist."

"And the natural cynicism, I see." Anne gave him a sagacious once-over. In his black evening trousers and jacket, complete with the usual white gardenia at the lapel, she thought he looked a little too formally rigged out to suit her overall impression of him. With his straight sandy-brown hair, his attractive, square-jawed, wholly American face, he looked as if he'd be much more at home in a suit of buckskin and fringed boots. "But you are dressed as finely as the others, Mr. Wycliff . . . What part are *you* playing?"

His tone was low and playfully conspiring. "I'm a chameleon, Miss Weston, very adaptable to my surroundings. Wherever I go, I manage to fit in. But I don't play a part. I'm always intrinsically myself."

"And who are you?"

"No one special. Just an orphan from Baltimore with the lucky knack of putting pen to paper."

"Why did you leave Baltimore?"

Jeffrey shrugged his wide shoulders. "There was nothing for me there. No family. No inheritance, certainly. I came where I thought there would be opportunity for advancement. And there is."

"You're ambitious."

"Very. I haven't any choice."

"Do you wish you did?"

Jeffrey's eyes gleamed with amusement. "Actually I find it rather challenging to have to grasp and claw my way to the top."

Anne raised a brow. "You're teasing me. But somehow I think you're still telling the truth."

He shrugged again, his expression coyly noncommittal. "New Orleans is fascinating, a place on the cusp of profound change. Writing about change, and maybe even inciting a bit of it with my seditious journalism, is very exciting."

"I've read all your articles since coming here. So far I've agreed with everything you've written, particularly on the subject of slavery and your abolitionist views. I've especially enjoyed your accounts of the derring-do of the Fox." Anne felt the warmth creep up her neck and flood her cheeks. Even after two weeks, just the thought of Renard made her blush like a schoolgirl.

Mercifully Jeffrey didn't seem to notice Anne's blush. Instead he grew sober and sincere, all remnants of teasing gone. "Yes. I've the highest regard and admiration for the Fox. If I weren't such a cynic, I'd call Renard a hero for the times."

"Don't let your cynicism keep you from so natural a conclusion, Mr. Wycliff," Anne replied, delighted to find someone who thought exactly as she did. She leaned confidingly close and impulsively laid her hand on his arm. "Renard *is* a hero."

"Who is a hero, Mademoiselle Weston? Could you possibly be talking about *me*?"

Anne looked up into the mocking face of Dandy Delacroix. She hadn't seen him since their encounters on the *Belvedere*. In the interim she'd tried to erase him from her thoughts, but had failed utterly to do so. She felt an unwilling attraction to him, and felt desperately guilty about it. She reasoned that she was only responding to the external male charms he obviously possessed, not the real man inside. But she still deplored her weakness, especially after she'd actually been kissed by someone truly heroic—Renard.

Lucien Delacroix was even more handsome than she remembered. And more smug. His dark, sardonic gaze held her transfixed for a moment, till he broke eye contact to glance down—then stare most pointedly—at her gloved hand still resting on Jeffrey Wycliff's arm.

A rebellious part of Anne bristled at the notion that Delacroix disapproved of her physical contact with Jeffrey. Who was he to pass judgment on her? If she wanted to behave in such a friendly fashion to a man she'd just met, it was no concern of *his*. Following this willful line of reasoning, Anne left her hand on Jeffrey's arm another lingering moment.

Finally she offered that same hand to Delacroix with a defiant smile. "Mr. Delacroix. Charmed to see you again."

He kissed her hand, the light pressure of his lips sending an odd, shivery feeling through her.

"Charmed to see *you*, mademoiselle. You are a vision, as always. I trust you are comfortably settled in your new home?"

"Quite comfortable, thank you. Do you know Mr. Wycliff?"

Delacroix's gaze shifted to Jeffrey, his expression cool and impatient, as if he'd rather not take the trouble to acknowledge him. Jeffrey stood up, and they shook hands. "Monsieur Wycliff and I have met before."

"Yes, we have. I did a piece on gaming hells in the city, and Mr. Delacroix was one of the gentlemen who figured prominently in it."

Delacroix smiled blandly, apparently unconcerned by the derogatory suggestion of Jeffrey's
words. "I was winning splendidly that night. Perhaps you should have stayed longer and taken
notes on my celebratory party afterward and included it in your article? Readers nowadays have
such a taste for anything that smacks of debauchery. Whatever sells the news, eh?"

Jeffrey pursed his lips and said nothing. Anne
had to admit that Delacroix had turned the tables
on him. He was a cad, but he was clever. His gaze
shifted back to her. His eyes gleamed wickedly
and, in the dim light, appeared as black as his
jacket. "What do *you* think of debauchery, Mademoiselle Weston?"

"I've had little experience with it," she replied
with a prim smile, though she knew her eyes must
be alight with amusement.

"Ah, if one can't live a debauched life, one can
at least read about people who do. Let me re-
phrase my question. Do you like reading about
debauchery?"

"I like a good novel now and then," she admitted, holding back her smile and wanting to kick
herself for finding him so entertaining. "But in
novels the people who behave badly—as debauched people generally do—usually die at the
end."

Delacroix nodded sagely, his dark hair full and
lush in the candlelight. "Very appropriate, I'm
sure, and instructive to the youth. But Mr. Wycliff
writes about real people doing real things. As is
frequently chronicled in the newspaper, bad people sometimes never get caught and never pay for
their crimes."

Anne nodded. "That's why we need heroes, Mr.
Delacroix. And I believe I've found one in this fel-

low Renard. Mr. Wycliff writes about him all the time. Do you know who I mean?"

Delacroix shrugged his wide shoulders. "Everyone knows Renard. Seems a foolish fellow to me, risking his neck for nothing."

Anne immediately bristled and was about to take up her usual argument for abolition when Delacroix smoothly diverted the conversation. "How do you like New Orleans? It appears that New Orleans likes you." He motioned toward the people filling the box, the men seeming anxious to make their way to Anne's corner for introductions. There were three females, too, eyeing Delacroix as if he were a giant bonbon. Katherine had them all detained at the door while Reggie handed out champagne. Anne wondered how Delacroix had politely managed to get past her talkative aunt so quickly.

"I like everything I've seen so far, but I've seen very little, really. Aunt Katherine has been busy receiving calls from old friends and generally settling in. I'd love to tour the city, but Uncle Reggie won't allow me to go out alone—even with my abigail and a footman or two in attendance—and he won't accompany me, either. He claims it's too hot to go gadding about during the day."

Anne recognized the slightly complaining tone of her voice and tried to correct it. She didn't want to seem ungrateful. More bracingly, she added, "He's not grown accustomed to the climate yet, the poor dear. Sometimes I wish I were a man and could go and do precisely as I pleased. Then I wouldn't be a trouble to anyone!"

"I don't blame your uncle," said Delacroix, flicking an infinitesimal speck of lint off his jacket sleeve, then returning his penetrating gaze to her face. His black eyes had a provocative glint; his smile was lazy and sly. "Such a charming bit of English fluff as you wouldn't last ten minutes on the streets of the rough-and-tumble Vieux Carré."

"I say, Delacroix—" Jeffrey began to object. Indeed, Delacroix's use of language was a bit out of line, but Anne almost liked the bluntness of it. She laid a gently restraining hand on Jeffrey's arm.

"What do you suggest I do, then?" she asked Delacroix.

He cocked his head to the side and studied her. The firm line of his masculine jaw was limned by candlelight. "I would offer myself as escort, but I'm sure you know that in *my* debauched company you would be in more danger than ever."

"Indeed," she murmured, a strange thrill running down her spine.

Their eyes held for a lengthy moment, then he seemed to recollect himself, assumed a bored pose, and drawled, "My advice to you, Mademoiselle Weston, is to mind your elders."

Again she bristled. "If I were a twenty-three-year-old man, I'd certainly be allowed outside my house without an army of escorts. It's not fair!"

"But you obviously are not a man—a fact for which I, for one, am most thankful." Delacroix splayed his right hand over his ivory brocade waistcoat and bowed, his eyes closed as if in homage to her fair sex, the long lashes black and beautiful against his skin.

Another instinctive, unwelcome response to the arresting beauty of the man made Anne's heart race. Furious with herself, she turned to look at Jeffrey, hoping to be diverted by comparing the two men—one so honorable, the other such a scoundrel. Standing slightly back, as if removing himself from the "scoundrel's" polluted presence,

Jeffrey eyed Delacroix with a mixture of anger and . . . envy? No, he was no help at all.

"Miss Weston is a suffragist, Delacroix," said Jeffrey. "In our discussion during the first act, she revealed that she believes women should have all the freedoms and rights of men." He turned and smiled at Anne. "But I do think your uncle has a point. Voting in the elections is one thing—and I fully support your views on that matter—but allowing you to go about town without the protection of an escort is another thing."

Anne conceded this point with a tiny sideways inclination of her head and a chagrined smile. She found it much easier to accept advice when it came from someone other than Delacroix. He had a way of raising her hackles without even trying.

"Why am I not surprised that Mademoiselle Weston believes that women should be allowed to vote?" said Delacroix, gazing down at her with a sort of idle curiosity that was insufferably patronizing. "She is very different from the Creole man's ideal of womanhood."

"You wound me, sir," said Anne with sweet, biting sarcasm. "For, as you must know, it is my fondest wish to be the Creole ideal of womanhood."

Anne was surprised by the deeply masculine rumble of amusement that came from Dandy Delacroix. Wide-eyed, wondering how such an energetic sound could come from such a lazy fellow, she studied the strong column of Delacroix's throat while his head was thrown back in laughter. She marveled at the show of straight white teeth, the expanse of broad chest, the black hair falling forward onto his forehead. The vital image was fascinating and pleasing. And—as it finally occurred to her—very insulting.

What she'd said wasn't that amusing. But he wouldn't stop laughing. She realized that he must be laughing at her modern views on women's rights, which ranked with her deepest convictions about rights for all human beings. *How easy it is for him to laugh at my convictions*, she thought indignantly, *since he has none of his own*.

He thought her an oddity, a British buffoon. She thought him very rude.

Suddenly the three women at the back of the box made their way to the front and gathered around Delacroix. Feeling suddenly suffocated by full skirts of taffeta and silk, Anne stood up and drew closer to Jeffrey, unconsciously grabbing hold of his hand.

"Delacroix," cooed one dashing young blond, slipping her hand into the crook of his elbow, "do tell us what makes you laugh so deliciously!"

"*Oui*, Lucien," said another clinging female, this one a brunette. "What is so impossibly funny? I love your humor, you wicked man!"

The third woman hovered close, looking ready to dive in and claim another arm if Delacroix should happen to sprout one. It was obvious none of the women had come to Katherine's box to be introduced to Anne. They were there to see Delacroix.

Seeming momentarily to stifle his laughter with some difficulty, he patted the gloved hand of the blond woman and said, "We're disturbing the elegant tranquillity of Madame Grimms's opera box, ladies. I suggest we repair to the hall where we can be as merry as we choose." He leaned close to the brunette and whispered quite audibly, "Or as we dare."

"Darling Lucien," she replied, caressing his arm, "with you I would go anywhere!"

Delacroix smiled wickedly, then nodded and winked at Anne as a sort of farewell as he breezed by with the two females clinging to his arms and the other less fortunate one trailing adoringly behind. They had barely gone through the door when he let loose with another hearty laugh.

"Good God!" said Reggie in an appalled undertone as he sidled up next to Anne. "What deplorable manners!"

"Nothing more than one might expect from Delacroix," said Jeffrey, his voice dripping with scorn. "I don't understand what all those females see in the fellow—except his money, of course."

Anne was sure she still detected envy in Jeffrey's voice, despite his disapproval of Delacroix. She wasn't certain how she felt. Insulted, yes. Summarily dismissed, yes. A little hurt, yes. But how could such a man have the power to hurt her?

"Anne, dear, I've a host of people to introduce you to." Katherine's voice broke through Anne's troubled thoughts, and she realized that a veritable army of dapper-dressed, smiling gentlemen was descending upon her. She also realized that she was still clinging to Jeffrey Wycliff's hand.

She was embarrassed. She darted a look at Jeffrey, found him grinning down at her, and hastily untwined their fingers. "You must excuse me, Mr. Wycliff," she mumbled, so low only he could hear. "I forgot myself in the confusion of the moment."

"I like you best of all, Miss Weston, when you forget yourself," he whispered back.

Anne couldn't help smiling, which was just as well, since politeness required that she look agreeable while being introduced to society's best.

* * *

"What's wrong, *cher?*" Micaela's golden-brown eyes were full of sober inquiry and compassion. She reached up and pushed a lock of hair away from Lucien's forehead. They sat together on a sofa in her small, elegantly decorated parlor. Micaela's voluptuous figure was draped in an alluring diaphanous dressing gown Lucien had carefully picked out for her, but she might as well have been wearing a gunnysack.

Lucien leaned forward, propped his elbows on his knees, and cradled his head in his hands. "Nothing's wrong, Micaela. I'm just tired."

There was a long pause. Finally, gently, she suggested, "You are tired very much lately, Lucien."

"Yes." What else could he say? It was a good excuse. At first he'd tried to forget Anne by spending more time in bed with Micaela, but that had proved fruitless. And in the past week—even before he had seen Anne and talked to her tonight—he'd entirely lost any desire to be with Micaela sexually. How did one tell his mistress he only wanted to . . . talk?

After that scene at the opera, leaving Anne so rudely, he felt like an absolute villain. He'd hurt her. He had seen it in her eyes. But he'd felt himself slipping, slipping . . . Slipping into the grasp of something he didn't want to face at this point in his complicated life. He liked Anne Weston too damned well, and a few more minutes in that opera box with her and he might have wrestled her to the floor for wicked purposes. He'd acted in self-defense. He got out of there as fast as he could, leaving a trail of insult and hurt in his wake.

Micaela's hand slid down his arm. "You are full of anger tonight, Lucien. At me, *cher?*"

Lucien stirred himself, caught Micaela's caressing hand, and absently held it. "No, not at you. At me."

"Why? Did you do something bad?"

Lucien lifted his head and smiled wryly at her. "Yes. Are you surprised?"

She smiled back, encouraged. She snuggled closer to him. "I can make you forget ..." She twined her arms around his neck and kissed him. Lucien felt nothing.

She drew back, a look of puzzlement on her face. She was exotic, incredibly beautiful, and wonderfully primitive in her lovemaking. But she wasn't Anne. He closed his eyes for an instant and imagined she was. He went further and imagined Anne's golden hair scattered on a pillow, her blue eyes hazed with passion, her sweet, sly tongue silenced by his kisses ...

"Lucien?"

He opened his eyes. Micaela drew back and settled into the crook of the sofa, studying him.

"I'm sorry," he said at last, feeling the inadequacy of the word but not knowing what else to say.

"It's all right, *cher*," she answered. "Tell me about her."

He made a sound of surprise, laughing softly. "Is it so obvious?"

"*Oui*. So ... tell me about her. I will listen."

Lucien shook his head. "No, I don't want to talk about her." Anne was the last thing he should be talking *or* thinking about. He made an effort to smile at Micaela and said, "Thank you, Micaela, for being so understanding. Right now, though, the thing I need the most is a good strong cup of coffee."

Micaela smiled back. "Whatever you want, *cher*." Then she rose and went to the kitchen.

* * *

Anne sighed and stared out of the carriage window as they drove slowly home through the Vieux Carré. It was raining, and the roads were thick with mud, the gutters swirling with dark brown water. The city was well-lighted by the oil lamps that hung by chains at each streetcorner.

Reggie had made it clear to Anne that he disapproved of the way she'd behaved with Wycliff, allowing him to monopolize her throughout the evening. Anne had no ready excuse to offer her uncle because she knew she had behaved irresponsibly. She'd paid far too much attention to Jeffrey Wycliff.

She'd probably encouraged him to think romantically of her by impulsively grabbing his hand during Delacroix's rude exit. And earlier she'd touched his arm with her hand, keeping it there far too long for propriety. But she'd left her hand on Jeffrey's arm for so long only to irritate Delacroix. Now Anne couldn't imagine why he incited her to behave against her own good judgment just to spite him. She couldn't explain it to herself, much less to Reggie.

Her behavior with Jeffrey was much easier for Anne to understand. Reggie's snobbishness about Jeffrey's orphaned background and his distrust of Jeffrey's ambitions and intentions toward her had conspired to make her more determined to get to know him better.

For once Katherine stayed out of the fray, and, after several minutes of heated discussion with her uncle, Anne decided to put the subject to rest. Laughing, she fell back against the plush squabs of Katherine's well-sprung carriage. "I'm flattered by all this vigilance on my account, Uncle Reggie, but you're jumping to conclusions. You act as though

I'm ready to marry Jeffrey Wycliff. I *do* like him—very much—and I do admire him, but I'm not mad to marry him! Don't worry, I don't intend to be hasty about anything as serious as that."

These few heartfelt words seemed finally to reassure Reggie. He, too, relaxed against the cushions, his face disappearing in the shadows. They continued their slow drive to the Faubourg St. Mary in noncontentious silence, allowing Anne to drift into private speculations about the most interesting of the men she'd met so far in America. Jeffrey, Renard, and Delacroix. Yes, Delacroix.

But first Jeffrey. He seemed to Anne to be exactly the sort of man she'd hoped to meet in America. He was self-made, ambitious, and involved in meaningful work. He was attractive, too. But the thing that most drew her to Jeffrey was something she was wise enough to keep from Reggie. They were both avid fans of Renard. On that basis alone, Anne knew they could be good friends. Whether something romantic was possible between them, she didn't know. So far he hadn't made her heart leap into her throat as Renard had.

Renard. He was her romantic ideal. Their chance meeting on the *Belvedere* had become to Anne like a sharply focused, golden dream. She had no hope, certainly no expectation, of ever seeing Renard again. But once in his arms was better than never, even though, after her brief but thrilling encounter with Renard, she would always compare other men to him. With such daunting competition, would a regular fellow ever be able to win her heart and hand?

Then there was Delacroix. Anne shook her head and smiled, but it was a bittersweet smile after the way he'd behaved tonight. He was an enigma. There was something about him that stirred her.

Was it curiosity? He was clever ... Was she charmed by his wit? Or was she really so shallow that she could disregard his conceit, arrogance, bigotry, and loose morals, and simply be enthralled by his physical beauty?

She didn't know. But something about Delacroix had made her heart race more than once ...

She closed her eyes. American men were a diverse lot, she thought sleepily. Diverse indeed.

Chapter 6

Midmorning sunshine slanted across the ruby-red and peacock-blue Persian rug covering Katherine's drawing room floor, the light that streamed through the tall French windows illuminating the exotic art that hung on the walls and the strange artifacts and barbaric-looking sculptures that littered the tabletops.

A vase of roses stood on a wrought-iron stand next to the sofa, the deep yellow buds exactly matching the color of Anne's walking gown. She was reading Jeffrey's latest article in the *Picayune*, and he was watching her. All was quiet except for the occasional rustle of paper and the muted tick of the ormolu clock on the marble mantel.

When she finished, she folded the paper and set it down, drew a long breath, and smiled at Jeffrey. "Isn't Renard wonderful? Did he really do all that? How is it that you're always the first reporter to know what the Fox does, Jeffrey?"

After three weeks of almost daily association—either at public functions and private parties, or at the Grimms mansion—Anne and Jeffrey were now the best of friends and called each other by their Christian names.

"Which question shall I answer first?" he asked her, grinning.

85

"All of them, and in order, you tease," said Anne.

"Well, yes, Renard is wonderful. We've always agreed about that. And, yes, he did orchestrate the escape last night of five slaves from the Latrobe house on Bourbon Street, getting them out of the very heart of the city without being apprehended. As to how I know about these things before anyone else ..." He shrugged his shoulders.

"You won't tell me? How rude of you, Jeffrey." Anne playfully slapped him on the shoulder. "I thought we shared everything."

"Not everything, Anne." He glanced toward the entryway and lowered his voice. "We've never kissed, and certainly not because of a lack of interest on my part. Perhaps we've just lacked the opportunity? Where *is* the old watchdog, anyway?"

Anne laughed. "If you mean Uncle Reggie, I'm just as surprised as you are that he's not here. I'm sure he would be if he knew that Aunt Katherine had left us alone to fetch her bonnet. I'd almost believe she planned this. She's been gone several minutes."

"She likes me."

"Yes, I know. She's always liked men of the literary persuasion. But more than likely she's having the servants pick flowers at the last minute to take to the cemetery. She has three husbands' tombs to decorate for All Saints' Day, you know. It's a beautiful day, and the place will be awash with fresh-cut blooms. You're welcome to come with us, Jeffrey."

Jeffrey grimaced. "No, thanks. I don't like cemeteries, even when they're decorated for a party. Having no relatives at least saves me from obligatory postmortem visits to them."

Anne winced and smiled, amused by his phraseology but still rather shocked by his lack of sentiment. "That's rather callous of you."

"No, just honest. Now, back to the matter of the kiss . . ." He darted another look toward the entryway and scooted an inch closer to her. "Your aunt likes me, but do *you* like me?"

"Of course I do."

"More to the point, do you like me well enough to kiss me? If you do, this would be the perfect time to tell me . . . and to show me."

Anne looked up into Jeffrey's eager face. His brown eyes were clear, his intentions direct and sincere, his expression ardent. She liked him, she really did. But she wasn't sure she wanted to kiss him. He took her hand and chafed it between his two. His palms were cool and rough. She looked down and studied his square-tipped fingers, the wide knuckles, and the clean, close-clipped nails. There was an ink stain on his thumb. For some elusive reason she found herself mentally comparing his honest workingman's hands to Delacroix's, whose hands were more like those of an artist or a musician—lean, sensitive, strong yet graceful.

"Anne," prompted Jeffrey in a gentle but urgent tone, "you've given me reason to hope that I'm something more to you than a friend."

He was right. She'd been flirting with him since the night of the opera when they'd met for the first time. She had supposed all along that when the opportunity presented itself, she'd happily give him the kiss he was asking for. But now she wasn't so sure it was the right thing to do. She didn't know if Jeffrey could ever be more than a friend. Maybe it was just too soon.

"Jeffrey, I do like you. And you're very special to me. Only . . ."

"Only what, Anne? I know I'm no Renard, but

I hope you aren't comparing me to him. Any man would come up short against such a fellow."

Anne blushed. He'd hit on the exact truth. She was comparing him to Renard. He didn't know, either, that she'd actually met Renard and shared a kiss that she could compare with Jeffrey's. She knew it was nonsense to continue mooning over the romantic outlaw, especially with a very real man with some excellent qualities sitting right next to her. If Jeffrey didn't exactly make her heart race, maybe it was only because she'd grown so comfortable with him. Maybe if she kissed him it would make a difference in her platonic feelings. Guilt won in the end; she supposed she owed him at least one kiss.

"All right."

He grew very still. "You mean you'll let me kiss you?"

"That's exactly what I mean." She closed her eyes, preparing herself, then suddenly got a brilliant, unscrupulous idea. Her eyes flew open just in time to see Jeffrey close his. "First tell me how you get your information about Renard, Jeffrey."

Jeffrey sat back, amused and exasperated. "You minx! That's blackmail!"

"So it is. Now tell me."

Jeffrey chuckled, lifting a hand to tuck a stray curl behind Anne's ear. "I can't tell you specifics."

"Why not?"

He grew sober. "Because it would be dangerous for you. The men I pay to be moles, to ferret out information for me, aren't the most savory fellows."

Anne's brows furrowed. "I can't imagine you consorting with unsavory people, Jeffrey."

Jeffrey's clear brown eyes took on a shrewd look that made him appear hard and threatening. It unsettled her. He didn't look at all like the amiable friend she'd come to know. "Remember, Anne, I told you I'm a chameleon. I blend in wherever I go."

When the strange expression disappeared from Jeffrey's face as quickly as it came, Anne thought she must have imagined it. "These 'moles' you pay to obtain information for you, are they associates of Renard's? Does he have traitors in his midst?"

Jeffrey looked surprised, then admiring. "You're a quick one. Most of my informants pass along rumors from the street. Rumors are unreliable, but sometimes quite true. However, I do have one informant who is a close, trusted partner in Renard's local organization, which is kept small for safety's sake."

"Has this traitor told you who Renard is?"

"No. He's only given me tidbits so far, things to use in my articles—nothing that might jeopardize the operation. He likes the money. I think he has an opium habit, like a lot of the scruffy fellows I deal with. He's edgy. He sweats a lot."

"He sounds like a threat to Renard," Anne said worriedly.

"Not yet. But he might become a threat in time. The reward for Renard's capture grows larger every week. The fellow might decide to betray Renard and cash in on the money. It could buy enough opium to last a millennium."

"Some men would do anything for money," Anne mused.

"Well, money equals power," said Jeffrey matter-of-factly. "Now, where's my kiss?"

After that last comment, Anne was not as disposed to kissing Jeffrey, but it seemed there was no getting out of it. She closed her eyes and waited. She felt his lips touch hers and was encouraged that she felt no revulsion. Actually, it was rather nice. Then he wrapped his large hands around her waist and began moving his lips over hers, ever so softly. But when he slipped his tongue into her mouth and his hands begin to roam up and down her back, she stiffened.

Anne put her hands on Jeffrey's chest and pushed, but he only held her tighter. His breathing was fast and irregular, and she was getting just a little frightened and . . . angry. She abruptly turned her head away and pushed harder against his chest. He let her go.

"Lord, Anne, I'm sorry," he said instantly, dragging his hands through his thick, straight hair. "I lost my head. You're so damned—I mean, you're so beautiful and sweet, for a minute there I forgot myself and just couldn't let go."

Who was she to throw stones, anyway? She'd lost her head when Renard had kissed her that night on the *Belvedere* and done things Reggie would lock her in her room for a year for doing—if he only knew about them.

"It's all right, only don't do it again."

"I can't ever kiss you again?"

She waggled an admonishing finger in his face. "*If* I ever let you kiss me again, you had better stop when I want you to."

He squeezed her hand. "I promise. Really, Anne. I'm sorry I—"

Reggie marched into the room. "You're sorry you *what*, young man?"

Jeffrey seemed to have been momentarily struck dumb by Reggie's unexpected appearance, so Anne improvised. "He's sorry he can't go with us to the cemetery."

Reggie looked sour. "*Is* he? He should thank his

lucky stars he doesn't have to escort Katherine
Grimms to the resting places of the three unfortunate men she called husband. It certainly gives *me*
pause."

Katherine swept into the room, her arms full of
white chrysanthemums. "Are you afraid of bogeys, Reginald, or is it voodoo? I daresay you
won't find either at a Christian cemetery during
the full light of day."

Reggie sucked in his cheeks and puffed out his
narrow chest. "After spending a month under
your roof, Katherine, I daresay I shan't be afraid of
anything ever again. I was only anticipating that I
might be overcome with sympathy for your departed husbands. Not because they died, mind
you, but because they were each once leg-shackled
to you!"

Katherine laughed out loud, a hearty laugh that
made all the crystal in the room sing. "Reginald,
sometimes you're downright amusing. If you
don't watch out I might set my cap for *you!* And
you've seen what happens to all my husbands."

Apparently Reggie found this lightly delivered
threat absolutely petrifying, much scarier than
ghosts or even voodoo curses, called gris-gris by
the superstitious locals. His mouth fell open, and
he suddenly developed a pronounced twitch in his
right eye. Anne and Jeffrey could barely contain
their amusement as Reggie hastily excused himself
and backed out of the room.

Laughing, Anne asked, "Do you think he'll still
come, Aunt Katherine?"

Katherine buried her nose in the fragrant bouquet of flowers she held against her large bosom.
"Oh, he'll come," she said. "Much as he dislikes
the whole business, he'd never think of letting us
go alone. He's too much of a gentleman—and a

fusspot over you—to neglect his perceived 'duty.' Shall we go, dear?"

Jeffrey said good-bye, catching Anne's eye with a significant loverlike look that made Anne's stomach a little queasy. She was very afraid she was going to have a problem on her hands if Jeffrey continued to act like a mooncalf over her.

Katherine had planned their visit to the St. Louis Cemetery to coincide with the hour when most of the Catholic Creole population would be at Mass. That way, the cemetery would be much less crowded. They alighted from the carriage and walked through the neat rows of tombs, which had been whitewashed prior to All Saints' Day by the families of the departed. Because of the high water table in the area, there were no underground graves.

The tombs were of varying shapes and sizes, and there were tall oak, magnolia, and loblolly pine trees scattered around the well-kept grounds. Everything was so bright and clean, Anne didn't find the experience the least bit depressing. And there were flowers everywhere.

They had parked closest to the Protestant section of the cemetery, which was fenced off from the Catholic-only section and the area in the back that was specifically designated for the burial of blacks. Katherine and her first husband had bought a substantial plot of cemetery ground, and she had since put each of her husbands to rest in tombs that adjoined one another.

"There's still plenty of room for my own tomb, although I hope I won't be taking up residence any time soon," Katherine joked.

Katherine, Reggie, and Anne were standing in

front of the tombs, the latter two casting their eyes over the epitaphs inscribed on the front of each.

While Katherine began arranging flowers on the end tomb, Reggie's attention remained fixed on the epitaph of her first husband. He looked grave and thoughtful. Anne moved closer and read over his shoulder, "Herein lies my beloved husband, Nathaniel, and our son, David. May the angels rejoice in the arrival of two splendid, soaring souls who enriched my life beyond my dearest dreams."

Anne was shaken. "Aunt Katherine? I didn't know you had a son." She and Reggie looked at each other, then looked at Katherine, who kept her back to them as she continued with her task.

"Oh, well, I don't suppose I talk about it very much. I told your mother and father years ago, right after it happened."

"They never said anything."

"It was so long ago, I daresay they might have forgotten. They knew I didn't like talking about it."

Instantly chagrined, Anne said, "I'm sorry, Aunt Katherine, I didn't mean to bring up something painful to you."

"I thought you might notice the inscription. I guess I should have prepared myself for the possibility." She turned around, her face flushed. She smiled, but Anne detected a sheen of tears in her eyes. "Nathaniel was killed in a riverboat accident. I was eight months pregnant at the time, and the shock brought on labor. The baby—I called him David after his paternal grandfather—didn't survive."

She smiled again, the corners of her mouth trembling a little as she seemed to reminisce. "He was beautiful, just like his father. Nathaniel and I had intended to have several children, but life doesn't always cooperate with one's plans. And complications during the delivery made my chances for more children impossible, so I was very lucky, indeed, to find two wonderful men after that who loved me even though I was barren."

"I'm sorry, Aunt Katherine," said Anne again, feeling stupid and awkward. She'd never seen her aunt so close to tears.

"Never mind, child. It does me good to talk about it now and then, at least once a year when I clean the tombs and decorate them for All Saints' Day." Her voice took on its usual bracing pitch and tone. "But you see, I'm a survivor. Life is too rich and full to waste time regretting."

But Anne's heart was full of regrets for the sorrow her aunt must have suffered all those years ago as a young woman, and, though they were softened by time, the memories still obviously brought her aunt pain. Katherine went back to arranging her flowers, and Reggie remained silent, his jaw set, his eyes fixed on the ground.

Just when Anne thought she couldn't possibly feel more blue-deviled, a cloud snuffed out the sun. She looked up and saw that, as so frequently occurred in New Orleans, a storm was brewing. But Anne didn't really mind, because the sudden showers usually lasted only a short while.

"Would you mind if I wandered around a bit, Aunt Katherine?" said Anne, feeling the need for private reflection.

Katherine spoke over her shoulder, not looking at her or Reggie. "Oh, do, Anne! The cemetery is beautiful this time of year. Why don't you go, too, Reginald?"

Reggie cleared his throat. "Well, if you don't mind, Katherine, I noticed a few weeds around the lee side of . . . er . . . Nathaniel's tomb, and I thought I might pull them."

Katherine's busy hands stilled for a minute, but she didn't turn around. It was a good thing she didn't, because Reggie's face was so red, it was obvious he'd rather not be looked at just then. "If you'd like, Reginald. The whitewashing took me so long the other day that I worked till dusk. I'm sure I missed a few weeds when I tidied up."

"Certainly . . . understandable, of course," mumbled Reggie. "I'll just lay down these flowers . . ."

Anne laid her flowers on the ground beside Reggie's bunch, kissed him tenderly on the cheek, and walked away. She knew that, despite the barbed comments exchanged between her aunt and uncle, they felt an underlying mutual respect. And today they'd actually shown their tender sides to each other. Anne was sure they'd still argue, but she felt as though a threshold had been crossed. Maybe now they'd allow themselves the luxury of an occasional lapse of animosity and actually enjoy each other's company. Or at least tolerate each other!

The sun was dodging in and out of the clouds. Anne was in shadow one minute, in bright golden sunshine the next. She strolled leisurely through the cemetery, skirting the edge of the Negro burial grounds. She wanted to go in and read the inscriptions, but she was afraid she'd be thought of as an intruder by the black people inside who were visiting the last resting places of their loved ones.

Finally she was in the Catholic section. Here the tombs were the largest and closest together, the flowers the most profuse. But very few people were about; as Katherine had predicted, most of them were attending Mass.

In the oldest parts of the cemetery, the tombs

were so high and so close together that walking through them was like passing through the narrowest of alleys. Her visibility was limited. She heard voices without seeing who was talking, like disembodied whispers drifting from another plane of existence. This fanciful idea was dispelled when someone, quite solidly mortal, now and then appeared from behind a tomb when she least expected it.

She imagined that after dark the cemeteries could be very efficacious for committing crimes, or for romantic trysts. Even in broad daylight, especially when the sun was behind a cloud—as now—she sensed an aura of mystery and secrecy about the place. She remembered her aunt's joking remarks about bogeys and voodoo, and a chill went through her. She was being silly, of course, but still—

"Oh!" Suddenly Anne was face to face with a gray waistcoat. Someone had come around the corner of a tomb at a very fast pace. She was surprised they'd avoided a painful and embarrassing collision. She looked up—way up—and stared at the most attractive black man she'd ever seen.

"Pardon me, mademoiselle," he said, stepping to the side and tipping his elegant beaver hat. He smiled briefly, his light gray-green eyes flashing in the sunlight that had just reappeared. "Are you all right?"

She smiled back. "Yes, quite. I was just a little startled." He was backing away, still looking at her. She thought she saw a spark of admiration in his expression, and it pleased her. "You seem to be in a hurry, so don't worry about me. Go on about your business. I'm sure it's important."

"Oui, mademoiselle, it is." He smiled, tipped his hat again, and walked quickly away. His skin was a light copper color, and, judging by his smart suit of clothes, she assumed he was a *gens de couleur*. His accent was cultured, and his bearing was professional. He was obviously educated. She watched him until he made a turn and disappeared.

She continued her walk, but stopped when she thought she caught a glimpse of a familiar figure down another alley between tombs. She backed up, held on to the cold marble edge of a tomb, and peered around the corner to see.

It was Delacroix. He was dressed in riding clothes: a black jacket, white jodhpurs, and tall black boots. A plain white shirt and stock completed the outfit to elegant perfection. His several rings winked in the sun that had just crept out from behind a cloud.

But Anne had no intention of creeping out from behind *her* hiding place. She found Delacroix fascinating, and this was an opportunity to watch him while she remained unobserved. She'd tried many times to analyze her interest in Delacroix and why he made her feel slightly off-balance whenever he happened to be nearby, but she'd never come to a logical or satisfying conclusion.

The fascination he held for her was all the more confusing because she disapproved of him and everything he stood for. He was an infuriating flirt without a serious thought in his head. However, he wasn't without wit, so there had to be quite a lot going on inside that handsome head of his. But what? He was nothing like the kind of man she'd come to America to find. He was a . . . curiosity. Yes, a curiosity. That must be it. That must be why she couldn't keep her eyes off him.

He was leaning against a tomb, his arms folded over his chest, his long legs crossed at the ankles.

He was hatless, and his hair was a wind-blown riot of black waves, glistening in the sunlight. His head rested against the tomb, his face was tilted to the sky, and his eyes were closed.

Anne was reminded of the way he'd looked that night at the opera when he'd thrown back his head and laughed at her sarcastic retort about wishing to be the Creole ideal of womanhood. He'd exuded a kind of vital, masculine energy, and the memory of it had come unbidden to Anne's mind many times over the past weeks. But the memory came with some pain attached to it as well. He'd left her rudely, with a woman on each arm and another one practically hanging on to his coattail.

Her eyelids drooped slightly as she continued to stare. The sun beat down on her shoulders, making her feel lazy and contented and a little ... sensual. The smell of flowers filled the humid air. She leisurely perused his form from head to toe. It wasn't quite fair for one mortal man to possess so many perfect physical parts ...

He moved, and she ducked behind the tomb, resting her hot cheek against the cold stone. Her breathing was strangely quickened. She closed her eyes, gathering her composure. She was just embarrassed, she told herself. Embarrassed to be sneaking looks at a scandalous rogue—

"Mademoiselle Weston! Fancy meeting you here."

Anne opened her eyes and pushed away from the tomb, standing ramrod straight. She snatched one quick look at his face and was afraid she saw amusement dancing in the depths of his black eyes. Because she feared to look again lest her suspicions be confirmed—that he knew she had been watching him and found the fact humorous—her distracted gaze darted everywhere.

"I . . . I'm here with my aunt and uncle. She's decorating the tombs of her three husbands."

"Ah, yes." There was a pause. "But aren't they buried in the Protestant section?"

"Yes. But I thought I'd look around a little, you know."

He stepped closer. Anne could feel his gaze raking her face, and her temperature rose another degree. "Perhaps you overdid it?"

Her eyes flicked to meet his. "Wh—what do you mean?"

He smiled. "You were leaning against the tomb with your eyes closed." He raised a hand and lightly traced his forefinger along the curve of her cheek. "Your face is flushed, and your beautiful eyes look a little feverish. Though it is November, the autumn here in New Orleans is much different than where you come from, *n'est-ce pas?* You must be very hot."

"Yes, I am a little worn down by the heat," she exclaimed too quickly, happy to be supplied with an explanation for her blushing embarrassment and unusual posture when he found her. Trouble was, as long as he continued to stand so close and to touch her so tenderly, she'd never recover from the "heat." *Why was he being so kind?* she wondered. She glanced around again, half-expecting a dozen of his female fans to come out from behind the surrounding tombs.

"You must sit down." He reached out and caught her elbow. "Come with me."

Anne's heart leaped into her throat. "Come with you? Where to?"

He laughed softly, seductively. "Don't be alarmed, *ma petite.* Come . . . just around the corner." He led her along with a gentle, supportive hand. Anne could hardly reconcile this courteous gentleman with the careless cad from the opera. "My family's plot is close by, and there's a bench you can sit on. It's in the shade where you can cool off."

"My aunt will miss me."

"Don't you mean your uncle? It doesn't strike me that Madame Grimms is much of a worrier, but your uncle is another matter."

Anne gave a nervous laugh. "Too true. Uncle Reggie does worry about me. All the more reason why I ought to go back."

"But if you collapsed on the way, I'd never forgive myself. Here. Just sit and rest for a spell. Then I'll escort you back to the heathen section of the cemetery myself."

Anne laughed and sat. "You're very kind."

He sat down beside her, crossed his legs, and casually draped one arm over his knee. Anne found herself admiring his legs again, and his hands—rings and all. He wore an enormous emerald on his left hand that was probably worth half her dowry.

Desperate for something to talk about, she blurted, "Why aren't you at Mass?"

He smiled. He had begun to play with his emerald ring, turning it around and around his finger. The movement was oddly arousing. She looked away. "Dear Mademoiselle Weston, can you really picture a rogue like me in church?"

She could picture him there, all right . . . surrounded by women. She pushed the thought away and said, "You went riding instead?"

"*Oui.* Do you ride, *cher?*"

"I did in England, but I haven't here."

"Ah, you would love to ride on Bocage. There

are acres and acres of lush green fields along the river."

She nervously smoothed her skirt with a damp palm. He couldn't actually be inviting her to go riding with him, could he? "I ... I'm sadly out of practice, I'm afraid."

"We have a poky old mare you could ride—"

She laughed. "I'm not that out of practice!"

He joined in her laughter. "I did not think so. And I have just the mount for you. A perfect match. A young filly with a light step and a long blond mane. She is frisky and is always tossing her head."

Although she was still rather uncomfortably warm, Anne was beginning to enjoy herself. "Are you implying that I am frisky, Mr. Delacroix?"

"*Oui.*"

"And that I toss my head about like your horse?"

"You lift your small chin in a defiant pose, which is most alluring. Both you and my golden filly are haughty, beautiful creatures."

Anne shook her head, smiling ruefully. "I'll bet you say that to all the girls." *And I'll bet they're just as ridiculously charmed as I am.*

Delacroix smiled and shrugged, leaving her to wonder.

"What kind of horse do you ride, Mr. Delacroix?"

"A black steed."

"To match your eyes?" She blushed, immediately sorry she'd mentioned his eyes. It seemed too intimate a comment.

Those black eyes gleamed with mischief when he answered, "No, to match my wicked soul, *cher.*"

"I don't believe you're as wicked as you pretend."

His smile faltered for a moment, then returned just as broad. "You think I'm pretending?" he asked her in a low, provocative tone. "Shall I prove it? Shall I show you how wicked I am?"

Up shot her temperature again. She laughed nervously. "You are a scoundrel, Mr. Delacroix, teasing me so! But I must remark on the fact that while you didn't attend Mass, you are still here at the cemetery on All Saints' Day. You must feel some reverence for the religious holiday."

She felt him shift on the bench, his arm grazing her shoulder, his thigh stirring her skirt. His mood shifted, too.

"I've five brothers buried here. I'm the oldest child, and, even though it was years ago, I remember each of them as clearly as if we'd just tumbled on the grass together yesterday, playing soldiers."

Anne's sympathy was instantly stirred. "I'm sorry, Mr. Delacroix."

"*Merci.*"

"Do you mind my asking—no, never mind."

"It's all right. It's natural that you'd be curious. They all died within a week of one another in a yellow fever outbreak. My parents were devastated. I just barely survived."

"Are you the only child left, then?"

"No, I have five sisters and one brother. They are considerably younger than I am because they were all born after the others died."

Anne shook her head, hardly capable of imagining the pain everyone involved must have endured, and then the courage it took to start another family. "Your mother must be a strong woman. I don't know if I could bear losing so many children like that, especially all at once, and then go on and have more."

"Not all Creoles are as frivolous as I am, you

know. With her limited experience, and within her limited sphere of influence, my mother is strong, loyal, and loving."

Anne felt the heat suffusing her cheeks again. "You are gently chastising me for my mocking comment that night at the opera, my implication that I do not admire Creole women and would never want to emulate them. I was wrong to lump them all together." Anne smiled sheepishly. "I fancy myself so fair and unprejudiced, then I say something so bigoted."

"Ah, mademoiselle, we all make mistakes. In our dealings with people, we so often find that there is more than meets the eye."

It was suddenly overcast again and had started to sprinkle lightly. Anne hardly noticed, because she was staring at Delacroix, dwelling on his last words. At last she said, "I quite agree with you, Mr. Delacroix. For example, *you* present yourself to the world as a frippery sort of fellow, but there seems to be much more beneath your light facade."

He laughed harshly. The sound was unexpected, intrusive. He stood up and extended his hand. "Are you rested, mademoiselle?" His arrogant drawl was back in full force. "It begins to rain. Besides, I should not wish for your uncle to think I'd absconded with his niece. I haven't dueled in a fortnight, and I don't wish to interrupt such a long stretch of good conduct. I promised my mother, you see."

"I'm quite rested," she replied stiffly, offended again. It seemed Dandy Delacroix's moods were mercurial, and the man's character too complicated to understand. She took his hand and stood up, but when she tried to pull free, he held fast.

Then, with a little tug, he had her next to him, face to face, with only inches between them.

"Wh-what are you doing, Mr. Delacroix?" she mumbled, her gaze resting on the sly slant of his finely molded lips.

"I'm thinking of proving to you that I am, indeed, quite wicked, mademoiselle. I only promised my mother that I wouldn't duel. I never said I'd refrain from seducing frisky females in the cemetery."

Anne felt mesmerized. She watched as he bent his head and his lips drew closer, then curved in a rueful smile.

"It is customary to close one's eyes when one is about to be kissed," he whispered.

She closed her eyes. But instead of the warmth of Delacroix's lips, Anne felt the first cool drops of rain. An instant later it was storming in earnest, large drops of water falling in buckets.

"Lucky girl," he murmured. "Saved by Providence on All Saints' Day." Then he hurried Anne along, back toward the Protestant section of the cemetery and the shelter of her aunt's closed carriage. Dazed and bemused, Anne moved like someone in a dream. Later, much later, she would try to understand what had happened, and why she'd almost let him kiss her . . .

Chapter 7

"In England a woman of quality would
never send her niece out on a shopping errand," grumbled Reggie, trailing Anne closely as
she meandered through the stalls of the marketplace with a large basket dangling from her elbow.
"That's what servants are paid for, for heaven's
sake."

Anne bent to examine a bunch of plump purple
grapes. "Everyone comes to the market," she said,
paying for the grapes and placing them in the basket. "That's probably one reason why I enjoy running these little errands for Aunt Katherine. At the
market all races and social classes mix harmoni-
ously."

"I don't know how you can describe a place
with so much discordant noise as being harmonious," argued Reggie, waving away a grinning mulatto boy who was hawking brass bracelets he'd
cleverly displayed by adorning his own thin arms.

Feeling festive and hoping to improve her uncle's disgruntled mood, Anne stopped a pretty girl
who was selling *boutonnières* and bought one for
Reggie. It was a tiny bouquet of Spanish jasmine,
carnations, and violets.

"Here, hold my basket, Uncle."

"I'm happy to take your basket. I've been wanting to carry it for you all afternoon. But you're as stubborn as your aunt—what's this? What are you doing, Anne?"

"I'm pinning this *boutonnière* to your lapel. Perhaps the beauty of it and its sweet smell will lighten your mood!" Having completed her task, she patted her uncle's arm and smiled up into his face. He was peering skeptically down his nose at the cluster of flowers, but even as Anne watched, his expression softened. He lifted the lapel and inspected the *boutonnière* closely. "Humph! They *are* rather lovely, aren't they?"

"Yes, you gruff old goat. Now smile for me, please."

Reggie tried hard to be uncooperative, but eventually a smile emerged from beneath his large mustache. He pinched her chin. "You're a minx, Anne. But if you really want my mood to improve, might I suggest we find a place to sit down? My feet are killing me."

"There's a coffee shop just over there," said Anne, standing on tiptoe and pointing. "Wouldn't you like a cup of coffee, too, Uncle Reggie?"

Reggie grunted, which Anne took for a yes. She knew he hated to admit that he had come to enjoy coffee almost as much as tea. They wove through the crowd and found an empty table and two chairs, and Reggie ordered for them both. Reggie had barely set down the basket and heaved a weary sigh when Anne saw him wince.

"What is it, Uncle Reggie?"

"Oh, it's that tiresome swain of yours. You'd think we could pass one day in peace without running into the fellow."

Anne glanced around the marketplace. "My swain? Who can you mean?" For one ridiculous moment, she thought of Delacroix. The fact that she'd nearly allowed the scoundrel to kiss her must have muddled her brain! She had regretted her weakness a thousand times since that fateful afternoon in the cemetery. Delacroix was not the kind of man on which a sensible woman would risk her heart.

"Don't look," whispered Reggie, slumping in his chair. "Maybe he won't see us—drat! Too late!"

Anne turned in her seat and saw Jeffrey striding toward them, a broad smile on his handsome face. "Why, it's Jeffrey! Sit up, Uncle Reggie, you look very sulky and rude in that posture."

Reggie begrudgingly sat up and composed his face into a semblance of politeness.

"Anne! Fancy bumping into you!" Jeffrey tipped his hat to Anne and nodded respectfully to Reggie.

"I don't suppose you recall last night at dinner when Anne told you we were coming to the market this afternoon?" said Reggie peevishly.

Jeffrey shrugged, looking ingenuous. "Did you, Anne? Well! I'm terribly glad to see you."

"Yes, it's been all of eighteen hours since you last saw her," drawled Reggie.

"Only eighteen hours?" said Jeffrey with feigned shock. "But it feels like a lifetime."

Anne laughed. "You goose. Sit down and join us for a cup of coffee. And don't mind Uncle Reggie. He doesn't like these jaunts to the market. They put him in a bit of a snit."

Reggie sniffed and said nothing, pretending to watch the people as they passed by. Anne still couldn't understand why Reggie disliked Jeffrey so much. It was probably because he hadn't gotten past his original opinion that Jeffrey was too "common" for her. But Reggie ought to know that that sort of attitude only made her all the more determined to be Jeffrey's friend.

When Jeffrey had pulled a chair over and sat down, he inquired, "Where's your aunt today?"

"She's visiting a friend of hers, a Madame Tussad. She goes every Saturday and sends Reggie and me on some errand to get us out of the way," said Anne. "It's rather mysterious, actually. She always insists on going alone to see her."

"She's probably a vulgar acquaintance she doesn't dare introduce you to, Anne," opined Reggie. "Delphina Street isn't exactly a fashionable address."

"My guess is she's an invalid, and Aunt Katherine doesn't wish to appear as though she's advertising a charity visit. But whoever she is, she's awfully important, because Aunt Katherine never misses a visit. She goes every Saturday afternoon like clockwork."

Jeffrey listened politely, but Anne could tell he was indifferent to such mundane chitchat, so she asked, "What are you doing today? Are you researching new information for another article about Renard?"

Jeffrey smiled ruefully. "I believe I'm growing rather jealous of what used to be my favorite subject to write about."

Anne raised her brows. "Used to be?"

"Sometimes I think my link to Renard is the only thing you like about me, Anne."

"Don't be silly. You and I got on swimmingly right from the start. But if you'd rather not talk about Renard—"

"Well, the thing is, I *have* discovered something very exciting about the Fox . . ." Jeffrey's voice trailed off, and he glanced nervously at Reggie, who pretended not to listen while he continued to watch passersby. Just then their coffee arrived, and while Reggie fished in his pocket for some coins

and ordered another coffee, Jeffrey leaned close to
Anne and whispered, "I'll come over tomorrow
night and tell you everything. I'm almost certain I
know what Renard has planned next. And I mean
to be there when it happens."

After such a disclosure, Anne didn't know how
she was expected to carry on a normal conversation. She was aflame with curiosity. And now it
was her turn to be jealous. Jeffrey was going to be
a part of the excitement! He might even see Renard, which was something she'd longed to do for
weeks! If she were a man, she could go with Jeffrey on this adventure, no questions asked. *It just
wasn't fair!* she fumed to herself.

"Have you been to Congo Square yet, Anne?"

"I'm sorry, Jeffrey. What did you say?" She
glanced up and saw him looking at her meaning-
fully. He was trying to convey to her that she was
acting oddly and arousing Reggie's suspicions.
She'd been daydreaming, idly stirring her coffee
till it was probably tepid. Jeffrey was right; she
must put off thinking of Renard till later.

"I said, have you been to Congo Square?"

She took a swallow of coffee and smiled wistfully. "I've heard about it. That's where the slaves
gather on Sundays to dance." Anne gave Reggie
an accusing look, which he pretended to ignore.
All this pretending was starting to annoy her. "I've
longed to see it ever since I got here." Just as she'd
longed to see Renard. She figured her chances of
seeing either were pretty dim. She felt her spirits
flagging.

"Well, tomorrow's Sunday . . ." Jeffrey turned to
Reggie. "Why don't we drive down after lunch to-
morrow? All of us, sir. You, me, Anne, and Mrs.
Grimms, of course. It's quite a spectacle."

Reggie sniffed. "By all accounts I've heard, it's a spectacle not fit for a lady's eyes."

"Gentleman *and* ladies gather to watch, sir," said Jeffrey. "Mrs. Grimms has gone quite often in the past."

"Mrs. Grimms is Americanized, I'm afraid. Our notions of what's proper and fit for a lady's eyes— particularly as the entertainment falls on a Sunday—are quite different in England, Mr. Wycliff," said Reggie with a superior mien. "I promised Anne's parents to look after her as if she were my own daughter. I pride myself on the fact that I've succeeded in doing that admirably well. Pagan dancing is not an activity one watches, particularly on the Sabbath."

"I've always rather thought of it as a cultural lesson, sir," Jeffrey persisted. "The slaves dance their native dances, using tom-toms and hand-made stringed instruments that are rather crude, but which keep up the rhythm splendidly. Their dances are all quite authentic. It's the one opportunity the slaves have to feel really free, I suppose. Feeling as you do about slavery, and as I know Anne feels, I'd think you'd enjoy seeing the black people participate in an activity indigenous to their true origins."

"Don't try to shame me into yielding to you, Mr. Wycliff," said Reggie with a stern look. "One might have an intellectual or a compassionate curiosity about many things—say, Chinese water torture, or childbirth—but that doesn't mean one should be allowed to witness them firsthand."

"Unless you're a man," said Anne, matter-of-factly. "Then you might do as you please."

When Reggie opened his mouth to protest, Anne said, "No, don't. I don't want to quarrel today, Uncle Reggie. It's too beautiful a day for that,

and I want to enjoy myself here at the market before it's time to go home. Jeffrey, didn't you order
a coffee?"

Jeffrey got up to inquire about his coffee, and
Anne concentrated on her own quickly cooling
drink. She was feeling glum, quite trapped by con-
ventions. And Reggie's mood had deteriorated
again, thanks to Jeffrey's showing up unexpectedly. She was studying her uncle's grim face over
the rim of her cup when someone else unexpectedly came into view. Delacroix.

Anne could see him in profile as he seemed to
be examining a bouquet of orchids. He was with a
woman—an incredibly beautiful woman. The quadroon was dressed in an aquamarine tignon and a
gown of the same deep, bright blue. She was
snuggled close to Delacroix's side, her thigh flush
against his, her long, slim fingers tracing circles on
the smooth bulge of his upper arm.

Observing the woman's behavior, engaged as
she was in such a public display of affection, Anne
concluded that she must be Delacroix's mistress.
Not even the star-eyed females who flocked to
him at parties and the opera had dared to touch
him as intimately as this woman did.

An odd feeling was twisting Anne's insides till
she could hardly breathe, the sharp, unpleasant
sensation lessening somewhat when she looked
away from Delacroix and his mistress. If she didn't
know better, she'd think she was jealous.

Then Reggie saw him. "Good God, there's
Delacroix. I suppose he'll want to sit with us, too."

"Don't you like him, either, Uncle Reggie?" she
asked, then added, "At least you can't accuse him
of trying to be my swain." Anne was distressed to
note a trace of wistfulness in her voice.

"Actually, Anne, I do rather like him, though I

can't say why. Maybe, as you say, it's because he hasn't chased after you. That wouldn't do at all. Lord, doesn't he have a way with the ladies?"

He paused while they both studied Delacroix. Today he was wearing a cream-colored jacket and trousers, making his dark good looks all the more striking. The woman was just as striking in her bright colors and seemed extremely pleased to be exactly where she was—practically plastered to Delacroix's side.

"They make a handsome couple," observed Reggie.

"Maybe we shouldn't look at them," said Anne, determinedly turning to face Reggie. "If he catches us watching, he'll come over."

Reggie's eyes suddenly widened. "No, now that I see who he's with, I'm sure he won't dare to." He blushed, shot Anne a harried glance, shifted in his chair, and cleared his throat. "That is . . . I mean . . ."

Exasperated, Anne shook her head. "It's all right to say it, Uncle Reggie. I'm not a complete dolt. I know he's with his mistress. In fact, I figured it out before you did."

Reggie stiffened and refused to meet Anne's eyes. "It isn't proper to discuss such things with you, Anne. And it's very unladylike of you to try to discuss them with *me*. Suffice it to say, Delacroix's too much of a gentleman to introduce you to his . . . er . . . companion. Even if he sees us, he won't approach us. Mark my words."

Wouldn't he? Anne wondered.

Maybe it was curiosity that drew her gaze back to the beautiful couple in the contrasting colors. Maybe curiosity kept her eyes fixed to Delacroix's face as he paid for the flowers, wondering if he'd look at her, wondering if he'd acknowledge her if she caught his attention.

He turned as if he sensed someone watching him. When their eyes met, Anne didn't flinch. She didn't look down shyly or pretend to be surprised, or react in any of the coy ways that would have been usual under the circumstances. She boldly held his gaze—the seconds ticking away like the emotion-charged countdown of a firing squad—till *he* looked away. Then he took his companion's elbow and led her through the crowd and out of sight.

"There are so many things I don't understand, Uncle Reggie," said Anne, sighing. "People, feelings, attitudes. It's all an enigma."

Reggie watched Jeffrey moving toward them, a cup of steaming coffee in his hand, the same self-satisfied smile on his face. "Yes, Anne," he said tiredly, a deep line appearing between his brows. "There are many things I don't understand, either. People frequently are not who, or what, they seem."

Reggie was looking at Jeffrey as he talked, but Anne couldn't imagine that he was referring to her American friend. She'd never in her life met anyone more open and genuine than Jeffrey Wycliff.

Maybe Reggie was talking about Katherine, who had surprised them both at the cemetery with a soft side she apparently hid most of the time.

Or maybe he was talking about Delacroix. To Anne, Dandy Delacroix was the ultimate enigma, the most perplexing mix of human parts and passions she'd ever met.

She wondered where he was taking his mistress. To a little cottage where a sudden rain shower wouldn't interrupt their kisses? That awful, unwelcome twisting feeling returned.

* * *

Dressed as Renard, Lucien climbed the tree outside Anne's bedchamber. His mask, shirt, boots, and trousers blended with the shadows. It was just after midnight, the sky a velvet expanse of muted black, the stars and moon obscured by low-lying clouds. A rumble of thunder echoed distantly. The air was thick with moisture and the verdant scent of wet earth.

He'd watched till he saw her light go out, then waited to make sure she was asleep before climbing through her bedroom window. He didn't want to scare her, and he didn't want the household alerted by her surprised outcry, either. He wasn't sure how she'd react to seeing him, or what he wanted to do once he got inside . . . but he was about to find out.

As he easily, quietly climbed each limb, his anticipation sharpened. He'd been imagining such a risky venture for weeks. Every encounter with Anne had intensified his desire to see her, and for her to see him again . . . as Renard. She liked Renard. She and Renard believed in the same things. As Delacroix, he was always at a disadvantage. They had nearly shared a kiss at the cemetery, but she'd been fighting her attraction to him all along. Then today at the market, he could see that her defenses were up again. She'd watched him and Micaela scornfully, throwing him a challenge with those magnificent blue eyes of hers.

Tonight he was meeting that challenge his own way. Of course, he had no business pursuing the girl, but—damn it!—he couldn't seem to help himself. It was dangerous for both of them, but no woman had ever felt so right in his arms. He was willing to take risks to hold her again.

He swung over to the window ledge, balanced,

then gently eased up the half-opened window, pushed aside the curtains, and let himself down. He was inside. He stood very still. He could see nothing in the dark room and had no idea where Anne's bed was located.

Deprived of sight, he found his other senses were sharper. Anne's scent was in the room. Light, sweet, floral. He listened for the soft sounds of her breathing and was disturbed when, after a couple of minutes, he still heard nothing. Then he realized he was the only person in the room . . .

. . . Till the door opened and Anne entered, holding a lamp in one hand and a goblet of milk in the other. Lucien was frozen to the spot, waiting for the inevitable scream and the lamp or the milk, or both, to fall to the floor with a loud clatter. But she didn't scream, and she didn't drop anything.

In the instant she saw his dark silhouette against the pale curtains, her eyes widened and her hands trembled, making the flame dance and the milk slosh and spill. She hesitated only a second, then closed the door softly behind her and advanced.

Lucien swallowed hard. Brave girl, he thought. Brave and foolish.

She looked like an angel. Her golden hair waved over her shoulders. The lamplight gave her face a soft, ethereal glow and reflected in her eyes like shining stars. A pale, flowing nightdress molded to her exquisite shape as she took one deliberate step after another . . . toward him.

Lucien lifted a warning hand and stepped back. "Anne . . . don't come any closer."

She stopped abruptly. "Why?"

"Turn out the lamp."

"I don't understand. Why did you come? I'm *glad* you came, but—"

"Snuff the light, then we'll talk."

She looked doubtful.

He grinned. "Don't worry . . . I'll find you in the dark."

Was that a blush that rose to her cheeks, or just a trick of shadows and lamplight? She gave him one last look, then padded to a nearby dresser, set down the lamp and the milk, and turned out the light.

Darkness, a few steps, and he had her in his arms.

His mouth claimed hers with an urgency that was born of weeks of yearning. Why had he ever wondered what he'd do once he got inside her room? Holding her and kissing her were as inevitable and natural as the sun rising in the morning and setting at night.

Her lips were as pliant and fresh as a tender rosebud, the nectar just as sweet. She melted against him, all her lush curves molding against his taut muscles, inciting him to heights of passion he'd never dreamed existed. Her small, curious hands wended their way up his back and around his neck, the fingers playing at the edge of the scarf that hid his hair. His hands circled her waist and pulled her closer, closer . . . It was wonderful, it was magical, and it was dangerous.

He pulled back. Both of them were breathing fast and shallow. "Now do you know why I came?" he asked. "I had to hold you again."

"I never dreamed . . ." she murmured. She gave a soft laugh. "Well, actually I've dreamed of nothing else since that night on the *Belvedere*."

He caressed her back. "I'm so glad you dream of me, *cher*, as I dream of you. But coming here, it is insanity, *n'est-ce pas*? I can just see the headlines now: *Renard Caught at Last . . . in Woman's Bedchamber!* Hardly heroic."

Her hands came around from the back of his head to trail lingeringly over his shoulders and the hard planes of his chest. A thrill ran down his spine. He heard her sigh, sweet and low. "You will always be a hero to me, Renard. But, tell me, do you make a habit of visiting women in this manner?"

Lucien laughed, hoping he sounded convincingly devil-may-care. He didn't want her to know that she was the only woman he'd ever climbed through a window to visit. There had never been anyone important enough to him to risk capture. And, truth to tell, any lady's bedchamber he'd ever wanted to visit before had been easily accessible through the normal means of entry. He'd been welcomed with open arms. Too bad Anne's arms were the only ones he wanted now.

"Where does your abigail sleep, *cher?*"

"In the next room, through a connecting door."

"Christ! Then I'd better go. You showed admirable restraint, but she might scream if she sees me."

"In this dark room I can hardly see the nose in front of my face," she reasoned, "and neither could Sarah if she woke up. Besides, she is a heavy sleeper."

"Still, I don't want to take any more risks than necessary, for both our sakes."

"But you just got here," she complained, a petulant note in her voice. He could imagine her pouting, and it made him want to kiss her again. His pulse quickened.

"I have to go before I *can't* go. Don't you understand, *cher?*"

"Then one more kiss," she suggested breathlessly.

"Your kisses make me dizzy. They make me

forget everything but you and how I want to make love to you."

He felt her tremble. "One more kiss, Renard," she taunted, holding her lips close to his. "I dare you."

He laughed. "You aren't a bit shy, eh?"

"Not with you."

They kissed again. Lucien felt every inch of him spring to life as she opened herself to him with sweet, virginal abandon. He caressed her back, kneading the firm flesh, reaching lower and lower till his hands cupped her rounded buttocks. He pulled her hard against him, against the heated swell of his manhood. She gasped, and her head fell back. God, how he wanted her! And maybe she wanted him just as much . . .

There was a shuffling sound and a moan from behind a nearby wall. Lucien's head reared up. "Is that your abigail?"

Anne's voice was muffled, dazed. "I don't know. Probably."

"I have to go." He put her at arm's length, steadied her, then let go.

"Renard! When will I see you again?"

There was a hesitation. "I don't know." He moved toward the window.

"What if I want to send you a message?"

"It's best you don't know how to find me." He pushed the curtains aside.

"You don't trust me?"

"It's not safe, *cher*. Good-bye."

"Not good-bye, Renard," she said stubbornly. "Till we meet again."

He knew she couldn't see him, but he smiled. She was a frisky filly, all right. "*Oui, ma petite.* Till we meet again." Then he climbed out the window and down the tree. After his quick descent, he looked up. She was leaning out the window, her hair cascading down like that of a princess in a fairy tale. She threw him a kiss, which he caught and held against his heart. Then he turned and hurried away, hidden by the shadows of a dark night.

Anne paced the floor of her bedchamber. She'd attended church that morning with Reggie and Katherine like the dutiful little Anglican girl she was, but now that services were over, she was wild to do something a dutiful little Anglican girl would never do in a millennium.

Last night's dreamlike tryst with Renard had served only to underscore her feelings of confinement and frustration. She had lain awake hours after he left, reliving his kisses and caresses, her nerves still vibrant with longing. She wondered why he had actually come to her bedchamber. It seemed too wonderful and incredible to believe he'd risk capture just to kiss her! But he remembered her from the *Belvedere*, which meant that their encounter on the mist-shrouded deck that night so many weeks ago had meant something to him, too. Maybe not as much as it did to her, but *something*.

Oh, how she longed to see him again! To talk to him. To discover who he was behind the mask. She hoped that he was as curious about her as she was about him, that she was not just some sort of romantic conquest. She had to admit that it was a possibility that Renard dallied with many women, climbing in through their bedroom windows to steal a kiss and sometimes something more, but she wanted to believe she was special.

He was her hero. He represented all that was free and exciting, while her own life seemed as restrictive as a prisoner's. Anne sank down on the edge of her bed, looking wistfully toward the window through which Renard had come and gone. She had to get out. If she didn't get out for a couple of hours, she'd scream.

The logical destination was Congo Square to watch the dancers. Reggie had made it clear he wouldn't take her, and Aunt Katherine, for some unfathomable reason, had seemed disinclined to oppose his authority in this matter; she wouldn't go without Reggie. That left Anne with no recourse but deception. It rankled her, at the advanced age of three-and-twenty, to have to sneak away to a harmless afternoon's recreation!

After lunch, Reggie and Katherine retired to their separate chambers to read and nap. Anne had complied with this American custom of resting on Sundays, generally spending the afternoon outside in the garden lounging and reading under a leafy tree. But today the idea of staying close to home was as appetizing as eating worms. She was in no mood to be biddable or docile. She was feeling rebellious.

Anne looked at the cabinet clock that stood against the wall. An hour had passed since her guardians had gone to their rooms, and she figured that both of them ought to have fallen asleep by now. She was already dressed to go out, neat and proper in a maroon silk walking dress, sturdy half-boots, and a black velvet bonnet with a starched, netted veil that, when pulled down, would lend her a little anonymity.

In her small beaded reticule she had money for a hired coach; a clean, scented, neatly pressed handkerchief; and a bottle of smelling salts. No lady ever left her premises without these essentials. Now she must slip out the front door without the servants observing her. Because Sunday was as relaxed and casual for the servants as it was for the owners of the house, Anne didn't think that slipping away unobserved would be too difficult a task.

And it wasn't. In less than five minutes Anne was a block away from her aunt's house and waving down a cab. In no time at all she was being let out at Congo Square. Anne paid her fare and generously tipped the driver. He responded with a friendly leer and a wink. Anne felt a little unnerved, but she supposed that one of the disadvantages of going about town unescorted was that people, including cheeky cabdrivers, might think her rather fast. This infuriating fact only made her more determined to do exactly as she pleased.

For at least three blocks she'd heard the chant-like singing of the dancers, the drumbeating, and the hand clapping. Now, as she stood just outside the square, the rhythm of the music seemed to thrum through her blood. And the sight of what must have been nearly five hundred black dancers, male and female adults of a wide range of ages, was overwhelming.

Enclosed in a fenced area surrounded by ancient sycamore trees, the dancers writhed with movement. Anne wished that Jeffrey were with her to explain the different dances. Then she realized that he actually could be there, hidden somewhere in the crowd that pressed against the fence to watch. She glanced around, hoping to pick him out from the dozens of other suited gentlemen.

When an elegant-looking Creole couple passed by and stared at her, Anne realized she must look rather conspicuous, gaping from a distance like a child standing at the entrance to a circus tent but afraid to go in. She lowered her netted veil and moved into the crowd, eventually working her way to the very front when several people vacated a large area. Anne turned her full attention to the dancers.

They were barefoot and dressed in what looked like hand-me-down finery from their white owners. But despite their faded, ill-fitting clothing, the dancers had a dignity about them that Anne admired. They seemed oblivious to the people watching them, caught up in the mood of the music, the rhythm of the drums, the mesmerizing resonance of the singing. Many of them appeared to be going through the motions with their eyes half-closed, almost trancelike in their concentration.

One dance ended and another began. Before, they had been doing little more than stamping their feet and swaying, but now the men and women paired off. The singing and the beating of the drums merged into a frenetic rhythm that seemed to urge Anne's heartbeat to keep time. She felt flushed, energized, excited. Beneath her skirt, her toes tapped in tune with the beating of the drums.

Now, instead of wishing Jeffrey were there to explain the dances to her, she wished Renard were there to share the excitement with her. But she couldn't imagine him in such a normal situation, in the bright light of day, and outfitted in ordinary clothes. He was her dark, dangerous hero of the night.

The dancing was growing more and more daring and exotic by the minute. The men were circling the women, then wriggling at their feet like snakes. Here and there couples seemed to be actually emulating the act of . . . sexual intercourse! Anne watched, fascinated, and—yes!—stimulated! Now she knew why Reggie objected to her coming there. He'd absolutely die if he knew where she was, what she was watching, and how it was making her feel!

While she didn't think there was anything wrong or immoral with what the dancers were doing, she was beginning to feel like a Peeping Tom. The dancing suddenly seemed too private to watch, and it occurred to Anne in a blinding revelation that this was yet another example of exploitation of the African people. They weren't even free to gather together and dance without an audience. Everything they did was monitored, confined, supervised. They were slaves.

Anne turned away, suddenly just as anxious to leave the place as she'd been to get there. She nudged her way through the crowd as tears stung her eyes. She wanted to go home, to separate herself from the mass of curious onlookers. She wanted no part of such exploitation.

Anne managed to work her way through the dense crowd and headed for the street. Blinking away the unwanted tears, she looked up and down the block for a cab. Seeing none, she started walking. She would hail a cab as soon as she saw one, but she had no intention of standing around waiting.

There was always the chance she'd see someone she knew. That could be either a blessing or a curse. Running into Jeffrey would be heaven, but meeting people of society who would condemn her for going out alone would be just the opposite. She was in no mood to defend herself and wasn't about to make up some outlandish story to justify her behavior.

She caught her skirts in both hands, kept her chin up, and strode with dignity along the banquette, headed north to the Faubourg St. Mary and home. Looking neither left nor right, she stared straight ahead, taking refuge behind her dark veil. She'd gone four blocks and was passing an alley when her arm was grabbed from behind.

Forced to stop so abruptly, she was nearly jerked off her feet. Furious as well as frightened, she turned to confront the person who had so rudely detained her. He was a tall, heavy, middle-aged man with a mottled complexion and a nose as red as a radish. His suit of clothes was worn and unkempt, his blond mutton-chop whiskers overgrown and bushy. Judging by his foolish, leering grin and glassy eyes, he was drunk.

"Now where's a pretty thing like you goin' in such a hurry?" He looked around, the slight movement making him weave on his feet, then pushed his face close to hers. "And all alone, it seems." His breath reeked of liquor and lunch, supporting her theory that this fellow had had one too many tips of some potent brew along with his midday meal at the local pub.

Anne tried to pull away, but the man's grip on her upper arm was as strong as his breath. His thick fingertips pinched into her tender flesh till she knew she'd have bruises.

"I demand that you release me, sir," she said. Anne looked up and down the street for possible help, but there was only one couple at the far end who were headed in the opposite direction. She'd have to scream to get their attention, and she didn't want to make a scene. She could imagine Reggie's horror if she was brought home by a city patrolman.

The man chuckled. "You *demand* I release you, eh? You've got a feisty way about you. And such a pretty way o' speakin'. From jolly ol' England, ain't you, love?"

Anne tugged at her arm, glaring up at the man. "You are breaking the law, sir," she ground out between clenched teeth, "and if you don't let me go this minute, I'll scream for help."

"Ain't no one about, missy. They's all down at the square watchin' the heathens dance. And how you reckon I'm breakin' the law?"

"You're holding me against my will. That is a form of assault, sir."

"Oh, assault, is it? I thought maybe you was figurin' on yellin' rape, or somethin'." His grin widened and his gaze lowered, lingering on her breasts. Alarm made Anne's heart skip a beat. "And here I ain't even kissed you yet."

"If you don't let me go this minute, I'll scream." Anne repeated her threat in a low, precise voice. She wanted him to understand every word. She was giving him one last chance.

His brows lifted, and his mouth curved in a nasty smirk. "That's what you said before, missy."

"This time I mean it." Anne held her breath. She felt his fingers loosen a little on her arm, which gave her hope, then, suddenly, he yanked her into the alley and pushed her against the brick wall, holding her captive by pressing his heavy body against hers.

Now Anne couldn't scream at all. The breath had been knocked out of her when she'd hit the wall, and by the time she got it back, the man had pushed up her veil and covered her mouth with his hand.

She struggled, kicking and thrashing, but her captor was incredibly strong and only shifted his weight and moved his legs till she was completely confined by muscle-bound thighs and the sheer bulk of the man. They were connected in the most unbearably intimate way.

Beyond the terror of finding herself at the mercy of this man and not knowing exactly what he meant to do to her, Anne registered the disagreeable odor of human sweat, musty clothes, and breath that reeked of gin and onions.

Anne's eyes widened as the man lowered his face to hers, his greasy-looking lips puckered up for the kill. She didn't take the time to wonder why, but when Anne closed her eyes against the inevitable reality of what was coming next, she conjured up a vision of beautiful hands decorated with emerald and diamond rings, and the chiseled profile of Dandy Delacroix.

Chapter 8

With her eyes squeezed shut and the man detaining her engrossed in the business at hand, neither of them was aware at first that someone else had joined them in the alley. Anne's first clue was a sound that reminded her of a woodpecker's single thump against a tree trunk—hollow and dull. She opened her eyes and saw a surprised look on the face of her accoster. He held her just as tightly, but it was obvious his concentration had been jarred. By a knock to the noggin? she wondered. In unison they turned their heads and discovered they were not alone.

Anne's heart leaped with joy and relief. As if she'd conjured him up, Delacroix stood in all his arrogant splendor not three feet away. Today he was dressed in black, his watch chains and fobs glinting silver in the sunlight, his hat worn at a jaunty angle.

He looked calm, almost bored. His stance was relaxed, but subtly belligerent. He leaned slightly forward, his hands, glittering entirely with diamonds, rested with languid grace on the knob of a walking cane. Most of his weight was thrown on one hip, his right leg bent minimally at the knee. His obsidian eyes were hooded, filled with lazy malice.

127

"Monsieur, I suggest you let go of the lady or suffer the consequences."

Anne had never been so glad to hear that languid, imperious drawl.

"And who are *you?*" the man said scathingly, skimming his bloodshot gaze over Delacroix's impeccable appearance. "I suppose it was you what hit me on the bean, with that cane you've got there, eh?"

Delacroix arched a black brow. "I plead guilty."

"Well then, I'm givin' you fair warnin', pretty boy, that if'n you so much as raise that little stick of yours again, I'll take it from you and give you a whackin' with it you won't soon forget."

Delacroix's eyes narrowed to glittery slits. "*Merci*, monsieur. So kind of you to warn me of your intentions. But don't forget, I warned you first."

The man threw back his head and laughed, his grimy neck revealed for Anne's unwilling inspection. Delacroix waited for the foul fellow's mirth to pass, his expression devoid of emotion, his gaze fixed impassively on the villain's face. But Anne could feel the tension in the air. She could see it in Delacroix's taut arms and legs. His relaxed pose was deceptive. He was like a coiled wire, ready to spring.

"Lord, I needed a good laugh," said the man, letting go of Anne with one hand while he wiped his watery eyes. "No fella what goes about dressed as slick as you wants to mess up his duds over a female. Now go on with you, I've got a kiss to collect."

Delacroix straightened up and leaned his cane against the brick wall. Unhurriedly he removed his right glove—only his right glove—and tucked it into his jacket pocket. Then he stood with his feet slightly straddled and his arms crossed loosely over his broad chest. "I haven't the slightest intention of going away, so I suggest you let the lady go, and, as the Americans say, put up your dukes."

The man heaved a beleaguered sigh, blowing his rotten breath Anne's way once again. "You're like a pesky mosquito what won't buzz off, ain't you? Well, guess you're just a bug what needs swattin', is all. Stay put, missy. I'll be fetchin' that kiss in a minute."

He let Anne go.

"Go home, mademoiselle," said Delacroix, looking at her for the first time, his expression stern. But Anne shook her head and scurried only a few feet away, deeper into the alley. She pressed herself against the opposite wall at a safe distance to watch. Strongly opposed to violence, Anne had no desire to see blood fly, but she didn't think she should leave Delacroix alone with this huge brute of a man. Heaven knew Delacroix had a strong-looking body, but did he know how to use it to best advantage? Dueling was one thing, fisticuffs was another. Delacroix might need her help.

Apparently resigned to her stubbornness, Delacroix turned his attention back to the man, who looked ready to pounce. Anne cast desperately about for a weapon. She spied a plank of rotten wood and picked it up. Ruefully she acknowledged that perhaps a lady ought to carry a derringer in her purse rather than a scented handkerchief, a bottle of smelling salts, and pin money.

With a drunken roar the man lunged. Delacroix swung once, hit the man square on the jaw, and sent him sprawling.

The entire ugly affair was settled in less time

than it took to say *sacre bleu*. There had been no scuffle, no grunting, sweating, or thrashing about. With one neat clip to the jaw, Delacroix had flattened his foe. Dazed, Anne moved tentatively forward, as if afraid the man, like a wounded bear, might rise up and attack. He was facedown, a dribble of bloody drool hanging over his bottom lip. She stood over him, then nudged his arm with the toe of her boot. There was no response. He was out cold.

Anne looked up into the face of her savior. Not even the first dew of perspiration dotted his upper lip. He was as cool as an English lake in spring. He was as unruffled and contained as a lone rooster strutting for the hens in his own personal barnyard. Anne was speechless.

"Mademoiselle? Are you quite all right?"

Anne dropped the board she'd been prepared to do battle with, and shook her head wonderingly. "You knocked him out. You completely leveled him with just one punch."

Delacroix frowned, working the fingers of the hand that had delivered the decisive blow. "*Oui*," he said dismissively. "He was drunk and dirty, and I had no desire to wrestle with the fellow. Rest assured, I did him no permanent harm. He'll sleep it off in a few hours, wake up wondering how he got where he is, then stagger home only a little the worse for wear." He scanned her from tip to toe, a furrow of worry between his brows. "But I repeat, mademoiselle, are you unharmed? Are *you* only a little the worse for wear?"

"Yes, yes, I'm perfectly fine," she answered impatiently. "But tell me, Mr. Delacroix, how did you do it? I'd no notion you knew how to fight!"

Delacroix shrugged. "I sometimes spar for the sport of it. As I am frequently in the company of females, I constantly have to be ready to defend myself against jealous ex-beaux, husbands, etcetera. However, rescuing damsels in distress is my specialty, and my favorite reason for using my pugilist skills." He smiled slyly. "I usually get a kiss as a reward for my efforts."

"Well, I'm afraid that's out of the question," said Anne, quickly looking away as the heat crept up her neck and flooded her cheeks with warmth. After kissing Renard so intimately last night, she felt it would be inappropriate to kiss Delacroix even as a reward for saving her. It confused her, though, that she still felt attracted to Delacroix after her tryst with Renard. "But I do sincerely thank you for coming to my rescue. How did you know where I was and that I needed help? I saw no one on the street when that lout dragged me in here."

Delacroix turned to pick up his cane. "I saw you at Congo Square. When you left, you did not take a cab, and I supposed you meant to walk home alone. That was foolish, mademoiselle, as foolish as coming to watch the dancing by yourself."

Anne was instantly defensive. "No one would bring me. What else could I do?"

"You could have stayed home."

"But nothing happened to me!"

Delacroix's black eyes flashed. "Nothing happened to you because I had the presence of mind to follow you when you left Congo Square."

"I wonder you recognized me in that throng of people."

"Pigheaded females stand out in a crowd, mademoiselle."

"So do peacocks with a flock of hens in tow, Mr. Delacroix, but I didn't see *you!*"

Delacroix smiled, as if amused and pleased by

her description. "You think me a peacock, eh? I have been called worse."

"Doubtless you have!"

"However, I'm sure you meant to insult me. Enchanting, mademoiselle. Is this how young ladies in England are taught to thank their gallant protectors? By insulting them?"

"*You* insulted *me!*" Anne gave a huff of impatience. "Oh, I *do* appreciate your intervention in this case, Mr. Delacroix, but I daresay the oaf only meant to dally with me. You know . . . kiss me, etcetera."

"It is the etcetera that ought to worry you. He may have meant only to dally with you at first, but passions have a way of running amok. He was drunk and very dangerous."

Anne sulked. He was right, and she hated to admit it. Indeed, she had been in grave danger of being raped, and she owed her salvaged virtue to Delacroix. Feeling unaccountably irritable, she changed the subject. "Why did you follow me from Congo Square?"

"I told you why." He extracted his glove from his jacket pocket and pulled it on, neatly and methodically tucking down the material between each finger. Anne watched, mesmerized as always by the lean shape and beauty of his hands. "I thought you might run into trouble." He glanced up, his eyes brimming with wry humor. "And, you see, I was right."

"I live just a few blocks away. It really wasn't such a foolish or unreasonable thing to attempt, you know, walking home such a little distance." She gestured toward the prone figure of the man. "*He* was just an unfortunate fluke. Besides, why should you bother to safeguard a female you hardly know? It couldn't have been convenient to traipse after me as you did."

"*Oui*, it was damned inconvenient. I left some rather scintillating company."

Anne took this to mean that, just as she'd assumed, he had been with fawning women. Or perhaps he had been with his mistress. For some reason, either possibility made her feel more argumentative. "Then there must have been some other more compelling reason why you followed me," she insisted.

Delacroix rolled his shoulders in a gesture of exasperation. "Is it a crime to be a gentleman? Other than the fact that it's never safe for a female of your tender upbringing to walk out alone, an additional reason to keep *your* sort on a short tether is the fact that *you*, mademoiselle, seem to attract trouble."

Anne stuck out her chin defiantly. "*My* sort! There's no reason for you to categorize me that way. Uncle Reggie keeps me perpetually on that hypothetical short tether you just mentioned, so I haven't even had the smallest opportunity to attract trouble since I left England!"

Except, of course, when she'd interrupted Renard's escapade on the *Belvedere*. But there was no way Delacroix could know about that.

They glared at each other.

"Mademoiselle, I have observed you in society since we met on the *Belvedere*. You've made no secret of your rebellious nature. Such an unconventional, unfeminine attitude always attracts trouble."

Anne put her hands on her hips and leaned forward. "Is that so?"

"*Certainement*. You don't suppose I followed you because I've got some sort of *tendre* for you, do you? Believe me, *cher*, you're not my sort. Not my sort at all."

Anne leaned closer, till they were practically nose to nose. "If I *were* your sort, Mr. Delacroix, I believe I'd have sufficient reason to instantly slit my throat. Real men don't piddle their time away gaming and wenching—"

"Don't they?" he murmured.

"And they don't spend all their time and money on themselves. Real men do something important with their lives, like fighting for a cause, or raising a family, or building a school, or ... or ... *something!*"

By now, Delacroix's jaw looked as hard as granite. His eyes glistened like sizzling bits of blackest coal. Anne smiled triumphantly, thrilled to have nettled him out of his usual bored ennui. "And *real* men don't—"

Anne was startled and silenced when Delacroix grabbed her by the upper arms. He removed what little distance was left between them by pulling her flush against his chest. Then he walked her backward and leaned her against the wall. Dazed, Anne didn't put up the least resistance.

She could feel the cool, round contour of a watch locket against her right nipple—which had become instantly, embarrassingly hard. She felt the blood rush to her head, to her fingertips, to her toes, as if her heart had suddenly decided to pump full-throttle. Behind the locket, Delacroix's chest was broad and warm.

She was close enough to see the shadow of evening stubble on his jaw, to see how dark and stormy his eyes got when he was in a rage. But it was a contained rage, for which small blessing Anne was extremely grateful.

"My poor, dear *enfant*," he said with menacing

calm, "I don't believe you have the slightest notion what real men do." His breath was pleasant, suggesting the taste of mint and lemon and afternoon tea. Reflexively she gave her bottom lip a quick swipe of her tongue. He caught the movement and riveted his gaze to her mouth. "So . . . as you are so regrettably unenlightened, why don't I *show* you what real men do?"

This was Anne's second time against that wall within the short space of ten minutes. She'd been pinned there unwillingly the first time by a disgusting, dangerous stranger intending to deflower her. Now she wasn't sure how she'd gotten herself pinned again, and she wasn't sure whether it was unwillingly or not. Delacroix's hold on her was quite different from the stranger's. It was strong, but it wasn't restraining. She knew she had only to push him away, and he'd release her.

So why didn't she push him away? She didn't like him. She didn't like him at all . . .

"You fight with the fury of a wildcat, *cher*. Do you kiss with the same passion?"

Anne felt her control slipping away as Delacroix's lips moved closer and closer. She supposed it was too late to pray for another rain shower to dampen their ardor.

She saw the lips curve in a smile. "Remember, *ma petite*, close your eyes . . ."

She closed her eyes. They kissed. She was fully involved, completely bowled over by an onslaught of sensations she'd never experienced before.

Well, almost never . . . She'd felt very much the same while being kissed by Renard!

His lips were firm and warm, coaxing and claiming her willing cooperation. Her own lips parted in a gasp, and he traced the smooth surface of her teeth with his tongue. She opened her mouth a fraction more and shyly touched the tip of her tongue to his. The kiss deepened. He made a sound of pleasure—a throaty, masculine sound that pierced through the remnants of Anne's composure, leaving her quivering and weak with desire.

And curious. Her mind reeled with the sensual possibilities of exploration. Her trembling hands moved from his upper arms, around to his hard back, and up to the nape of his neck. Thick fringes of his ebony hair lapped over the edge of his collar, and she wove her fingers through it. It felt like silk.

Delacroix's hands had, till then, been flat and unmoving against the small of her back. Now they moved, too, clasping her waist, pulling her closer. Oh, so close. She could hear the drums from Congo Square in the distance, their primitive beat seeming to vibrate through every nerve in her body. Anne felt deliciously wicked, wanton, abandoned to all sense of propriety. She was oblivious to time, to place, to everything but the man who held her, kissed her . . .

"*Cher?* Shall I wait for you in the carriage, or will you be . . . brief?"

Spoken with a tinge of amused sarcasm, the low-pitched, mellifluous, wholly feminine voice coming from where the alley opened onto the street shattered the spell that held Anne in thrall. Simultaneously Delacroix and Anne pulled apart, their arms dropping hastily to their sides, as if they were two guilty children caught wrestling in their Sunday best and endeavoring to look innocent.

He looked at her; she looked at him. Delacroix appeared totally out of character—blissfully mauled, bemused, as if he'd been startled from a trance. She had the disturbing suspicion that she looked just as strange, just as disheveled and compromised. Then they both looked at the person who had interrupted them. It was Delacroix's mistress.

A few beats of silence fell. Anne stared at the beautiful quadroon, dressed in a stunning gown of bright pink, a white, lacy tignon on her head. She held herself with regal grace, as if she were somehow above the scene she'd just stumbled onto. She stared back at Anne, a cool curiosity in her expression, a faint smile on her lips.

Under this condescending scrutiny, Anne felt more and more foolish by the instant. And all the rushing, swelling, fitful throes of passion shrunk and expired. Now Anne felt shame. She dropped her gaze to the ground. She did not dare look at Delacroix. But perhaps he was embarrassed, too ...

"You, of all people, Micaela, know I can never be 'brief.' So much pleasure is lost in haste, n'est ce pas?"

Anne's head reared up at the sound of Delacroix's mocking drawl. She couldn't believe it! He wasn't the least bit embarrassed. He was completely himself again, his eyelids drooping in his usual expression of haughty boredom. His mouth—the mouth that had so cleverly enticed her to forget any sense of propriety to which she had previously aspired—curved into a self-satisfied smirk. Anne was mortified, angry, and, for once, speechless.

"What a shame, cher," he said to her, "that such a pleasant interlude was cut short, eh? Life is unpredictable. Who knows when we might be able to take up where we left off?"

Anne was speechless, but she had full command of her hands. She slapped his face.

Delacroix barely flinched from the blow, though she'd put all her strength behind the swing and knew she'd hurt him. He rubbed his jaw and looked ruefully at her. "I suppose I deserved that."

"I suppose you did." She barely recognized her own voice. It was hoarse, faint, trembling.

Anne's conscience told her that she was just as much to blame for the intimacies between them as he was. She hadn't pulled away, and she'd participated with as much ardor as he had. Maybe more. But with Delacroix's mistress standing by, Anne's embarrassment overrode all sense of fairness. As a lady, she had a duty to put the decadent dandy in his place.

"Come, mademoiselle, I will escort you home." He reached for her arm, but she moved quickly away.

"Nonsense, Mr. Delacroix," she said haughtily. "You have someone waiting for you. I wouldn't dream of wrenching you away from her scintillating company yet again. Besides, I daresay there shan't be room in the carriage for all three of us. I shall walk home alone, just as I meant to do from the beginning." She turned and took a step toward the street.

He detained her by swiftly catching hold of her arm. "Even a simpleton would have concluded by now that it is dangerous for a female of your type to walk alone."

"Are you speaking of the danger from you, Mr. Delacroix, or from that fellow lying facedown in the dirt? Because, as I recall, I was in just as much danger of being compromised by you as I was by—"

"You are safe with me," he said wryly. "I promise you."

"I wasn't safe from you a moment ago—"

"Nor I from you," he returned.

Anne stiffened. "Sir, you are *no* gentleman!"

"The truth stings your pride, *n'est-ce pas?*" He rubbed his jaw again where she'd slapped him. "For today at least, I can vouch for my own good conduct. Can you?"

Anne lifted her chin. "I can vouch for mine." She indicated the mistress—who still watched with an amused expression—with a sideways nod of her head. "Is *she* the safekeeper of your conduct, Mr. Delacroix? Are we to have a chaperone?"

"No." He turned and spoke gently to the woman. "Micaela, go and wait in the carriage, *s'il vous plaît.* I will walk the lady home. I dare not leave her to her own devices."

Anne stamped her foot. "I don't need your assistance!"

Micaela arched her fine brows. "Of course, *cher*, I will wait for you in the carriage if that is what you wish. Certainly you must see the lady home. Take good care of her, but don't take too long. *Au revoir, cher. Au revoir,* mademoiselle." She turned with a swish of skirts and was gone.

"I hope you're happy," snapped Anne, "mortifying me in front of that woman! Now if you *don't* mind—" She tugged at her arm, which he still held in a firm grip.

"I meant what I said. You're not walking home alone. Now come along." He ruthlessly pulled her arm against his side, their elbows locked, in the usual manner of promenading couples. "And unless you wish to make a scene, don't struggle and try to dash off. I'll run right after you, creating a diversion for Sunday strollers which will make both of us prime fodder for the gossip mill for weeks. The choice is yours, but I hope you're not so pigheaded that you can't acquiesce—for once!—to reason and common sense."

"Very well," said Anne, angrily jerking her veil over her face again. "Walk me home if you're so determined to be ridiculous. But don't expect conversation."

He guided her toward the street. "Believe me, *cher*, I neither expect nor desire conversation. But I advise you, unless you wish to be thought quite unnatural, erase that scowl from your face and try to look more pleasant. I'm never seen with unhappy females. Show your teeth."

"Pompous toad!" she mumbled as they emerged into the sunlight.

"Insufferable brat," he retorted in an undertone.

And thus did they return to Prytania Street, strolling along at Delacroix's usual elegant pace, with smiles on their lips, pleasant greetings to acquaintances they chanced upon, and a steady stream of whispered insults exchanged with enthusiasm between them.

He left her at the gate. "Don't bother to invite me in, mademoiselle," he said mockingly. "Though I'm sure you wish to thank me properly for my invaluable assistance—"

"Humph!"

"—since we were so sadly interrupted during your last attempt at thanking me—"

"Scoundrel!"

"—but I am persuaded to think that you'd rather enter the house the way you left it—on tiptoes."

Anne did not deign to reply. She rudely turned her back on Delacroix and marched with stiff dignity through the gate and down the flowerbordered walkway to the front door of the house. She had her hand on the doorknob, ready to turn it, when a perverse notion made her glance back over her shoulder to see if Delacroix watched from the gate.

He was still there, but he seemed to have only been waiting for her to notice him, the cad! He smiled sardonically and tipped his hat, then turned his back on *her!*

Anne entered the house and slammed the door behind her. She stomped halfway down the hall, past a startled, sleepy-eyed footman, when Reggie suddenly appeared, saying, "And just where have you been, young lady?"

Chapter 9

Anne swept past Reggie and headed for the stairs. "Please, Uncle, don't make me explain now."

He hurried after her, his heels clicking on the parquet floor. "Why not? Why can't you explain? What's the matter with you?" A note of concern crept into his voice. "Did something happen—?"

"No, nothing happened." Anne picked up her skirts and began ascending the stairs.

"Then why can't you tell me where you've been? I noticed you weren't in the house or anywhere on the grounds an hour ago. I was just about to send for the police." There was a pause while Reggie waited for a reply. But she couldn't reply without feeling foolish, because she'd suddenly discovered she was about to cry. "Anne! Stop this minute and explain where you've been or else I'll lock you in your room till . . . till your thirtieth birthday!"

Anne stopped, half-laughing, half-crying. "Oh, Uncle Reggie, how can you be so *gothic!*" A tear brimmed over, dripped off a lower lash, and slid down her face. She turned around and looked at her uncle, standing in his burgundy brocade dressing gown at the bottom of the stairs, his spectacles perched on the end of his prominent nose, his

142

brow furrowed with worry. "I'm a grown-up woman, you know. You can't lock me away from the world forever."

His expression softened. "But, my dear, you're crying. Whatever's the matter?"

"Oh, I've made a fool of myself, I'm afraid." She wiped away the tear, turned around, and slowly descended the stairs, her chin on her chest, her eyes downcast. When she reached the bottom step, Reggie handed her a snowy-fresh handkerchief— which item he always seemed to have in bountiful supply for just such emergencies—and, with an arm thrown around her shoulders, led her into the library and sat her down in a massive wing chair by the empty fireplace.

While he poured them both a glass of sherry from a crystal decanter set out on a nearby table, Anne put her uncle's handkerchief to good use. She wept a little, scolded herself soundly for being such a watering pot, wiped her eyes, and blew her nose. Reggie waited patiently, hovering over her with a glass in each hand. Finally she looked up and smiled, received her drink with a mumbled thank-you, then took a long sip.

Like a nurse administering a dose of cod-liver oil, Reggie watched till Anne had swallowed the wine. Satisfied, he sat down in a chair opposite her, crossed his legs, took a medicinal swallow himself, and said, "There, my girl. I hope you're feeling a little more the thing now. Will you talk to me?"

"Yes, of course I will." Anne looked chagrined. "But I must start with a confession."

Anne proceeded to tell Reggie everything, from sneaking out of the house, going to Congo Square, and deciding to walk home alone when she couldn't find a cab. He occasionally interrupted with a question or two and an exclamation of alarm.

When she got to the part of the story about the drunk pressing unwanted attentions on her, Reggie stood up and stared down at her, his eyes bulging. "Where *is* the fiend? I'll call him out! I'll ... I'll—"

Anne tugged on Reggie's wrists, making him sit down again. "No, you won't. There's no need. He didn't get very far. He didn't even kiss me. Mr. Delacroix came along just in the nick of time and saved me."

Reggie visibly relaxed. "Delacroix, eh?" Then he looked perplexed. "But I don't understand. How was he able to save you? Did he have a gun?"

"Delacroix didn't shoot him."

"Just threatened to, eh?"

"No. He knocked him out."

Reggie's mouth dropped open. "I say," he continued after a period of slack-jawed astonishment, "I had no notion the fellow was willing to muss up his clothes in an alley brawl. It was deuced good of him. I'm prodigiously grateful, and shall have to thank him in some way. He brought you home, I suppose? But I daresay he was embarrassed to be seen and went immediately back to his lodgings to bathe and change." Reggie appeared to be trying not to smile. "Was he a sight, Anne? Were there watch fobs and rings strewn around on the ground?"

"No, Uncle. Mr. Delacroix rendered the fellow unconscious with a single hit to the jaw." She grinned ruefully. "Not even a ruffle was stirred."

The smile spread unreservedly over Reggie's face. "Bless my soul! I always did like the fellow and never knew why. *Now* I know why. He's got gumption, and he rendered you an invaluable service." Suddenly Reggie sobered. He slumped in his chair, looking thoroughly drained.

"What, Uncle?"

"You might have been hurt, Anne. Merciful heavens, you might have been ..."

"Raped. Yes, I know."

Reggie shook his head. "I don't know how we shall *ever* be able to thank Delacroix enough."

Somewhere in the middle of these raptures, Anne decided that she would not tell Reggie about Delacroix's own amorous advances in the alley. She had considered telling him at first, while her hurt pride still rankled, but her conscience clearly told her that she was as much to blame for the intimacies as Delacroix.

Besides, Reggie would be livid. And her uncle certainly wouldn't understand about her own part in the passionate proceedings. She wasn't sure she understood it herself.

"I'm very tired, Uncle. I think I'll go lie down for a while."

Reggie jumped up, immediately solicitous. "I should think so! If I'd known you'd endured such an ordeal, Anne, I'd have sent you to bed right away." He caught her elbow and moved with her toward the library door.

"Oh, posh!" she scoffed with good humor. "There's nothing wrong with me that a half-hour nap and a hot bath won't fix."

"You've have a nerve-shattering experience. You'll have dinner in bed and then stay upstairs till morning—"

"No, I most certainly will not. Jeffrey's coming over after dinner, and I mean to receive him. I don't suppose you'd allow him in my bedchamber, would you?"

"Good God, I don't even like him sitting with

you in the parlor. Anne, don't be stubborn. Just for once do as I ask."

"I frequently do as you ask, but not tonight. I'm a grown woman, remember? I have to be able to trust my own judgment, even if it means making a mistake. You might advise me, but you cannot dictate."

Reggie sniffed. "I won't. Not anymore. Not now that I've seen the shenanigans you resort to when you're determined on some course of action I disapprove of. It *is* all right if I escort you to your room, isn't it? You *will* indulge your old uncle just a little bit, won't you?"

Anne smiled up at Reggie. "If it eases your mind, Uncle, you might *carry* me up the stairs if you're able."

Reggie gave a bark of laughter. "Hah! Not I! But maybe Delacroix could. I'm beginning to think the man's capable of much more than we ever allowed."

Inwardly Anne agreed.

Later, in her dressing room, steeped in a porcelain tub full of hot, scented water, she tried to reason out her attraction to Delacroix. She concluded, as before, that it had to be purely and simply a physical attraction. She didn't like his high-handed ways, his lazy self-indulgence, his cavalier attitude about women and flirting and kissing . . . She didn't like his ethics, his morals, or his political beliefs. Anne disliked and disagreed with him on all these essentials.

Of course, now and then he *did* show signs of being almost human; he had rescued her that afternoon, he had spoken feelingly and affectionately of his family that day in the cemetery, he even had good taste in his mistress and seemed to treat the lady well. But he always ruined these few favorable impressions by immediately afterward saying or doing something despicable or shallow.

Anne sighed, squeezing a spongeful of water onto an upraised knee. The demoralizing truth of the matter was that, despite his infuriating, arrogant ways, Delacroix had the face and figure of an extremely well-favored man—a well-favored man who knew how to kiss rather splendidly. And Anne's "primitive" side would like nothing better than to kiss him right back, no matter how despicably he behaved.

Appalled at her own self-acknowledged lust, Anne sank down into the suds till she was completely immersed except for her eyes and nose. She had enjoyed Renard's kisses, too. In fact, both men kissed rather splendidly. Very much alike. But she could understand her ardent response to Renard. *He* was worthy of being lusted after. Why had she responded with equal fervor to a scoundrel like Delacroix?

Good heavens, she thought despairingly, *is sultry Louisiana turning me into a fast woman?*

"Is she the one?"

Lucien turned his head on the pillow and peered across the dimly lit chamber at Micaela. He lay fully clothed on the bed. She stood at the door in a filmy white nightdress, holding a tray of coffee and pastries.

"What do you mean? Who are you talking about, Micaela?"

"The blond lady in the alley."

Lucien tensed, the pleasant drowsiness replaced by bunched muscles and edgy weariness. But he tried to appear unaffected by her words as Micaela moved toward the bed, setting the tray on a table just next to it. She hiked a shapely thigh onto the mattress—stripped of covers—and leaned forward, resting her hand lightly on his chest. "Is she the one you almost told me about weeks ago, when I suggested that you had found someone?"

Lucien's jaw set. He hated Micaela's perceptiveness. He didn't want to admit to himself, much less to her, that Anne had become so important to him that she'd made it impossible for him to make love to any other woman. It was a frightening thought.

He hedged. "Micaela, you're a beautiful, desirable woman. I haven't made love to anyone else since I moved you in here."

Micaela shrugged, tracing slow circles on his hard chest with her fingertips. She was like that, very sensual and always touching. Why would any sane man find her undesirable? "Lately you are very tense, *cher*. You brood like a man with a heavy heart. You might not make love to anyone else, but you haven't made love to me, either. Not for many weeks."

Lucien forced a smile. "You used to complain that I was insatiable."

Her gaze trailed up and down his supine body, her long thick hair falling forward as she bent closer. "You know I enjoyed our lovemaking very much." She looked up at his face and into his eyes. "But you will marry someday, Lucien. Is this English woman the one who will be your wife?"

He laughed uneasily. "Lord, the man who marries that little termagant will rue the day."

But Micaela didn't laugh. "I'm very serious, *cher*."

Lucien sobered, too. He caught her hand and lifted it to his lips, kissing the palm tenderly. "Are you worried about your future? You know I've arranged to leave you the house and plenty of money to start off married life comfortably ... and with someone worthy of you, I hope. Perhaps that young smithy I see ogling you at the market whenever we go there."

Micaela's cheeks took on a delicate tawny color. A tiny smile curved her lips, then disappeared. "It's not me I'm worried about, Lucien. It's you. What if this English girl is the love you've been waiting for? What will you do about ... about the other part of your life?"

Lucien had never told Micaela about his alter ego, Renard. Their association had been caring and physically satisfying, but not intimate in the same way that two people in love shared thoughts and secrets. Neither of them had any romantic illusions about their relationship, but it was more than business. They were friends. And Micaela had an uncanny way of reading him. Was it possible that she knew he was Renard?

He kept his face perfectly expressionless when he asked her, "What do you mean, 'the other part of my life'?"

Micaela's gaze was steady. And sincere. "You know what I'm talking about."

"Do I?"

"Yes. And since you won't confirm my suspicions, that's all I'll say. But someday, cher, you'll have to make a choice. I've never seen you so taken by a woman as you are by this one. There have always been flirtations, of course, but I suspect that in this girl, you've met your match."

Lucien did not reply. Micaela hadn't said anything he hadn't already thought a million times. The conflict between his necessary masquerade and his consuming passion for Anne Weston was tearing him apart. Today in the alley he'd had another taste of heaven. But this heaven was fraught with hellish pitfalls for her and for him. The most tormenting yet satisfying result of their embrace was the conviction that for some odd reason Anne had responded to him. She had responded to Dandy Delacroix . . .

But Anne was the last thing he should be thinking about today. Tonight he and Armande had another slave escape planned. It would accomplish the freedom of at least three more slaves living under intolerable conditions right there in the city. Their mistress viciously beat them. Lucien had been setting the groundwork for this escape for several weeks.

He had been thinking, his gaze unfocused. The clock on the mantel struck the hour: six o'clock. Now his eyes sought Micaela's. She'd been waiting, her expression solemn, expectant, caring. "Micaela, I would never tell you anything that might endanger you. Who I am and what I want are complicated questions right now. I won't say Miss Weston isn't important to me, but I don't know yet whether she can be a part of my life." He sighed heavily.

"All I want is for you to be safe and happy, Lucien."

"I want the same for you, *cher*," he told her, smiling affectionately. "But now I must get up and go home before I fall asleep."

Micaela sighed and stood up, smiling at him rather wistfully. "Sometimes, Lucien," she said, "I wish you weren't such an honorable man."

He gently grazed her cheek with the back of his hand. "I'm usually not nearly as honorable as I should be," he said ruefully.

She walked him to the door. "Will I see you soon?"

Their gazes locked. They both knew that the

next time he visited would most likely be the last. "Yes, Micaela, I'll see you soon."

After dinner that evening, Anne and Katherine left Reggie and walked into the parlor to wait for Jeffrey Wycliff. Anne was especially glad to leave Reggie to his English habit of lingering over port because she wanted to talk to her aunt alone before Jeffrey showed up.

Immediately after they'd sat down on the striped damask sofa near the fireplace, Anne said, "Aunt Katherine, I wonder if you'd do me a favor."

Katherine had leaned her cane against the sofa and was busily arranging her skirt. She glanced up. "Well, of course, dear, if it's at all possible."

Anne nervously smoothed her own silk burgundy skirt. "I hope it's possible. I want you to somehow get Uncle Reggie to leave Jeffrey and me alone for a few minutes tonight."

Katherine's busy hands stilled. Her sharp gray eyes fixed on Anne's face. "Indeed? Might I ask why you wish to be alone with Jeffrey? Or is the answer obvious?"

Anne bit her lip and squirmed a little in her seat. "No, the answer is not obvious if you're implying that I want to give Jeffrey an opportunity to court me. I don't."

"Then why do you want to see him alone? You'll only encourage him."

Anne leaned close and said in a conspiratorial whisper. "He knows something about Renard—some information I'm dying to be told."

Katherine's attention seemed instantly caught. "You don't say? What sort of information?" Then she turned away, twisting the knob of her cane in her large, elegant fingers.

"Jeffrey has some information about Renard's latest plan to help slaves escape to Canada. Isn't that terribly exciting?"

Katherine's brows furrowed. "How can Jeffrey possibly know these things?"

"He has connections."

"What connections?"

"I don't know." She decided not to tell her aunt that Jeffrey actually had an informant inside Renard's ranks. She didn't think he meant for her to share that information. "Just some people who work as moles, grubbing out interesting tidbits for Jeffrey's newspaper articles. He's quite thrilled, though, because this time he actually seems to know Renard's rendezvous point and when he plans to be there."

"And Jeffrey means to tell you all this?"

"No, I imagine he doesn't mean to tell me anything at all. He plans, I'm sure, to dangle his knowledge like a carrot in front of my nose without giving me the teeniest bite—the tease! My only hope of ferreting out the information will be if Reggie is out of the room."

"What can you possibly do with this information, Anne? I know you're rather taken with the stories of Renard, but surely you don't intend to chase after the fellow? He's an outlaw."

Anne gave a huff of exasperation. "I'm not a simpleton, Aunt."

Finally Katherine grudgingly agreed to get Reggie out of the room. When Jeffrey arrived, Anne still didn't know what Katherine's plan was, but she trusted her clever aunt to come up with something. Reggie immediately joined them, nodded with stiff formality to Jeffrey, and said a perfunctory "How d'do?" Then he sat down to read the newspaper. Although Reggie was usually falsely cordial to Jeffrey, tonight he was downright rude. He had not forgiven the man for putting the idea of Congo Square in Anne's head in the first place.

Fifteen maddening minutes passed while Anne waited for her aunt to make her move. Finally she did. She fainted. After a start of surprise, Anne took her cue.

"Oh, dear! Aunt Katherine! What's the matter?"

Katherine's fainting scene was so believable, even Anne was a little alarmed. She might have thought her aunt was really ill if Katherine hadn't winked at her while Reggie dashed away to fetch a restorative glass of watered wine.

Katherine revived while Reggie hovered over her, patted her hand, and looked fit to be tied. He mentioned sending for the doctor more than once, but Katherine refused, finally convincing him that all she really needed was a bit of fresh air. It occurred to Anne that Reggie was more than a little upset by Katherine's slight swoon, and that Katherine was really enjoying the extra attention he was giving her.

Reggie assisted Katherine to her feet and, with much attention and care, guided her out of the drawing room and into the hall without an apparent thought or a backward glance at Anne and Jeffrey. Perhaps because she'd left her cane behind, or perhaps because she was still playing out the farce, the notoriously vigorous Katherine Grimms leaned on Reggie's arm the whole way.

"Well," said Anne, chuckling softly. "That was some show!"

"Anne, come here."

Anne turned around, surprised by the coy sound of Jeffrey's voice. She discovered him sitting on the sofa and patting the cushion next to him. "Just what do you think you're summoning me to do, Jeffrey?"

Jeffrey grinned. "I'm not a dolt. I saw Katherine wink at you when Reggie fetched the wine and I know she didn't really faint. There can be only one reason why you'd go to so much trouble to get rid of your uncle. I only wonder that your aunt was a party to the mischief."

Anne crossed her arms and arched a brow. "What reason is that?"

Jeffrey shrugged. "So we can be alone. If this isn't an invitation to kiss you again, what else can it be?"

Anne shook her head and crossed the room to sit next to him on the sofa—but well out of arm's reach.

"You're a conceited dog, Jeffrey. I've not got you alone to kiss you. Have you forgotten? You promised to tell me what you know about Renard's planned escape tonight."

Jeffrey's face fell. "Renard again!" he said with a bitterness that took Anne by surprise. "Is he all you think about? Or do you just think about him when you're with me?"

Anne's own good humor instantly fled. Jeffrey's sudden contemptuous manner of speaking about Renard confused her. It seemed ridiculous that he could be jealous of a man to whom Anne had absolutely no access, but ... *was* Jeffrey jealous of Renard?

"I thought we shared an admiration for the Fox," she said in a reasoning voice. "I thought you enjoyed talking about him."

"Yes," said Jeffrey, raking a hand through his hair. "I *do* admire him, and I *do* like discussing him with you. But, as I've told you before, I don't like talking all the time, especially when I want to be kissing you instead of talking to you."

"Well, I'm sorry to disappoint you," said Anne, a little nettled and afraid she was going to be denied her longed-for treat in hearing what Jeffrey knew about Renard, "but I didn't get rid of my uncle so you could kiss me. I told you I'm not ready for that yet." Silently she added, *I don't know if I'll ever be ready—not with you.* "You told me you'd tell me all about Renard's planned escape, and I knew you couldn't tell me with Reggie in the room. That's the only reason I asked Aunt Katherine to help me out."

Jeffrey sighed and shook his head. "Very well. I ought to be used to your missishness by now." After a moment of heavy silence, he managed a grimacing sort of smile. Anne was relieved to see even this small sign that he was returning to his usual friendly manner toward her.

"Let's not waste any more time. Tell me, Jeffrey. Tell me what you know about Renard."

Jeffrey sat staring at his hands for some time, then looked up at Anne soberly.

"Well?" she prompted, mad with impatience.

He sighed. "I can't tell you anything."

"You're angry with me, and this is your way of getting back!" she exclaimed.

"No, that's not true. I really can't tell you anything. It's too risky, for you and for everyone involved."

"Then why did you say—?"

"I wasn't thinking. I was wrong to make you think I could tell you anything. I'd forgotten all about my promise to confide in you till you brought it up just now, ruining my more pleasing ideas about why you'd got rid of your uncle."

Anne frowned and was silent for a moment.

Then she said, "Can't you even tell me what time you're going to be having this wonderful adventure? When the hour comes, I can think of you and imagine being there."

"You'll be fast asleep by then. Believe me, you're best off sleeping blissfully in your bed while we fellows face danger."

Anne decided to let this arrogant comment pass, then tried a different tack for prying information out of Jeffrey.

"You will be careful, won't you? It would be dreadful if you fell off your horse and broke your neck."

"You know I don't have a horse, Anne. And—thank God!—I won't be needing one to—" He stopped short and looked suspiciously at Anne.

"Does that mean the rendezvous point is nearby? Perhaps inside the city?"

"No more questions, Anne." He stood up. "I know what you're up to, and you won't get another word out of me."

She looked up at him beseechingly.

Jeffrey groaned. "And to be sure I don't cave in to your little female tricks, I'm leaving."

Her beseeching look changed to a scowl.

Jeffrey sighed. "You're miffed with me, which is another compelling reason to make this an early evening." When Anne didn't answer, he reached for his hat. "Good night, Anne." But when he began walking away, Anne felt guilty. She stood up and held out her hand.

"Wait, Jeffrey."

He turned around and looked questioningly at her.

She smiled. "Are we still friends?"

For a long moment he just stared at her. Then he walked back, caught her chin in one of his large hands, and kissed her hard and full on the mouth before she had time to protest. He laughed at her surprised expression. "Anne, we're more than friends." Then he put his hat on his head at a rakish angle and strode toward the door. Seconds later, as she stood rubbing her jaw where Jeffrey's fingers had pinched into her skin, Anne heard the front door close behind him.

She should have been angry that he'd kissed her, but at the moment it was the least of her concerns. She'd barely registered the sensations of his lips on hers. She was thinking ahead. She was making plans, considering possibilities. She was going to be at that rendezvous point tonight right along with Jeffrey. There were ways of getting there without her friend's help. Well, he *would* be assisting her, but he'd never know he was, and he'd never ever know she was there. Even if she was noticed some time during the planned escape, no one would recognize her. She was going in disguise.

Anne excused herself early that night, her mind busy with thoughts of Renard and the adventure ahead. She'd told her aunt and uncle she was having the housekeeper, Theresa, mix her up a sleeping potion. She knew one or both of them would check on her in her room before they retired to their own bedchambers, and she planned to look sound asleep, although she had no intention of actually taking the medicine. Naturally Reggie had commended her good sense in wanting to get an undisturbed night's rest.

As she ascended the stairs to the upper floor, Anne's only regret in leaving so soon after Reggie and Katherine returned from the garden was that she couldn't observe how the two of them behaved toward each other after the "swooning" episode. She had a feeling that a turning point had been reached in their relationship. She was sure an attachment was growing between them.

Reggie had been seriously alarmed by Katherine's supposed indisposition, and Katherine had thoroughly enjoyed his gentle solicitude. Could two such disparate personalities be happy together? Anne thought they were almost as dissimilar in their attitudes and philosophies as she and Delacroix!

Intriguing as the subject was, however, Anne had more important things to think about at the moment. Before going to her room she took a detour to the deserted servants' quarters and sneaked into the small chamber where Reggie's manservant, James, slept. She got what she needed, then left without being seen. She made another short jaunt to Reggie's room. Once inside her own room, she hid the borrowed items in her wardrobe, then rang for her abigail, Sarah, to help her into her nightgown and comb out and braid her hair. Then Anne sent her downstairs for the sleeping potion.

While Sarah was gone, Anne couldn't resist opening her wardrobe and reaching in the back for the black suit of clothes she'd taken from the closet of Reggie's manservant. He was shorter and more slightly built than Reggie, and his clothes actually came close to fitting her. The tailored trousers and jacket were sober and inconspicuous, as befitted his station, and would lend her the anonymity she needed to succeed in her masquerade.

Her plan was to leave the house as soon as she thought Reggie and Katherine were asleep, walk to Jeffrey's boardinghouse, then wait till he came out. It was fortunate that he'd pointed out his lodgings to her one day while they were driving down Camp Street, an offshoot of Canal Street in the American District.

Jeffrey's conversation had not clearly indicated when the slave escape would take place, just that it would occur at an hour when she was normally sound asleep. She hoped she'd get there in time. He had, however, obligingly let it slip that he was going on foot to the rendezvous point. As she was an excellent walker, Anne knew she could easily follow him.

Anne heard Sarah's footsteps coming down the hall, so she hastily put the clothes back in the wardrobe and shut the doors. Sarah carried a cup of steaming tea. "Here, miss. Theresa says the stuff what'll make ye sleep is in the tea. Drink it all up, she says."

"I will, Sarah, as soon as I'm settled in bed."

Sarah nodded, lifted up the mosquito netting, turned down the coverlets, and plumped Anne's pillows. While her back was turned, Anne took the opportunity to dump the tea into her chamber pot. "There ye go, miss," said Sarah, turning around to face her mistress. "You'll be as comfy as can be."

"I'm sure I will," said Anne with a smile. Sarah knew about her run-in with the drunkard in the alley. By now Anne supposed that most of the servants had heard various versions of the story. She handed Sarah the teacup. "I've already finished my tea and will be sleeping like a babe in no time."

"Lor', miss, ye drunk it already? Wasn't it hot?"

"Not intolerably so." She climbed into bed and pulled only the sheets to her chin. The night was too warm for anything heavier. "As I am sure he'll wish to know, please tell my uncle I took my sleeping potion."

"Yes, miss, I will." Sarah arranged the mosquito netting so that there were no openings, curtsied, and smiled. When Sarah closed the door behind her, Anne immediately turned on her back and stared across the dark room at the open window. It was still hot. Hot in November. The weather here was nothing like England's. And in England she'd never be lying in her bed contemplating such a daring adventure.

Anne frowned. Reggie would say it was stupid. Most people would think it was stupid, and very dangerous. And maybe it was. But she had such a strong compulsion to see Renard again—even from a distance—that she felt she had no choice but to follow the driving instincts that urged her on.

Last night he'd been in that very room, holding her, kissing her. Anne closed her eyes and remembered the sensation of his lips on hers, his hands moving over her bare skin. No one had ever made her feel so sensual, so alive.

No one, that is, except Delacroix! She hated to admit it, but both men had the same devastating effect on her. She'd had intimate encounters with them both in the last twenty-four hours, and if she was honest with herself, she'd have to admit that sometimes the memories got confused and intertwined.

The curtains moved in the incoming air as if in slow motion, a languid breeze rolling across the room to the bed. Anne welcomed its cooling effect on her flushed cheeks. The moon was nearly full that night, and the room had a dim, preternatural glow about it. Nothing was really in complete shadow. The furniture, the cushions, the bric-a-brac, everything was still and solid, everything but the curtains belling in the breeze.

She might have slept if she weren't so full of expectancy, so full of thoughts of Renard ... and Delacroix. Anne shook her head in the dark. How she wished she could keep that scoundrel from weaseling his way into her thoughts!

She heard movement and lowered voices outside her door, then the knob turned carefully. Quickly she rolled on her side and closed her eyes, forcing herself to relax completely. She must look convincingly, peacefully dormant.

She sensed the light of a lamp falling across her face, the darkness behind her closed eyes brightening infinitesimally.

"She's done up, the poor dear," whispered Reggie.

"Yes," said Katherine. "The herbs seem to have done the job well enough."

"We really must do something for Delacroix," said Reggie. "He might have actually saved her life, the little scatterbrain."

"Yes," agreed Katherine. "We'll do something to show our appreciation."

There was a pause, during which Anne supposed she was being studied. She felt a little foolish, though thoroughly loved. How often was a twenty-three-year-old woman so completely mollycoddled?

In another moment the light withdrew and the door was closed. She opened her eyes and listened while her doting relatives moved away, each to his or her own room. She wondered with what feelings they parted tonight.

Just to be safe, Anne waited another ten minutes or so after the last squeak of a floorboard was heard in the hall, then she threw off the sheets, flipped up the mosquito netting, and got out of bed. She lit a lamp, turned it low, then quickly

donned the trousers and jacket over her chemise.
She pulled on a pair of sturdy half-boots, then finished the outfit with the hat she'd borrowed from
Reggie's room. She had wound her braid in a cor-
onet and secured it with several hairpins. She
hoped none of it would come loose and hang
down her neck, revealing to everyone the true nature of her sex.

She studied her reflection in the mirror and acknowledged that she'd be instantly known for a
fraud—or at least an oddity—if she were trying to
go about town in the daylight hours. But in the
dark she hoped to get by with such a hastily de-
vised disguise.

Now she had only to wait a few more minutes
before leaving the house to walk to Jeffrey's lodgings. She looked at the mantel clock. It was forty
minutes past ten. She sat down at her dressing
table and stared at her reflection, waiting,
waiting . . . The tick of the clock sounded through
the silent room, its slow-creeping measures of time
completely out of rhythm with Anne's racing
heart.

Soon she would see Renard again. Soon.

Chapter 10

Anne walked quickly through the quiet residential streets of the Faubourg St. Mary, discreetly keeping in the shadows of the trees as much as possible, crossing to the other side if it looked as if she was about to encounter someone on the banquette. Her disguise was adequate, but it was best not to take chances.

Jeffrey lodged in a respectable boardinghouse on Camp Street, just down the block from the new St. Patrick's Church and not far from Canal Street and the Vieux Carré. The closer Anne got to Canal Street, the more people she saw, and the more nervous she got. It was one thing dreaming up a daring scheme in the safety of her bedchamber, and quite another actually to undertake it.

But despite her anxieties, she did not regret the deception and danger in which she found herself hopelessly tangled. She had to see Renard again, and this appeared to be the only way to accomplish what had become an all-consuming desire.

Last night's encounter in her bedchamber played over and over again in her mind, spurring her on. She had no way of knowing when or if he'd ever visit her again. He was elusive, a dream that had to be pursued. He certainly hadn't been knocking on her aunt's door lately, or—like

Delacroix—turning up like a bad penny everywhere she went.

The night was balmy, the air redolent with scents both good and bad. The stars hung low, their brilliance softened and blurred at the edges, as if shining through the thin translucence of Chinese lanterns.

Mrs. Cavanaugh's Boardinghouse, a moderate-sized two-story building surrounded by a tidy garden, was just ahead, the gables and shutters limned by moonlight. Jeffrey had made the point once that he was plump enough in the pockets to have his own house, but, being a bachelor, he found it more convenient to come and go as he pleased at Mrs. Cavanaugh's.

But when discussing the advantages of having his meals and laundry taken care of, Jeffrey always made it quite clear to Anne that he'd give up these admirable arrangements at the drop of a hat if a woman he couldn't resist marrying came along. He'd said it in that coy way of his, leaving Anne no doubt that he thought of her as just such an irresistible woman.

Anne determinedly put Jeffrey's troublesome infatuation out of her mind. Tonight her thoughts and feelings were consumed with the idea and image of her hero, Renard.

Anne stared up at the only lighted window in the house, an upper outside window with the shade pulled down. She decided that it must be Jeffrey's room. When a shadow from inside suddenly loomed over the shade, Anne realized how exposed she was standing there in the moonlight. If Jeffrey happened to look out, he couldn't help seeing her. She crossed the street and scanned the area for a good hiding place. She saw a large rhododendron bush near the street, in a corner of someone's small yard. Hidden behind it, she could still command a comprehensive view of the boardinghouse.

Anne was just about to take up her position for spying when she heard fast-paced footsteps on the banquette. She snatched a glance up the road and saw two gentlemen quickly walking her way. She'd have to wait till they passed by before she could hide, and she wondered how she was going to manage to look inconspicuous in the meantime. Surely it would appear odd to the gentlemen if she simply stood there twiddling her thumbs!

Anne couldn't think of a better plan on the spur of the minute, so she remained where she was. But she struck a nonchalant pose, hooked her thumbs in her trouser pockets, thrust out her chin a little, and fixed her eyes on the boardinghouse across the street. She hoped to appear so sure of herself and relaxed that she would excite no interest at all. No such luck.

"Monsieur." One of the men made a slight, polite bow, touching the narrow brim of his hat. Anne watched him out of the corner of her eye, keeping her chin up and her face averted. "Might we be of some assistance to you? Are you looking for an address at this late hour?"

She replied in a lowered voice, her tone brusque, hoping to sound convincingly male. She hadn't planned on talking to anyone. "No ... er ... thanks. I'm waiting for someone."

The man did not respond. After a tense pause, Anne braved a look at him. She was startled to see that he was the same man she'd nearly run into at the cemetery a few days before—the handsome black man. He was looking at her keenly, as if he recognized her, too, or perhaps simply saw through her disguise. She tried to brazen it out, but she was afraid her nervousness showed.

"Armande?" The other man was talking now, nudging the first man on the arm. "Come along, brother, this fellow doesn't need our assistance."

Anne glanced at the second man. He, too, was a mix of races, just as handsome as the first man, but younger looking. He was visibly sweating, shifting nervously on his feet. They were both well-dressed—and in a hurry. The older one, called Armande, was carrying a small valise.

"Come, Armande," the younger man said again, impatience in his voice. "We've got work to do."

Armande was finally prodded to movement. With one last puzzled, interested look at Anne, he hurried off down the street with his brother.

Anne wasn't sure what suspicions Armande had about her, but he was gone, and that was all that mattered. She blew a relieved breath, then waited for them to turn a corner and disappear before she took up her position behind the rhododendron bush. The shadow that had moved over Jeffrey's shade was gone, but an instant later it reappeared, then slid away again, as if he were pacing restlessly in his room. *He's as excited as I am!* thought Anne. She smiled in the dark. On the matter of Renard, she and Jeffrey would always agree. They were both drawn to him, to his heroic lifestyle that was the active, expanded realization of their own ideals.

Now the waiting began. She didn't want to sit down because the wet grass would stain her borrowed trousers. Though it was probably just an hour or so, the wait seemed like an eternity, and by the time the light went out in Jeffrey's room, Anne's legs were stiff and her back ached. These minor discomforts were, however, quickly disre-

garded when Jeffrey let himself out a side door of
the boardinghouse and made for the street. Even
though it was dark, Anne couldn't mistake that
swaggering, long-legged stride. It was Jeffrey, all
right.

She followed him at a discreet distance. Though
it must have been after midnight there were still
occasional people on the streets. Anne darted in
and out of shadows, usually managing to hide
when someone approached, but her throat tightened with fear whenever a man passed by. She
dreaded a repeat of the scene in that alley yesterday, particularly since there was no Lucien
Delacroix in the vicinity to help her out of it.

Jeffrey was just ahead, of course, and she could
call to him for help if necessary, but she didn't
want anything—not even her own defense—to in-
terfere with Jeffrey getting to his destination on
time. Her whole hope of seeing Renard depended
on Jeffrey being in the right place at the right time.

The right place was apparently the cemetery, in
fact the same cemetery where Aunt Katherine's
husbands were buried, the same place where
Anne had held a conversation with Delacroix, and
where she'd seen that man . . . She remembered
thinking how appropriate the atmospheric burial
grounds were for trysts and dangerous assigna-
tions, for romance and skullduggery.

Now Jeffrey seemed just as anxious as she was
to keep out of sight. Mindful of possible watchful
eyes, he stealthily stationed himself in the shadows of a rose arbor in a yard across the street from
the Catholic section of the cemetery. She hid herself behind a bush in the yard next door, the slick,
leathery leaves of another rhododendron pressing
against her cheek.

She crouched down and congratulated herself

on stalking Jeffrey so expertly that he never suspected he'd been followed. She was settling in for another long wait when she heard the dull, plodding echo of a horse's hooves on the road. She parted her protective greenery and watched the excruciatingly slow approach of what appeared to be a rickety farmer's wagon full of cargo. In the moonlight she could make out barrels, baskets of produce, and what looked like huge sheaves of tobacco tied together in large bundles.

It seemed an odd hour to be transporting merchandise to the market or the dock, but she'd seen other cargo-laden wagons on the road that night, and supposed that busy farmers made up their own schedules. Unless, of course, that was no field hand bent nearly double over the horse's reins, his wide-brimmed straw hat pulled low on his forehead ... Did Renard use disguises other than his usual uniform black? Whoever the driver was, he looked as though he'd dozed off, swaying with the movement of the wagon.

With no one to urge it forward, the piebald mare stopped completely and dropped its muzzle to the short tufts of grass that grew in the middle section of the road in a thin line, tore a juicy mouthful, and proceeded to chew. Anne watched all this with keen interest. The scene looked perfectly harmless and unrehearsed. Was it real, or was it part of Renard's plan?

Suddenly the driver roused himself, sleepily knuckled his eyes, stretched, and stepped down from the wagon. Anne immediately realized that the driver couldn't be Renard. He didn't have Renard's physical build, the details of which Anne remembered with surprising exactness, as if she'd been seeing him on a daily basis. But she'd only seen him twice, and both times primarily in the dark.

The man led the horse into the shadows of a pair of tall sycamore trees that skirted the boundary of the cemetery and were planted so close together that their upper branches intertwined. Now the wagon bed was in complete darkness. The driver reappeared from the lee side of the wagon and stooped to inspect the horse's outside shoe. The driver was fully illuminated by the moonlight and seemed the natural object for watching, but Anne couldn't help wondering . . .

Her gaze veered into the shadows where the wagon was practically hidden from view. She looked hard. Did she imagine it, or were the bundles of tobacco shifting and moving about? She squinted and strained to see. Someone was crawling into the wagon bed and hiding under the sheaves of tobacco! And there was another dark figure following him, and another figure just emerging from behind one of the tall tombs. Yes, Jeffrey had definitely hit on the right time and the right place! Slaves were being stowed away and driven out of town in a farm wagon! But where was Renard?

Anne watched intently, her breath caught in her throat, her heart hammering against her ribs, as three escapees crawled into the wagon. All during this short process, the driver continued to fuss with his horse's shoe and pretend to be oblivious to the goings-on at the rear of the vehicle. When all three slaves were safely inside, the driver hiked himself onto the seat and picked up the reins. Anne's disappointment smarted like a scraped knee. Wasn't she going to see Renard at all? Or was he hidden in the wagon, too? But surely someone would have had to escort the slaves to this point.

Suddenly Renard appeared at the rear of the wagon. Like a flat stone thrown over the surface of a lake, Anne's heart skipped and skittered. There was no mistaking the dark figure of her hero—so tall, lean, and upright! His movements were assured and economical as he hurriedly arranged the tobacco and made certain nothing was showing that might draw suspicion to the wagon.

As Renard straightened from this task, the driver, without seeming to glance back, gave an almost imperceptible sign—a half-turn of his wrist—which Renard duplicated. Then the driver deftly flicked the mare's rump with the tethers and the horse lifted its head, and, still chewing, leaned into the first plodding step of its "getaway" pace.

This was all done without a hitch, and Anne could imagine the smile curving beneath Renard's mask as he stood in the shadows. But it was too soon to smile. Behind Renard, Anne saw movement. Shapes shifted in the dappled shade of the trees. Obscure silhouettes slid over the cold marble tombs, slithering, like phantasmic predators, ever closer to Renard. Could they be members of a posse, alerted to Renard's whereabouts and bent on capture? Anne was afraid that was exactly the case, yet Renard continued to stand there, apparently unaware of the imminent danger.

Terror gripped Anne's throat and strangled the words of warning that formed on her lips. Unable to command her voice, she pushed aside the screen of leaves and ran toward Renard, waving her arms. He seemed to startle when he saw her, stepping forward with one foot, then hesitating.

But of course he would hesitate, Anne reasoned. A man springing out from behind a bush, franti-

cally waving his arms, might be a trap. The driver
stared, too, surprised to immobility, like a deer
caught in lantern light.

There'd been no time to spare for thoughts of
her own danger, but the sickening whine of a bullet as it passed close by Anne's head made her all
too aware of the risk she'd taken. Somehow she
found her voice. "Renard!" she called, but he was
already moving. However, he wasn't moving
away and out of danger. He was moving toward
her! In half a second he collided with her and
yanked her to his side, pinning her there with an
iron arm around her waist and forcing her to keep
up with him as he raced down the road.

Beyond the rattle of her teeth and the rush of
her own blood pulsing wildly through her veins,
Anne heard hoofbeats on the road, the mare no
longer plodding, but charging down the quiet
street as if it were chased by wolves. The wagon—
all loose rotten wood and squeaky bearings—
lurched and clattered behind. Raised voices
echoed from the shadows of the cemetery. Angry
words intermingled with scuffling boots and the
whinnying of nervous horses.

Even as she pushed herself to the very limits of
her strength to keep up with Renard, Anne knew
it was hopeless. How could they possibly outrun a
mounted posse? But suddenly she saw a horse, its
dark shape blending into the dense shadows beneath a full-leaved, drooping willow tree at the
edge of the cemetery. Renard tossed Anne onto the
saddle, quickly untwined the tether from a tree
branch, then leaped into the saddle behind her.

"Hold on tight," he whispered fiercely in her
ear. But Anne didn't need to be told to do something that made such incredible good sense. Both
their lives were in the balance, and now that it

looked as if she'd have something worth remembering in her dotage, Anne had never felt so determined to reach old age. She clung to the saddle pommel like a drowning man to a tossed ring of life-preserving rope.

Anne could feel Renard's powerful thighs press against her hips as he spurred the horse forward, his chest bearing down on her as he reached for the reins and flicked the horse's neck. "Hiyaaa! Go, Tempest!" he shouted, and they shot forward with such force, Anne's head popped back to thump against Renard's chin. She could hear his teeth clack together on impact.

Just as they gained the road, she glanced back and was relieved to see that they were pursued by only three men, not a fully organized posse. No doubt the men were bounty hunters, keeping their numbers small so there'd be fewer of them to split the reward among them.

In a moment they were on the road, a mere horse's length behind the wagon but, fortunately, several lengths ahead of the pursuing horsemen. But Anne knew they were not out of shooting range. Renard's broad back stood as a barricade between her and the firing guns, but she took no comfort in this fact. She couldn't bear the thought of Renard being shot.

Renard did not intend to be anyone's bounty, dead or alive. Handily managing the racing horse, he jagged back and forth without pattern, making for an unpredictable target. Eventually they gained on the wagon and pulled alongside it. Renard extracted a gun from a holster strapped to his hip and twisted in the saddle to take aim.

There was the deafening crack of gunfire at close range. Above the ringing in her ears, twice Anne heard the dull impact of a bullet and the shrill cry of a frightened horse thrown off-balance by a floundering rider.

With only one rider left in the saddle, the chase seemed all but over. The hoofbeats of the remaining horseman slowed, then halted completely. Renard turned in the saddle. Anne had turned, too, and was peering hopefully over Renard's shoulder when she felt the searing, stinging path of pain across her temple.

Blood, warm and sticky, immediately oozed from the wound and trailed thickly down her cheek and around the curve of her jaw. Her face washed cold. She felt faint, distanced, teetering. There were only pinpricks of consciousness left . . . Then there was nothing.

Lucien felt Anne go limp. He grabbed her around the waist and held tight. She must have fainted. He marveled that she'd lasted as long as she had during all this excitement.

Despite her disguise, Lucien had recognized Anne the minute she'd jumped out from behind that bush. He'd long ago memorized her every movement and mannerism, the nuances of her body language as familiar to him as his own. For weeks he'd watched her from a distance and longed to be close to her, as close as last night in her bedchamber, as close as now. But not under these circumstances, damn it! Now, in addition to the strong feelings he'd had for Anne all along, his heart swelled with gratitude. The little scatterbrain had risked her life to save his.

Thank God the chase was over, the favorable ending of it achieved, he knew, only because of the two casualties. Lucien hoped fervently that the wounds he'd inflicted were as trivial as he'd intended them to be. He'd aimed for the pursuers' arms and legs, but it was hard to be accurate from the back of a galloping horse.

But, just as the note had warned, Jeffrey Wycliff—or one of his informants—had known about tonight's mission and leaked it, intentionally or unintentionally, to the wrong people, forcing this confrontation and the resulting bloodshed. It was the first time Lucien had had to resort to gunfire to avert capture. His stomach churned with anger. Was this just the beginning of other botched missions? So few people were involved in the planning and execution of these escapes—people he trusted—that he didn't have the slightest idea whom he ought to suspect. Whom was Wycliff in cahoots with?

Armande turned now and waved to Lucien, veering the wagon to the right as they reached a fork in the road, slowing it to a pace that would keep the ancient conveyance intact till the rendezvous point with out-of-town compatriots. Armande would continue north on River Road and Lucien would go east, toward Bocage.

There was a remote cabin on the outskirts of his estate, a sultry niche deep in the cypress woods near a critter-infested bayou where no one but Lucien and Armande ever went. They had arranged to meet there in the morning and report on the completed mission.

It was a favorite place for the two of them to put their heads together to plan strategies for the cause, or just to relax on the porch with a cheroot, listen to the lulling singsong of the crickets, and watch alligators pretending to be drifting logs, their beady eyes peering out from under mossy headdresses. Tonight Lucien would take Anne there to recover from her swoon.

He slowed his horse to a canter, then a walk,

nuzzling his chin against a tuft of hair at Anne's brow. He smiled and squeezed her close, desire and admiration for her, like shafts of sunlight, beaming brightly, warmly, into the dark, cold corners of his cynical soul. She was a game one, foolish and headstrong, but pluck to the bone. When had he started to care so deeply for her?

Yes, he cared for her. Maybe he even loved her. It was a thrilling but unwelcome possibility. He didn't want to love her. He had no business loving anyone, not while he was committed to the masquerade of Renard and the risks it entailed. How could Anne possibly fit into such a crazy existence? Did he have the right to try to make her care as deeply for him if it endangered her life? He lifted his chin and let her head fall back into the hollow under his jaw. He kissed her forehead, his lips drifting down her hairline . . .

And tasted the metallic bitterness of blood. *Mon Dieu!* She'd been shot!

Lucien would have panicked, or wept, or cursed if he'd had the leisure of time, or if the stakes hadn't been so damned high. But he had no way of knowing how serious Anne's injuries were until he could examine them by candlelight, and that could not be accomplished on the road in the dead-dark of night. So all emotions were checked for now, all energy channeled into getting Anne to the cabin as fast as possible.

He spurred his sweating horse to a gallop, Anne clasped tightly against his chest, his large hand curved around her jaw to keep her head against his heart, to keep her delicate neck from snapping like a doll's. Hardened by a career of risk and danger, Lucien was still nearly overpowered by a nauseating, gut-wrenching fear. What if he was too late? What if he lost her?

He was off the main road now, urging his horse to an even faster gallop as he rode down a country lane. Skirting the manicured lawns of Bocage, the slave quarters, and the acres of sugarcane fields, he headed for the dense security of the cypress woods. The closer he got, the rougher the terrain became. Given this fact, he was probably riding too fast, but he trusted his horse to follow the thin trail familiar only to those few who used it frequently.

Tempest sidestepped dangerous snarls of overgrown ground cover and circumvented rocks and shrubs that loomed up seemingly out of nowhere. Finally the ground got mushy, and Lucien knew they were almost into the woods, and once inside, he would have no choice but to slow down. Time. Time was the enemy.

Lucien prayed. He prayed to all the saints he knew by name, and all the saints he didn't know by any stretch of a sinner's imagination. In his mind's eye, he was on his knees, the endless sky the roof of his cathedral, each star a candle lighted for Anne. For sweet, sweet Anne.

Chapter 11

They were deep in the woods now, their progress slow as Lucien maneuvered his horse around the trunks of large cypress trees, thin fingers of moonlight barely penetrating the overhanging, moss-laden branches. The verdant closeness of the swamp made many people claustrophobic, but Lucien welcomed the dense foliage—tonight more than ever—as a means of hiding from the encroachment of unfriendly civilization. Fireflies winked in the dark stillness.

The trees cleared slightly, and he saw the cabin, its weathered wood gleaming silver-gray. It was really nothing more than a fishing shack, perched on the muddy banks of the bayou. Footwide planks of wood, supported by moldy rope, served as a sort of walkway over the mud from the crude hitching post to the warped and blistered front door. But inside this unprepossessing structure the cupboards were stocked with food, medicines, bandages, and sundry supplies that made the old cabin a valuable haven for Lucien and chosen others. Anne wasn't the first refugee he'd brought there, but he'd never been more relieved to see the place, or felt more urgent in his mission.

He eased off the horse, carefully pulling Anne with him and supporting her sagging body

against his. She felt so slight and insubstantial, he
experienced another rush of uncontrollable fear.
He caught her under the knees and carried her to
the cabin, making a distracted mental note to water and tend to the exhausted horse later, when he
was sure Anne was out of harm's way. He prayed
God he had it in his power to secure Anne's safety.

He lifted the latch in the door, which was never
locked, and, turning sideways, toted his light baggage inside, kicking the door closed behind him.
He knew where the bed was and needed no light
to guide him. He laid her down, the supporting
bed boards creaking as Anne sank lifelessly into
the soft, moss-filled mattress.

He walked quickly to a pantry, found a tinder-
box, and struck a light, shakily holding it to the
wick of a thick candle. He darted a searching, worried glance at Anne, then hastily found and
lighted three more candles. He took two of these,
placing one on each side of the bed on small tables.

He sat down on the bed and leaned forward,
gently taking hold of Anne's chin and turning her
head to the light. Lucien's stomach tightened with
distress, every nerve in his body cringing in sympathy. There was so much blood! Too much of it to
see the wound, or to assess its seriousness.

Tamping down his rising panic, he stripped off
his black gloves—sticky with Anne's blood—
found a flagon of fresh drinking water, and
poured a goodly amount over a clean cloth he'd
taken from the medicine chest. He dabbed gingerly at the wound till he'd sponged away most of
the blood. All during this process, Anne didn't stir
at all. Such pale inertia was unlike her. Before,
whenever he'd seen her, she'd been vibrant with

life, so passionate and energetic. What had he done to her?

Lucien's fears were considerably mollified and his guilt slightly assuaged when he got a good look at the wound. There had been no penetration of the bullet. It had only grazed her, leaving a shallow scrape about an inch long. Lucien let loose a heavy sigh, relief flooding through him like a tranquilizing dose of bone-warming, muscle-loosening liquor. With the application of that herbal disinfectant Armande had mixed up recently and a clean bandage, she'd heal in a matter of days, the wound probably leaving no permanent mark. He didn't relish the idea of Anne having a lifelong reminder of this night in the form of a scar on her beautiful face.

When Lucien applied the disinfectant, Anne showed the first signs of returning to consciousness. Her head rolled on the pillow, and a soft, low moan escaped her lips. Lucien worked faster. He didn't want her waking up till he'd completely cleaned and dressed the wound. Once he'd accomplished this, he'd snuff out all but one of the candles. And the one that remained lighted wouldn't be placed anywhere near his general vicinity. Anne mustn't see any more of him than necessary.

When Lucien was ready to tie a strip of material around her head and secure the bandage at her temple, his hands faltered for a moment. She'd braided her hair and wound it in a tight bundle, secured by a dozen pins. He'd love to see it loose.

Lucien's fingers hovered longingly over the coil of gleaming braids. He itched to see the long silken curls cascading over the white pillow casing. He'd imagined it that way so many times ... Moments passed, his indecision as palpable and heavy in the surrounding air as the swarm of mosquitoes that had been drawn by the scent of blood.

The insistent, incessant whine of the mosquitoes was what finally prodded Lucien to movement. This was no time to indulge his romantic fantasies! He had to get Anne's wound properly dressed. He quickly tied the strip of cloth around her head, securing the bandage. He batted away a half-dozen or so mosquitoes, then pulled the net down and over Anne's still form, tucking it snugly under the edges of the mattress.

"There, *cher*," he murmured, "you are protected from the bite of the insects." He pulled a straight-backed reed-bottomed chair next to the bed and sat down, sighing deeply, smiling with self-derision. "But who will protect you from me?"

The question was not rhetorical. He knew he was a threat to Anne's immediate safety and ultimate happiness. She could have been killed tonight. He had had no idea that she was quite so intrepid, that she would go to such lengths to see him. Unless he could draw a promise from her to behave more circumspectly, she'd assuredly put herself in harm's way again. And there was still the problem of how to return her to Prytania Street without exposing her to damaging gossip.

He wondered if she'd been discovered missing yet. If so, he hoped Reggie would keep his wits about him and conduct a *discreet* search for her. If word of her escapade leaked out, society would not look kindly on a young woman who'd dressed like a man, chased after an outlaw, and spent several hours alone with him in a remote cabin. Never mind that he'd only brought her there to recover from an injury; details that might lend the story a more respectable slant would be disregarded.

As his gaze rested on Anne, Lucien felt the tug of another smile—this one tender. She never gave the gossips a second thought, but went about her business, answering to her own conscience and no one else. Just now she looked as sweet and vulnerable as a child. Her knees were drawn up slightly and turned to the side. One arm rested on her stomach; the other was curled up over her head, her hand lying open on the pillow. Her long lashes made feathering shadows on her cheeks, where there was finally a slight flush of color.

She looked so innocent. Like an angel. But he knew how strong-minded, how ruthlessly determined she could be. She believed in Renard, she believed in the cause, and she had willfully flouted conventional wisdom to be, for a short time, part of her hero's life.

Lucien's smile fell away. If she knew that Renard was also Dandy Delacroix, would she still think of him as a hero? He was only a man, after all, completely undeserving of such awe and admiration. He knew she fancied herself in love with him—with Renard—but she could only be in love with the legend, not the man, because she didn't know the man beneath the disguises, behind the masquerade.

He'd been playing the parts for so long now, Lucien wasn't sure who he was, either. It was too simple to say he was a mix of both Delacroix and Renard. He wasn't. He was something beyond the sum total of both. How could Anne love a man she'd never met?

Even if Anne's love was genuine, and not the manufactured infatuation of hero worship, would it be right to accept her love? He had a feeling his career as Renard couldn't last more than a few more weeks—he needed that much time to carry

out a plan he was devising to stop permanently
Bodine's escalating brutality to his slaves—but
anything could happen in a few weeks.

Tonight was proof of that. Someone had infil-
trated the tight ranks of his operation. Lucien
knew his time as Renard must come to a natural
end, but he'd no intention of obliging his enemies
by celebrating that end dangling from a noose. But
fate might see his abolitionist career conclude in a
different manner than he envisioned . . .

In the interim Anne would be in danger, too.
The best plan all around would be to discourage
her from caring about him, to keep her at a safe
distance. But could he? He had gone to her house,
kissed and caressed her in her own bedchamber,
but there had always been the safeguard of her abigail sleeping in the next room. Completely alone
with her now, he wanted nothing more than to
hold her in his arms and make love to her all night
long.

When she woke up, he'd guard his identity . . .
and his heart. He would show her that he was an-
gered by her risky behavior and discourage her
from falling in love with an outlaw. It would be
hard, but he was doing it for both their sakes. He
ruefully remembered Micaela's comment about
him being an honorable man. Could he be honorable tonight, or would he give in to his deepest
yearnings?

Lucien heard his horse whinny, a reminder that
the animal needed water and his bridle removed.
Close by was another smaller shack that he used
as a makeshift stable, complete with hay and oats.
He would put Tempest in there for what was left
of the night, safe from alligators that sniffed out a
sweating horse from yards away and stalked it
like any other warm-blooded prey. Even now there

could be unwanted visitors outside the door—the long-toothed, beady-eyed, low-bellied kind.

With one last look at Anne, who slept peacefully, Lucien stood up, opened the door, and went outside. There was a rustle in the grass that grew tall along the water's edge and a ripple in the water itself. By the flash of terror in Tempest's eyes and the way his nostrils flared, Lucien realized he'd come outside just in time, just when an alligator was about to pay a predatory call. Lucien hurriedly led the horse to the shack several yards upshore, rubbing Tempest's long nose and crooning soothing words. He tended to the animal's needs and firmly latched the door shut behind him. Then he jogged back along the path to the cabin.

When he opened the door, a firefly drifted in with him. His gaze darted to the bed, seeking reassurance in the vision of his sleeping angel.

But she wasn't asleep. She was sitting up in bed, staring at him most disconcertingly, all four candles ablaze and flooding the room with light.

Anne was disoriented. Her head felt like a balloon, light and airy, as if it might float off if it weren't attached. Her memory came in bits and pieces—bits of chaos and pieces of fear. Slowly she put them together and came up with one fantastic scene after another. The cemetery, the slaves escaping, the bounty hunters, the mad dash across country on Renard's horse, the gunshot, the pain . . .

A shiver coursed through her. She touched the bandage that was tied snugly around her forehead and winced involuntarily. It hurt like the dickens, but obviously she'd not been mortally wounded.

She must have fainted more because of the shock than because of the actual physical injury.

She looked around, familiarizing herself with the strange environs. She was in a bed with clean, simple bedclothes underneath her and nothing on top, which was fine because it was too hot for covers. The bed was swathed in mosquito netting, making everything outside this man-made cocoon appear hazy and slightly unfocused. The fuzziness of her vision might also have something to do with the throbbing pain behind her right eye.

Four globes of light pulsed and flickered, one on each side of the bed, and two across the small room on the flat shelf of what looked like a pantry cupboard. She assimilated these facts and grew comfortable with them before she attempted to unravel the unknown aspects of her situation. Had Renard brought her there? If so, where was he?

The door opened. An instant before she hadn't even known where the door was. Renard came in the room. As before, he was dressed in black, his head tied up in a close-fitting scarf, hiding his hair completely. A mask covered his face from forehead to mouth, with slits to see through. He wore a long-sleeved shirt, tight-fitting trousers, and tall boots—all black. While a single firefly flickered and bounced around him, he didn't move. He just stared back at her.

Then suddenly he was in motion, moving quickly to the pantry and snuffing out both candles with a hiss of breath, then leaning over Anne's bed to extinguish the candle on one side of her with a thumb and forefinger. He picked up the other candle and placed it on the mantel of a small fireplace behind him. This lighting arrangement made it impossible for her to see Renard's face. He was in the shadows—black melding into black—

but she was fully illuminated, exposed. She objected and told him so.

"Renard, why are you hiding from me?"

"Hiding?" He leaned against the wall opposite the bed, his shadow merging indistinguishably into the shadow of the pantry cupboard. "I'm right here, *cher*."

"I can't see you."

"That's the whole idea."

"But you can see me."

"And the sight of you brings me more pain than you can imagine."

"I . . . I don't understand."

"You have been injured because of me."

"No, it wasn't your fault!"

"Why did you come to the cemetery tonight, Anne?" His tone was stern and disapproving. "It was very foolish of you. You were in grave danger. You might have been killed."

Anne felt awkward and foolish. He was right. "I wanted to see you," she said, instantly embarrassed by the petulance in her voice.

There was a pause. "And you would take such risks to see me? Why? You don't even know me."

Anne twisted her hands in her lap, feeling less and less like a mature woman, and more and more like a silly, inexperienced schoolgirl. But the dark that obscured Renard's face lent her courage. She raised her chin. "I could ask you the same thing, you know. Why did you risk exposure by climbing into my bedchamber window? You don't know me, either."

"I know you better than you think."

"How is that possible?"

"I have been watching you."

The thought that Renard had been surreptitiously watching her sent a thrill through Anne like a bolt of lightning. "But how? Where?"

"Never mind. Let's get back to my question to you. Why are you taking such risks for a man you don't know?"

"I do know you. At least I know the substance of your character. When I first ... met you on the *Belvedere*, I was very much impressed with your ..."

She hesitated, so he supplied, "With my kisses?"

"With your mission, monsieur!" Anne felt her face heat up. "You're making it very hard for me to tell you how much I admire what you do." A shrug of her shoulders expressed her loss for words. "It's so noble."

His weary sigh sounded in the darkness. "I don't think of it as noble. I think of it as necessary. I do what I can. As time passes, more and more abolitionists will become involved in what is coming to be known as the Underground Railroad. Soon I will be nothing more than one among many."

"Will that suit you, monsieur, being one among many?"

"Eminently. I don't do this for the newspaper coverage, you know."

Anne continued to feel tongue-tied and unusually shy, which didn't seem right after the intimacies they'd shared just the night before. "It's good of you, monsieur, to discount the fame."

"You mean the notoriety, don't you?"

"Many people think of you as a hero." Softly: "I do."

"Because I cut a dashing figure in black?" His voice dripped with scornful sarcasm.

Anne was offended. She felt her uncharacteristic shyness receding. "Of course not! As I said, I approve and applaud what you do. Even if your fingers dripped with jewels, if you behaved heroically, you'd be a hero to me." Anne couldn't imagine how she'd come up with such an example. She'd been describing Delacroix! But *he* was no hero. He was a scoundrel.

But her conscience rebelled at this pat summation of Delacroix's entire identity. He'd saved her from danger, hadn't he? Wasn't he a hero, too? More to the point, *why* did he constantly intrude on her thoughts, even when she was with Renard?

Her head throbbed. She rubbed her temple, feeling confused, frustrated. An edge of impatience crept into her voice. "You are angry with me tonight, monsieur, and you won't listen to me and believe me. Why is it so hard to accept that I admire you and what you do? Truthfully, I'm not merely besotted by your dashing image." Though it didn't detract from his appeal, either, Anne silently admitted.

Renard's broad shoulders shifted in the dark. She could hear the whisper of cloth against rough wood wall. The firefly seemed attracted to him, too; it bobbed around his head, lighting first one feature, then another in a fleeting orange glow.

"I know you despise slavery, mademoiselle," he said in a tone that conceded her point, but only reluctantly. "I know you would do more for the cause if you could, and are chafed by the limitations of your sex." In a lighter tone, he added, "You would be a man, eh, mademoiselle? Then you would set the world on its pompous ear."

Anne thought about this interesting idea for a minute, but there was never any question in her mind that she much preferred being a woman. Her attraction to Renard was more than sufficient proof of that. "No, I don't want to be a man. I enjoy being a woman." She lingered on this thought, hoping the implication was not lost on Renard. "But I *am* attracted to men who are the sort of man I'd be *if* I were a man. Does that make sense, monsieur?"

He did not reply. His silence unnerved her. She wanted to fill the empty space with words. Preferably with truth. Anne drummed up her courage. "I'm very much attracted to you, Monsieur Renard. I think I might even be a little . . . in love with you. I have to know . . . do you feel something for me? Is that why you came to my bedchamber?"

"I shouldn't have come," he said bluntly, deflating Anne's hope of a similar confession from him. "I only contributed to your infatuation with a fantasy, a hero of your imagination."

"You're wrong," said Anne stubbornly. "I don't know why, but it seems as if I've known you forever. There's something between us . . . a familiarity I can't explain. It's as though I see you all the time, instead of just that once on the *Belvedere* and then in my room last night—"

"That is impossible," he quickly interjected.

She sighed. "Yes, I know. Which makes it all the more strange for me to feel so at home with you. And when you kissed me . . ."

The firefly, as if cued, hovered near Renard's lips. They were finely molded, firm and sensuous. "Yes?" he prompted her softly. His lips stayed slightly parted. Anne imagined the feel of them on her own lips, trailing down her neck, lingering in the hollow under her ear.

No, that was Delacroix! She shook her head to clear it of the intrusive image, but only succeeded in making her head ache worse. "When you kissed me, it felt so natural, so right. So exclusive."

"Exclusive, eh?"

"Yes, as if you were—"

"As if I were the only man for you."

She'd made her point. Eagerly: "Yes."

"If that is so, *cher*, then I must conclude you have never felt the same in any other man's arms, *n'est-ce pas?*"

Once again Delacroix's image intruded. Those dark eyes, the thick lashes, the wicked smile. She remembered the kisses in the alley. She'd felt exactly the same in his arms as she had in Renard's. Just as natural. Just as right. Just as exclusive. She had to tell Renard the truth.

"The truth, mademoiselle," Renard prompted, as if he'd again read her thoughts.

"There has been one other man with whom I've experienced similar feelings."

"But you don't love this man?"

"No, I don't love him," she said, the words rather too strongly underscored with feeling. Then, less emphatically, "I can't love him. I deplore his lifestyle. He is a slave owner."

"Is this your only objection to the fellow?"

"Isn't it enough?"

Another long pause. "*Oui.* It is enough. But what if he weren't a slave owner?"

"There are other objections." Irritably, her head pounding like the drums on Congo Square, she said, "But why do you ask me about this man? He means nothing to me. Less than nothing."

"I ask because he and I are the same—"

"The same?"

"—the same in that we both make you feel strong emotions. How can you love me and not love him?"

Anne had no reply. She took reprieve in complaining about her headache. In truth she was beginning to feel quite overpowered by it. "My head aches abominably."

Instantly Renard was alert. "*Mon Dieu*, I'm such an imbecile. I talk while you suffer. *Un moment, cher.*" He moved to the cupboard, opened a door, and pushed around bottles and dishes. "First I will get you some water, and some food if you're hungry. And then a cup of tea, laced with Armande's special headache remedy."

"Armande?" Anne remembered the two men on Camp Street. Armande was the tall one, the one she'd also seen at the cemetery the day she ran across Delacroix. Her brain was trying to pull together some disjointed thoughts. Something just out of reach was taunting her. "I know an Armande."

Renard stopped his busy movements abruptly, looking over his shoulder. His face was fully in the light of the candle, but Anne's vision seemed to be getting worse; everything was a blur. His wary stance seemed oddly at variance with his casual tone of voice. "You know an Armande? One of Madame Grimms's banker friends, I suppose."

"No. I don't exactly know him. He's a mulatto, I think."

Suddenly the room capsized and went black in splotches. Anne fell back on the pillow and tried unsuccessfully to hang on to consciousness. The next thing she knew, Renard was sitting on the side of the bed, holding a cup of something. The mosquito netting was draped over on itself, uncovering the details of the room. Renard had put the candle on the table by the bed, and she could see the color of his eyes. Dark, dark chocolate. "Here, *cher*. Drink this, and you'll feel much better."

Anne wanted desperately to feel better. Then

maybe she could think straight. Things were eluding her, things that would be eminently clear and logical when she was feeling more herself. She felt weak but sat up so she could drink. Something seemed to shift inside her head, and the pain throbbed harder than ever. Renard supported her neck. She held on to the cup, but his hand covered hers. The long fingers, the curve of the wrist looked familiar.

"Your hands . . ."

"Drink, Anne." She took a sip from the cup. It was tepid and tasted like black tea laced with something bitter, with a generous measure of sugar added to counteract the bitterness.

"Drink more." Renard tipped the cup higher. Anne complied, completely trusting him.

"Now lie back against the pillows and rest."

Again she obeyed, closing her eyes and easing down into the pillows. But when she felt the bed lift under her, she opened her eyes and caught Renard's wrist before he could stand up completely. "Stay with me."

"I can't."

"I won't rest unless you sit beside me. Please?"

He hesitated. "I have to move the candle."

"I don't care, as long as you come back."

He repositioned the candle, setting it on the mantelpiece where it had been before. He came back and stood over her for a minute, then sat down. His face was in shadow. She reached up and touched his mouth. Warm breath spilled over her fingers, sending a tremor down her spine. He removed her hand and put it on the bed, pressing it flat for a minute as if emphasizing his next words. "Don't touch me, Anne. I can't bear it. Touch me, and I'll have to leave."

Anne felt suddenly flushed. "I'm hot." She

tugged at the front of her jacket. "This is too confining." She fumbled with the buttons. Exasperated, she let her hand plop to the bed.

Renard's cool palm pressed against her forehead. "It's probably the effect of the medicine making you feel hot, though it's certainly a warm enough night to begin with." He began to undo the buttons, his fingers nimble and quick. The way they brushed against her skin was distracting. And very pleasant. She felt her nipples pucker against the soft muslin of her chemise.

With the jacket open, relatively cool air whispered across Anne's exposed neck and chest. She felt much better already, although she wasn't sure if it was the medicine or the loosened buttons or the man sitting next to her that was doing the magic. But then Renard withdrew, apparently intending to put the mosquito net between them again.

She stopped him by catching hold of his hand. "What are you going to do with me?"

"I'm going to take you home as soon as you're up to the ride. Rest now, and let the medicine work."

"You know all about me. You know where I live. You know who my aunt is. You know my name. You even know everything I feel about you . . . but I know nothing about you."

He sighed. "It is for the best, *cher.* I wish you understood. Now please rest, Anne."

"Only if you stay."

"I said I would."

"*Inside* the netting."

"Only if you lie still, and . . . don't touch me."

"Won't you please just hold my hand?"

Another hesitation. "Just." He took her hand. "Now be quiet and go to sleep."

As Anne held on to Renard's hand, she couldn't resist running her thumb along the fine bones and ridges. They felt beautiful, maybe as beautiful as Delacroix's. She wished she could see them.

Later, when she opened her eyes, she realized she must have slept for a while; the candle had burned down some. She felt marvelous. The medicine had obviously worked wonders. Her headache was gone.

The lone firefly hovered and hummed just outside the netting. Anne smiled. It had attached itself to them like a minuscule pet. She felt warm breath on her ear and turned her head, finding herself nose to nose with Renard. He was asleep, his head on the pillow, one leg bent on the bed, the other hanging to the floor. He still had hold of her hand, their fingers laced on the pillow between them.

It was the natural thing to do. She moved closer. And she kissed him.

Chapter 12

Lucien had succumbed to sleep only after promising himself that he would keep one foot on the floor. His reasoning was simple, if possibly self-deceptive. He told himself that if he didn't actually lie down beside Anne, he'd remain in control.

Keeping his boot sole pressed to the wood planks of the cabin floor represented Lucien's last holdout against temptation, but it was a damned uncomfortable position. He'd had to twist his torso at an unnatural angle to lay his head on the pillow beside Anne while at the same time keeping that blasted foot on the floor. He awoke to a distinctly unpleasant sensation in his lower back. *Pain*. And something else ...

Anne's lips shyly, tentatively touching his. He groaned and pulled her against his chest, burying his face in her fragrant neck. Her breasts were firm and round beneath him. He could feel the nipples—as hard as pebbles—even through the material of her borrowed jacket. Her arms convulsed around his back, pulling him closer.

Now there was no question about it; the foot-on-the-floor exercise had definitely been self-deceptive, and a dead failure. His control had slipped through his fingers like a length of cool, sleek silk—trembling fingers that reached reflexively for Anne's braided hair. He wanted the pins out. He wanted them out *now*, damn it. At this point, only the toe of his boot maintained contact with the floor, an apt metaphor for the amount of control he had left. Next to nothing.

"Shall I help you?"

Lucien's hands stilled. Anne's shy question recalled his derelict conscience. She was too innocent and too willing. She had no idea what she was getting into, and he had no right to touch her. His hands dropped to her shoulders. He waited for his breath to slow, his leaping pulse to settle into a more natural rhythm.

"Please don't stop," came Anne's sweet plea, so close he felt her breath caress his ear. "I want you to kiss me. Please kiss me, Renard, just as you did last night."

Lucien groaned and sat up, turning his back to her. The foot was firmly in place again, from heel to toe, flat on the floor. "God, Anne, don't tempt me."

The bed creaked as she pushed up on the pillows. Her palms rested on his back, warm and soft. "Why not? Don't you want to kiss me again?"

"Of course I want to, but I can't."

"Why not?"

"Because this is different. This time things could get . . . carried away." Her hands began moving, making little circles of pressure on the tight muscles of his back. It felt wonderful.

"What if I told you I wanted things to get carried away?"

"Then I'd say you're a fool." His tone was purposely derisive. "Why can't you realize how dangerous it is to be connected with me in any way? Especially like this."

He felt her hands lift away from his back. He was glad. At least one part of him was glad—his conscience. The rest of him felt bereft. He yearned for her as he'd never yearned for another woman. So many times he'd imagined her beautiful hair rippling over the pillow like a river of gold, her arms outstretched, welcoming him, beckoning him to settle into her warm softness. Tonight it could be that way.

Lucien's jaw tightened. Yes, maybe it could be that way, but with one big difference. He'd never imagined making love to Anne as Renard the out-law, and in the dark. He wouldn't be able to really see her, to worship her with his eyes as well as his hands.

Lucien rubbed his eyes with thumb and forefinger. There was no question that he couldn't allow her to see him. But how could he accept Anne's love dressed like some damned thief, mask and all? Maybe it was appropriate, though ... given the circumstances. Wouldn't he be stealing something that didn't belong to him, could never belong to him as long as he pursued his present life?

Without turning around, he asked her, "How do you feel, Anne?"

"I feel wonderful." Her tone was rich, seductive, very sure.

"Good. Then you're well enough to ride?" His own voice had none of her confidence. He seemed rooted to the spot; afraid to turn and look at her, but loath to stand up and begin the grueling process of separation. The long ride home with her fitted between his thighs, the heat of her, the intox-icating, womanly scent of her would be an exquis-ite torture. And, in the end, he'd still have to send her into the house and up to bed alone. Without him. Lucien's heart felt as though it had been squeezed dry.

There was a soft, tinny sound behind him. *Plink, plink.* Pins. Anne was loosening her hair.

Slowly Lucien turned. He had no choice. He had to see.

There was just enough light from the candle for Lucien to see far too much for his tenuous self-control. She'd lain back against the pillows, her hair fanning out on all sides, muted candle-glow gilding the multitude of waves. Stars of reflected light shone in her eyes, too. Her arms were raised, beckoning him, just as in his dreams.

"Anne, I can't . . ."

"You can." She lifted one hand and tugged playfully on his shirtfront. She smiled, her lower lip quivering slightly. She was adorable. She was half-woman, half-child. "You must, *cher.* I love you."

Lucien cursed himself even as he gave up the hard-fought battle against his own desire. He wanted her more than anything he'd ever wanted in his life. She was offering him heaven, and he couldn't refuse it.

Lucien bore Anne down into the cool, plump softness of the pillows. He caught and plundered her willing mouth. She kissed him back with trembling eagerness. Her slender frame arched against him, and her arms wrapped around his neck.

"Sweet Anne," he murmured, his lips trailing down her throat. "Sweet Anne, what have you done to me?"

She sighed softly, her hands sliding up the taut muscles of his back to the nape of his neck. "I've loved you. Will you love me back, Renard?"

Who could resist such a plea, such an invitation to paradise? But by giving in to what they both wanted, was he condemning her to a kind of hell?

He pushed up on the heels of his hands and looked down at her. The candle was sputtering, its last flicker of light about to extinguish. Anne's face was obscured by shadows. He could just see the pale shining of her eyes; the delicate, classic features of her face; the curve of her cheek. Her lips were parted, her quick, sweet breath stirring the air between them. With a shaky hand, he tenderly brushed away a tendril of hair that had caught against her lower lip. "I can't promise you anything, Anne. I don't know yet what will happen when I—"

She lifted her hand and laid her fingers lightly against his mouth. "I don't want promises, *cher*. I just want tonight."

He claimed her mouth again, possessive, passionate. He would give her exactly what she wanted, what they both wanted. Tonight he would love her with the fervor of weeks of denial. He'd make sure she would never forget and never regret the next few hours together. He would make her his for all eternity.

His hand reached up and covered her breast, his thumb and forefinger catching the tight nipple and rolling it gently through the muslin of her chemise. She gasped, and an answering thrill coursed through him.

Again he pulled back, straining to see her. But even as he did, the candle went out completely. Dark. Everything was dark, except for the frail glow of moonlight that sifted through the threadbare curtains at the windows. The dark was a curse and a blessing—a curse because he couldn't see her, but a blessing because she couldn't see him. Did he dare take off his mask?

"Renard?" Her hand reached up to touch his face, the delicate fingers trailing an inquisitive path down the tightly fitted mask. There was a soft intake of breath as her fingers came to the edge, where flesh touched flesh. The smooth nail of her forefinger lightly grazed the stubble along the sharp angle of his jaw, then rested on his lips. He could feel her pulse in the pads of her fingers. Her heart was tripping a light, frenzied beat, like the capering dance of his own heart.

He swallowed, tamping down his escalating need, trying to ignore the heaviness in his loins. He wanted to go slow with Anne, to pleasure her.

"I was just wondering how best to remove your trousers, *cher*." His voice was a raspy whisper, but with an edge of excitement, like a thirsty man approaching a cold, fresh-flowing stream. "It seems you've got them pinned to your chemise."

Her soft laugh floated in the air. "Yes. Sorry to inconvenience you, my love, but I was afraid they'd fall off."

He smiled, her fingers still resting lightly on his lips. She traced his smile, dipping with slow luxuriance into all the curves. Then she took one of his hands and lifted it to her own lips, where there was an answering smile.

"You have a beautiful mouth, Renard," said Anne. After a slight hesitation, she added, "I'd like to touch the rest of your face. Would you . . . take off your mask?"

Lucien stiffened. He wished nothing more than to take off his mask, along with the rest of his clothes. "I don't know, Anne."

"It's too dark to see you. If you really don't want me to know who you are—"

"I don't," he interjected quickly. "It would be too dangerous."

She sighed. "Are you afraid I might expose you?" She sounded hurt.

"No, of course not. It's for your own protection. It's best you don't know who I am."

There was another pause. "Do I know you?"

"No," he answered, telling himself it was the truth. She didn't really know him. She didn't know Lucien Delacroix. She only knew the Dandy, his cursed masquerade.

"I understand if you don't want to take off your mask, but—"

"But what, *cher?*" His hands slid slowly along her collarbone and over the cap of each shoulder.

"Will you ... will you take off the scarf you've got tied around your head? I want so much to feel your hair."

Lucien debated. The room was in almost total darkness. And hair was hair, wasn't it? Certainly his wouldn't feel much different than any other man's. She'd never recognize him by his hair. "Yes, *cher,* I'll take off my scarf if you'll do me an immense favor."

"What favor?"

"Will you help me undo those damned pins holding up your trousers?"

"I'll help you, with that and with anything you ask." He could hear the smile in her voice and pictured it on her wonderfully sensuous mouth.

Lucien propped himself on one locked arm, then reached around to untie the tight knot at the back of his head that held his scarf in place. He threw the scarf on the floor and ran his fingers through his slightly damp hair. It felt good to let his scalp breathe, though freeing his hair to do as it pleased—in this humidity and without the assistance of a comb—would make it an unruly tumble of curls. Dandy Delacroix always kept his crop neatly brushed, the springy waves tamed. Surely she'd not make a connection between the two of them.

Together they undid the pins holding the trousers to her chemise. The room was silent as they single-mindedly worked to remove another barrier to their mutual pleasure. Silence, except for the quick fan of their breath mingling in the air between them.

Mindful again of slowing down the delicious process of seduction, Lucien turned his concentration to the generous swell of her breasts before removing her trousers. He held one breast in his hand, then bent his head and, through the thin material of the chemise, took her nipple in his mouth. He twirled his tongue around the hard bud, pulling and pushing gently with the ridge of his teeth.

He heard the hiss of Anne's breath, felt the tug of her fingers in his hair. It hadn't taken her long to find a home there, among all those curls. She moaned with unmistakable pleasure, which increased his own enjoyment tenfold. She arched against him, her legs moving restlessly. Lucien responded by slipping a leg between her two, lifting his knee to nudge them apart. Then he eased himself atop her till they were connected intimately from head to toe, his erection against the rise of her mons.

"There are too many clothes between us, Anne."

"Y-yes. Too many."

"Are you ready, then?"

"To . . .?"

He chuckled. "To take them off, of course." He felt a little nervous, a little green. He assumed she was a virgin since she was well born and generally well protected. It had been a long time since he'd had to consider the complexities of making love to a virgin. It was humbling, too, if he was, as he hoped, the first man for her. He didn't want her to be frightened, or to feel rushed. He waited.

She reached up and started undoing the buttons on his shirt. The way her fingers brushed against his bare skin underneath made his breath catch. Soon his shirt was open, then she was tugging on it, pulling the tail out of his trousers. He smiled through the exquisite agony, glad she wasn't shy.

He shrugged out of his shirt and sent it flying through the air to find a resting place somewhere on the floor with the scarf. As he braced above her on the bed, her hands moved without hesitation to his chest. The feel of her palms pressing against his chest, moving slowly down to where the thin line of hair disappeared into the band of his trousers, nearly sent his control completely out the window. God, how would it feel to lie with her completely naked?

The thought inspired him to ease gently away from Anne's questing hands and off the bed. "I'll be back," he whispered, then he sat in a chair and struggled out of his boots. They were damned difficult to remove without a bootjack or a manservant to help, and he wasn't feeling particularly patient. Then, without ceremony, off came the trousers, too. He thought, rather sheepishly, that maybe it was a good thing Anne couldn't see how rigid he was. It might scare the living daylights out of her.

While Renard took off his clothes, Anne wasted no time. Her head felt fine—all of her felt fine—and she had no intention of lying about like a helpless female. She sat up in bed and pulled off her jacket, dropping it on the floor by the bed. Then she hooked her thumbs in the waistband of her trousers and pushed, scooting out of them, inch by inch. The trousers slid over the bedcovers and onto the floor at the foot of the bed.

She pulled off her stockings and tucked them under the pillows. Renard had apparently taken her boots off when she was unconscious. Dressed as she was only in her chemise, she felt the air hit her exposed skin like a dip in the cool sea. She debated whether to take the chemise off, decided that Renard might think her too forward, then lay back on the pillows and waited.

The mattress dipped under his weight as he sat down on the edge of the bed. His shadow loomed above her in the dark. She sensed his hesitation, his regret. "What is it, Renard?"

He sighed. "I wish we could do this with all the candles blazing. I want to look at you, Anne."

She thought of asking him to trust her. To light all the candles. To reveal himself to her, figuratively and literally. But she didn't. He wasn't ready. So she said instead, "It doesn't matter. We can see each other with our hands and our lips and . . . our hearts." She propped on one elbow and reached out to him with her free hand. And he came.

They sank down together into the pillows. The impact of bare flesh against bare flesh—legs tangled, hearts beating wildly—made Anne weak with desire. He was a patchwork of textures, rough here, smooth there—satin and sandpaper. He bent his head and kissed her deeply, their tongues twining and teasing, his hands in her hair.

At this most intimate moment, Anne again thought of Delacroix. A fleeting memory of his kisses intruded. She remembered the similar way they incited her passion, but she thrust the thought aside. Delacroix had no place in bed with her and Renard.

He rolled her to one side, putting enough distance between them to caress her. He smoothed his hand along the swell of her hip, down into the valley of her slender waist, then up where the narrow sleeve of her chemise rode the delicate cap of her shoulder. He hooked his thumb under the fragile material and tugged, gently slipping the chemise down her arm. He eased her onto her back and did the same to her other shoulder, moving the chemise down till the wide neck of the garment bared her breasts.

He bent and trailed his lips along her collarbone, lingering at the base of her throat, where her pulse fluttered like a frightened bird. But she wasn't frightened. She was mad with wanting him, with needing him to hold her closer and closer. The weight of his manhood pressed against her stomach, suffusing her womb with honeyed heat. There was a wetness between her legs, a tremor in the muscles of her thighs.

Then he moved lower still and took the tip of her breast in his mouth, the nipple tender and engorged. He suckled there, the titillating play of tongue and teeth making her stomach contract. He moved to the other breast and did the same. She buried her hands in his hair, her fingers clutching in the lush curls.

Her head fell back, her body wallowing in the pleasure of it all. She heard herself moan, and wondered at the power of this joining of man and woman. Images of the slaves at Congo Square, their writhing, rhythmic mating dance, floated through her consciousness. She could feel the beat of the drums in her blood.

Anne knew she was ready. She regretted nothing. Whoever Renard really was, she loved him. Though she had freely shared her own feelings, he had said nothing of love. He desired her, and for now that would have to be enough.

Suddenly he surprised her by rolling onto his back and pulling her atop him. She splayed her hands on his chest, half-reclining, his erection still pressed against her stomach, her legs straddling one of his powerful thighs. As he did—possibly more than he did—she wished for a room full of blazing candles. She could tell, just by touch, that he was beautiful.

He seemed to be waiting. His long fingers were curled around her upper arms, unmoving except for the slight up and down motion of his thumb along her sensitized skin. She caught her bottom lip between her teeth, suddenly anxious. Everything had seemed to be going along wonderfully. She'd loved every minute of it, so far. She knew they weren't finished. They couldn't be finished. Her nerves still sang like telegraph wires. Her body was heavy and aching. But perhaps, just at this point, she was expected to do something.

"Do you want to touch me, Anne?"

She wasn't sure what he meant. Hadn't she been touching him all along? Shyly she said, "I don't know what you mean."

"Without me . . . distracting you, would you like to . . . er . . . explore a little?"

"Oh." Now she understood. And she couldn't be more pleased. "Yes, I do. I do want to touch you."

She'd start with his stomach. Sitting up, she straddled his hips. His manhood slipped between her thighs, its long hard length pressing against her woman's core. Wryly she wondered how Renard could think she'd not be "distracted" by a little detail like that. Later, if she stoked up enough courage, she was going to explore that part of him as well. She felt her face warm at her randy thoughts.

His abdomen was hard and flat. He held his breath while she lingered over the perfectly segmented row of muscles that flowed from hips to ribs. And his chest was wonderful, every tendon and sinew gloriously defined beneath the light dusting of hair. By touch, his shoulders were even broader than they appeared to be, and fluid with strength. He was ideally suited for an artist's model. Oh, he *was* beautiful!

Now she reached up to touch his face, reconciled to being allowed access only to his mouth and the square angle of his jaw. Her fingers explored the contours of his lips, soft yet firm. For a moment she paused, overcome with a sense of familiarity, as if she were acquainted with the shape already. Not just from last night, but from another time.

Her hands stilled, her thoughts trying, by twists and convolutions, to organize into something cohesive. But how could she think straight when her muscles were strung like a tight wire, her heart was pounding like a trip-hammer, and the very core of her sexuality was wet and burning with need? He lifted his hips just then, his manhood rubbing against her. She closed her eyes and bit her lip.

"Oh, please, don't move," she whispered.

"Why not?" he asked, a teasing note in his husky voice.

"You know why. Because I'm not done exploring, and if you keep that up, I'll soon be reduced to a state of idiocy."

"You and me both," he confessed, chuckling. Anne liked that. She liked knowing that he wanted her as much as she wanted him. And he wasn't afraid to tell her so.

Her fingers had wended their way up the sides of his jaw, expecting any minute to feel the coarse cloth of his mask, but it wasn't there! *It wasn't there!* She gasped.

In a state of cautious delirium, she slowly moved her fingers over his cheekbones. High and sharp. Aristocratic.

Then the bridge of his nose. Straight, no bumps. And the tip was just right—not too long.

His forehead was high, expansive. She smiled. A gypsy would look at that noble brow and say he was intelligent and philanthropic, but she knew that already.

His brows were thick and arched. She could imagine them waggling wickedly.

Her fingers fluttered down to his eyes, carefully testing to make sure they were closed first, then skimming her thumbs over the lids. Deep-set, the lashes long and thick.

She sighed. "You're beautiful."

He gave his head a little shake. With a mix of embarrassment and amusement he said, "Men are usually called handsome, *cher*. You're the one who's beautiful." He let loose a ragged breath. "Are you finished exploring? Because I don't think I can refrain from distracting you much longer."

"Well, there's just one more part of you I'd like to explore."

"One more?"

She sat back, scooting down till she straddled his knees. Then she ran her hand up his thighs—the muscles hard and taut, just like the rest of him—found the coarse cluster of hair at the apex of his thighs, and wrapped her fingers around the proud jut of his sex. He was hot and tumid, marvelously male.

He groaned, and in one fluid movement had her flat on her back. "Anne," he rasped, "you minx! You're as curious as a monkey!"

"But a little more attractive, I hope. *N'est-ce pas?*"

He growled again and kissed her smiling mouth. And then all conversation was abandoned, every teasing remark, every light thought forgotten as they kissed and caressed each other with the reverence and intensity of first-time lovers. Anne felt a rising tension in her stomach, a tremulous languor in her legs. That most private, sensitive part of her suffused with heat and pleasure.

A piece of her wanted their lovemaking to go on and on, but she knew, logically, unavoidably, there had to be an ending to such bliss. She'd go mad if she remained in such a state of pleasurable delirium for too long. Even now her body cried out for release. She clutched him, her fingers digging into his shoulders.

"Are you ready, *cher?*" His voice was strained, as if he was barely in control.

"Yes," she whispered, going very still.

"It will hurt a little the first time."

She felt a small tremor of fear, but nodded her understanding, and tacit consent.

"Don't be afraid," he soothed, stroking her hair as he braced above her on an elbow. "I'll be gentle."

She nodded again, trusting him completely. He moved his free hand down between her thighs, kneading the tender skin beneath the crisp curls. To be touched in such a private place was so intimate, yet felt so right. Another wave of pleasure shuddered through her. Reflexively she arched against him.

"Patience, sweet Anne, patience," he crooned. His fingers touched the hot, moist core of her. It felt so wickedly good, she thought she might pass out. She was so tense, so slick with need. Then he slid one long finger into the narrow channel of her womanhood, probing, stretching, preparing for her consummation.

"Please, Renard," she begged him, hardly knowing what she was pleading for. "Please . . ."

But *he* knew. He settled himself between her legs again, elbows braced at either side of her shoulders. He shifted forward, then slowly entered her.

She was filled with him, the wonder of it suspending her somewhere between agony and ecstasy. The power of their joining overwhelmed her with emotions, until she didn't know whether to laugh or cry from joy.

Then came a quick thrust of his hips, and he was deep inside her, past her virgin's barrier. Anne gave a gasp of pain, and he held her and kissed her till it abated, till the pulsing demands of her body came to urgent life again, stronger than ever. She lifted her hips, taking him even deeper inside her.

She heard him groan. "Sweet Anne," he whispered hoarsely.

He began the rhythm, plunging, then pulling back. Again and again. Anne was in heaven, every part of her blissfully lost in the consuming act of love. It only got better and better. Too good to endure for long. Too sharp, too intense to last.

Her core exploded with sensation. Muscles convulsed, expanded. Her mind slipped. The world contracted. Waves of intense pleasure washed over her. Blood surged into all her extremities, her fingers and toes pulsing with tingling warmth.

"Renard!" she cried out, holding him to her.

She felt the muscles in his chest and arm pull taut as he cried out her name. Then one last powerful thrust, and, shuddering, he filled her with his seed.

Later, lying side by side, they clung to each other in the dark. Outside, the crickets sang their courting calls to the heavens, the moon rode the sky, and daybreak came inexorably closer. Anne knew that if she slept, she'd wake up alone. The room would be filled with light, and Renard would be gone.

But still she smiled. Everything was changed. She belonged to him, now and forever. Contented, she watched the lilting dance of the firefly, hovering jealously outside the net. Then she closed her eyes and slept.

Chapter 13

When Anne awoke, the room was filled with the hazy semilight of approaching dawn. She wasn't alone, as she'd expected to be, but it wasn't Renard who hovered over her. And it wasn't Renard's hand brushing against her temple. It was a black man's. It was ... Armande. She'd been right about him. He was the same man she'd seen last night while she waited outside Mrs. Cavanaugh's Boardinghouse, and the same man she'd nearly run into at the cemetery on All Saints' Day.

He wasn't looking at her when she first opened her eyes; he was fussing with the thin linen strip that held the gauzelike square of cotton against her wound. He was being very gentle. She watched him with overt curiosity. He was something to look at, all right, despite his worn and baggy clothing. The dun-colored shirt and trousers were a far cry from the natty outfit he'd been wearing on Camp Street, but the humble clothing didn't take away from his attractiveness. This morning he looked like an extremely handsome but down-on-his-luck farm worker.

Then it hit Anne like a ton of bricks. *He* was the farmer from last night, the one who had driven the wagon! Armande was Renard's trusted cohort, a well-rounded fellow who could drive rickety wagons full of slaves and tobacco hell-bent-for-leather down the muddy Louisiana roads, and still mix up a potent tea that cured a headache within minutes of drinking it!

His gaze shifted, and he looked straight into her eyes. He showed no surprise. "You're awake."

A delayed sense of modesty made her look down to check that she was covered. She was, from neck to toe. And underneath the light quilt, she felt the soft lawn of her chemise. She hoped it was Renard who had put it on her. She swallowed her embarrassment. "Yes."

He nodded, a small, serious smile nudging his lips upward. "How do you feel?"

"I feel wonderful, thanks to Renard." She'd meant no double meaning, but she blushed anyway. Trying to cover her confusion, she rushed on. "And thanks to you. It was your mix of herbs that got rid of my headache last night. How did you learn such witchery?"

Armande's finely arched brows lifted, and his smile quirked up on one side. "You think it's witchery, do you? I'm a physician, Mademoiselle Weston, taught by the finest medical men in Paris."

Anne winced and made an apologetic smile. "I'm sorry. I didn't mean to imply that you were a witch doctor."

His smile broadened, his hazel eyes brimming with humor. "I'm not offended."

"It's just that our family doctor back in England never uses herbs." She shivered. "But he does use leeches."

"Ah, yes, modern science at its finest," Armande murmured dryly. "And people think voodoo is primitive."

Anne laughed.

"*Oui.* You are right, mademoiselle, my methods and my medicines aren't always the most traditional. But I've studied science and folk remedies and mixed the two to my own satisfaction. I'm not so narrow-minded that I can't give credit where credit's due, taking the best from both worlds."

Anne thought he must have applied that philosophy to other parts of his life, too. He'd obviously successfully mixed in both the black and the white worlds. Although there shouldn't be major differences between them, at least in matters of opportunities and justice, there obviously were. He, like Renard, was trying to correct the injustices.

He was looking at her, serious again. She wondered if he guessed her thoughts. "Did your antiseptic paste do the trick?" she asked him.

His gaze shifted. He picked up a small damp towel from the table and wiped his hands. His fingers were long and graceful, the nails clipped short and clean. He had perfect hands for a surgeon. "There is no infection. Your wound should heal quickly and leave no scar."

Anne nodded, only half-attending. Looking at his hands had brought to mind thoughts of another pair of graceful hands, memories she'd been working hard to keep at bay. Renard holding her, loving her ... But it was impossible. The memories flooded back. Every inch of her body felt imprinted with his touch. Her heart yearned for him.

Her eyes roamed the room. The cabin was even smaller than she had imagined last night by flickering candle-glow, but it was clean and neat. On the pantry shelf, she saw the candle that had burned to the quick last night, leaving her and Renard in the dark. She'd never be afraid of the dark again . . . She wondered where the firefly had gone. With Renard?

"Why don't you ask?"

Anne gave a little jerk. She lifted startled eyes to Armande. She'd been a thousand miles away, yet still in the same room. "Ask what?"

"You're wondering where he is, aren't you?"

Anne's eyelashes fluttered down. She stared at her hands, her fingers tightly twined together in a prayerlike pose. "Not really. I expected him to be gone. He wouldn't let me see him in the daylight." But she wished that he had said something about seeing her again. Last night had been very special to her. She hoped that it had been special for him, too—at least something more than a single night's passion.

"I met him here this morning," Armande continued, not contradicting her statement about Renard shying away from being seen. "He asked me to take you home as soon as you were awake. He's concerned that your aunt and uncle will have called out the city patrol by the time I get you back, but he was just as worried that a ride home might exhaust you and bring on some return of your symptoms."

Anne looked up. "Did . . . did he leave me a message?"

Armande's expression remained carefully neutral. "No, mademoiselle. There was no message."

Anne swallowed her disappointment. "How is it that I'm allowed to see you, but not him?"

"He has his reasons, mademoiselle."

"Reasons that he won't share with me," she mumbled irritably. Anne was tired of being kept in the dark for her own "safety." Was Renard really just protecting her, or was he also using his masquerade as a way of keeping emotional distance between them? Anne hated herself for doubting him, but she'd been loved and abandoned. What sensible woman wouldn't have doubts?

Feeling more testy by the moment, she said, "Aren't you afraid I'll describe you to the police?"

Armande looked back at her, his nicely shaped mouth curved in a wry smile. "Not in the least, mademoiselle. Renard would have nothing to do with a tattle-tongue that couldn't be trusted." He spread his hands in an expansive gesture. "My life is in your hands."

Anne was slightly mollified by Armande's inference that Renard at least trusted her, but she wanted a lot more than that from a man she'd just given herself to, body and soul. "That's all very well, but if I can be trusted with *your* life, why won't Renard trust me with—"

"That is not the issue, mademoiselle. Renard is worried about your safety, not about his."

"Yes, of course, my *safety*," muttered Anne.

Armande shook his head at her, then dropped the towel and whisked his hands together as if finished with the subject as well as the task of washing up. Brisk, businesslike, he said, "Now tell me, when do you generally get out of bed in the morning, mademoiselle?"

"About eight."

"And your aunt and uncle?"

"Breakfast is served at ten. I don't usually see them till then."

Armande leaned against the wall opposite Anne's bed, his arms crossed, the fingers of one hand pulling thoughtfully on his chin. "It is barely six o'clock. I hope we can get you inside the house and up to your room without either of them knowing you were gone."

"The servants will be up by now, and we're still

quite a ways from the Faubourg St. Mary, aren't we?" She reached up and touched her bandage. "And what about this?"

"Tell them you slipped and fell against the edge of your dressing table."

"And I bandaged myself?"

He grinned. "You're a resourceful woman. They'll believe you."

Anne frowned. "Not Uncle Reggie. Lately he doesn't trust me very much."

Armande raised his brows in an expression of mock disbelief. "He doesn't trust you? Goodness, I can't imagine why. How many times have you sneaked out of the house recently?"

"Don't vex me, Armande," Anne warned him with a reluctant smile. "I'm a little tetchy this morning."

"You're just hungry. I'm sure you ordinarily have a sunny disposition. I've got some bread and cheese for you, and a cup of wine. It's nothing fancy, but you could probably use a little food on your stomach after last night's excitement. You must be very tired."

Again Anne found a double meaning in seemingly innocent words. Indeed, last night had been very exciting in many ways. She wondered how much Armande knew about last night. She dismissed the embarrassing thought and took refuge in pragmatism. "How much time do I have to eat?"

"About five minutes." He moved to the pantry, prepared a plate of food for Anne, poured the wine from a rustic-looking crock, then set it on the table beside her. "Eat, then get dressed. Your clothes are there on the chair." He waved a hand toward the other side of Anne's bed, in a dim corner of the room.

"Thank you," she said, sitting up against the pillows to eat, pushing her tangled hair out of her eyes. "Where is your brother?"

Armande looked startled for a minute, then said, "Christian? He's at home ... I hope."

"Did Christian help last night with the escape?" When Armande made a face, as if he didn't want to answer, she said, "Yes, I know. I'm as curious as a monkey, so Renard tells me. You don't have to answer if you don't want to."

Armande shrugged. "I have a hard time talking about my brother. Yes, he helped with the escape, but not directly. He's actually only minimally involved in what we do, but it's our hope that by being part of something this important, he'll ... straighten out."

"A bit wild, is he?" said Anne with smiling sympathy. "Must be his age."

"I hope that's all it is," said Armande. He stood awkwardly for a minute, then moved toward the door. "I have to saddle the horse. I'll leave you to eat and to dress." He hesitated, his hand on the latch. "Will you be all right? You don't need assistance, do you?"

Anne blushed. "Thank you, but no. I shall manage very well by myself."

Armande grinned, looking genuinely relieved. "Thank goodness. I don't know how I would have explained to Renard that I was required to help you dress, or convince him that I did it with my eyes closed."

Anne blushed even more deeply, if that were possible. "Then ... then he does care about me?"

Armande's smile faded. Seriously he answered, "I can't speak for Renard, mademoiselle." He turned the latch. "But he has shown much concern for you. You must trust him to do what's best for both of you."

After Armande left, Anne stared at the door. She mentally groused over the taciturn nature of Renard's right-hand man. He could tell her so much, but he obviously had no intention of doing so. She must trust Renard to do what was best. What did that mean? Why did Renard and his friend have to be so cryptic, so vague? If she was ever going to know anything about Renard's true identity, or his real feelings about her, she was obviously going to have to wait till he was ready to speak for himself. And that might never happen.

As things stood, Anne had no idea when or if she'd ever see Renard again. What if she was just another conquest in a string of conquests? It was a painful, sobering thought, and she ate her food and drank her wine glumly, not really tasting it but well aware that she needed the energy it gave her to get through the morning.

She dressed, then braided her hair and tucked it under the hat again. She'd ride back to town on the back of Armande's horse, keeping her hat brim pulled low over her forehead. No one would recognize her. Certainly no one among her set of acquaintances would even be out of bed yet.

When they reached her aunt's house, she'd hurry through the kitchen and past the servants, hoping none of them would comment to her aunt or uncle about her strange clothing and the odd hour she was coming in the back door. There was little chance she would get away without having to offer some explanation, though, and she'd been mentally constructing another lie. She hated lying, but Reggie would have a hard time handling the truth of her latest escapade.

Finally they were on their way. The swampy

country they traveled through didn't look even remotely familiar to Anne, and by the time they emerged from the lush foliage and onto River Road, if not for the flow of the river to use as a compass, she'd not have known which way was north and which was south. Thankfully they weren't required to travel through the heart of town to reach the Faubourg St. Mary, and they completed the journey without being troubled by anyone.

Word of the escape probably wasn't out yet, though Jeffrey had likely worked all night writing an exclusive for the *Picayune*. Anne wondered how Jeffrey would relate the story and how she would figure into it. She saw the printed column in her mind's eye: "*An unknown male youth alerted the Fox to suspicious shadows in the cemetery ...*" She amused herself for several moments speculating on all the possible ways the story could be written up, and wondered if Jeffrey would recount it as accurately as she could.

An alley connected Katherine's backyard with the yard of her closest neighbor to the north. Armande used this approach to the house and let Anne down just outside the far gate, keeping his horse and himself well-hidden from view behind a full-leaved hickory tree. He kept astride the horse, handing down a small container. "Take this paste and apply it to your clean wound every night and every morning."

"Thank you, Armande."

He shrugged. "For what?"

"For being my friend today. For trying to reassure me"—she grinned ruefully—"even though you told me nothing."

Armande doffed his floppy-brimmed farmer's hat, sweeping it in grand and gallant fashion. He smiled warmly. *"Au revoir*, mademoiselle, till we meet again."

Anne lifted a hand in farewell, her heart touched yet saddened by his parting words. *Till we meet again.* Renard had not said those words to her last night, and he hadn't even left a single word of farewell, of love, or even of friendship with Armande to pass on to her. Anne's spirits flagged.

She watched him ride away, then turned reluctantly to the gate that led into Aunt Katherine's well-kept, inviting backyard. She'd spent many happy, reclusive hours there. Today she was entering it a changed person. She'd never be happy again until she was reunited with her love. She hoped that didn't mean she was condemned to a lifetime of unhappiness.

But while she was left in doubt about his feelings for her, she had no doubts about her feelings for him. She loved him, and she'd spend every waking hour worrying about him. The appearance of those bounty hunters last night suggested that Renard's operation was hardly impenetrable. Someone was leaking information. *Who was the snitch?* she wondered.

Suddenly extremely exhausted, Anne wended her slow way up the red brick walkway to the back entrance of her aunt's house. Glancing up at the windows she knew belonged to Uncle Reggie's bedchamber, she thanked Providence that he wasn't an early riser.

Reggie hadn't slept a wink all night. He'd risen early, far earlier than his usual hour, dressed, and wandered outside to sit on a marble bench under one of Katherine's banana trees. He was bedeviled by the most ludicrous thoughts, romantic thoughts, the sort of thoughts he'd never expected to take root in a head as hardened as his was to such fanciful notions. And worse still, Katherine Grimms—the cane-swinging, liberated female with a voice like fingernails on a schoolchild's slate board, and with the bearing of a navy admiral commandeering a fleet of battleships—was the center of all these tender feelings.

In spite of himself, Reggie smiled. Last night, when she had swooned, he'd had the English starch scared out of him. He realized that he would be devastated if something happened to Katherine, and his nurtured dislike for her had disappeared like morning mist in the path of the climbing sun. He admitted it; he liked Katherine Grimms very much. Very much indeed. Now, what was he going to do about it?

Reggie brooded. He looked for answers in the Eden-like paradise of Katherine's yard. It was not yet seven o'clock in the morning and mid-November, but the air was warm and sweet with the scent of a hundred flowers and fruit trees. The chirps and whistles of birds echoed in the tall trees that were scattered harum-scarum over the three or four acres that made up the Grimms estate. Now he better understood why Anne liked sitting out here on Sundays.

Anne? Had he conjured her up? No, because if he had, she'd not be dressed like a man, nor would she have a bandage tied around her head and a stricken look on her face at the sight of him. She had just walked around the edge of a profusion of bushes, apparently from the back of the yard. He sat in a copse of sorts, surrounded by trees and vegetation, not easily seen from any direction. Finding him there well before his usual hour of rising had obviously given his niece a shock.

"Uncle Reggie?"

He braced himself. What mischief had she gotten herself into this time? "The very same, Anne. Whom did you expect?"

"N-no one," she stuttered. "But least of all you."

"Come closer, Anne," he said softly. "How have you hurt yourself, child? It can't be a mortal wound," he added grimly. "I see you're still walking."

He expected her to take him to task for calling her "child," but she didn't. And, indeed, she was no child. Watching her cross the few feet that separated them, he was struck anew with how womanly she really was, despite her masculine apparel. He was trying not to overreact to her odd appearance and behavior, or assume the worst possible explanation for her wandering in the yard at seven o'clock in the morning. But the closer she got, the more clearly he could see that she was extremely upset about something. His protective instincts reared up.

He scooted along the bench, making room for her to sit beside him. As she sat down, he took her hand in his. "Good God, Anne, what's happened to you?"

Anne lifted her downcast eyes and looked earnestly at him. He speculated that she might be deciding how much to tell him. Her eyes were very clear and blue. Again he was arrested with the notion that she'd suddenly grown into a woman, seemingly overnight. She sighed heavily. "I was thinking of lying, but I've decided to tell the truth. I did something very foolish last night. I went to see Renard."

Reggie could not immediately respond. He knew she was smitten with the outlaw, but he'd taken it for granted that she had far too much common sense to actually seek out Renard's dangerous company. He cleared his throat, but his voice still had a telltale rasp in it when he said with deceptive calm, "I must have misunderstood you. You can't have gone alone to that outlaw's lair."

"I didn't go to his lair," she asserted, lifting her chin a fraction. "I'm not a complete dolt." She got an odd look about her then, which Reggie was terribly afraid meant that though she'd not set out to go to his lair at the beginning, she'd certainly ended up there. "Jeffrey had been given a tip about Renard's next escape plan. I got enough information out of him to establish the approximate time the escape would take place. I stationed myself outside Jeffrey's boardinghouse and waited till he came out, then secretly followed him to the rendezvous point."

"What happened at the rendezvous point? Did Renard show up?"

"Yes." She ducked her head, her eyes fixed on her hands, the long, slim fingers splayed over her knees. "Do you think you would be willing to wait for further explanations, Uncle Reggie? You can read all about it in the *Picayune*. Jeffrey saw it all. There will be plenty of details." She made a trembling smile. "Just insert my name in the part played by the 'young man.' "

"How can you ask me to wait, Anne? You've been injured, and I don't even know how and by whom! Who bandaged you? Did anyone—" He blushed with embarrassment and bottled fury. "Did anyone take advantage of you?" He thought he'd burst a blood vessel when Anne blushed a most revealing, gloriously female shade of rose. "If that outlaw laid a finger on you—!"

Anne's head reared up. Tears shone in her eyes.

Her voice was thick with emotion as she said, "Renard didn't hurt me, Uncle Reggie. He saved my life." She touched the bandage. "There was gunplay. This wound was caused by a bullet that grazed my forehead. Renard protected me. If not for him, I might be dead." By now Anne was shaking. "Don't ever, *ever* think Renard hurt me, Uncle Reggie," she ended on a fierce note. "He'd never do that. Never."

Reggie was too stunned to think at all, much less speculate on Renard's motives concerning his niece. Every detail of the story faded into insignificance when compared to the fact that his own sweet Anne had nearly been killed.

He stared at her for a startled, horrified moment, at her wide blue eyes shadowed with a new maturity, at her slim shoulders shaking with a delayed reaction to the horrors and hard-learned lessons of the night before. Then he pulled her against his chest, tucked her head under his chin, and stroked her hair with a gentle hand.

"There, there, my girl," he soothed. "I shan't ask you another thing . . . for now. And I won't blame anyone for anything till I know more about the situation. Just calm down and lean against your old uncle till you feel better."

He felt her relax against him. She clung to him like the child she used to be, till eventually her convulsive shivering stopped and a soft sigh escaped her lips.

"I'm so tired, Uncle Reggie," she said. "I think I want to go inside and go to bed now."

"Yes, my girl," he answered firmly. "To bed you'll go, and that's where you'll stay till I say otherwise."

Anne managed a weak laugh. She squeezed his neck affectionately. "I'll let you bully me now, but soon I'll have recovered my old vim and vigor and be wanting my way again."

Reggie heaved a beleaguered sigh. "Yes, Anne, I know. I expected no less." Then he stood up and escorted his troublesome niece into the house.

carried his trousers ... into the house.

Chapter 14

Lucien stepped out of his carriage and onto the banquette in front of Katherine Grimms's stately mansion. He held in one hand a potpourri bouquet of flowers, the multicolored blossoms and leafy stems so tall and profuse they tickled his chin. He was dressed in a dark green jacket and black trousers. His brocade vest was the palest of yellows, closely imitating in color the fresh rose attached to his lapel, the bud still damp with morning dew. He was correctly and elegantly attired for a morning call, but this was no ordinary visit.

"Take the horses around the block, George, *s'il vous plaît*," Lucien advised the driver with a flick of his wrist. "I shan't be long." George nodded and drove off.

Lucien surveyed the front of the house, his eye straying to Anne's bedchamber window. The shutters were closed against the heat and brightness of the late morning sun. He imagined her lying on the bed, resting, he hoped, and being tenderly cared for by her aunt and uncle. His heart ached at the bittersweet memory of last night. He could never regret the magic hours they'd spent together making love, but he'd had no right to take her virginity when he could give no promises in return.

How could he have lost control to the point of

involving Anne in his life when he had no guarantee of a favorable outcome for his own destiny? And what was he doing now, standing in the hated guise of Dandy Delacroix in front of Anne's home?

As each day passed, Lucien's contempt for the part he must play in society had grown by leaps and bounds. Being considered only as a pleasure-seeking wastrel with no ambition beyond his own comfort and gratification was wearing thin. It had proven to be an effective screen against any connection to Renard, but he was looking forward to a time when deception would no longer be necessary.

But what then? Even if things ended the way he planned for Renard, he still wasn't sure what his next step should be, or where his ambitions would ultimately lead him. He wasn't even sure who he was anymore. Without the mask, without the facade of lazy debauchery, who the hell was he? He should have considered all these complexities before allowing Anne to give herself to him so completely. He thought grimly that perhaps he wasn't so different from Dandy Delacroix, after all. Anne deserved better.

But he couldn't brood in front of her house all day. He should do what he had come to do and leave. Ostensibly he'd come to inquire about her state of mind and physical well-being after her harrowing experience in the alley. After he'd received Reggie's grateful note early yesterday evening, it would not be considered odd or inappropriate for him to pay such a visit. But, of course, that was not the real reason he'd come.

It hardly seemed possible, now, that the alley incident had occurred just yesterday. So much had

happened since then. So much had changed both
for himself and for Anne.

Sweet Anne ... It had been torture leaving her
that morning. He'd longed to watch the sun rise
and fill the room with light—to see her in the af-
terglow of their lovemaking. But he had not come
to her aunt's house hoping to see her. That would
be foolish. On the contrary, Lucien felt very confi-
dent that Reginald Weston was keeping his niece
in her bedchamber and denying her visitors—
possibly for punitive reasons, and assuredly because she was not yet fit to be seen with that gash
on her forehead.

Lucien's sole purpose in this visit was to find
out for himself how she had fared after Armande
left her at the back gate early that morning. He
had a method in mind to secure this information,
and it did not involve talking to Anne, or even her
uncle.

Setting his hat at a rakish angle over his right
brow, Lucien slowly made his way to Anne's front
door. He was admitted into the vestibule by a
doubtful-looking butler and kept waiting in the eclectic parlor some fifteen minutes. Normally he
would have been intrigued by Katherine's collec-
tion of artifacts, but as the minutes dragged by he
became worried.

Certainly if Anne hadn't been able to sneak into
her room that morning and attribute the graze on
her temple to a tumble against her dressing table,
there would be a bit of a commotion in the house.
Reggie would demand the truth, and Anne would
be hard-pressed not to tell it. He knew her, and
she was too damned honest for her own good.

What if she was sick? Lucien felt a surge of
dread and doubt. Parts of last night had been grueling, traumatic. Not their lovemaking, surely, but

how could he have possibly thought that making love to her could make things *better*? He was about to stand up and pace the floor when Reggie walked quickly into the room.

"Mr. Delacroix! How nice to see you! Sorry to keep you waiting so dreadfully long, but I was ... er ... unavoidably detained."

Lucien stood up and offered the older man Dandy Delacroix's usual lazy handclasp. Handshaking was an American custom, and Reggie seemed to view it suspiciously still, but he shook hands nonetheless. Lucien noticed that Reggie's palm was clammy, his overall manner harried and distracted. However, he seemed to be trying very hard to be pleasant and hospitable, probably because he was genuinely grateful to Lucien for saving Anne from the threatening advances of that drunk yesterday.

"I don't wish to inconvenience you, Monsieur Weston," he began, "but your note was so kindly written ... perhaps it was too kind. I really did little to deserve your gratitude."

Reggie motioned for Lucien to be seated, then sat down himself in an opposite chair. "It could not possibly have been too kind a note, Mr. Delacroix," Reggie assured him. "You rendered Anne an invaluable service for which I shall always be indebted to you."

"I only did what any man would do," Lucien disclaimed modestly. "You must know how little I enjoy discussing my dubious merits—"

Reggie sat up straighter, making a stiff nod, a manly acknowledgment. "Indeed, sir, I understand completely. No gentleman likes his praises sung too loudly or too long. Never fear, the subject is closed. I feel the same about such matters myself. Understand completely—only doing your duty."

Lucien smiled his approval. "I simply came to see how Mademoiselle Weston fares today. She's not too overcome by yesterday's ordeal?"

Reggie frowned and looked at the floor, tapping his chin with a thoughtful forefinger. Suddenly he looked up at Lucien. "I hope you won't take this question amiss, Mr. Delacroix, but I *must* ask it. You *are* keeping everything that happened in that alley in the strictest confidence? You know how people talk, even when the party is completely innocent of wrongdoing ..." His voice trailed off. He appeared distressed, as if he knew he'd been insulting but couldn't help himself.

Truly, thought Lucien, this man cares deeply for Anne and considers her welfare and reputation above everything else. If only *he'd* been as honorable and considerate last night! "Mum's the word, Monsieur Weston," he assured him. Then, earnestly, "I'd never do anything to hurt Mademoiselle Weston—if I could possibly help it."

The two men's eyes locked for a moment. There was a puzzled curiosity in Reggie's light blue eyes that seemed to grow clearer instant by instant—like the dawning of understanding. Lucien looked away, panicked. Could Reggie tell? Could Reggie see in his eyes how he felt about Anne? Perhaps he'd been *too* earnest. Perhaps he'd been too—

"Are the flowers for her, then?"

Lucien turned his gaze back to Reggie. There was a reserved pucker about the older man's mouth, a shuttered look around the eyes. But the expression as a whole was not unkind. Lucien gathered his scattered composure. Here was Renard, for Christ's sake, the so-called daring outlaw, falling to pieces in a perfectly safe drawing room in the company of a perfectly civilized gentleman!

His concern for Anne, his consuming desire for her, could be a potent weapon in the hands of an enemy.

"*Oui*, the flowers are for Mademoiselle. I thought they might brighten her room"—he made a vague gesture with his free hand—"brighten her day, perhaps. Delicate females depend on such pretty things to amuse them, *n'est-ce-pas?* To coddle and wheedle them through life's difficulties."

Reggie nodded. Their eyes met again in complete understanding. They both knew Anne was no ordinary "delicate" female who expected to be amused and coddled out of difficulties, but neither said so. Reggie stood up and pulled the bell rope to summon a servant. "I'll have them put in a vase and sent to her room. She'll be delighted, I'm sure. So kind of you . . ."

He sat down again, his gaze fixed on his flower-burdened guest with a new intensity. Under such keen scrutiny, Lucien was tempted to squirm. "You do understand that I'm not allowing her visitors just yet?"

"Perfectly." A chambermaid came in and, after receiving Reggie's instructions, took the flowers and left the room. "But I had hoped to see Madame Grimms today. Is she in?"

This request seemed to surprise Reggie as much as, or maybe more than, anything else Lucien had said so far. It was obvious Reggie was curious about Lucien's possible business with Katherine—suspicious, even—and very protective of his womenfolk.

Ah . . . A light went on somewhere in the dim, overtaxed recesses of Lucien's brain. He had supposed for some time that Reggie and Katherine did not get along. Perhaps it had just been a rather prickly mating dance. There was no denying now that he detected protectiveness in Reggie's manner toward Katherine. And protectiveness came of love . . .

"Mrs. Grimms is sitting with Anne," Reggie said hesitantly. "But if you'd like me to fetch her, I would be happy to take her place at Anne's bedside."

Lucien frowned. "I thought you said Mademoiselle Weston was doing well?"

"We're not exactly nursing her," Reggie assured him wryly. "While she's relatively quiet, we're using the opportunity to take her to task, to set down new rules, you see."

"I see." Lucien heaved an inward sigh of relief. Anne could use some hard-nosed chaperoning for a while. Then he wouldn't have to worry about the little baggage so much. In the next few days he'd be busy enough keeping himself alive, much less Anne.

"I'll go and get her."

His thoughts full of Anne, Lucien frowned again. "Get Anne?"

Damn! He'd slipped up and used her Christian name, and irrationally supposed Reggie was bringing Anne downstairs when Reggie had already told him that she wasn't receiving visitors. Neither mistake was lost on Reggie. "Of course not Mademoiselle Weston," he quickly corrected himself, smiling gamely, brilliantly. "You said she was not receiving visitors, and rightly so. A slip of the tongue, n'est-ce pas? Silly me . . . of course you meant Madame Grimms."

Reggie returned the smile with meticulous politeness and bowed himself out, saying, "Of course. As you say . . . a slip of the tongue. Sit down, Mr. Delacroix. I'll have Theresa bring in a tea tray."

"*Merci*. But that's not necessary—"

"Katherine likes tea this time of day. No trouble at all."

Lucien watched Reggie back out the door, cursing himself for being such an ass. He walked distractedly to the window, pushed aside the heavy drape, and looked out, seeing nothing, feeling nothing but his own ineptitude. How was it that he could keep his wits about him when dealing with the dangers of a criminal's life, yet hadn't been able to hold on to them at all in this situation, simply because Anne was just a few rooms away?

God . . . just a few rooms away. Upstairs, in that bedchamber, in that bed . . . Dark, warm, vivid images of last night flashed through his mind. The feel of her was like nothing he'd ever imagined.

"Lucien?"

Lucien pivoted around at the familiar use of his name, at the welcome voice of his friend. Katherine stood just inside the door. He relaxed, his usual facade not needed now. "Is it safe to talk?"

She reached behind her and closed the door. "It is now."

Lucien made a doubtful face. "Reggie has instructed Theresa to bring tea."

"We'll have sufficient warning. The door squeaks. I won't allow Theresa to oil it."

Lucien grinned. "You frequently hold clandestine conversations in this room?"

Katherine shrugged, dismissing his teasing with a serious look. "Never before with you. Why are you here, Lucien? It must be very serious for you to take this chance. It couldn't wait till next Saturday, when you could send word through Madame Tussad?"

Lucien sighed and sat heavily in the chair

Reggie had recently vacated. "I had a good excuse to come. Reggie sent me a note, thanking me for saving Anne from the certainty of being . . . er . . . compromised."

Katherine sat down in the opposite chair. "You mean raped, don't you?"

Lucien winced. "Probably. The foolish girl. She's just like you, Katherine. Too intrepid for her own good."

Katherine raised her brows. "Is that why you like her so well?"

Lucien tried to avoid a direct answer. "I've always admired courage and resourcefulness in a woman."

"Don't hedge. I asked you if you liked her."

"Of course I like her, but—"

"But perhaps not as well as she likes you?"

"I don't know how much she likes me."

"Then you're a fool, Lucien. She likes you well enough to sleep with you. And knowing my niece, that means she's in love."

Lucien liked Katherine's straightforwardness, but just now it embarrassed him and definitely inconvenienced him. He didn't want to be taken to task over something he knew he was guilty of. He had no defense.

"Did Anne tell you everything?"

"Everything. Except, of course, that you'd bedded her. I figured that out for myself. And now you've confirmed it with that guilty look. Where was Armande all that time?"

"Escorting the slaves out of town. He returned to the cabin at daybreak."

"Anne gave the impression that Armande was there the whole time. The assumption, the hope that Anne was never alone with Renard is the only thing keeping Reginald from falling to pieces."

"How much does he know?"

"Only the broad details. He won't press Anne, but he's a highly intelligent man and very intuitive. He's figuring things out as he goes, I'll wager. Anne actually confided in him first, you know. He was sitting in the garden this morning when she dragged in dressed like a man and looking a bit worse for wear."

"Does Reggie know anything about your connections to Renard?"

"No." Her stern mouth relaxed, curving ruefully. "Neither he nor Anne is privy to my involvement in your nefarious crimes, Lucien." She got a sudden inquisitive look on her face just then, and Lucien feared the next question—as well he might. "How did you make love to my niece without her knowing who you really are?"

"You put me to the blush, Katherine," he evaded, but still he felt the blood pulse close to the surface of his skin.

"You aren't going to tell me?"

"Suffice it to say she doesn't yet know that the hero she ... admires is really the wastrel she loathes."

"Anne is just as intelligent as her uncle. She'll figure out who you are soon enough."

He nodded. "Probably much sooner than I would like. That's why she mustn't see me for a while. Even in the dark, people note similarities."

Her brows lifted. "Indeed."

"I need time. I'm hatching a plot that—God willing—will stop Bodine's abuse permanently. I can't deal with Anne and Bodine at the same time."

"This plot against Bodine is something you've wanted to do for a long time. I'm sure you're putting yourself in considerable jeopardy to accomplish this, Lucien. Why now? Why the sudden need to hurry up the business?"

"I'm ending my career as Renard, Katherine."

"I'm glad!" she said emphatically. "It's time. Can I attribute this disinclination to flirt with death to my niece's influence?"

Again he evaded. "As you know, there's a leak, Katherine. I have an unsettling feeling that I'm about run out of luck."

"Yes, so do I." She brooded a moment, biting the outside edge of her lip, contemplating the floor. "You did get my note, then, warning you that Wycliff was bragging to Anne about knowing your rendezvous point?"

Lucien reached over and squeezed Katherine's hand. "Yes."

"Thank God," Katherine murmured wryly. "I had the devil of a time last night finding a private moment to scribble that hasty message. I was afraid the young groom I sent wouldn't get it to you in time."

"He did. And forewarned, we were very careful . . . at first. But when we'd managed to get the three men inside the wagon without the least sign of trouble, and Armande was actually at the ready to flick the horse's ear and take off, we began to relax. A foolish and precipitous act. The bounty hunters crept up from behind us, through the cemetery."

"How were you alerted?"

Lucien blinked. "Anne didn't tell you?"

"Anne's explanation about last night was short and sketchy. She said we'd read about it in the *Picayune*."

"Wycliff got his story, then. It should report that a certain anonymous 'young man' saved my life by risking his own. As you must know, Anne was that young man."

Katherine was silenced. While the ormolu clock on the marble mantel ticked away the seconds, Lucien watched her absorb the shock. Anne nearly killed. Anne in love with an outlaw. Anne no longer a virgin.

"Are you ready to draw and quarter me?"

"More than ready." She sighed heavily. "I didn't take Anne away from her family in England so she could throw away her future, Lucien. You are a good man, but a man of strong passions. It appears you've allowed those passions to rule you where my niece is concerned. She deserves everything that's best in life, and if you don't think you can give her the best, then . . ." She didn't finish the sentence; she didn't need to. "I don't want her hurt, Lucien."

"Neither do I," he replied soberly.

Katherine reached across the distance between them and took Lucien's hand. She squeezed hard. "I know you will do what's best."

Lucien was grateful for Katherine's show of confidence, even while she was obviously angry with him for compromising her niece's future happiness. He was determined to "do what was best" for Anne, but no matter how carefully he made his plans, there was always a chance that something could go wrong . . . dreadfully wrong. Till he could be more sure of the outcome, he still couldn't make promises to Anne, or to her aunt.

Lucien had another concern, too, that he didn't dare voice aloud to Katherine, and tried not to dwell on himself. Anne still didn't know that he and her hero, Renard, were one and the same. What if she had nurtured such a hatred for

Delacroix, the wastrel and cad, that she couldn't
accept who Lucien really was?

Katherine interrupted his brooding thoughts.
"As Renard, what are your immediate plans? Am
I involved?"

He stood up. "I'll let you know, Katherine. I
dare not stay longer. Reggie's already suspicious
of my wanting to speak to you." He cocked an inquiring brow. "You don't suppose he's jealous?"

Katherine stood up, too, busily smoothing non-
existent wrinkles out of her blue bombazine skirt.
"It's too early to suppose anything," she mumbled. When she looked up, her face was delight-
fully flushed. "You'll keep me abreast of
developments, Lucien?"

"Certainly," he replied, distracted from his own
troubles by his enjoyment of the girlish bloom that
had spread over her handsome features. "And
you'll keep me abreast of ... developments, too,
won't you?"

"Out of here, you rapscallion," she said with a
haughty sniff, her lips fighting a smile. "I shan't
put up with your nincompoopery!"

Lucien playfully threw up his hands in defeat,
then bent to kiss Katherine's cheek. Just then the
unoiled hinges of the parlor door announced
Theresa's arrival with the tea tray. Lucien immediately put a proper distance between himself and
his hostess, transforming himself in the wink of an
eye into the persona of Dandy Delacroix. His lips
smirked, and his eyelids drooped lazily.

"*Certainement*, Madame Grimms," he drawled.
"I understand completely. If you say your literary
club is not interested in hearing Monsieur LaPriell
expound on the social benefits of slavery—" He
spread his hands in a helpless gesture. "Well, then
I suppose I must believe you. But I thought you

might be a little more open-minded about allowing a dissenting voice among your ranks. How
else can you make educated choices?"

Recognizing her cue, Katherine opened her
mouth to deliver a sharply worded set-down
when another voice intruded. "Some choices are
self-evident, Delacroix. At least to an honorable
man"—Jeffrey Wycliff inclined his head to
Katherine—"or woman."

Lucien turned to see Jeffrey sauntering in behind Theresa and the tea tray. Another maid was
carrying a vase holding the flowers he'd brought
for Anne. Lucien wondered why she was bringing
them to the parlor, when Reggie had expressly instructed her to take them to Anne's bedchamber.

Jeffrey was dressed in his customary conservative gray suit and hat, but there was something
different about him today. He looked more smug
than usual. A very definite self-satisfaction shone
from his clean-shaven face. Lucien's eyes dropped
to the rolled-up copy of the *Picayune* Jeffrey had
tucked under his arm. He'd apparently brought
the newspaper fresh off the printing press so he
could impress Anne with his story about Renard.

"Monsieur Wycliff, *bonjour*," he said, ignoring
Jeffrey's baited implication that he wasn't an honorable man. Katherine thought he was honorable,
and her opinion counted much more than Jeffrey's
did. He bowed politely, but was nearly overcome
with an irrational urge to bloody the cocky brag-
gart's nose. "Your timing is exquisite. I was just
leaving, and now you may keep Madame Grimms
company at the tea table."

Jeffrey nodded cordially to Katherine. "Mrs.
Grimms will understand that I don't have time to
stop for refreshment this afternoon. Actually I've
come specifically to see Anne." His gaze lifted

abruptly to Lucien's face, as if trying to catch a re-action to the familiar use of Anne's name. Lucien kept his expression as vacuous as possible, while inwardly his vague dislike for Jeffrey Wycliff took on substance.

"You will be disappointed, I'm afraid," Lucien couldn't help saying. "Mademoiselle Weston is in-disposed today and not receiving visitors."

"Oh, she'll see *me*," Jeffrey asserted.

"Jeffrey, I'm afraid Reginald won't allow it," Katherine interjected.

Jeffrey smiled charmingly as he walked across the room. "I beg to differ, Mrs. Grimms. Wild horses couldn't keep Anne away from me today." He pulled the paper out from under his arm and waved it like a taunting schoolboy. "I have a first-hand account here of Renard's latest derring-do. Nearly freed his last slave this morning. There was a very close, very exciting encounter between Ren-ard and a band of bounty hunters."

Lucien frowned. A band of bounty hunters? Did three men constitute a band?

"Goodness!" exclaimed Katherine, feigning sur-prise. "Yes, I'm quite sure Anne will want to read the article, Jeffrey, but I'll have to take it up to her room. She had a rather nasty fall last night against her dressing table, and the wound has left her a bit woozy." She moved forward, holding out her hand.

Jeffrey backed away, tucking the paper under his arm again. Lucien noticed that Jeffrey didn't react at all to the news of Anne's fall; he seemed too full of himself at the moment to have much concern for the woman he'd been determinedly wooing for the past several weeks. "Oh, no, I can't let you do that. I absolutely have to watch the ex-pressions flit across that beautiful face of hers as she reads this." He waggled a finger at her. "You can't take that pleasure away from me, Katherine."

Katherine laughed, but the sound was forced. She was obviously losing patience. "But, as I told you, Reginald won't allow—"

"She was standing at the window, looking out, as I came up the drive. I showed her the paper, and even from a distance I could see her eyes light up like fireworks on the Fourth of July. 'I'll be down, Jeffrey,' she called. 'Wait for me.'"

Jeffrey shrugged and smiled an insincere apology. "Can you blame me for doing exactly as she asked, Katherine? I imagine that Anne has been for the past five minutes cajoling and arguing with her uncle. If you were a wagering woman, whom would you bet on to win the argument?"

Fully acquainted with Anne's strength of will, Lucien had no doubt Anne would win. Judging by the warning glance she darted his way, Katherine suspected the same outcome. He had to get out of there before Anne showed up. That was why the flowers had been brought into the parlor; the dratted girl had never intended to stay in her bedchamber.

"It's unfortunate that I can't stay to see Mademoiselle Weston," said Lucien, easing his way to the door. Suddenly he turned, flashing a brilliant smile. "I hope she likes the flowers." He glanced at the huge bouquet that the maid had placed on top of the grand piano.

Jeffrey followed the direction of Lucien's gaze and frowned. Jealousy was written all over him. It gratified Lucien that he was able to take the edge off Jeffrey's huge ego. "But how fortunate for you, Monsieur Wycliff," he continued, "to have such influence with Mademoiselle Weston that she disregards physical discomfort and defies her uncle just to see you." He stopped and wrinkled his brow. "But I'm rather puzzled . . . does she go to all this trouble because of her regard for you, or because of her fascination with the Fox?"

Lucien stayed only long enough to see the effect of his words on Jeffrey's smug countenance. Jeffrey did not disappoint; he turned a shade brighter than the pink roses in Anne's bouquet.

Satisfied, Lucien bid Katherine a pleasant *adieu* and left. As the butler closed the door behind him, Lucien thought he heard the soft tap of Anne's slippers on the stairs. He sighed and forced himself to keep walking to his waiting carriage.

Chapter 15

As Anne read the article Jeffrey had written, she felt the blood slowly drain from her face. She was glad she held the newspaper directly in front of her, positioned in such a way that it hid her ashen complexion from the view of her aunt and uncle, and especially from Jeffrey.

She couldn't believe it. She couldn't believe he had stooped so low. But then Reggie had always mistrusted Jeffrey. He had always thought the brash American was too ambitious. Apparently her uncle was right.

Enough time had lapsed for Anne to have read the article twice over. She sensed Jeffrey's fidgeting. He was eager to hear her response. He was waiting for her praise and adulation—for feminine worshipful sighs, no doubt. And since she could not reveal that she had firsthand proof that his account of the story was pure fiction, she must certainly give him all he expected.

She rallied herself for the playacting. It would be difficult, to say the least, but she would make short work of it, plead fatigue and a headache, then send Jeffrey on his way.

She lowered the newspaper and discovered two expectant faces looking at her—Jeffrey's and Aunt Katherine's. Reggie was sitting at a distance, pre-

243

tending indifference. He was miffed with Anne because she had insisted on seeing Jeffrey even though he had been unable to persuade her to sit for a polite ten minutes with Delacroix. He thought Delacroix deserved to be told again that she was grateful for his intervention in the alley. But Anne could not bear to see him, a man she'd so recently kissed and felt passion for, when last night she'd given herself heart and soul to Renard.

Just the thought of Delacroix confused her. Despite her love for Renard, she still remembered Delacroix's kisses with something akin to wistfulness. She didn't know how to justify such feelings. The only explanation that made sense to her was that she was fickle and wicked. It put her out of temper to be faced with the possibility of owning such character flaws, and she dealt with it by avoiding the source of these unpleasant emotions—Delacroix himself.

Avoiding Jeffrey was not necessary. She had no confused feelings about the man or his kisses. And she was curious to read his article about Renard and the slave escape. Perhaps there would be exciting details she'd missed in all the confusion. Perhaps there would be news about the condition of the bounty hunters. And—truth to tell—she could not resist reading about herself, and had wondered how Jeffrey would describe her part in the escape.

Anne couldn't have been more surprised when she found herself entirely omitted from the article, as if she'd never been there last night, as if the young man she'd masqueraded as simply didn't exist! Instead Jeffrey had written a highly creative version of the story, casting himself in an aggrandized role of foolhardy hero. All this, when he'd obviously stayed safely hidden behind the rose arbor the whole time!

According to the bold black script of the *Picayune*, Jeffrey Wycliff, humble newspaper reporter, had risked life and limb to warn Renard about the bounty hunters. He had run into the street without a weapon, frantically waving his arms, to alert Renard. While dodging bullets, he'd managed to waylay one of the three bounty hunters before the fellow took to the road in pursuit of Renard. He'd wrestled him to the ground and taken away his weapon before the fellow dashed off into the shadows of the cemetery.

If memory served her, Anne had counted three bounty hunters in pursuit when she and Renard left the area. So even that part of Jeffrey's story was fabricated. He couldn't have waylaid one of the bounty hunters unless there had been four altogether. And there weren't. The wrestling match was just another figment of his writer's imagination, a clever ruse to gain a little hero worship for himself.

Anne forced a brilliant smile. "So, Jeffrey, last night was even more exciting than you'd hoped."

Jeffrey was leaning forward in his chair, his elbows propped on his knees, his square-tipped fingers steepled. His smile broadened. "I should say it was!" He waited, expecting more.

She had no choice. Reluctantly she said, "What a hero you are! Why, without your intervention, Renard might have been killed last night. You must be very proud."

Jeffrey sat back in the chair and crossed his legs, right ankle over left knee. Anne might have imagined it, but she could have sworn his chest puffed out a good two inches. "It was nothing more than any honorable man would do under the circum-

stances. I couldn't let them catch Renard un-
awares, leaving the poor fellow without a fighting
chance. And, naturally, I support Renard's cause
and couldn't allow money-grubbing bounty hunters to kill him for something so ignoble as a paltry
reward."

"The reward's not so paltry, I hear," said Anne,
her jaw beginning to ache from holding a false
smile for so long. "And if they don't believe in the
abolition of slavery, and consider Renard a menace
to Southern society, why shouldn't the bounty
hunters try to catch him?"

"Indeed, Jeffrey," Katherine piped up from her
seat next to Anne on the sofa, "men do all sorts of
things to further themselves in the world. Dishon-
orable things, dishonest things."

Anne flashed a surprised look at her aunt. It almost sounded as though Katherine knew Jeffrey
had lied about last night. But there was no way
her aunt could know, because Anne hadn't told either her or Reggie about her part in warning Renard. They only knew that she had been wounded
while she and Renard rode away from the bounty
hunters. The only way Katherine could possibly be
privy to the truth was if Renard himself had told
her. And that was impossible.

"Well, thank God, I don't have to depend on
such low means to earn a living," said Jeffrey,
sighing happily. "Though it wouldn't surprise me
if this little coup earns me a considerable hike in
salary and more column space in the paper." He
leaned forward again, his eager face offending
Anne's sensibilities, tempting her to slap it
soundly. "Someday I'll own the paper, Anne, lock,
stock, and printing press. Mark my words." Then,
in a lowered voice, "I'll have all the gals in New

Orleans chasing after me then. Won't you be jealous?"

Anne squeezed her hands together, willing them to stay put in her lap. She managed an arch smile. "I should think all the 'gals' will be after you as soon as they've read today's newspaper. You're a hero, aren't you, Jeffrey? A hero like Renard." She supposed that was what he'd always wanted.

He laughed, a sort of manic exhilaration evident in his posture, his expression. "Can you believe it?" he pressed her, obviously wanting even more flattery. "Can you believe that I was *really there*, and that I was actually lucky enough to be part of Renard's success last night? It's something the two of us have wished for and talked about so many times, Anne!"

"Indeed, Jeffrey, it *is* rather incredible," said Reggie, rising from his chair and sauntering over. Anne couldn't tell by his expression what Reggie was thinking. He had his English reserve tightly buttoned up, like a protective emotional overcoat. "One wonders why you don't abandon the drudgery of a nine-to-five job at the newspaper and pen novels."

Confusion passed briefly over Jeffrey's face, but he recovered quickly. "But novels are fiction, Mr. Weston. I prefer the drama of real life."

"And you certainly do have a dramatic flair, Mr. Wycliff," said Reggie, stretching his lips into an unconvincing smile. "However, I'm afraid your eloquent prose has wearied my niece. I think you'd better go now."

Anne took her cue. "Yes, I am rather tired, and my head hurts a little."

Belatedly Jeffrey made a show of sympathy. "What was it your aunt told me you did? Fell against the wardrobe or some such thing?"

Anne laughed weakly, touching the small bandage partially hidden behind the forward sweep of her hair. "Yes, clumsy me. I fell against my dressing table."

Jeffrey stood up, compelled to depart, with Reggie so obviously eager to get rid of him. He bent and took hold of Anne's hand, squeezing it affectionately. Even to Anne, her fingers felt icy, incapable of absorbing warmth from Jeffrey's. He seemed startled by their coldness, their stiff nonpliability. He laughed nervously. "It must be true what they say—all that rot about household accidents being the most common. Imagine it, while I didn't get the smallest scratch hobnobbing with criminals, you injured yourself sitting snugly at home. *Can* you imagine it, Anne?"

"Well, *my* imagination is quite stretched to the limit," said Katherine pleasantly, but with a thread of steel in her voice. She lent her considerable influence to hasten Jeffrey's departure by standing up as well.

With both of Anne's tall guardians hovering near, Jeffrey wisely moved toward the door. "Well, good-bye, then," he said to Anne. "I hope that little scratch won't keep you away from the theater. And the Taylors' ball is on Friday. Will I see you there?"

"I don't know, Jeffrey," Anne said doubtfully, lifting her hand in a brief farewell. She really wasn't sure how she felt about going out in public in the near future, but there was one thing she *was* quite sure of. She couldn't tolerate another tête-à-tête with Jeffrey. He had ruined her trust in him. Their friendship was over.

"So good of you to come, Jeffrey," said Katherine, herding him into the vestibule. Soon after that Anne heard the door close, and her aunt came back into the parlor. While Jeffrey was being shown out, Reggie had continued to stand over Anne. She felt his concerned gaze like a tangible thing. Katherine moved to stand beside Reggie. Anne looked up at her two loving relatives, worry etching lines in their kind faces.

"You knew he was lying, didn't you? So you took pity on me and threw him out by his coattails."

"It was my pleasure," said Reggie dryly. "I've been longing to throw him out from the first." He paused, then very gently added, "It's quite natural for you to feel disillusioned, you know."

"Please don't fret about me," she said softly. "I'll get over it." Though she was holding back tears, Anne grinned ruefully. "Thank you, Uncle Reggie, for not saying, 'I told you so.' "

"My dear girl, did you really think I would?"

Anne ducked her head, the tears too close now for concealment. Reggie's pristine-white, neatly folded handkerchief suddenly appeared in her lap. Through her blurry vision, she saw it, picked it up, and dabbed away the tears.

"I'm such a watering pot," she complained, blowing her nose.

"It was you who warned Renard, wasn't it, Anne?" asked Katherine.

"It was, but that's not why I'm so upset. I'm upset because—"

"Because Jeffrey lied to impress you, to impress the people at the paper, and to make himself out a hero—like Renard. His ambition has cost him his integrity," said Reggie.

"It cost him your friendship, too, I'll wager," said her aunt sadly. "I was fooled, too. I thought him a much better sort of chap."

"I wish now," said Anne, lifting her misty eyes

to look at her uncle, "that I'd come down to see Delacroix as you wanted me to."

"Why, love?"

"Because he's certainly more of a hero than Jeffrey. Despite his wastrel ways, he's proven to be much more honorable, hasn't he?"

There seemed to be no need to respond to the obvious truth of this statement, and, after a pause, Reggie said, "Do you agree with me, Anne, that you ought to stay at home for the next few days, refusing visitors? We can tell people you've got a head cold or some such thing. You need the time to recuperate from all this tomfoolery, and that way we can also avoid having to tell the dressing table fib to half of New Orleans. I must say, it will get rather tiresome explaining your injury. In a week, you can cover the wound with some cosmetics and arrange your hair to hide it, as Sarah attempted today."

His eyes widened, as if he'd hit on a wonderful idea. "In fact, why don't all three of us hibernate for a while? We can be a cozy family of three. I know I could use a little respite from society." He looked—rather shyly, Anne thought—to Katherine for her reaction.

Katherine was pink with pleasure. Her eyes sparkled. Apparently the idea of holing up with Reggie for a week didn't strike the chord of terror it might have done just a month or so before. "I should be delighted to hibernate for a while," Katherine admitted. Reggie beamed. "But I must make one exception," she said. "I never miss my visit with Madame Tussad. I must go and see her this Saturday, just as I always do. Agreed?"

"Agreed," said Reggie, trying not to grin too broadly. He turned to Anne, as if just remembering that she had a vote to cast as well. "Anne?"

"Agreed," she said, smiling.

She needed time, too, she realized. Time to rethink all her prior conceptions and biases about people, about appearances. Time to untangle the mixed images of scoundrels and heroes, emerald rings and black masks. Time to relive last night, every whispered endearment, every caress as Renard made love to her in the dark.

Time to figure out what that night of bliss with Renard really meant in her life, or if it would ultimately mean nothing at all. She had no guarantees she would ever see him again, much less be held in his arms. Such uncertainty was difficult to bear, especially since the thing she wanted most in the world was Renard's arms around her once more.

Lucien was drawn to Katherine's house like a magnet. She had sent word through Madame Tussad that she and Reggie were going to keep Anne at home for a few days, but Lucien yearned to see Anne again—even if only from a distance.

Until he confirmed his suspicions about the leak in his organization, and until his plans for Bodine's downfall were firmly in place, he had intended to stay away from Anne for safety's sake—both hers and his. But he couldn't resist walking by the house late at night, sometimes waiting in the shadows across the street and hoping she'd appear at her bedroom window. And she did . . . twice. Both times for far too short a time to satisfy his overwhelming desire to see her.

He thought she looked wistful those nights as she leaned out and took deep breaths of the cool night air. He wondered, and hoped, that she was thinking of him. Or at least thinking of Renard . . . Did she hope he would climb the tree again and visit her bedchamber, make love to her right under the nose of her abigail sleeping in the next room? He was tempted. Oh, how he was tempted.

One day, feeling frustrated, he walked past the house in the morning. He didn't expect to see her; he was only indulging a particularly intense urge to be near her. He was shocked when, just as he was about to cross the street and hurry away, she walked around the corner of the house carrying a basket of fresh-cut flowers.

They both stood completely still, their gazes locked across the long expanse of lawn that separated them. He wasn't sure what would have happened if Katherine hadn't rounded the same corner an instant later and taken Anne's arm, leading her back toward the porch. Anne resisted, seeming to be explaining to Katherine that someone they knew was on the street and ought to be noticed.

Katherine turned and waved, cheerfully and dismissively, without slowing her ruthless march to the front door. "Can't stop to chat, Delacroix," she called. "Delightful morning, isn't it? Goodbye!"

Lucien understood her determination to keep him and Anne apart, approved it, and fervently hated the necessity of it.

He bowed low, throwing Anne a kiss in a dashing, devil-may-care gesture worthy of Dandy Delacroix's most roguish technique. She continued to stare at him, turning her head to watch him even as her aunt pulled her inexorably away. He smiled, tipped his hat, and sauntered away, hoping he looked breezy and carefree when inside his heart pounded like a trip-hammer.

Anne hibernated with her aunt and uncle for a week and a half. Many notes of regret were sent out each day as invitations were declined. Jeffrey came by every evening, and every evening he was sent away frustrated.

Anne enjoyed her seclusion but missed Renard dreadfully. She pined for him especially at night, when memories of their lovemaking drifted in on cool night breezes, caressing her skin as his hands had caressed her. One night, as she stood at the window, she felt as though he were outside watching her. She peered wistfully into the shadows, sending him a mute invitation with her eyes, then calling herself a fool when he never came. It was her imagination, she decided. Mere wishful thinking wouldn't bring Renard back to her. Nothing would bring Renard back if he didn't love her.

Anne read the newspapers eagerly, hoping for at least some word of him from that source, but he was keeping out of the news these days. Rumors were rife, and Anne suspected they were spawned and spread by Jeffrey. *He* was in his element, the toast of town since the story broke about his encounter with Renard. There was no proof to link him with the outlaw except for this one chance meeting, and he couldn't be arrested for aiding and abetting an outlaw because the bounty hunters were not affiliated with the authorities.

Anne supposed it irked Jeffrey considerably to be denied the opportunity of talking over his popularity with her, but she hoped he'd find other, more willing female ears to listen to his boasts.

Anne saw Delacroix once as he was walking past the house. Aunt Katherine hurried her inside before they had a chance to exchange a single word, which Anne thought was rather odd. But Katherine made some excuse about avoiding everyone till they formally made their reentrance into the whirl of social activities.

But what was really odd about the brief encounter with Delacroix was Anne's reaction. When she noticed him on the sidewalk in front of the house, she was stunned by how glad she was to see him. Her heart seemed to leap into her throat. He looked his usual self, very dapper in a russet jacket and black trousers, the rings on his fingers winking in the late morning sun, but he looked different, too. She felt no repugnance, not even when he threw her a kiss. She'd wanted to catch it and hold it to her heart.

By now Anne was sure she was as fickle a woman as ever walked the earth. How could she love Renard, yet still be so attracted to another man? Especially when that other man was a scoundrel.

As for Reggie and Katherine, Anne had never seen them happier. They whiled away their time playing cards, strolling in the yard, snipping dead heads off the rose bushes, reading poetry and travelogues, and generally getting along like two doves in a cote.

Now their occasional arguments were more the tolerant give-and-take of differing opinions, rather than the childish bickering of before. In fact, these disagreements gave spark and spice to their harmonious existence. They had learned to understand and respect each other. They were in love. She wondered how soon they'd acknowledge that fact to each other.

One day as Anne sat with them in the parlor, taking afternoon tea, Reggie sighed deeply and set down his cup with a clatter.

"What is it, Reginald?" asked Katherine.

"We have to go back out there, you know," he replied glumly, casting his eyes wistfully about the room, his fond gaze resting finally on Katherine's face. "All this peace and comfort has to end. Just thinking about it gives me a headache."

Katherine echoed his sigh. "Yes, I suppose you're right. Madame Tussad tells me it's rumored we have yellow fever in the house. A few cases have been reported in the city recently."

"Good God!" said Reggie, appalled.

"So, before a few alarmists have us laid out in the parlor with our toes turned up, we'd better show our faces somewhere."

"Well, I'm ready," said Anne determinedly. "I've had plenty of time to pull myself together, and my wound is hardly noticeable."

"Then it's settled," said Katherine. "Shall we go to the opera tonight?"

"Might as well," said Reggie. "I can't think of a better place to get such immediate and widespread exposure. Sitting in our box, all smiles and blooming health, ought to convince the populace we aren't laid up with yellow fever."

"I thought the fever came only in the summer, Aunt Katherine."

"Generally it does. But we've had a very mild autumn. It could be a particularly hearty strain that's been around for a while."

"Well, I hope it stays far away from here," said Reggie fervently, looking nervously at Anne. "I shouldn't like to see you abed with such a malady, Anne." His anxious gaze shifted to Katherine. "Or you."

There was a wealth of feeling in those two simply spoken words. Flustered, Katherine hastily replied, "I haven't had the fever once since moving to New Orleans. They say newcomers and the fairskinned are the most susceptible, but I guess I'm too stubborn to succumb to it. Either that or my hide's too thick for the disease-ridden mosquitoes to puncture it."

"Thank God for that," said Reggie solemnly, lifting his cup for another sip of tea, then pausing just before his lips touched the rim. "What will you wear, Katherine?"

Startled, laughing, Katherine inquired, "Where to, Reginald? My wake?"

"No. To the opera tonight. Perhaps your purple silk?"

Katherine blushed prettily. "Do you think it suits me?"

"Yes."

Her lashes fluttered down, her thumb caressing the smooth china handle of her teacup in a distracted gesture. "Then of course I'll wear it."

Anne smiled to herself. She might have been a fly on the wall for all the notice her two guardians could spare her. Their eyes and thoughts were for each other. It made her feel wonderful watching people coming together in love. Wonderful and a little wistful. Would she have a happy ending, too?

Hat in hand, Lucien stood in the little parlor of his house on Rampart Street. He was dressed for the evening, decked out in his favorite black jacket and trousers, pristine white shirt with a few elegant ruffles, and a muted gray vest. Micaela stood opposite him, her arms crossed, smiling.

He felt tense. His business with Micaela was awkward.

Micaela sensed Lucien's discomfort and broached the subject first. "You've come to say good-bye." Her smile remained, relaxed and genuine.

He smiled back, relieved, sheepish. "Yes." He paused. "You do understand, Micaela?"

"Completely, *cher*. I have been expecting this for some time."

"Have you?"

"There is another woman."

Lucien shifted nervously. "My life has become very complicated lately, Micaela. I can't afford to have anything, or anyone, distracting me."

Micaela laughed softly, stepped forward, and smoothed her hand along the sleek silk of his lapel. "But I so enjoyed distracting you the many months we were together. You were a wonderful lover. I hope you have not spoiled me for—"

"For your young, brawny smithy? I'm sure I haven't. When two people love each other, experience is the least important aspect of lovemaking. Passion surpasses expertise, and expertise comes with time."

"Your woman . . . she is lucky, Lucien."

Lucien frowned, unnerved by the way Micaela kept referring to another woman in his life. How could Micaela be so sure of him, when he wasn't even sure of himself? His business with Renard was far from over, and there were times when he wondered if he was ending the masquerade too soon. Had he done enough for the cause? More to the point, had he purged himself of the hate that had engulfed him since that summer twenty years ago when he'd been forced to beat his best friend with a whip?

"I will pray for you."

Micaela's words brought him back to the present. He smiled. "Do. I'm not sure how much influence I have with the saints these days." He reached inside his jacket pocket and handed Micaela a small scroll of paper tied with a string. It was the deed to the house. Inside the paper was a wad of bank notes, enough money to open a substantial account for her and her new husband.

Completely unembarrassed, Micaela took the scroll and tucked it inside a pocket of her gown. She knew what it was, and, without glancing at the roll of money, she knew Lucien had been generous.

"We've had a good relationship, Micaela—a real friendship. There were times in the past year when I'd have gone completely crazy without you."

Micaela smiled archly. "It was my pleasure, Lucien."

He laughed, pinched her cheek, then gave her a brief, light kiss on the forehead. "God bless you, Micaela, with many children and many happy years with that young man of yours."

"The same good wishes for you, *cher*, wherever you go, whatever you do."

Lucien recognized the undercurrent of concern in Micaela's parting words. She understood so much, but he'd never once suspected her of leaking her suspicions about him to the wrong people. She was a remarkable woman in many ways. But she wasn't Anne. No one was like Anne.

Micaela walked him to the door. He turned at the bottom of the walkway that connected with the banquette and waved. Her slim silhouette was outlined by the glow of candlelight behind her. He couldn't see her face. She waved back, then closed the door.

Lucien stepped into his carriage, and the driver immediately set the horses to a lively trot. He was meeting Bodine at the opera, the two of them to sit together in Bodine's box like best friends. Tonight he was planting the seed for the blackguard's downfall. And for Renard's final coup.

Even though he hated the day-to-day need for

deception, Lucien sometimes wondered if he'd miss the excitement of setting up Renard's little capers. When the masquerade was over, would he be bored by the tranquil tenor of normal life? Did his duty lie in the occupations of a normal life? He had much soul-searching to do.

Lucien reflected briefly on his parting from Micaela. She was a pragmatist, and she'd made the severing of their amicable arrangement easy for him, and for herself. No regrets, just mutual good wishes for each other.

Then his reflections returned to the subject of most of his waking thoughts: Anne. A surge of excitement went through him. Would she be at the opera tonight?

Chapter 16

Anne was already itching to go home. The opera was by Rossini, and the singers were wonderful, but Jeffrey had joined them in the box as soon as the curtain fell on the first act. Worse still, it appeared that he planned to stay for the whole performance, happily oblivious to Katherine's unusual reserve and the patent lack of an invitation to join them. But they had been on such familiar terms before, it would have taken a more sensitive man than Jeffrey to catch on to the fact that he was suddenly *de trop*.

Anne pitied him. He'd compromised his integrity, but she thought she partially understood why it had happened, why his ambitions had begun to rule him. He'd had to struggle for everything he had, for everything he was. Of course, that didn't excuse him for finding his principles expendable. But people made mistakes, and Anne hoped Jeffrey would learn to handle himself more honorably in the future.

For the present, however, she was having difficulty tolerating his preening enjoyment of the instant fame his *Picayune* article had gained him. Most of the opera glasses in the theater were trained on their box. This could partly be due to the appearance of Anne, Katherine, and Reggie after more than a week's absence from the social scene, but it seemed more likely that they were staring at Jeffrey. He was heady with happiness, his handsome, boyish face flushed with success. And he was oppressively attentive to Anne. She didn't know how to repel him without being downright rude.

Her vexation with the situation was making her hot. She pulled out her fan, a large feathered creation that matched the deep burgundy flounce of lace on her off-the-shoulder bodice. The gown itself was ivory alpaca, tightly cinched in at the pointed waist and trimmed with tucks.

Anne energetically plied the fan through the stifling air. Sarah had arranged Anne's hair in a becoming coiffure that helped cover her scar, although the faint red mark didn't amount to much, anyway. Armande's salve had worked wonders in quick healing. But Anne didn't want to think of Armande, because it made her think of Renard, which filled her with longing and frustration. Deaf to Jeffrey's pandering patter, she cast her eyes restlessly over the hundreds of faces that filled the opera house.

There had been an empty box just across the theater and up one tier. Now, suddenly, it was occupied. Anne's gaze riveted on the two figures who had entered the box during intermission. They were Delacroix and Bodine, settling themselves in their chairs.

Delacroix looked very handsome, as usual. As on the other morning when she'd chanced upon him passing the house, she felt strangely drawn to him. She had long ago admitted to herself that she was attracted to Delacroix, but tonight the familiar tingling along her nerve endings caused by the sight of him was magnified tenfold. She concentrated on him, looking for a logical reason for such an abrupt and illogical increase of awareness.

He hadn't even raised his head yet; he was still busy with small adjustments to his seating—pulling out opera glasses, turning his chair slightly toward the stage. His hair was thick and wavy and brilliant black in the candlelight. His lashes shadowed his high cheekbones, the sharp angles of his face stirringly masculine.

Then, suddenly, he looked directly at their box. Her heart fluttered as their eyes met. Their gazes locked for a moment, then he looked away, whispered something to Bodine, and left the box.

Anne was in a frenzy of anticipation. Her mouth went dry, her hands trembled. She mentally calculated the minutes it would take Delacroix to walk around the building to where she sat, because surely he was coming to see her.

She was glad. She had been wanting for some time to thank him properly for his intervention in that alley incident, and this would be the perfect opportunity. She wouldn't exactly have to say the words, but a contrite look and a warm handclasp ought to convey her apology for behaving like a brat that day. She told herself that was the only reason she was so eager to see Delacroix's tall, elegant figure enter her aunt's opera box, but she knew she was kidding herself. There was something else making her heart dance a merry jig. Something else that would perhaps be clearer once she saw him up close . . .

He entered the box. He was detained by a couple of Katherine's friends who were just leaving. They were elderly women, but Anne could see how effective his charm was even on women who were supposed to be past youthful follies.

Anne stared at him. His shoulders . . . She'd forgotten how wide they were, how snugly they fit inside his Paris-tailored jacket. She could imagine her arms around those shoulders, her fingers in that glorious hair. She could imagine kissing those sculpted lips, touching the bridge of his nose, trailing her fingers along the line of his jaw.

The opera house buzzed with conversation, with the rustle of satin and silk, the chime of bracelets astir, the soft snap of dozens of fans moving the air. But for Anne everything suddenly went quiet. She froze. As still as a stone she sat, simply watching him, all her senses hungry for more. Deep inside her, a small ache blossomed in her chest, then grew and grew till she thought her heart would burst.

Then the two women finally left and Delacroix moved toward her. Their eyes met again. There was something in the expression of those dark eyes . . . Below the tranquil surface, a storm raged. Beyond the assumption of calm civility, there was a man consumed with passionate yearning. She recognized it immediately, because she was sure her own eyes reflected the same intensity of emotion. Her heart nearly stopped. Her mind reeled with shock. She knew him. *She knew him*. The moment was electric and would be seared in Anne's memory for a lifetime.

She knew him . . . *Renard*.

"Cat got your tongue, Anne?"

Anne registered that Jeffrey was speaking. He pushed his face close to hers, trying to command her attention, trying to catch her eye. But her eyes were for Delacroix. The room shrank to insignificant size, and looming in the center of it was the man of her dreams . . . in the guise of a scoundrel!

She wanted to laugh. She wanted to leap from her chair and throw her arms around his neck. In front of God and man, she wanted to wrestle that counterfeit cad to the floor and have her way with him.

These were delicious, delirious thoughts, but Anne did not allow them to show on her face. The joyful discovery of her hero's identity, and the relief of knowing she wasn't a fickle, loose-moraled female who could lust after two such disparate men as Delacroix and Renard, was sobered by the abrupt realization that her knowledge could be dangerous. If she allowed anyone to know what she knew, Delacroix's life could be in grave jeopardy.

He had affected his usual facade of boredom—the languishing posture, the drooping eyelids. But Anne knew that he was fully aware of her discovery that Delacroix the rogue and Renard the fox were one and the same. His dark, shuttered gaze seared through to her very soul. His soul, too, was bared for her to see his longing. She knew he ached as she did. She knew he was holding back as she was.

"*Bonjour*, mademoiselle," he said finally, taking Anne's gloved hand and kissing it. A thrill coursed through her. With an obvious effort, Delacroix pulled his gaze away from her and made a curt bow to Jeffrey, who returned the cool salutation with an equally brief and frosty nod of his head.

"*Bonjour*, Mr. Delacroix," said Anne. He was still holding her hand. They both seemed to realize they could be causing speculation by such lengthy hand-holding, and drew back abruptly. Anne made a gallant effort to appear normal. "How . . . how are you this evening?"

"Quite well, and you?" His voice lowered. His lips curved into a seductive smile. "You are more beautiful than ever. You have a certain glow about you I've never seen before."

Anne felt the color rise to her cheeks. She knew he implied that their lovemaking had given her that glow.

Then suddenly Reggie was there, extending an open hand to Delacroix. The fact that Reggie had initiated this American custom testified to his honest regard for Delacroix. Anne supposed her uncle would never forget what Delacroix had done for her. How would he feel if he knew his niece's savior was Renard ... and her lover?

"So good of you to come over, Mr. Delacroix," said Reggie. He winced a little. On the way to the opera he'd complained of a headache. "I wasn't sure if you understood, or even noticed, my little hand signal."

Anne was disappointed. Apparently Reggie had summoned Delacroix to the box; he hadn't come simply to see her. While she knew he wanted her, could sense the frustration and yearning he felt, Anne still didn't know if Renard—or should she say Delacroix?—ever planned to make her part of his life. He could obviously choose from dozens of women. Perhaps she was just another conquest.

"I was distracted for a moment by ... something else, but when I finally understood that you wanted me to come over, naturally I was delighted."

"I'm glad." Reggie smiled, but Anne could tell it required an effort. Apparently his headache was worse. "But I must confess I asked you over for something more than an ordinary courtesy call. I'm afraid I've got a dreadful headache and need to go home. I was wondering if—"

"Reginald!" expostulated Katherine. "You never said a word!"

"I didn't want to ruin your first night out in nearly a fortnight, Katherine, but, indeed, I was beginning to wonder how I was going to manage to sit through the whole performance."

A furrow of worry between her brows, Katherine leaned forward, prepared to stand up. "What nonsense!" she scolded. "Of course you don't have to sit through the performance. Goodness, Reginald, what nincompoopery is this? I wish you'd spoken up. Anne and I are ready to go home immediately."

Reggie laid his hand on Katherine's shoulder, gently compelling her to remain seated. "I wouldn't dream of dragging you away from such bravura performances. I was wondering what to do when I saw Delacroix across the way and thought perhaps he could—"

"How can I be of assistance, monsieur?" Delacroix instantly inquired.

"You can escort my two charges home at the end of the opera." He frowned, rubbed his temple. "You did bring your carriage?"

"I'm delighted to report that I did indeed bring my carriage tonight. But even if I hadn't, I'd have sent home for it for the privilege of such enchanting company."

"Why didn't you ask me to take Anne and Katherine home, Mr. Weston?" questioned Jeffrey, respectful but peevish. "I know I don't have a carriage, but I'd have gotten them a cab."

"The doorman might have hailed them a cab, Mr. Wycliff," said Reggie with dampening logic. Jeffrey opened his mouth, but Reggie forestalled him, saying, "Yes, I know, you'd have been happy to escort them, as well. I didn't want to inconvenience you. Mr. Delacroix has proven very helpful in past, and I trust him implicitly." When Jeffrey's face turned bright red at the implication that *he* wasn't trustworthy, Reggie realized the *faux pas*. "I'm sorry, Mr. Wycliff, you mustn't mind me. I've got such a devil of a headache, I'm not saying precisely what I mean. No offense meant."

"But, Reginald, I don't want to stay for the opera," asserted Katherine, trying to stand up again. "There won't be anyone to take care of you when you get home."

Reggie's light grip on Katherine's shoulder increased. While his smile was weak, his resolution was firm. "My devoted manservant James, would take umbrage at that remark. Truly, Katherine, it would make me wretched to drag you home over a silly little headache. I just need to sleep it off. I'll be perfectly fine in the morning."

"But you're making me wretched by refusing to allow me to——"

"Just this once, Katherine, don't argue with me."

The simple, succinct request finally got through to her. Staring with concern into Reggie's pain-filled eyes, she realized she would only be doing him more harm by continuing to argue. "Very well. But I expect James to appraise me of your condition as soon as we arrive home."

Reggie laughed, wincing at the same time. "I will, though I think you're fussing over nothing. Isn't that something you've always accused *me* of doing?"

Katherine sniffed. "Well, go home then," she said brusquely, probably to cover up her worry. "Don't tarry while your head's pounding like a kettledrum. Mr. Delacroix will see us home in splendid form, won't you, Mr. Delacroix?"

"Just as *I* could have done, if I'd been given the chance," muttered Jeffrey.

"Rest assured, Mr. Weston," said Delacroix, "I

will take the utmost care of your two charges, as you so quaintly call them." He slanted a sly look at Anne, a look brief but fraught with meaning. Anne's pulse quickened.

"Then I'll be off," Reggie announced, relief in his voice. "Without the endless lines of carriages ahead of me, I should get home in no time at all. Good night, Anne." He leaned over and kissed her on the forehead. "Good night, Mr. Wycliff." He gave Jeffrey a brief nod, but for Delacroix he attempted a full-fledged smile. "Much thanks to you, sir, and a good evening." Lastly he turned to Katherine. It looked as if he wanted to kiss her, too, but he restrained himself. "Good night, Katherine," he said softly, then he was gone.

Directly after Reggie left, the lights dimmed and the curtain rose on the second act. Delacroix went back to Bodine's box, but first assured Anne and Katherine that he would return to collect them after the performance. Visitors to the box had kept Bodine company during Delacroix's absence, but it would have been rude for him to desert the horrid man for the entire evening, Anne reasoned.

Now that she knew who Delacroix really was, she understood his supposed friendship with the slimy likes of Bodine. She was sure he used the show of public camaraderie to support the image he'd honed of a decadent slave-owner. He wanted people to think that he and Bodine were two birds of a feather, so to speak.

Or ... he could be setting Bodine up for a big fall.

That second idea made Anne's stomach clench with fear. If only a fraction of the rumors she'd heard about Bodine's atrocious treatment of his slaves were true, it would be Renard's dearest wish to stop him. It would be a risky business, though. Bodine would be just as ruthless to someone he caught trying to free his slaves as he was to the slaves themselves.

"What has Delacroix done to earn your uncle's undying gratitude and complete trust, Anne?"

Jeffrey's mouth was quite close to Anne's ear. His tone was snide, accusing. Her first impulse was to push him away, but she checked the urge with considerable effort and decided to tell him an abbreviated version of the truth. "A couple of weeks ago, I went to Congo Square to watch the dancers."

His look was reproachful. "You did? You never told *me!*"

"No, I was embarrassed. I ran into problems on the way home and Delacroix rescued me."

Now he was incredulous. "From what? What could that dandy possibly rescue you from? A small dog he beat with his cane?"

Anne kept her gaze fixed on the stage. "No. A rather *large* man tried to ... er ... seduce me. Delacroix punched him in the face."

There was a pause, then the words burst out. "I don't believe it! We *are* talking about the same man, aren't we? *Delacroix?*"

"The very same," Anne replied, keeping her voice carefully inexpressive. "Now, if you don't mind, Jeffrey, I'd like to listen to the—"

"Lord, it sounds as if you're smitten with the fellow!" Out of the corner of her eye she saw him cross his arms and slump in his seat like an angry child.

She couldn't resist baiting him a little. "I *do* like him."

"He's a slave owner, Anne! A care-for-nobody fribble with as much backbone as a snake."

"He's not so bad after you get to know him. Besides, some snakes look nasty, but are perfectly harmless, while other snakes look harmless, and are actually *quite* nasty. Appearances can be so deceiving." She lifted her opera glasses to her face and leaned forward, pretending to pay rapt attention to the performers on stage and effectively conveying her wish to be left alone.

She felt Jeffrey glaring at her in the semidark. She imagined he was at a loss to know why she was suddenly so unsociable, when before she'd been almost too friendly. He sank into a sulky silence. This suited her exactly. She wanted to think. She was stunned by the revelations of the evening and had had no time to assemble them into some reasonable order. It seemed incredulous, but Delacroix truly *was* Renard!

It seemed logical for Renard to have assumed such an extreme opposite persona in public. No one would ever suspect Dandy Delacroix of risking his neck to free a handful of slaves. Anne couldn't imagine now how she'd overlooked the similarities between the two men for so long. But nothing was as clear as hindsight.

At the next intermission Jeffrey departed, leaving no question in Anne's mind that he was angry and jealous. Upstaged by Renard, he'd fabricated an adventure that cast him in the star role of hero. Anne allowed herself a faint smile, imagining how Jeffrey would react if he knew that Renard and Delacroix were the same man.

Katherine fidgeted and sighed heavily throughout the whole performance, seeing and hearing as little as Anne did. Their enjoyment of the opera was nullified by other considerations. Katherine wanted to get home to Reggie, and Anne looked eagerly forward to—and dreaded—the ride home in the carriage with Delacroix. It would be agony and ecstasy. He'd be so close, yet so out of reach.

She allowed herself a glance across the room at Bodine's box, but it was too dark to see Delacroix sitting there. She sighed. She looked forward to the day when she could gaze at him in the light. To make love to him in the light. To open her heart to him and share his deepest thoughts in the light. That day would come, she vowed, if it was the last thing she ever did.

Lucien knew he had business to attend to with Bodine, but ever since he had returned to his seat, his thoughts were full of Anne, nothing but Anne. He kept remembering the look on her face when she realized he was Renard. There had been shock, certainly, but not the horrified disbelief Lucien had feared. It seemed Anne was bright enough to realize that Dandy Delacroix was also part of the masquerade. She ought to realize, too, though, that she had never really come to know the real man behind both disguises. Lucien ruefully acknowledged that even he didn't know exactly who that man really was.

Standing so close to Anne in the box, holding her hand and kissing it, had been torture. He had yearned for her for the past several days, but even his precious and poignant memories of their night together hadn't prepared him for the reality of actually touching her. He wanted her more than ever.

He was formulating a plan to get her alone tonight, his mind consumed by thoughts of kissing Anne, holding her, making love to her ...

Lucien sighed, passing a shaky hand over his forehead. That was the problem. Anne was a distraction he couldn't afford as long as he had business as Renard. But—damn it!—he was in too deep to turn back now. He had to see Anne. He had to be with her.

He gritted his teeth, promised himself that he would see her later, than determinedly made Renard's business a priority. With his eyes fixed on the stage, Lucien said, "I have a proposition for you, Bodine."

He felt Bodine shift in his chair. He'd been dozing through a particularly exquisite aria. "What kind of proposition?" he inquired in a thick voice. He yawned hugely, not bothering to cover his mouth with his hand. "If it's got something to do with that money I won from you last night, I'm not taking anything but cold cash."

Lucien assumed an offended tone. "You know I'm good for it. In fact, I've got it on my person and had planned to hand it over to you directly after the performance."

"Then what's the problem? Why are you offering me some sort of proposition?"

"We're friends. I just thought I might make things more interesting for you. I know your tastes. Wouldn't you prefer a warm body over cold cash?"

Bodine grunted derisively. "I can get all the warm bodies I want. If not on my estate, there's Sadie's brothel."

"But you told me yourself, you hate paying for it."

"I never do, unless Sadie's got a virgin. Virgins are worth paying for."

"That's how I thought you'd feel. Just how much is one worth to you, Bodine?" Lucien turned his head. He'd caught Bodine's attention. The lights from the stage reflected in his bleary eyes—eyes that were suddenly sharp with avarice.

"Are you suggesting I forfeit what you owe me for a virgin you've got tucked away somewhere?"

"*Exactement.*"

Bodine licked his lips. "How do I know she's worth it? Before I commit myself to this little proposition of yours, you'll have to show her to me."

Lucien laughed. "This is not a contract, Bodine. This is just one night of rutting, *n'est-ce pas?*"

"I want my money's worth. You owe me a lot. Never seen you play so ham-handed before."

"You can't see the girl. She doesn't arrive on Bocage till tomorrow."

"She doesn't arrive? She's a new slave, then?"

"*Oui.*"

"How old?"

"Barely old enough to have her menses. I know you like them young, as well as virginal."

"What does she look like?"

"Slim as a reed, but with wonderful breasts. Her skin is a little lighter than creamed coffee. Her face is oval, her nose straight, her lips full and red." Lucien flicked a speck of lint off his jacket sleeve. "I'm quite sure you'll like her."

Lucien heard Bodine swallow. In a husky voice he said, "If she's such a prize, why don't you take her?"

"I told you before, I have a mistress. Besides, I don't like children in my bed. However, my sexual tastes are not under discussion at the moment. Yours are. I'm offering you quite a treat, but if you aren't interested . . ." He shrugged his shoulders in a gesture of dismissal.

Bodine rose to the bait. "Damn it, Delacroix," he growled, "You know damned well I'm interested. But she'd better be all you've made her out to be, or

I'll want the full amount of the gaming debt, too. Do you understand?"

"*Certainement.* I'm not worried. You'll be satisfied. She's a jewel." He turned away, lifting his opera glasses to his face.

Frustrated by Delacroix's offhand attitude, Bodine snarled, "When, then? When can I have her?"

"Tomorrow night, there's a ball at Rosedown—"

"So?"

"Meet me there. As you know, Rosedown is the closest neighboring plantation to Bocage. After late supper is served, I'll take you to Bocage and direct you to the right cabin. By that time of night, the other slaves will be in their bunks and asleep, for the most part. I'll isolate the girl, but it's always best to keep these things as quiet as possible. It peeves the other slaves when young girls are raped."

"I don't like the use of that word."

Lucien lowered the glasses and gave Bodine a sweet smile. "I had no notion you were so prim about your vocabulary."

"I could care less what your 'notions' are, Delacroix. Just don't disappoint me tomorrow night, or you'll be everlastingly sorry. Understand?"

"Perfectly."

Applause thundered through the house. The performers were taking their bows, curtain call after curtain call. Bodine left without a word of good-bye. Lucien waited for the lights to come on, then he stood up and brushed off his sleeves with energy, as if ridding himself of the vile contamination of Bodine's company. He felt filthy. There was a foul burning in his throat. He couldn't wait to get outside, into the fresh air, into the pure presence of the woman he desired more than anything.

He smiled at the thought of Anne, his heart thrilling at the prospect of sharing his carriage with her. He'd hoped for a little more time before she figured out who he was, but tonight she'd taken one good look at him and had known.

So she might as well know all, he decided as he strode down the hall to Katherine's opera box. And, if Katherine cooperated, he was going to spend a little time alone with Anne. He'd never made love in a carriage, but the idea had considerable potential. He couldn't help himself—his steps lengthened.

Chapter 17

Even though Anne was sure it was as spacious as all other vehicles of the same type, the carriage seemed minuscule. And all its perceived tiny corners were filled with the presence of Delacroix, making his nearness almost unbearable for her. Her full skirts and Katherine's crowded the space between the seats, forcing him to stretch his legs to the side. There was a lighted lamp inside the carriage, and Anne enjoyed several surreptitious glances at those incredible long legs of his.

The trip to Prytania Street was slow-going behind dozens of other opera fans, but they would eventually arrive at the Grimms mansion, and Anne dreaded the inevitable end to such agonizing bliss.

There was so much they needed to say to each other, so many questions Anne wanted to ask! But with Katherine in the carriage, it was impossible to speak freely. Most of all, Anne wanted to touch Delacroix. That was the hardest part—not touching him when he was so close.

And Katherine did not help Anne through the ordeal by keeping up her usual chatter. She was distracted, worried about Reggie. She seemed hardly to notice with whom she shared the carriage, and spent most of the time staring out the window, counting off the landmarks till they got home.

"Did you like the opera, Mademoiselle Weston?"

Anne was startled to note that Delacroix had abandoned his usual lazy drawl. The clear, melodic tones thrilled her. He sounded like Renard. Her heart beat faster than ever, the blood surging through her veins. She snatched a glance at Katherine, but her aunt was too preoccupied to notice and comment on the sudden change of rhythm in Delacroix's voice. Nevertheless, Anne thought he was taking unnecessary risks by not keeping strictly in character. Katherine was no dolt.

"I always enjoy anything by Rossini." She paused, toying with a dangerous notion of her own—innuendo. "Tonight was the most exciting performance I've ever experienced."

One dark brow climbed to a roguish peak. "Indeed? The most exciting ... er ... performance you've *ever* experienced, mademoiselle?"

She blushed. She hadn't meant for him to take the double meaning quite so far. "On the stage, sir," she answered demurely. His eyes gleamed in the lantern-glow, black and devilish.

"I hope you won't think I'm too forward, sir—" she began, breaking the charged silence.

"*You*, mademoiselle? Too *forward*?" He feigned shock.

She tried to subdue a saucy smile, failing utterly. "I was just wondering if you would mind if I call you by your Christian name."

He smiled back at her, slid a glance at the inattentive Katherine, then looked back to Anne. He leaned confidingly close. Anne's breath caught. He smelled vital, masculine, clean. Like that night in the cabin. Her stomach tightened; her throat went dry. "Do you think it proper to call me by my first name, Mademoiselle Weston? It implies an . . . intimacy, *n'est-ce pas?*"

Anne swallowed. Nervous, she licked her lips. He watched her avidly. This close watchfulness did nothing for her composure. "We are friends, Mr. Delacroix." She paused, then coyly returned his own frequently used catchphrase. "*N'est-ce pas?*"

He sat back against the carriage squabs, fluctuations of light and shadow from outside the window passing over his chiseled features. A faint smile played about his lips. "Yes, we are the best of friends. I saved you from a lech, didn't I?" he finished with an ironic smile.

Then he waited, building Anne's anticipation. He was a master at withholding, she thought ruefully, building her to peaks of excitement before giving her what she wanted. Hadn't he proven that in the cabin? But the wait had been well worth it. "Please do call me Lucien."

"Lucien," she repeated, rolling the sibilant sound over her tongue like melted chocolate. She had always liked his name, even when she considered him a scoundrel. When she suddenly realized how besotted she might appear, she snatched another glance at Katherine. This time her aunt was paying attention. She shifted an inquiring look between her and Lucien.

Lucien, always ready to do his part, looked perfectly unconcerned and harmless. Anne endeavored to appear just as nonchalant. She was rewarded for her efforts when Katherine's face relaxed. But only for a minute. Her aunt's puzzled look was replaced by one of worry. She got right to the point.

"I'm concerned about your uncle."

"I know you are, Aunt Katherine. I'm a little worried, too. But I think Uncle Reggie's just got a headache, as he said."

"You know how protective he is of us . . . of *you*, that is. He's never left us in a public place before."

"And he wouldn't have tonight if Mr. Delacroix hadn't been available to take us home. He was prepared to sit through the entire opera with that wretched headache."

Katherine's face softened with tenderness. She sighed. "I know. Such foolish nincompoopery!"

Anne glanced out the window. They were turning onto their street. She tried to inject enthusiasm into her voice for her aunt's sake. "We're almost home. In less than five minutes, we'll have scouted down James and know exactly how Uncle Reggie's doing. Maybe his headache's gone by now, and he's waiting up for us."

This idea cheered Katherine considerably. She immediately grabbed handfuls of her skirt, ready to leap out of the carriage even before the horses drew to a complete halt. Anne turned her attention back to Lucien. She expected him to look as wistful as she felt, as disappointed as she was for the quickly approaching conclusion to their forced togetherness. Instead he looked exultant, eager. His eyes glimmered like wet coal, so black, so full of . . . mischief? What was he up to?

The carriage rolled to a smooth stop. Too impatient to wait for the coachman to open the door, Katherine reached for the handle. Lucien beat her to it, turned the latch, and stepped outside, reaching up for Katherine's hand to assist her in getting out. Katherine took his hand and stepped down, but just as she was about to pass him and head willy-nilly for the front door, he detained her.

Still clasping her hand, he pulled her close and

whispered in her ear. Katherine listened for perhaps half a minute, shook her head vigorously, then stretched on her toes to whisper something back. When she appeared to try to step away, he detained her and whispered in her ear again. Judging by the stiff manner in which Katherine held herself, she didn't like, or didn't agree with, whatever Lucien was saying.

Anne found this intense exchange most intriguing. What on earth were they arguing about? If nothing else, it was rather rude to talk secretly in plain sight of a third party! But they continued to whisper till Katherine's shoulders drooped slightly, as if she were giving in.

Then, without a backward glance, she marched down the walkway toward the front door. Lucien ignored Anne's outstretched hand and called up to the coachman, "Drive down River Road till I rap three times, George, then head back here at a leisurely pace." He got in the carriage, shut the door behind him, and pulled down the leather shades on both sides, enclosing them in complete privacy. Then he sat back and smiled wickedly.

"Close your mouth, *cher*," he advised her.

She took his advice, overcome by the implications of what had just occurred. "You're kidnapping me?"

"Regrettably, only for a short while."

"What could you have possibly told my aunt to have persuaded her to let me go with you?"

"It wasn't easy. She's miffed with me."

She gave a short, nervous laugh. "This is most—"

He crossed his arms, grinning like a satyr. "Improper?"

Her fan slipped through nerveless fingers and

clattered on the carriage floor. "If Reggie finds out—"

"Reggie is most probably snoring away in bed. James will have dosed him with a sleeping potion."

"But if he's not asleep, and waiting up for us—"

"That's unlikely. And if he *is* waiting up, Katherine's prepared to tell him the truth."

Anne leaned forward. Her lips could barely form the words. "The *truth?* But—"

"Your aunt knows all about us."

Anne's voice rose to a squeak. "She knows that we . . . *made love?*"

"Yes."

"She knows who you are?"

"Yes."

"But . . . but *how?*"

Lucien leaned forward and traced her cheek with his knuckle. Anne felt a shiver run down her spine. "Your aunt knew that Dandy Delacroix and Renard were the same man from the beginning. In fact, she helped me set up the operation and is an integral part of it. Have you never wondered about the clockwork regularity of your aunt's visits to a certain Madame Tussad? And their solitary nature? She always goes alone, as you may recall."

"I assumed it was charity, or a long-standing friendship she didn't want to share with anyone else."

"Madame Tussad is Armande's cousin."

"Oh!"

"Sometimes we meet there together. Other times pertinent information is simply passed along. Your aunt has been very valuable to me, and to the cause. Someday you must get her to tell you all she's done. Mostly she's a strategist and strong moral support. In short, she's a brave and brilliant woman."

Anne's reticule slipped from her grasp and fell next to her fan, and she plopped back against the carriage cushions. Amused, Lucien picked up her dropped articles and placed them in a far corner of the seat. "Good God," she murmured, truly shocked. "This is too much to take in in one night. First to find out that you have been living a double life, one as a man I've hated, and the other as a man I've admired and loved. And now to learn that my aunt is part of your operation!"

"You never really hated the Dandy, did you?" asked Lucien. "Tell me truthfully, sweet Anne."

She smiled shyly and shook her head. "No. Actually I thought I was wicked because I was so attracted to him. To *you*. It was a relief when I found out tonight that all along I've been lusting after just one man."

"Lusting, eh?" His eyes lighted up like obsidian just picked from a volcanic rockpile, still lava-hot, still throbbing with life from the core of the earth. The power he had over her was humbling, frightening, exhilarating. He took one of her gloved hands and slowly began to unfasten the tiny pearl buttons, from elbow to wrist.

"What are you doing?" she asked, snatching back her hand. Just from this small sexual overture, this tiny step in what was probably going to be a full-fledged seduction, Anne could feel the honeyed heat gathering at her woman's core. But she didn't want it to be so easy for Lucien to seduce her. She was angry and wanted answers.

Lucien looked surprised. "I'm taking off your gloves, *cher*."

"I . . . I can see that, but I don't think that's such a good idea."

Lucien smiled. "But I think it's a wonderful idea. And only the beginning of something even better."

Anne raised her brows imperiously. "Where have you been for the past week and a half, Lucien? I've been sick with worry."

He reached again for her hand; again she drew back. He pursed his lips, amusement twinkling in his eyes. "Anne, don't be angry," he soothed. "I couldn't come to you. It was too dangerous. Don't you think I would have come if I could?"

Anne squared her shoulders, lifted her chin. "I don't know what to think. You were right when you said in the cabin that I really don't know you. I'm crazy to let you charm me into submissiveness."

He leaned forward and, without touching her with his hands, kissed the sensitive hollow behind her ear. "And I'm simply crazy about you," he breathed.

She felt her resolve melting. His lips felt like heaven against her skin. "You're a scoundrel, with women flocking after you like ants to a sugar bowl."

His hands gently, tentatively clasped her shoulders, and he ran his palms down her arms, making gooseflesh wherever he touched. "Your lips are like sugar, Anne. Sweet, so sweet."

He touched a forefinger to her chin and slowly coaxed her head to turn. Their lips met in a brief, whisper-soft kiss. She moaned softly. "You're a rogue, Lucien."

"A rogue with a mission."

"A mission?"

"To loosen these damned buttons," he said wryly. Bemused, intoxicated by her consuming desire for him, she watched him apply himself with single-minded intensity to the task of undoing her buttons. It occurred to her then that he was rather adept at the procedure, as if he undressed women on a regular basis. The idea made her feel rather prickly. Then, unbidden, unwelcome, the image of his mistress loomed up in her mind. He had both gloves off now, and he bent his head to kiss her wrist. Filled with unexpected heartache, she pulled her hand away.

Half-amused, totally frustrated, Lucien looked into her face. "*Cher?* What's wrong now?" His lips tilted in a rueful smile. "Are you feeling shy?"

Anne bit her lip, averted her gaze. "You have a mistress."

There was a pause, a sigh. He lifted her chin again, forcing her to look at him. "I *had* a mistress. I don't anymore."

Anne's heart soared. "You don't?"

"Not since I kissed you, *cher.* Your passion made everyone else pale in comparison." He smiled, his eyes full of teasing affection. "That night in the cabin was the most exciting performance I've ever experienced."

Pleased but disbelieving, Anne felt warmth creep into her cheeks. She dropped her gaze. "Oh, Lucien, how can you tell such lies? She is experienced in the ways of pleasing a man, and I'm just—"

He took both her hands and spoke earnestly. "You're just the most passionate, desirable, beautiful woman I've ever known. Something stirred in me the minute I first saw you on the deck of the *Belvedere.* I wanted to make love to you before I even knew your name."

She shook her head, amazed, immensely flattered. But a tiny voice inside said, *He only speaks of desire, never of love.* She turned away.

"*Cher,* don't you want me anymore? Are you no

longer interested now that you know I'm just plain Lucien?"

She couldn't let him believe that. She placed her fingertips on his firm jaw. "I don't believe you can ever be just plain anything, Lucien. You are a good man, an extraordinary man to have risked so much to help others."

"But I need to be myself." His tone became grim, emphatic. "I don't intend to keep up this charade much longer. But first—"

"But first you're going to deal with Bodine."

He was surprised. "How did you know that?"

"You can't bear to let the most blatant abuser of slaves off scot-free. Bodine needs to be stopped, and he ought to be punished. How are you going to accomplish this, Lucien?"

"That is only for me to know. I won't endanger you again by including you, even in the smallest way." He touched the faint scar at her temple.

"But Lucien, I want to—"

He laid a quieting finger over her lips. "Shhh, *ma petite*. We have so little time together tonight, I don't want to spend it discussing Bodine. I want to spend it making love to you."

She trembled, but not with fear. "In . . . in a carriage?"

"Anne, you seem to think the thing impossible," he said, laughing. "Believe me, where there is sufficient motivation, anything is possible. And sometimes the most unexpected places bring the most pleasure."

Convinced, Anne wrapped her arms around his neck, twining her fingers behind it. She set aside her doubts, her worries. She might never see Lucien again, but she would take whatever she could get now, whether he loved her or not . . . She answered him by placing her mouth on his.

He groaned and pulled her into his arms and onto his lap, burying his face in her hair. "Anne, I never thought I could desire a woman as I do you. God help me, I'm obsessed with you." His lips trailed down her neck, leaving behind a shivery path of pleasure.

She turned her face to his questing kisses. His hands roamed over her back. Their kisses became deeper, more intense. She was blissfully lost to all reason and thought.

She shifted, straining to get closer, and nearly slipped off his lap. "This skirt!" she complained, grabbing his shoulders to keep from sliding to the floor. She'd never been so thoroughly disgusted by the dictates of fashion. Yards and yards of alpaca were an encumbrance to lovemaking!

Lucien laughed, caught her waist, and set her firmly on his lap again. "Don't worry, *cher*. I won't let you fall. And as for this trifling barrier . . ." He started gently tugging on the skirt, pulling it out from under her till her chemise and silk drawers were the only thing between her bottom and his lap. Her skirt billowed out on all sides of her, like a full-blown ivory rose.

"Straddle me," he ordered, his voice husky. Wide-eyed, curious, and aroused, Anne did exactly as he told her. Now she faced him. There was no mask, no darkness to obscure his beloved features, or to hide the desire in his eyes. With her open palms braced against his broad chest they kissed.

She'd almost forgotten how delirious his kisses could make her feel, how joyful. Their tongues tangled, dipped, and explored. Their lips roamed over each other's faces, throats. She kissed his beard-stubbled jaw.

He kissed the smooth ridge of her collarbone,

then moved lower, lower, till his lips and tongue played along the lace ruching of her low-cut neckline. His hands slid up slowly from her waist till they cupped her breasts from underneath. Anne instinctively leaned into his palms. When his thumbs came up and flicked both nipples, she moaned with pleasure.

"Oh, Lucien, how I wish ... how I wish ..."

"Say it, Anne. Say it." He bent and buried his face in her cleavage. Her hands tunneled through his hair, her eyes closed, her mind tilting, reeling.

"'Tis immodest to say it," she whispered, half-gasping, half-laughing.

"Nothing is immodest between lovers."

"I just wish I could be naked, lying next to you, feeling your body against mine. And I wish I could look at you in the light. All of you."

"Will you be satisfied tonight to see only part of me?" he asked tenderly. "If the carriage was stopped for some reason, I couldn't bear to have you exposed to the greedy eyes or the sordid speculations of others. But at least this is more than either of us was granted that first night in the cabin."

"And more than I ever dreamed possible when I left the house this evening," she agreed. "Just let me feel your bare chest, Lucien. Let me open your shirt."

She gently pushed his hands away as he started to undo the buttons of his vest and then his ruffled shirt. She wanted the pleasure all for herself. And as Lucien had done to her, she was going to make him wait.

She felt his eyes on her as she intently, slowly undid each button. His hands glided up and down her waist, teasing the undersides of her breasts, but not cupping them fully as he had before. He, too, was playing a teasing game. Soon Anne was stepping up the pace, too eager to hold back.

Finally she was able to slide her hands inside the opened shirt. His chest was hard with muscle and lightly dusted with soft swirls of black hair. Her palms tingled on contact, the thrill of touching him traveling up her arm and into every nerve of her body. His nipples were small and wine-colored. She lowered her head and lathed the taut buds with the tip of her tongue. He groaned and moved his hands up and over her breasts, squeezing gently, pressing her erect nipples between thumb and forefinger.

"Now my turn, *cher*," he growled as he undid the few buttons at the front of Anne's gown and carefully eased down the bodice to expose her breasts. Anne couldn't control her breathing, her chest heaved up and down. At first he only looked at her; he didn't touch.

"You're so beautiful, Anne," he whispered, his own breath seemingly suspended. "Your skin is so white, and your nipples are so richly tinted—like a damask rose."

If she was beautiful, that was good, because she wanted to be beautiful for Lucien. Only for him. If he didn't touch her soon, she'd go mad.

He touched her. His hands kneaded her breasts, his clever fingers teased her nipples, and then his head lowered, and he suckled at each breast till Anne knew the meaning of madness.

"Lucien," she pleaded huskily. "Now, Lucien. Love me *now*."

He moved her onto the seat next to him while he undid his trousers. Anne watched with unmaidenly interest as his erection sprang free, full and hard. He pulled her atop him. She eagerly straddled his thighs and pushed her skirts out of the way. Lucien reached under her, found the slit in her drawers, and sheathed himself in the tight, moist channel of her womanhood.

Anne was nearly overwhelmed with feeling. To be literally filled with the man she loved was the closest thing to heaven on earth she could imagine. Tears of joy welled in her eyes. Their gazes met and locked. "I love you, Lucien," she whispered, her throat tight with emotion. "I love you."

He began to move. He plunged deep, then pulled back, again and again, setting a rhythm that Anne eagerly, mindlessly followed.

Tension built, then exploded suddenly, as wave after wave of intense pleasure flooded through her. Lucien shuddered against her at the same moment, whispering her name like a benediction as his seed flooded her womb.

Spent and blissfully lethargic, she laid her head against his chest and listened to the strong beat of his heart as it gradually slowed. She was content, at home in the arms of the man she loved.

Later, their clothes restored to respectability, and with Anne sitting beside him on the seat with her head resting against his shoulder, Lucien picked up his cane and rapped three times on the ceiling. The carriage slowed, turned, and headed back to town.

"Must we return so soon?" asked Anne, grown drowsy in the aftermath of their lovemaking, lulled by the gentle rocking of the carriage. "I feel so safe in here with you, hidden from the world, as if we were encased in a warm cocoon."

He turned and caught her chin in the palm of his hand, tilting her face so he could see her. He looked troubled. "I wish it were possible to stay hidden away with you, but I can't. And I can't promise you—"

He didn't finish. He sighed and turned away, his hand falling heavily to his lap.

She would not press him. She did not want false promises or forced words of love. She prayed that someday he would give his heart willingly. She hoped he was holding back because the dangerous masquerade of Renard was still very much part of his life, and not because of personal doubts about his feelings for her. When he held her and made love to her, she felt truly cherished. She hoped she wasn't imagining such emotions on his part.

"Lucien, when will I see you again?"

He frowned. "I don't know."

"There is a masquerade ball at Rosedown tomorrow night. I haven't wanted to go, but Reggie says we're under an obligation to the Bouviers. They introduced me around town when I first came to New Orleans. *I* think they're a bunch of high-stickers and dreadfully snobbish and dull, but I shan't mind going if I know you'll be there. *Will* you be there?"

Still frowning, Lucien said nothing.

"What's wrong? I understand if you have other plans."

"No, I do plan to be there. I'll be in costume, but I suppose you'd recognize me in any masquerade by now." He smiled briefly, but was soon frowning again. "I'm not staying past supper."

Anne sensed that this information was all he intended to impart. She suspected that he had business to attend to at the ball, and perhaps after the ball, and he had no intention of revealing the nature of that business. But Anne knew with gut-wrenching clarity that Lucien's late-night business was with Bodine.

Her heart sank. So soon! The confrontation, the danger was coming so soon! If Lucien's plan—

whatever it was—was successful, perhaps he would be able to commit himself to her. But if something went wrong ... She squeezed his arm, cuddling closer. She couldn't bear it if something happened to him. He had become her life.

"What, Anne? What's the matter?" He peered tenderly into her face. She forced a smile.

"Nothing's the matter. I'm just going to miss you, that's all. Tomorrow night seems like a lifetime away."

He squeezed her arm and spoke intently. "Anne, even though we'll be able to see each other, we'll have to be very discreet. You'll have to pretend to dislike me. You must tell me now if you won't be able to do that."

"I've had lots of practice."

He groaned. "I'm not sure when we'll be able to be together like this again."

Or if we'll ever be able to be together again, thought Anne, her heart filled with doubt. But she only said, "Soon, Lucien. Soon."

He did not reply, and the carriage trundled down the road toward home and an uncertain future. More than ever, Anne knew just how much she would lose if things did not go as planned. In Lucien's arms, she'd known ecstasy and contentment. And because of these blissful feelings, she also knew fear.

Chapter 18

Katherine met them at the door of the Grimms mansion. They had said their good-byes in the carriage, so with one last kiss on the cheek for Anne and a warm handclasp for Katherine, Lucien turned and walked away. Anne watched till he boarded the carriage and waved from the window.

Katherine seemed eager to get Anne inside, muttering something about the servants. They went directly to Katherine's bedchamber, neither of them saying a word. When the door closed behind them, they both spoke at once.

"Aunt Katherine, I had no idea you were in league with Renard!"

"Anne, when did you figure out that Lucien was Renard?"

They laughed, more from a release of tension than from real mirth.

"First things first," said Katherine, moving to a table holding two crystal decanters. "Sit down, child, and let me pour you a glass of water. Or would you rather have brandy? I should say you deserve a stiff shot of something."

Anne sank into a wing chair next to her aunt's massive mahogany bed. "A strong cup of tea

292

sounds heavenly, but I suppose the servants are all abed."

"Yes, and I'm glad they are. I hope none of them saw you return to the house with Lucien. Your reputation would be in tatters." Katherine poured a snifter of brandy and carried it to Anne. "Here. Drink up. It will help you sleep."

Anne took a sip of the brandy, finding the immediate effect rather soothing. She had thought herself relaxed, but she hadn't realized how jangled her nerves had become since leaving the secure circle of Lucien's arms.

"Oh, Aunt Katherine, what difference does it make about my reputation? Why worry about that now? Everything has changed, and will change even more. Lucien wants to end his career as Renard as soon as he takes care of one last matter of business." She took another sip of brandy. "I'm sure you know what I mean."

"Yes." Katherine frowned. "Bodine. I told Lucien that he should feel no responsibility to take care of that dreadful man before ending his career as Renard. He's already done enough, and now that it's become obvious that there's a traitor within our small ranks, it's dangerous for him to continue the work."

Anne leaned forward, setting her glass on a bedside table. "Surely you don't think Lucien is in more danger than he was two weeks ago."

"I don't know, Anne. This last coup will be risky, but if there's anyone who can pull it off, it's Lucien."

Anne stood up and paced the floor. "You know the details of the plan, don't you?" She stopped in front of her aunt and faced her. "You know the time, the place, and the strategy. Lucien won't tell me anything, but *you* can tell me!"

Katherine shook her head firmly. "No, actually I don't know the details. Lucien is wisely keeping most things to himself these days, relying on very few people to help him. And even if I did know, I certainly wouldn't tell you. I don't want you involved!"

Anne took hold of her aunt's forearms. "You must know *something!* And can't you see, Aunt Katherine, I *am* involved. I've been very much involved since that night at the cabin with him. I love him so much, and if I just knew a little of what his plans were, if I weren't so utterly in the dark, I wouldn't worry as much."

"Don't fool yourself, Anne. Either way, you're going to worry. Besides, Lucien and I both know you too well to believe you can be told the details of his plan without somehow involving yourself. The best thing you can do for Lucien at this point is to stay out of the way. For once you must simply remain safely at home."

Frustrated, Anne resumed her pacing. "Have you and Lucien forgotten that I was useful to him when he met up with those bounty hunters? Things might have turned out quite differently if I'd stayed at home that night."

"Yes, you might have been killed if that bounty hunter's aim had been a scant inch more precise."

"Nonsense," Anne said with a huff, crossing her arms stubbornly. "What about Lucien? *He* might have been killed if—"

"Lucien is resourceful and clever," Katherine interrupted. "If you hadn't been there to warn him, something else would have alerted him to the danger." She moved close to Anne and put a gentle hand on her shoulder. "I'm not diminishing what you did, Anne. It was brave. And it probably did save Lucien's life. But don't you see that you're a distraction to him now? Let him do what he needs to do, so he'll finally be free to pursue some happiness for himself. And—if my guess is correct—for you, too."

Anne did not miss the wistful tone in her aunt's voice. "Oh, Aunt Katherine, I'm so selfish! I haven't even asked about Uncle Reggie. Is he feeling better?"

Katherine sighed deeply and moved to the window, staring out into the balmy, black November night. "He's sleeping, but he's restless. James gave him some laudanum." She turned from the window and made a weak smile. "If Reggie allowed himself to be dosed, he must feel awful."

Anne crossed the room and took her aunt's surprisingly cold hands, chafing them between her two warm ones. "You care for him very much," she said softly.

"So much, Anne, that I'm prepared to leave my beloved New Orleans if there's a chance that Reginald and I can be together."

"But why would you need to leave New Orleans? This is your home."

"Anne, home is with the person, or people, you love. But, as you must realize if you think about it, if it comes out that Lucien is Renard, my involvement in the work might be found out, too. I couldn't bear for Reginald to be implicated in this mess, or even embarrassed by my incarceration." She smiled grimly. "I'd even hie myself back to merry old England if Reginald wanted me to. He's made it clear enough that he doesn't exactly like the wilds of America."

"I'm not so sure about that—"

"I don't even know how he truly feels about me, so all of this might be unnecessary speculation— the pipe dreams of an old and foolish woman. I think I perceive a certain gentleness in his manner toward me of late, though. A certain protectiveness. But it's probably all in my head."

"Then it's in my head, too," said Anne, squeezing her aunt's hands. "I've seen the gentleness. I've seen the way he looks at you."

Katherine pulled away from Anne's grasp and returned to the window. "I dare not believe he loves me till he tells me so. Reginald and I have been at daggers-drawn for as long as I can remember. We're like water and oil, impossible to mix."

"You've been mixing rather well the last two weeks," Anne reminded her. She hesitated, then suggested coyly, "I think all that friction between you two over the years—when you've been thrown together for family weddings and funerals and such—has simply been the only acceptable outlet for your mutual attraction."

Katherine spun around like a child's top twisted into sudden motion. "Anne! Good heavens! What nincompoopery you speak!"

"Indeed, Aunt Katherine," said Anne, amused by her liberal aunt's maidenly reaction, "I speak only the truth, just as you've always taught me to do. I'm blunt, just as you are. It's not a coincidence that I'm Reggie's favorite niece and you are—quite simply—his favorite female overall."

"You go beyond blunt. Now you're spinning whiskers," Katherine said weakly.

"No, I'm not lying, and if you thought I was blunt before, what I'm going to say now will surely shock you. My advice to you, dear aunt, is to get my Uncle Reggie between those sheets"— she pointed to the bed—"where the two of you can work out your accumulated differences to the mutual satisfaction of both!"

Katherine was unable to articulate a scathing

retort—or any sort of retort, for that matter—
though her face turned red and her mouth worked
at the effort for several seconds. Finally she gave
up, clamped her lips together, and walked with
stiff dignity to the door. For a full minute she
stood with her hand on the cut-glass knob, her
face averted, gathering her composure and her
wits. Then she turned and faced down her grinning, unrepentant niece. She was trying to look
stern, but Anne detected the hint of a smile playing about her aunt's mouth.

"I can see that consorting with that scalawag
Lucien has caused you to abandon the finer points
of discretion."

Anne's grin broadened. "Careful, Aunt Katherine, you begin to sound like Reggie. I love him
dearly, but he tends to be a bit priggish now and
then. That's why you're so good for him. You're
much more broad-minded. Remember when he
blanched at the mention of 'bosom' in mixed company? How you took him to task!"

Katherine laughed aloud. "As you must know, I
can converse quite freely about all sorts of body
parts and the most delicate subjects as long as they
have nothing to do with me. Now go to bed,
Anne, and get some sleep. I just realized I was
about to march, affronted, right out of my own
room!"

Anne readily complied. She was truly tired. On
her way to the door she almost mentioned the
masquerade ball at Rosedown, but decided that
the less interest she showed in the ball, the more
likely that she'd be able to go. She didn't want
Katherine to know that she suspected that Lucien
would set the groundwork for Bodine's downfall
at the masquerade. She wanted to be on hand
when things first got rolling—when the curtain

went up, so to speak—even if she was denied a part in the final act. However, she hadn't given up on the idea that she'd be part of the final act, too . . .

At the door she turned, smiled her sweetest, most angelic smile, and bid her aunt good night.

The next day Reggie's headache was not better. In fact, though he got up at his usual hour and gamely tried to make chitchat at the breakfast table, by ten o'clock he went back to bed. This sort of prolonged indisposition was very unusual for Reggie, and Anne was worried. So was Katherine.

By noon they were standing by the side of his bed, trying to talk him into seeing the doctor. "What for?" he asked. "I just have a headache. Everyone gets headaches."

Katherine reached over and felt his forehead for the third time in ten minutes. "No fever . . ."

"You see, Katherine? There's no need for concern."

"What about your throat? Does it hurt?"

"As I've told you innumerable times, my throat feels fine."

"But you haven't got an appetite. I saw how you pushed that egg around your plate, trying to make it look as though you'd had a bite or two."

At the mention of food, Reggie grimaced. "Well, you're right about that. I don't have an appetite. It's probably a touch of influenza, which is why the two of you are being very unwise in standing so close to me. Go away and rest up for your evening at the Bouviers."

"You don't think we're going out and leaving you home sick, do you?"

"You and Anne are not sick, and the Bouviers will be offended if one or two of us don't go to their masquerade ball. It's the highlight of the social season, I'm told."

"I know, Reginald," said Katherine. "You forget that I've been attending Madeline Bouvier's balls for nearly a quarter-century. Missing just this once won't matter."

Reggie grew agitated. He was pale, but patches of hectic red appeared on both cheeks. There was a deep furrow of displeasure between his brows. "But it does matter ... at least to me. They paid particular attention to Anne when we arrived in the city, introduced her to all the right people. I won't have them thinking the English are rag-mannered ingrates. If you won't go, I'll go myself."

He threw off his covers and started to sit up. It was immediately obvious that the slightest movement made his head throb. Katherine was horrified. "Good God, Reginald, lie down, you stubborn fool! I'll take Anne to the ball if that will make you happy. All I want is for you to rest and get well."

Reggie lay back down, but he didn't gloat over his victory. He was in too much pain for that. He just lay there, very still, as James and Katherine hovered over him, straightening his pillows and retucking his blankets.

Anne watched his face, her heart full of sympathy. She could swear that behind that English stiff upper lip, Reggie was gritting his teeth. She'd watched the exchange between him and Katherine with mixed feelings. She was very concerned about her uncle, but worried about Lucien, too. She felt she needed to be at Rosedown tonight. But the matter seemed beyond debate. Reggie would not be satisfied—in fact he would not rest at all—unless both she and Katherine went to the ball.

"Fetch my writing paper and quill, Anne," said Reggie after a moment.

Anne moved to the Chippendale drop-front desk, saying over her shoulder, "To whom are you writing, Uncle? Can't it wait?"

"I'm going to ask Delacroix to escort you to the ball tonight."

"He can't!" said Katherine rather too quickly. Then, more casually, "He's not planning to stay beyond the supper hour."

Anne looked keenly at her aunt. Now why would she know that unless Lucien had made a point of telling her? Anne was more than ever convinced that Renard's plot against Bodine would begin to take shape that night at the Bouviers' ball. She didn't think her aunt had been lying to her about not knowing the particulars of Lucien's plan, but it appeared that she at least knew that tonight's masquerade ball was the setting for the opening scene.

It was settled that Anne and Katherine would be driven to the ball by one of Katherine's relatives by marriage—an ancient uncle on her second husband's side of the family, a Captain Miller, retired from the navy. He would lend the respectable chaperonage that Reggie demanded for both women. Katherine didn't bother to remind him that she used to go everywhere without male escorts before Reggie came to New Orleans. But just the fact that she refrained from this reminder was proof of her worry over his health—and evidence of her love.

Reggie got no better and no worse as the day progressed. After dinner, Anne went upstairs and put on her costume. She was going as an angel, the irony of which was not lost on Reggie when she showed him her costume before descending to the drawing room to await Captain Miller's carriage.

She pirouetted at the foot of his bed, holding between pinched thumb and forefinger the layers of diaphanous skirts, which were white shot through with gold threads. The bodice was crisscrossed with gold cording, the sleeves pert puffs of gathered lace. Sarah had cleverly made wings of white netting and a halo of starched piping, dipped in glittery gold paint. Anne had a half-mask of white, dotted with gold stars, which she would put on when they arrived at Rosedown.

"With your matching golden hair and that sweet face, Anne, I'd almost believe I'd died and gone to heaven." Reggie smiled wryly. "But we know you're no angel."

"And we know you're not going to heaven," she retorted playfully. This made him laugh, but it must have made his head hurt worse, too, because he quickly quieted and closed his eyes. Anne watched him worriedly till he opened his eyes again and managed a smile. She smiled back and bent to kiss his forehead. She thought he felt a little warm. Was he getting feverish?

"You don't think the décolletage a tad too low, do you?" said Reggie, flitting a prim glance over Anne's bosom as she straightened. "You are, after all, supposed to be an angel."

Before Anne could reply, Katherine's timely entrance, in the garb of a Tudor-period noblewoman, made Reggie forget all about Anne's décolletage. Katherine wore a purple velvet sheath tied around the middle with a length of gold cord, the skirt hemmed with fur. The long sleeves were fullest at the wrist, also bordered with fur. She wore an ornate headdress and a heavy gold necklace. She looked imposing, but, at the same time, very feminine in the flowing style and soft fabrics.

Reggie's eyes widened. "Who are you supposed to be?" he asked breathlessly.

Katherine gave an embarrassed chuckle. "One of King Henry's wives. I don't care which, but since three of his six unfortunate brides were named Catherine, I suppose I ought to be one of them. Catherine Parr, perhaps?"

"I'm as entertained by your choice, Katherine," said Reggie, speaking with surprised amusement, "as I was by Anne's. Henry was a cruel despot who used women for his own nefarious designs. He had two of his wives executed. There's no way in heaven you'd have married such a man or even tolerated his behavior. I find your choice rather ironic."

"As ironic as my choice to dress as an angel," said Anne.

"That's exactly why I did it," Katherine said, shrugging. "And because I thought the style rather becoming." She hesitated, averting her eyes. "It's purple."

"So it is," he murmured, a sparkle in his eyes.

She bit her lip, smiled, and darted him a quick, shy look. "Besides, since I've had nearly as many husbands as he had wives—"

"Posh! You've only had three . . . so far."

Anne thought this might be an appropriate time to leave them alone. Not that she thought Reggie would propose to her aunt from his sickbed, but she felt intrusive standing there observing their gentle flirting. She slipped out the door without either of them noticing her departure.

As Anne ascended the stairs, she heard the front door being closed softly and the butler murmuring something about "waiting in the drawing room" while he fetched the ladies. Anne debated whether she should alert her aunt to the early arrival of Captain Miller, then decided against it. She'd talk to the fellow for a few minutes, giving Katherine a little more time with Reggie. Aunt Katherine had called the captain ancient, so he must be at least eighty or so. Surely Reggie wouldn't think it improper if she entertained such an elderly gent for a few minutes without a chaperone.

At the foot of the stairs, Bentley the butler bade Anne a grave good evening. "Good evening, Bentley," she answered. "Don't bother to fetch Mrs. Grimms. She'll be down shortly. I'll keep our guest occupied till then." He nodded his understanding, but Anne didn't think he looked very pleased. She entered the drawing room.

As she breezed in, a tall man who was not in the least ancient turned from his inspection of one of Katherine's paintings to face her. It was Jeffrey. He was the last person she expected or wanted to see. Her steps faltered halfway across the room, then she forced a pleasant smile to her lips and continued on, saying, "Jeffrey, how are you? I didn't expect to see you tonight. Are you going to the ball?"

The look on his face when he first turned around was harsh and sulky. He was peeved. He obviously had not recovered from his displeasure of the night before. But Anne acknowledged to herself that her manner had indeed changed drastically toward Jeffrey, and it was only reasonable that he would want to know why. Tonight, however, was not a good time for such a complicated, and necessarily evasive, conversation.

How was she supposed to explain her change in behavior? How could she tell him that she knew he'd lied about his part in Renard's close call two weeks ago? She'd expose her own involvement that night if she did. And how could she tell him she was in love with another man without telling him who that other man was?

His expression had changed. He was looking her up and down, his gaze keen-eyed and lingering. She remembered that she was in costume and decided that that must account for his staring. After a couple of moments, though, the boldness of his stare had gone past excusing. He was ogling her as if he'd like to—

"Jeffrey, I asked you if you were going to the masquerade ball. As you can see, *we* are. Our carriage will be here in just a few minutes."

Finally, after one last leisurely perusal of her low decolletage, his eyes lifted to hers. He'd have to be blind and a fool not to catch the flash of anger there. He looked down for a minute as if he were embarrassed, manhandling the brim of his hat as he held it in his blunt-tipped fingers. But when his gaze met hers again, the sulky, belligerent look was back.

"You're beautiful, Anne. If there are such things as angels, you'd be a divine model."

"Pretty words, Jeffrey," said Anne, "but you're good at words."

His eyes narrowed. "What's that supposed to mean?"

Anne sighed, shook her head, traced the shape of a flower on the carpet with her slipper toe. "It's not supposed to mean anything." She didn't want to get into this. She had far more pressing matters to think about. "I'm sorry."

"Anne, look at me."

She schooled her features into blandness, then looked up. He searched her face and eyes intently, as if he was trying to find answers to his questions

without having to stoop to actually voicing those
questions out loud. He was battling with his male
pride. In the end, his need to know won out over
pride.

His voice was low, his tone tense and frankly
bewildered. "Anne, we were friends. I had hoped
to be more than that to you eventually. You gave
me reason to hope."

Anne nodded. "Yes, I did give you reason to
hope. I thought, at first, that we might be able to
be more than friends."

His eyes brightened a little, but she wasn't sure
if it was from anger or a spark of false hope returning. "What changed your mind? What made
you decide that you and I couldn't be romantically
involved? If I knew what I'd done wrong, maybe
I could . . . fix it."

Anne moved to stand by the grand piano. She
slid her hand over the smooth, polished lid in a
thoughtful gesture. "Jeffrey, when I came to America, I was looking for someone like you. In England, every gentleman I was allowed to associate
with seemed to have had everything handed to
him on a silver salver. These gentlemen had no
purpose in life, no ambition, no strong desire to involve themselves with people or causes beyond
their limited social circle."

She smiled at him. "You were so different. You
used your wits and your determination to succeed, and, against all odds, you did succeed. You
involved yourself in the world around you. In
your articles you championed the good, condemned the wrong. I truly admired what you'd
done with your life."

"Admired? As in the past tense?"

Sadly she said, "Jeffrey . . . you are *too* ambitious."

"What the hell do you mean?"

She turned away. "I can't explain."

He grabbed her arm and roughly turned her to look at him. "I deserve an explanation!"

"You're hurting me," she said with controlled calmness. "Let go of me immediately."

Jeffrey's mouth clamped together. She could see a muscle working convulsively in his jaw. She could imagine his teeth grinding together in frustration. They were at a standoff, face to face, eye to eye. Finally he released her.

"You're in love with someone else, aren't you?" he said truculently.

Anne gave a soft laugh that implied denial. "Why do men always assume—"

"I saw you gawking moon-eyed at Delacroix across the opera house last night. Christ, I couldn't believe it! Why you'd look twice at him is beyond me. He's everything you hate. He makes mock of everything you believe in. Then, when he came to the box because your watchdog of an uncle waved him over, I saw how he looked at you."

"Uncle Reggie likes Delacroix," Anne began, her heart pounding. Had it been so obvious what she and Lucien were feeling?

"Your uncle likes him because he doesn't think Delacroix's man enough to compromise you, that's all. And because he and your uncle are birds of a feather, all fuss and no fight."

Now Anne was angry. No one was going to talk that way about the two men she loved most in the world. And he was so wrong about them! If he only knew ... With much effort, she kept the truth to herself, but not the anger. Coldly she said, "If you persist in talking about my uncle and my friend Delacroix that way, I'll have to ask you to leave."

Jeffrey looked incredulous. "Your *friend* Delacroix? And I suppose you and I aren't even that
anymore? Not even friends! God, Anne, what's
happened to you?"

"My eyes have been opened, that's all. Now I
see people for who they really are."

"I suppose I'm included in that top-lofty summation of humanity," muttered Jeffrey. "You think
you know me now, and you don't like what you
think you know. Or, more probably, Reggie's finally convinced you I'm not good enough for
you."

Anne recognized what she thought was real regret in Jeffrey's voice. She didn't believe he was a
bad person, just on a slightly compromised path
right now, driven by his over-ambition. She
couldn't let him leave believing that she thought
he wasn't good enough for her. It could possibly
be the last time they'd meet privately, the last time
they'd talk so honestly. Impulsively she took his
hand.

"Jeffrey, I'm sorry. I'm so sorry if I've hurt you.
I've never thought of you as beneath me in any
way. I do want us to part as friends."

Jeffrey's expression, curious and eager when
Anne first took his hand, turned ugly. "Well, I've
sure as hell thought of you beneath *me*." At Anne's
shocked look, he squeezed her hand harder, ignoring her attempts to pull free. "I've thought of you
beneath me, naked and writhing in passion. And
that's just one position. I've thought of you,
dreamed of you in a hundred different ways since
the day I met you."

"Jeffrey, let go . . ."

He squeezed harder, pulled her closer till his
breath hissed across her face. "And if I can't have
you like that, I don't want you at all." Then he

pushed her away and walked swiftly out of the room, leaving Anne shocked and angry. She moved to a wing chair and sank into the cushions, crushing her wings behind her.

She'd certainly handled Jeffrey all wrong. His infatuation with her was as much her fault as his. How she wished she could go back and change her behavior over the past weeks!

After a few minutes of silent self-lecturing, she heard Captain Miller's carriage pull up outside. She took a deep breath, rallying her spirits. She couldn't change the past, but she could do her best with the future. She hoped her future would be a rosy one with Lucien ... but only if everything went as planned tonight.

Jeffrey leaned against an outside wall of a saloon on Bourbon Street. He looked casually to the left and the right, watching for the familiar stride of his favorite and most reliable mole. The one inside Renard's ranks. The one who would do just about anything for money. Jeffrey could understand that motivation. He planned to have plenty of money very soon. Things hadn't worked out with the English heiress, but there was another, less honorable route to take, and, after his interview with Anne tonight, he was prepared to take it.

Jeffrey rubbed two coins together in his hand, the other hand shoved in his pocket, one knee bent, the foot flat against the wall. He stared at the coins, heavy, golden, and shiny, like Anne's hair. He shook his head, bitterness burning in his throat.

He supposed it had been too perfect to work out. She was beautiful and rich, too, a fact he'd quickly made sure of before trying so hard to woo her. Winning her would have made him the envy of everyone in town. As when his embellished article had hit the press. Everyone had stared at him on the street, thought of him as a hero. It had felt good, damned good.

Marrying Anne would have been the best move of his life. He'd have finally convinced everyone else that he was good enough, that he'd put so much distance between himself and that hellhole foundling home in Baltimore that no one would ever remember where he'd come from.

But what the hell. There was another way to get rich. And once he had the money, he'd find another woman—one less complicated than Anne. He fantasized for one last time about her.

Yes, it was too bad. Too bad.

Then he saw his mole. Nonchalantly he eased into the alley next to the saloon, cursing when a drunk followed him and started retching. Jeffrey sidestepped the vomit, hoping none of it had splashed on his new trousers, then went halfway down the alley and waited. Soon a dark figure headed his way, gingerly making a wide circle around the pool of puke. The drunk had disappeared and was undoubtedly back inside the saloon, drinking again.

Now he and the mole were face to face. Jeffrey smiled, full of happy plans. "Christian, my friend," he said. "What's the word?"

Chapter 19

"I'm not your friend," said Christian, resting his shoulders against the opposite wall and glaring hatefully at Jeffrey. "We do business together, that's all."

"A thousand pardons," mocked Jeffrey, his good humor not in the least diminished by Christian's surliness. He was used to the man's mercurial moods. It was Christian's opium addiction, and probably his guilt, that made him so changeable. "Your note said Renard was assisting another escape."

Reluctantly Christian said, "He is."

Jeffrey waited, then finally prompted him. "So? Where and when?"

Christian wiped his nose, shifted against the wall, averted his eyes. "I'm not sure I'm going to tell you this time."

"Then why are you here?"

Christian turned his head and fixed Jeffrey with an accusing stare. "Where did those bounty hunters come from last time, Wycliff? I didn't tell you the location of the rendezvous point so you could sic bounty hunters on Renard. I told you so you could get your sensational story for that damned paper you work for." Christian looked disgusted. "And was it ever sensational."

Jeffrey shrugged, uncomfortable for an instant, but only an instant. "Adding a little drama is the usual procedure. And, for your information, I didn't alert those bounty hunters. I don't know how they found out."

"They found out because you had loose lips that week. Word got out on the street."

"I've kept *your* dirty little secret, haven't I? I could easily start rumors that would convince Renard you've been snitching to support your filthy opium habit."

"But you won't because you need me, not because you want to protect me. But, unlike you, I do have some natural human feelings. I won't have Renard and his men placed in unnecessary danger again. Lives could have been lost that night. If I tell you what's happening next, I must have your word that you'll keep the information entirely to yourself till the deed's done. Then, and only then, can you talk about it and print what you saw in the paper."

"That's easy enough."

Christian studied him for a minute, looking dissatisfied, indecisive. He shook his head, sighed. "I don't know."

"What do you mean, 'You don't know'?" What do you want? A promissory note?"

Christian pushed off from the wall and pointed a finger at Jeffrey. "If you cross me on this, I swear I'll kill you."

Jeffrey's stomach twisted at the succinct, soft-spoken threat, but he feigned unconcern. He shrugged.

"And no boasting ahead of time," Christian added.

Jeffrey bristled. "I don't boast."

Christian sneered. "You did to Anne Weston."

"What the hell are you talking about?"

"Why do you suppose she was there that night, too, dressed like a man?"

Jeffrey was stunned. "Anne?" he choked out at last. "Anne was the fellow who—"

Christian seemed to enjoy Jeffrey's shocked expression, his obvious humiliation. A small, superior smile tilted his lips. Jeffrey wished he could wipe that smirk off his face with his knuckles, but Christian was big and muscled. He dared not attempt it. "Yes, Wycliff. I wonder how she felt when she read your account in the *Picayune*, attributing the saving of Renard's life to your own doing. I understand she thinks quite highly of integrity. Did you ruin your chances with the girl by telling a tiny lie or two?"

"Shut up!" snarled Jeffrey. Suddenly everything became crystal clear. No wonder she'd suddenly become so distant, so cool. What a fool he'd been! But how the hell could he have possibly known that that skinny young man was Anne? Shapely, long-haired Anne tricked out like a man? He'd figured the fellow was one of Renard's cohorts, or fans. They'd ridden off together, hadn't they? Then another suspicion crossed his mind. A suspicion that galled him like no other.

"Renard and Anne . . . I know they outran the bounty hunters, but where did they go after that? She idolizes the man, but he wouldn't . . . ?" Jeffrey couldn't quite get the words out. He was seething with anger and jealousy. "Did Renard . . . bed her?"

Christian merely shrugged. "Do you think I know everything? Renard's sex life is his business, not mine."

Jeffrey swallowed this blow to his pride with considerable difficulty. Anne knew he'd been no hero that night. She'd followed him and hid herself, waiting, just as he'd hid and waited. So she knew that he'd only squatted inside a rose arbor and watched the drama played out by others. Even when he'd seen the shadows of the bounty hunters creeping up on Renard from the cemetery, he'd frozen.

As much as he admired the outlaw for his derring-do, he'd not had enough gumption himself to warn Renard of the imminent danger. But Anne had, he thought grimly. Anne had risked her own life to save Renard's. Renard had probably been extremely grateful for that, and, besotted fool that she was, she had probably been extremely accommodating.

"I haven't got time to stand here all night while you sulk," said Christian.

Jeffrey rallied, more determined than ever to carry out his plan. "You're the one withholding information. I'm just waiting to hear where the escape is going to take place, and when."

"How much will you pay me?"

"The paper will only allow me a hundred dollars bribe money a month, as you know."

"That's not enough." He turned to go.

"No, wait," said Jeffrey, desperate. "I've got some money of my own. Say another hundred?"

Christian paused, considered. "Three hundred altogether."

"Why so greedy all of a sudden?"

"I have a feeling . . ." Christian's brows knit together. "Renard's been more reticent lately with information. He's no fool. I'm sure he suspects a leak. Hell, he might already suspect me, and without your rumors to fuel the fire. I think he's going to disappear soon. This could be his last assisted slave escape." He smiled ruefully. "You won't need me anymore, and I'll have to get my money elsewhere."

"Then why don't you tell me who he really is?" Jeffrey said nonchalantly. "I'd pay you plenty for that information. You could have a neat stash put away."

"Do you take me for a fool? Why would you pay good money for information if you weren't going to turn it around and make more money? You're thinking it would make quite a headliner, aren't you? You'd really be a big shot at the paper then."

Jeffrey faked a hurt expression. "Do you think I'd do that to Renard? I'm on his side. I always have been. Everything I've ever written about him has been glowing. I could have alerted the authorities with that last information you gave me, but I didn't."

Christian looked at him keenly, suspiciously. "I used to believe you were on Renard's side, but I'm not so sure anymore. Sometimes I think you're on whatever side's most lucrative for you, that you're too ambitious."

Hearing Anne's words repeated by this pathetic snitch stung Jeffrey to the quick. He wanted this interview over as soon as possible. He pulled out a wad of bills and gave them to Christian. "Three hundred. You can count it if you want, but it's all there."

Christian took the money almost reluctantly. *The fool,* thought Jeffrey, *he's got too many scruples.* "Now tell me."

"The escape is planned for midnight, at the bayou behind the slave cabins on Bocage."

"Dandy Delacroix's plantation, eh?" Jeffrey smiled, cheered to hear that Delacroix's slaves were the escapees this time, even though in the end the slaves would not get away.

"But not Delacroix's slaves," Christian clarified. "The escaping slaves are coming from Rosedown."

Jeffrey took this disappointing news in stride. "Rosedown, you say? Yes, there's a ball there tonight, isn't there? A good time to sneak away, I suppose."

"Remember what I said about leaking this information before the deed's done, Wycliff," was Christian's parting threat. "If anything happens to my brother, I'll kill you." Then he turned and walked away, leaving Jeffrey alone in the alley.

He stood there for a minute, feeling the impact of Christian's words, feeling his blood chill and his heart beat hard and fast. For once, he told himself, he was going to have to be brave. If, as Christian speculated, Renard was going to hang up his mask, this was Jeffrey's last chance.

It was regrettable that Renard was going to have to pay the price for Jeffrey's financial windfall, but he didn't feel that badly about it. After all, he'd only pretended to champion the outlaw's cause. Renard had simply been an excellent subject to write sensational articles about, articles that had considerably furthered his own journalistic career. He admired Renard more for his image than for his ideals. But his admiration for the man was no reason to spare him. Money was money.

Jeffrey left the alley and headed down the street to the Calaboso and the police.

The ball was a crushing success. Americans and Creoles alike were invited to the home of the modern-thinking Bouviers; they didn't discriminate, as a lot of Creole families did. In fact, one of their daughters had recently married a rich American, which made the integration of the two cultures almost mandatory.

When they first arrived, Captain Miller, dressed in a simple black domino, retired immediately to the card room, and Anne and Katherine stood on the periphery of the dancing and took in the scene. Anne was enthralled. She'd never been to a masquerade in her life. This one was done on such a grand scale, it was overwhelming to imagine how much money had probably been spent on this single event.

It had been too dark to see the grounds around the house as they drove up in Captain Miller's sedately paced carriage, but the front facade, basking in the glow of torchlight, was quite interesting. It was a traditional plantation house, not a modern building with the classical pillars and lines so favored by the rich lately. Anne couldn't help wondering if Lucien's Bocage was similar. She knew the Delacroix estate adjoined the Bouviers'.

In the back of the house, down the hallway, was the ballroom. Obviously the room had been built to be used specifically for balls, and only for balls.

Anne looked up. Above the dancers were several huge crystal chandeliers. It must have taken dozens of servants—or slaves—to light all the tapers. Her eyes dropped again to floor level, where innumerable historical and fictional characters were represented, the myriad colors of their costumes flashing in the candle glow.

A daring Marie Antoinette danced with a Mohawk Indian brave. Caesar Augustus showed off his shapely legs in a short toga. Robin Hood flirted with a sultry Cleopatra. A medieval knight made the turns of the dance with ease despite his restrictive armor, while the nubile black cat in his arms held her tail instead of her skirt as they swirled and dipped to the lilting strains of a Viennese waltz.

Anne looked for Lucien, but so far she had not spied him anywhere. She smiled to herself, wondering what costume he'd worn. She'd teased him last night to tell her, but he'd insisted that he wanted to surprise her.

When the dance ended, several gentlemen immediately descended upon Anne. She agreed to dance with a man dressed like Napoleon. Despite his mask, she recognized him as Edward Dean, a friend of her aunt's. She was sure it wouldn't be difficult to recognize most of the people she knew, because only a few faces were actually obscured by cosmetics or fake beards or full masks. Some, like Captain Miller, wore only domino capes and masks over their usual evening wear. But where was Lucien?"

"Miss Weston," said Edward, peering down into Anne's face, "would you think me terribly forward if I told you how *heavenly* you look tonight?"

Anne smiled obligingly at the witticism. "No, Mr. Dean. However, I hope your Josephine doesn't get jealous if she sees you dancing with me."

"Don't worry, Miss Weston. You won't lose your head over it." Anne laughed, as she was supposed to.

The dance was almost over before she saw Lucien. He was conversing with King Henry the Eighth, who, on closer inspection, proved to be exactly the person Anne expected him to be talking to—Charles Bodine. As for Lucien, he was dressed like a frontiersman.

Anne couldn't believe it. When she'd first met Jeffrey, she had imagined him in just such a get-up, thinking that because of his resourceful American ways, he deserved a more rustic image. But Jeffrey could never have done justice to those tight-fitting buckskins and knee-high fringed boots. Nor could the beaver-tailed cap have sat so rakishly on Jeffrey's head, or the rifle looked so right hanging over his shoulder.

Anne's breath was suspended. Lucien looked even more virile than usual. Women would be flocking to him all evening. In fact, his coterie of females was already forming. Hovering nearby were two women, apparently just waiting for Lucien to look up from his close conversation with Bodine and notice them. Anne felt a stab of jealousy. If only she were more certain of Lucien's feelings for her, perhaps she wouldn't be so vulnerable to unwelcome anxieties . . .

While she was being twirled about the dance floor in Napoleon's arms, Anne couldn't tell if Lucien had seen her or not. When Napoleon returned her to her aunt's side, Anne said in a whisper, "Did you see Lucien, Aunt Katherine?"

"No. Have you?"

"Yes." Anne nodded in his direction. "He's over there, in the corner . . . with your husband, King Henry."

Katherine's eyebrows lifted. She looked, she pursed her lips. "How appropriate. One despot playing another. He treats his slaves like Henry treated his wives."

"Yes. Reggie would enjoy the irony, wouldn't he?"

Katherine's brows knitted. "Yes, he would. I

wonder how he's doing. How long do we have to
stay at this stupid ball before we can go home
and check on that stubborn old fool? I'd feel
much better if only he'd let us call for the doctor."

"You left word with Theresa and James to send
a message if Reggie got any worse, didn't you?"

"Yes, but—"

"Uncle Reggie would be angry if we left too
early. We haven't even seen our host and hostess
yet." Anne's voice lowered and grew slightly petulant. "And, though I know it's selfish of me, I'd
really like to dance with Lucien just once before
we leave. However, with so many women vying
for his attention, perhaps I won't get the opportunity."

Katherine squeezed her hand. "I'm sure Lucien
will dance with you if he gets the chance, but you
can't expect him to spend much time with you. A
single dance might not be wondered at, but people
know you two have opposite political philosophies."

Anne saw Lucien lead a woman dressed seductively as a Persian slave girl onto the dance floor.
When he took her in his arms for a waltz, he whispered something in her ear that made her laugh.
Anne's heart ached with longing. She wished he
were whispering in *her* ear.

Just then she and Katherine were approached by
several more acquaintances and were obliged to
socialize. Smiling determinedly they did their
duty. Reggie would have been proud.

Lucien could barely concentrate on what Mademoiselle Petit was saying. She smiled at him
through her transparent veil and murmured something about wanting to be part of his "harem," but

nothing she said or did was stimulating enough to keep his mind off Anne. Anne ... dressed as an angel. She'd always looked like something celestial to him, but were angels supposed to look so damned seductive?

He counted the minutes till he could take her in his arms and dance with her. Since that was all he could do in front of three hundred people, dancing would have to suffice. At least then he'd get a whiff of her light scent, be able to look down into those bright blue eyes, hear her voice, tell her how beautiful she was.

He decided to wait till just before late supper was served. He'd be leaving right after that, when people would be reorganizing and sauntering back into the ballroom, the card room, outside on the lawn. He and Bodine could slip away then without it being remarked upon. He'd take him to Bocage and start the beginning of the end. The end of Renard, and, he hoped, the end of Bodine.

He mingled. He pretended interest in all sorts of insipid conversations. He was insipid himself. He danced with scores of women, with whom he flirted shamelessly. He made each of them laugh, simper, and blush, then went on to his next partner. He played the part of charming rogue so well, heads turned in his direction all evening—some people smiling, some frowning.

Then the moment he'd been waiting for arrived. He'd been watching Anne surreptitiously all night. She'd certainly had no lack of dancing partners, either, and he knew he'd have to be aggressive in getting past all the would-be swains that clustered around her the minute she left the dance floor.

One dance had just ended, and in three minutes

another would begin. In that short interim he'd have to make his way across the room and gain possession of Anne's hand before someone else claimed it. And even if someone did claim it, he'd state a prior commitment. What the hell. He moved across the room.

He was there, she was there, all the swains were there. She looked up at him, unsmiling, rosy from dancing—or was she upset? He hoped the former. He bowed low, sweeping his beaver-tailed hat off his head and gallantly crushing it to his chest.

"Mademoiselle Weston," he intoned in his best drawl, "I believe this dance is ours."

"You're just a tad late, Delacroix," said young Richard Waverly, squinting belligerently through the eyeholes of a black mask under a huge sombrero. "She's already promised this dance to me."

"Sorry, Monsieur Waverly," said Lucien, "but hours ago I secured Mademoiselle Weston's promise for the last dance before supper." He turned to Anne. "You do remember, mademoiselle? You had just arrived . . . ?" Lucien raised his brows.

After a slight hesitation that confused Lucien, Anne took her cue. "Oh, yes. I do remember now, Mr. Delacroix." She turned a regretful face to Richard. "I'm sorry, Mr. Waverly. Perhaps the first dance after supper?"

Richard appeared placated with the promise of future bliss and bowed himself away. Lucien, however, did not miss the scathing look cast his way from under the retreating sombrero. Lucien couldn't have cared less. The prize was his.

He took Anne's hand and led her onto the dance floor. The strains of a waltz floated from the orchestra balcony. He drew her into his arms, but found her rather stiff. She averted her face.

"What's the matter, Anne?" he asked, concern making his tone harsh. "Has someone been annoying you?"

"Oh, yes," she remarked coolly. "A man has been annoying me all evening."

His jaw set. Grimly he asked, "Who? I'll land the fellow a facer. Did he dare touch you? Did he speak disrespectfully to you?"

Anne's blue eyes flashed up at him through her thick tawny lashes. "Indeed, I've been wanting him to touch me all night—"

"What?"

"—or at least notice my existence. But he's been far too occupied entertaining half the female population of New Orleans to notice little ol' me." Her accusing gaze slid away, and she turned her face again.

Lucien's tight muscles relaxed. He recognized jealousy when he saw it. Didn't the little baggage know it was important to maintain his roguish reputation? Especially tonight.

Actually he rather enjoyed her desire to keep him to herself. He felt the same way about her. But he couldn't resist teasing her a little.

"I danced with half the female population of New Orleans, Mademoiselle Weston," he said gravely, "because . . ."

She turned to face him, arched a dubious brow. "Because why, Mr. Delacroix?"

"Because the other half are too old to dance."

Anne's mouth pursed, but her eyes gleamed. Lucien hoped she was finding humor in the situation and not just getting angrier. "Madame Dupois is at least seventy. You danced with *her*. And, I might add, you danced with her before you danced with me."

"Madame Dupois is an exception to the rule. Although she has a touch of rheumatism and is definitely part of the female population expected to sit instead of dance, I was able to persuade her to do otherwise."

"You enjoy that, don't you?"

"What, dancing?"

"No, persuading women to do your bidding."

He grinned at her. "I plead guilty."

She shook her head, trying not to smile. "That's just what you said to the man in the alley when you knocked him on the head with your cane. Are you always so ready to own up to your crimes?"

"Always."

"Then someone should tell you that it's criminal for you to wear those buckskin breeches in public." She slid him a coy glance. "They make you look far too masculine."

"But if I hadn't been wearing them, I'd never have convinced Madame Dupois to dance with me. She may be seventy, but she's got a keen eye for a good leg."

Anne grinned. Lucien was thrilled to be finally winning her over again. "Conceited popinjay! But I must admit that the old gal has good taste. With you in that costume, even I might be tempted to do your bidding."

The distance between them was just enough that Anne could flick an interested eye over the entire length of his person. In the aftermath of her quick but thorough scrutiny, Lucien felt the blood pulse through his veins. It was as though she'd caressed him. Their gazes met, and he saw playful arousal reflected in the depths of her blue eyes. "Yes, the breeches are quite effective," she said demurely, "but I must confess I like everything I see."

Lucien had thought himself well past the age of blushing, but apparently not. He felt the heat in his neck, ears, and cheeks. He probably looked like a red-faced, half-strangled Johnny Raw in his first stiff, store-bought cravat. And though dancing had always been an easy, effortless activity for him, now he suddenly felt clumsy and nervous, mindful of watching his feet.

"Sweet Anne," he groaned, all the while trying to keep up his usual bored facade, "you've turned the tables on me. Now instead of me teasing you, you're teasing me. Do you know what you do to me?"

"I know what I'd like to do to you."

He missed a beat, tripped slightly, and quickly swept her into a smooth turn.

"You covered that nicely, Mr. Delacroix," she said, stroking his shoulder with the tiniest movement of her thumb. "No one would have suspected that we were about to tumble onto the floor, now would they?"

"If you persist in tantalizing me, Mademoiselle Weston, we may yet find ourselves prone on the ballroom floor, and in a position that might embarrass you in front of all these pillars of society." He smiled politely.

"Your hints of impending debauchery, Mr. Delacroix," said Anne with wide-eyed innocence, "trouble me not at all."

Lucien's hand on her waist involuntarily tightened. "You look like an angel, and, God knows, you feel heavenly in my arms, but you torture me with the wicked glee of a temptress from hell."

Her eyes danced with mischief. "You deserve it. Besides, would you have me any other way?"

He gave her a leering grin. "Right now, Anne, I'd have you anyway and anywhere I could!"

They both laughed but grew quickly serious, knowing that they spoke the truth in jest. They stared at each other for a long, lingering moment, till a couple brushed close by and recalled them to reality and prudence. Lucien returned to his droopy-eyed dandy's persona, and Anne smiled vacuously at passing dancers. When the music ended, he bent briefly to her ear and whispered, "Meet me in the garden behind the statue of the unknown woman," then bowed and walked away.

Anne was supposed to meet her aunt in the supper room, but she escaped through a side entrance and went around to the back of the house. She saw three other couples who would rather tryst than eat supper, cuddling and kissing in the moonlit Rosedown garden. She had no idea where the statue was, or even what it looked like, and she wandered deep into the lush greenery of trees and bushes searching for it.

At last, far away from the other romantic couples, Anne saw an ancient statue that looked as if it had been transported from some ruined villa in Italy. It was a woman in a long toga with outstretched arms. The look on her stone face was one of longing. Anne stood, staring at the statue's poignant expression, till a human arm reached out and tugged her into the shadows behind it. Enclosed on all sides by shrubs or stone, Anne was once again alone with Lucien.

"You didn't scream," he said, pulling her against his chest.

"I knew it was you. You're the only man I know

who grabs at me out of the shadows." She locked her arms around his neck. The pattern of moonlight through gently stirring leaves played over his face. She could just make out his smile, then she saw it disappear.

"I had to see you, hold you, one more time before—"

Anne's heart filled with dread. "Before what?"

He sighed. "Before the night is over."

"Because something important is happening tonight?"

"I only have two minutes, Anne. Two minutes that I don't intend to spend talking."

Before she could say another word, Lucien had covered her mouth with his. His lips were warm and firm, his kisses deeper and more demanding than ever before. She felt his passion and urgency and returned it completely. She pressed against him, her body touching his at every intimate point.

He broke their kiss, gasping, then caught her at the waist and lifted her, nuzzling her neck and chest with his lips. She slid down, and his hands cupped her breasts, his thumbs rubbing over the hard nubs of her nipples.

Blood rushed through her body, pooling in all the sensitive spots. Moisture gathered at her woman's core. Just in that minute of kissing, he'd made her want him desperately. And, judging by the hard jut of his manhood against her, he wanted her equally as much.

He kissed her again on the mouth, his tongue mating urgently with hers, driving her near madness with desire. She turned her head, saying breathlessly against his cheek, "Two minutes? Perhaps that's long enough to—"

He chuckled, but his voice was shaky. "No, it's

not nearly enough time to do justice to the passion I have for you, sweet Anne. Another time, another place."

She pulled away, holding his face between her hands. "Oh, yes, Lucien! Another time, another place. *Promise* me!" She felt tears stinging her eyelids.

She could feel his sudden reserve, his drawing back, even as she held him close. "It's time to go back inside. Katherine will be looking for you."

"I don't want to go yet."

"You have to. I'll watch you till you get inside." He gently pushed her away.

"I love you, Lucien."

"Good night, Anne." He turned slightly, his face suddenly completely obscured by shadows.

She crossed her arms in a viselike hug, as if she could hold in all the worry, all the fear. She looked longingly one more time at his shadowy figure, then turned and walked dejectedly toward the house.

"Be careful," she whispered under her breath. "Come back to me."

Lucien watched Anne go inside to sit at supper with her aunt. God! Making her leave him was like losing part of his own soul. He wished he could give her the assurances she craved; he hated seeing her so anxious. But in another minute he would meet Bodine at the spot they'd agreed on to escort the blackguard over a harvested sugarcane field to Bocage, and Lucien was achingly aware that the outcome of events in the next few hours would determine his future ... and Anne's ...

As supper was being served, Katherine looked in vain for Anne. She'd watched her dancing with

Lucien. She'd seen how they'd pretended indifference. She acknowledged that to the unsuspicious eye they had probably succeeded in making Anne appear as just another target for Delacroix's flirtatious assaults. But Katherine noticed toward the end of the dance that they were struggling, that they were doing everything in their power to maintain a very tenuous hold on their emotions.

Now she couldn't see either of them in the throng of people politely pushing their way into the supper room. She concluded with dismay that they'd sneaked off somewhere to relieve those feelings of frustration. She, too, knew what it was to be frustrated, but couldn't the hot-blooded little fools have waited one more day? Though Lucien had given her no details, she knew he was posing as Renard one last time tonight. She knew Bodine was involved, and she knew the operation was risky. Perhaps that was why Lucien had taken Anne somewhere private. Maybe he was afraid it would be their last time together.

"Mrs. Grimms?" Katherine turned at the obsequious voice at her elbow. It was one of the Bouviers' liveried slaves, a young man decked out in a white wig and knee-breeches. He held out a silver salver with a small folded paper upon it. There was no envelope, as if the note had been sent in haste. She took the note with trembling fingers. It had to be news of Reggie. She unfolded the paper and read the brief contents, feeling the blood drain from her head at the same moment.

The slave caught her elbow, steadying her as she swayed. Grateful for his support, Katherine forced herself to breathe deeply. Now was not the time to fall apart. Reggie needed her. He had yellow fever.

* * *

Jeffrey stood in a dark corner with his arms folded. He'd been watching Anne all night. Dressed as a specter, his face covered with a chalky paste, his eyes smudged and hollowed with black greasepaint, his lips bloodred, and his form covered from head to toe by a hooded cape, he'd had no trouble keeping to himself. He looked like a corpse—like death itself.

He'd seen the way Anne and Delacroix had looked at each other while they were dancing. He'd noticed how she'd glanced Delacroix's way all night. And Jeffrey had seen her leave the house to meet him in the garden. He'd even followed her, and while he couldn't see them, he could hear Anne and Delacroix murmuring to each other, kissing and caressing in the shadows. It was obvious they were lovers. The damned girl had barely allowed him a little kiss, but judging by the sounds that came from behind the statue, she had allowed Delacroix access to all her charms!

The hateful feelings coursing through Jeffrey's body showed plainly on his face, making him appear more frightening than ever. No one came near him. A superstitious lot, the Creoles especially kept their distance. He smiled grimly. Maybe they thought he really was a specter of the grave, a bad omen sent by dark forces to warn some unfortunate sinner of impending death.

The image suited his mood tonight. If he had his way, tonight would be the last night on earth for Renard. And Delacroix. Jeffrey bit the inside of his mouth till he drew blood. How could he have missed the obvious for so long? Now he knew. Now he knew that Anne didn't have it in her to love more than one man at a time. He knew Renard and Delacroix were one and the same.

He smiled again, less grimly. But such a smile on such a face gave an evil effect. He headed for the door, surprised to see Katherine Grimms hurry out before him, her expression full of worry. Outside, an elderly gentleman assisted her into a carriage, and they drove off helter-skelter. Jeffrey's curiosity was piqued, but he had an appointment to keep with the New Orleans Guardians of the Peace. He ordered his horse to be brought around, mounted the handsome steed he'd rented just for the night, then turned the animal west, toward Bocage.

Chapter 20

〰〰〰

Carrying a low-burning lantern, Lucien and Bodine walked side by side across the marshy field, keeping their separate thoughts, as silent and secret as oysters. Bodine was probably contemplating the treat ahead, the black virgin woman-child Lucien had promised him. Lucien was going over the details of the plan in his head, again and again. Everything seemed to be in order. As one last measure of security, though, he sent a prayer winging upward. *May the saints help me do this one final favor for the abolitionist movement*, he prayed. *May the saints help keep me alive for Anne and the future I hope we will have together.*

They were just yards away from the circle of slave cabins. House slaves lived in cabins near the manor house, but field hands were logically placed in cabins close to the acreage they worked. Lucien had chosen the outlying cluster of cabins to play out his farce on Bodine. Naturally he took him to the most remote cabin of all, standing virtually by itself in a grove of trees.

As they approached the door of the small wooden building, Bodine stopped and turned toward Lucien. The lantern glow played over Bodine's face, revealing the bloating and the deep lines of a depraved life. "This is it?"

"*Oui.*"

"There's no light inside the cabin."

"I told you, I don't want the other slaves to know about this."

"If she screams, they'll know."

"True." Lucien shrugged. "But maybe she won't scream."

Bodine found this idea interesting enough to spur him to movement. He walked toward the door, lifted the latch. Over his shoulder, he glared at Lucien. "You aren't going to stand out here all night, are you? I'll take as much time as I want."

Lucien spread his hands wide. "As much as you want," he agreed.

Bodine grunted, then opened the door and went inside. Lucien waited. Less than a minute later he heard a dull *thunk* and then the sound of a heavy body falling to a dirt floor. Smiling, he went inside.

Armande was standing over the unconscious body, holding an iron skillet. Lucien winced when he saw the size and weight of the weapon. "I hope you didn't kill him."

"Of course not," said Armande, offended. "I knew just where to hit him and how hard. He'll be out for several hours, long enough to serve our purpose."

Lucien looked around the small cabin. "Where is the bag?"

"Under the mattress. If something went wrong, I didn't want the evidence in plain sight."

"*Bon.*" He pulled the burlap sack from under the mattress and untied the rope at the puckered closure. "I don't relish this part," he said dryly. "We have to touch him."

Armande nodded, grimaced. "But at least by lantern glow we won't have to see much of him."

"True. I suppose we should be thankful for small favors, *n'est-ce pas?*"

"There's little time left, *mon ami*. We'd better get busy."

"*Oui*," said Lucien, then bent to the task.

Anne watched from behind the thick trunk of a sycamore tree. She was breathless from catching up with Lucien as he left the grounds of Rosedown. She had stealthily followed him and Bodine as they crossed the field to Bocage. Then she had seen Bodine go inside the cabin, and a moment later watched as Lucien followed. The cabin was softly lit from the inside by a low-burning lantern, but thin curtains covered the windows. She decided to wait and watch from a safe distance. She didn't want to jeopardize Lucien's plan, whatever it was. She just wanted to be on hand in case she was needed.

She'd been waiting only fifteen minutes or so when the cabin door opened and Lucien and Armande emerged, carrying between them the body of a large man. Anne bit her lip. The body of a large, lifeless-looking man!

My God, she thought, *they've killed him! They've killed Bodine!* She knew he wanted to stop Bodine's abuse of his slaves before ending his career as Renard, but she never dreamed he'd do something so drastic.

They carried the body around to the back of the cabin. The lantern dangled from Armande's elbow, illuminating a small patch of ground at his feet and casting thin, jumpy shafts of light over his sober face. Lucien was in darkness. They moved surprisingly fast, considering their luggage, and soon they were yards away from the cabin, surrounded by cypress woods.

Anne followed, keeping the same safe distance as before. Twigs caught and tore at her skirt, bark scratched her exposed skin, wet leaves rubbed against her face, and insects circled her head like buzzards around a carcass. Her slippers sank in the mud. Without the straps around her ankles, she'd have lost them completely.

She was sure they were close to the bayou by now. She wondered if they were going to bury Bodine, or perhaps leave him for the alligators. The thought made her sick to her stomach. Suddenly they stopped moving. She heard the soft snort of a horse. Lucien and Armande whispered to each other, then made grunting sounds, as if they were making a concerted effort to lift a large object. Were they putting Bodine on a horse? Why? Where were they going to take him?

The trees were close together, and what little moonlight had shone through the foliage before was now blocked by overhanging tree branches thick with Spanish moss. The lantern Armande carried didn't help her to see them better, either; the dim beams bounced erratically off objects, not shining long enough on anything for Anne to get a good look.

Then she realized that there was more than one horse. In fact, there were probably three. The lantern was swinging at least four feet above the ground. She saw the dark, sleek flanks of the horses, a brief flash of a horse's bit. She heard the suck of hooves in mud, the soft squeak of leather. Armande and Lucien were mounted, and Armande held the tether of the horse that carried Bodine. They turned north and trotted briskly away—or as briskly as they could through the swampy cypress woods.

It didn't occur to Anne till it was over that she'd been left quite alone in the habitat of alligators and snakes. It hadn't occurred to her, either, to call out to Lucien as he rode away. She was in shock, she supposed. Shocked that Lucien could commit murder . . .

If not for her fond wish to survive to a ripe old age, and her dislike of creatures that slithered up a person's leg uninvited, Anne might have stood there numbly for hours, contemplating what this new development meant to her relationship with Lucien. Instead, she turned and headed back toward the slave cabins.

It didn't take her long, and she breathed a sigh of relief as the clearing came into view. Her relief was short-lived, however. She saw horses picking their way slowly across the marshy sugarcane field. It was too dark to make out who the riders were, but she could bet they were the police. She counted five altogether. Had they somehow learned that Lucien was planning murder tonight? Did they know he was Renard? Had the snitch in his organization gone to the police with information that could put Lucien in prison for life?

They'd seen her; she heard murmurs among them as they approached. She stood there, tense, waiting. Then one rider separated from the others and pulled up in front of her. His cape billowed out behind him. His white face glowed with preternatural eeriness in the faint moonglow. Her heart nearly stopped. She was staring at the mask of death. Visions of voodoo and gris-gris and strange sacrificial rites flashed through her terrified mind. Then the specter smiled.

"Hello, Anne," said Jeffrey. "Out for a stroll?"

"Jeffrey," she said faintly. "What are you doing here?"

"I asked you first."

"You're with the police ..." Her eyes narrowed. "Why?"

"As if you didn't know," he said in an undertone, then turned to one of the officers. "She's a friend of mine. I'm going to take her up on my horse. It's dangerous leaving her out here alone."

The police officer moved his horse closer, staring down at Anne. "You don't think it would be even more dangerous to take her with us?"

"No," said Jeffrey. "I'll keep her well out of harm's way."

Anne was sure of this. After all, Jeffrey always managed to keep *himself* out of harm's way.

"Who are you, young lady?" asked the officer who was apparently in charge of the patrol.

"Anne Weston," she answered.

"What are you doing traipsing around in the middle of the night?"

"I was at the Bouviers' ball," she began, but she didn't know how to explain why she was walking the outskirts of Bocage, so fell silent.

Jeffrey, who was clearly a better impromptu liar than she was, supplied her with an alibi. "I was at the Bouviers' ball till just a few minutes ago. Don't be embarrassed, Miss Weston. I saw you leave with that young man—someone in a red domino mask and cape?" He turned back to the officer. "It was a tryst, sir, and now the cad has gone off and left her. Isn't that right, Miss Weston? By the way, Anne, this gentleman is Lieutenant Dutillet."

Anne decided it was better to go along with Jeffrey's story than to deny it. She lifted her chin. "Yes. He was a cad, all right. But I blackened his eye."

A couple of the officers snickered. "Well done, mademoiselle," said the lieutenant. "Now get her on the horse, Wycliff. We're losing precious time."

Jeffrey reached down, and Anne had little choice but to allow him to pull her up on the horse. She sat sideways on the front of the saddle, with one of Jeffrey's arms circling her waist. Despite her dislike of being in such close proximity to Jeffrey, she realized that there was no better place to be if she wanted to help Lucien. Obviously Jeffrey had turned traitor and was leading the police to Renard. She was confused, though, about what they expected to find. Had Lucien planned a slave escape tonight, as well as murder?

As they moved stealthily into the cypress woods, Anne whispered, "So, Jeffrey, you decided to go for the reward?"

His arm tightened around her waist, and he bent his head close to her ear. "I couldn't have you."

"Is that what you wanted? My money?"

His hands splayed on her midsection, his thumb caressing, straying much too close to her breast. "I wanted more than that, but the money made the package perfect."

She pulled his hand away and hung on to the saddle pommel for support. "I thought you were a champion of the cause. I thought you were on Renard's side."

"Not after he bed you."

Anne made a disparaging noise through her teeth. "I don't know where you got that ridiculous idea."

"My suspicions were confirmed tonight."

"What do you mean?"

"Never mind. Soon all my suspicions will be confirmed, and you'll regret playing me for a fool, Anne. Too bad you're so full of integrity, you can't forgive a fellow for being a little too ambitious, for being too human for your highfalutin tastes."

Anne had no reply to this. He was right. She couldn't forgive him, especially now. She wondered if he knew that Renard and Lucien were the same man. Somehow Jeffrey knew she'd made love with Renard, but had he also seen her leave the ball to meet Lucien in the garden? Had he seen her follow Lucien and Bodine across the sugarcane field? Had he put two and two together and come up with the truth?

"What suspicions are you hoping to confirm tonight, Jeffrey?" she ventured, trying to lead him into saying something revealing.

"You'll see," was his disappointing reply. "Now be quiet. We're getting close to the spot."

They were on the edge of the bayou directly behind the slave cabins. No one had lighted a lantern. The only light was the dim moonshine reflected off the still, gray-green waters of the bayou. Just minutes before, Lucien and Armande had headed this way. Where were they now? she wondered, her stomach knotted with tension. And what made Jeffrey think she'd keep mum if Lucien showed up? She was going to scream the minute she saw him. She was going to warn him to ride away, even if it meant she'd go to jail herself.

As if they'd planned their strategy beforehand, without discussion the men spread out, hiding in the shadows of the huge, moss-draped trees. And they waited. For what, exactly? Oh, how she wished Lucien had confided in her, instead of keeping quiet in an attempt to protect her!

Everyone, even the horses, was perfectly still. Anne stayed as still as the others, hoping to lull them into a false security. In the silence, the sounds of the forest were magnified. There were the deep, rhythmic croak of the bullfrog, the singing of the crickets, the constant buzz of insects, and the gentle lap of water against the shore. The air was warm and dank, smelling sweet.

Suddenly there was movement down-shore. The lieutenant raised a hand and held it in the air, poised like a snake about to strike. A horse appeared out of the lush foliage on the opposite side of the narrow bayou—a black horse. Tempest?

Anne opened her mouth to shout a warning, but Jeffrey clamped a hand over the lower half of her face and held her hard against his chest. She struggled, but his grip was strong—much stronger than she expected. The rider on the horse came into view. It was Renard!

The lieutenant's hand came down in a swift motion: the signal to give chase. The horses were spurred forward into the shallow waters of the bayou. Anne saw Renard immediately turn Tempest back into the cover of the woods, but with four lawmen chasing him, she didn't have much hope that he could outrun them. Having to maneuver through the tangled jungle of the cypress woods would work more to the benefit of the police. It could slow Renard down just enough that they might be able to surround him.

The posse of police had splashed across the bayou and disappeared into the woods before Jeffrey removed his hand and urged his own horse forward to follow at a slower pace. Anne was startled by the first crack of pistol shots, her hear thudding against her ribs. "We don't want to get too close to the action till the deed's done," Jeffrey told her, "but I do want to be there when they rope him in. I can't wait to see the look on his face!"

Anne could say nothing. Her throat ached with fear and frustration. At that moment she hated Jeffrey. If Lucien was killed, it would be his fault! She would have jumped down from the horse on the spot if she didn't want just as badly to follow the police. Although the air was warm, she was cold and shivering with dread. Feeling utterly hopeless, she closed her eyes and prayed to God that Lucien would escape.

They'd crossed the bayou and hadn't ridden far when they came upon the very scene Anne had been desperately trying to push out of her imagination for the past hour. Someone had lighted a couple of lanterns, the oil turned up high and burning brightly. All the policemen's faces she hadn't been able to see before were illuminated by yellow lantern-glow. They were off their horses, clustered in a tight circle, their heads tilted down. They were looking at something—or someone—on the ground. The lieutenant was on his knees.

Anne's deepest fears rose to the surface, finding voice in a long, shrill "Nooo!" She leaped from the horse, stumbled in the slimy undergrowth, struggled to her feet, and ran to the group of men. She yanked the arm of one policeman, pulling him aside so she could see past him, so she could see what they'd done to her beloved Lucien ...

Anne blinked through tears as she looked down t the prone body, all in black from head to toe.

Her head felt light, her vision was fuzzy. She couldn't focus, she couldn't even breathe.

"He's still alive," she heard the lieutenant say, and her hammering heart pounded even harder in relief. "Took a nasty blow to his head, though. Must have hit that low branch there." He made a vague gesture upward. All Anne registered was that he hadn't been shot. A bump on the head seemed less serious.

"Take his mask off," Jeffrey said eagerly. He'd come up behind Anne and stood very close. The others murmured their excited agreement. Anne felt ready to faint. Once they removed the mask, Lucien would be exposed as the Fox and all hope would be gone. They'd take him away and she'd never see him again. Her knees were shaking, ready to buckle. She watched as one officer lifted Lucien's head while the lieutenant untied the mask and lifted it off. There was a collective gasp.

"My God," said one of the men. "Charles Bodine! Who'd have thought?"

Anne's knees gave way and Jeffrey caught her and held her up with an arm around her waist.

"His reputation was just a cover, I suppose," said the lieutenant. "Lord, if I hadn't seen it with my own eyes, I'd never believe it. You're all witnesses, men. Bodine'll be put away for a long time on our testimony, and from this night forward, Renard is history. He's given us a good run for our money, but it's over. Thank God, it's over."

Anne couldn't have put it better. It was over! She was flooded with relief, delirious with happiness. Her strength returned and she pulled away from Jeffrey. She watched as Bodine was put on the black horse she now suspected was not Tempest at all. She listened as the cheerful men congratulated themselves for having finally outfoxed the Fox.

She should have realized before that the man in black couldn't have been Lucien. Bodine was the same height, but was heavier, not as well-proportioned. She'd been too upset, too worried to think clearly. She also realized that Lucien must be close by, because he had obviously been the one to cleverly orchestrate this deception.

Caught up in her own thoughts, Anne had forgotten Jeffrey. Now, as the police mounted their horses, she looked around and could just make out his shadowy form as he leaned against a tree trunk. His eyes were mere slits in a blur of gray-white, but she felt the palpable hatred emanating from them. A shiver coursed down her spine.

She turned away and found the lieutenant peering curiously down at her from his horse. "Just one question, Miss Weston," he said. "Why did you cry out earlier? Are you somehow connected to this outlaw? One of his admirers, perhaps?" He gestured toward Bodine, the large man looking pathetic and harmless with his arms dangling over the horse's flanks.

"Connected to that man? No," said Anne, the ring of truth in her voice too strong to disbelieve.

The commander nodded. "I see. Then maybe you screamed because you were afraid we'd mistakenly injured your swain?"

"My . . . swain?"

He grinned. "The cad whose eye you blackened. I guess you care about him more than you want to admit, eh?"

Anne made a convincing show of maidenly consciousness, bowing her head, averting her eyes. The lieutenant chuckled, then looked over toward Jeffrey. "You'll see she gets home?"

"Of course," said Jeffrey.

Anne's heart sank as the lieutenant turned and led his small posse out of the woods, headed for town. She wanted to call out to him, to beg him not to leave her with the monster Jeffrey had become, but she knew Jeffrey wouldn't hesitate to implicate her if he was cornered. He was angrier with her than ever, and she thought she knew why ...

Slowly she turned and confronted him. One lantern had been left behind, and Jeffrey moved into its circle of light, standing perhaps three feet away from her. The cosmetics he wore were streaked by sweat, the blacks and whites running together for a ghoulish effect.

"You know, don't you?" she said.

"That they got the wrong man?"

Anne stuck out her chin defiantly. "Whether they got the wrong man is a matter of opinion. Bodine is a vicious rapist and murderer. He has deserved to be behind bars for a long time."

Jeffrey crossed his arms and took a step closer, standing straddle-legged, belligerent. "But we both know he'll be incarcerated for crimes he didn't commit."

Anne didn't want Jeffrey to recognize how much he frightened her, but she took an involuntary step backward. "Renard's crimes were justified. I wouldn't even call them crimes. As I recall, you didn't used to, either."

He uncrossed his arms, dropping his hands to his sides. "But I hate the man now. He's still a hero. In your eyes, he's an idol to worship. In fac you've given him the biggest sacrifice of all—yourself. And now he's getting off scot-free." Jeffrey threw back his head and laughed mirthlessly. "Dandy Delacroix is the Fox! He's a clever one, all right. No one suspected, and now no one will ever know. It's a closed case. Bodine is as good as locked up for life."

"You're not going to tell anyone?"

"Who would believe me with all this theatrical evidence?"

"You've got the reward money, and the story. That ought to satisfy you."

He took one step closer. "But I'm not satisfied. Not yet. Sure, I've got a story, but no one will admire me for snitching on Renard. The police will be lauded and admired because they've been against Renard all along. But I'll be seen as a turncoat. I helped capture a man whose life I just saved two weeks ago. Do you comprehend my dilemma? Do you see the problem with my credibility from now on? Do you see that my integrity will be in constant question?"

"And rightly so," Anne couldn't help saying.

"Yes, I'll have to take my reward money and start fresh somewhere else—climb up from the bottom of the heap. But I'll do it."

"Then you should be satisfied."

"No, Anne. No, I won't be satisfied till I have one last thing. The thing that Renard had—the thing that Delacroix had, too—the thing I covet most of all. I want *you*."

"I told you, Jeffrey. I don't love you. I don't even—"

He laughed, the sound harsh and cold. "I 'n't want your love." He suddenly sprang forward, grasping her arms, his fingers biting painfully into her flesh. Anne was frozen with fear. "I just want this." Then he bent his head and pressed his mouth cruelly down on hers.

Chapter 21

S he had clamped her lips tightly together, but with his tongue and teeth, Jeffrey forced them apart, then plundered her mouth greedily. Anne thought she was going to be sick. Jeffrey's large hands pressed her arms to her sides so she couldn't scratch his eyes out as she dearly wanted to. Instead she twisted her head from side to side until he could no longer maintain his disgusting invasion of her mouth. He cursed and swung her around, pinning her against a tree trunk.

"We've done enough kissing anyway, my little angel," he rasped, his hot breath fanning her face. "I want some of the stuff you gave Delacroix in the garden. Or should I say Renard?" He laughed. "Do you like men in costume, Anne? Here's your chance to prove it!"

He yanked her arms behind her, making her cry out with pain. He held her wrists with one hand. With his other hand he grabbed her breast and squeezed painfully hard. Desperate and furious, she swiftly hiked her right knee up and caught him forcefully in the crotch. He yelped like a dog, but he didn't let go. Face contorted with rage, he grabbed the front of Anne's gown and ripped it, exposing her breasts to his lecherous gaze.

Anne squeezed her eyes shut. She prayed fervently for Lucien to rescue her, as he had in the alley. Where was he now, when she needed him more than ever? Jeffrey was like a man possessed. She was afraid of more than rape; she was afraid he might end up killing her . . .

There was a "whooshing" sound and a thud, like a large object falling. Then Jeffrey was literally yanked away from her. Anne opened her eyes. Lucien, dressed as Renard but without a mask, was holding Jeffrey up by the points of his collar against the trunk of another tree. This position made breathing impossible for Jeffrey, and even in the yellow glow of lantern light and through the runny coating of cosmetics, his face shone bright red.

Lucien's expression showed barely contained fury. "I ought to kill you, you bastard!"

Jeffrey clawed ineffectually at Lucien's forearms and made a choking sound.

"Oh, you don't want to die, do you? Well, the lady didn't want the attentions you forced on her, either." Lucien made a sound of disgust. "You're no better than Bodine."

Clutching the torn material of her gown to cover her breasts, Anne watched as Jeffrey's color changed from a flushed red to a deathly pallor. His eyelids fluttered. "My God, let him go, Lucien," she whispered. "His lips are turning blue! You're killing him!"

"No, he's just getting ready to pass out," said Lucien grimly. "But I'll put him down before that happens because I want him fully conscious to hear what I have to say. What about it, Wycliff? Are you ready to listen?"

Bug-eyed, Jeffrey nodded. Lucien released him, and Jeffrey slumped against the tree, rubbing his neck, taking in huge, noisy gulps of air. Lucie stood over him, watching scornfully. "I want you out of New Orleans. No ... I want you out of the state."

"Gladly," said Jeffrey in a raspy whisper, pushing up from his slouched position. "I'll be gone by tomorrow night. I want nothing more to do with you, or *her*."

"Watch what you say," warned Lucien in an ominous tone. "If you do or say anything that hurts Anne, or her reputation, I'll kill you. If you disregard this advice, and turn tail and run before I learn of your treachery, I'll hunt you down. Do you understand, Wycliff?"

Glaring at Lucien, rubbing his injured throat, Jeffrey reluctantly nodded again. With one last sulky glare at Anne, he staggered to his horse, mounted, and rode away toward town.

Instantly Anne was in Lucien's arms. With her face pressed against his chest, she said in a muffled voice, "Where did *you* come from?"

He took her by the shoulders and held her at arm's length, looking lovingly into her face. He inclined his head slightly to the side and tilted his chin, indicating the tree. "From up there."

"Were you there all along?" she asked, incredulous.

"All along."

"You saw the police, everything that happened?"

"Everything."

Anne knitted her brows. "What took you so long to get down here? You could see what Jeffrey was leading up to."

"Sweet Anne," said Lucien with a sigh, an apologetic smile curving his lips, "I'm only human. I was in the uppermost branches. I dared not start ʼown till the posse left, and I dared not come down at a breakneck pace. If Jeffrey heard me, I might have been shot like some poor helpless tree possum."

Anne's eyes widened. "Jeffrey had a pistol?"

"Strapped to his right thigh."

"Why didn't he use it just now?"

"I took it away when I had him against the tree. I've got it in my back pocket."

"Thank God!" said Anne.

"Yes, and thank God you didn't get yourself killed this time. You must have a guardian angel, Anne, whose sole job through eternity is to save you from your own foolishness. *How* did you follow me tonight? After we parted in the garden, I watched you go inside the house. How did you know something was afoot?"

Anne opened her mouth, ready to defend herself, but Lucien stopped her with a forefinger touched lightly to her lips. "Never mind. I know you've got a million excuses. I don't want to hear them. You'll charm me out of lecturing you, anyway."

Anne couldn't help smiling, though the corners of her mouth trembled a little at the effort. It seemed like years since she'd smiled. "You're a wonderful, incredible man, Lucien Delacroix."

He arched a brow. "Just a man? Not a hero? Not an idol, as Wycliff suggested?"

Anne reached up and tenderly caressed his jaw. "You'll always be my hero."

He looked away for a minute, tucking a loose strand of hair behind her ear. "Even without the mask and the daring rescues?"

Anne sensed his vulnerability, and it made her love him all the more. "Oh, Lucien, do you thin' Renard is all I love about you?"

His gaze locked with hers again. "The thought has crossed my mind."

"Then you're a fool!" she scolded him, her eyes brimming with tears. "Don't you know that—against my will!—I fell in love with Delacroix, too?"

Lucien grinned sheepishly. "He's a scoundrel."

"I know," she admitted, smiling back with glistening eyes. "But, mixed together, your diverse personalities make a very attractive man."

"An imperfect man," he amended soberly.

"An imperfect man who is perfect for me," corrected Anne. She trailed her hands along his shoulders, admiring their width.

"Then it wasn't, as that villain Wycliff suggested, a *sacrifice* you gave me that night at the cabin?" Lucien said in a low voice.

Anne's eyes darted to his. She giggled involuntarily. "Heavens, no! I should think *that* was obvious!"

"Or in the carriage, either?"

She smiled seductively. "I sacrificed a *little* comfort, but I was well-recompensed in other ways."

He laughed and caught her in his arms again. Then he pulled back, took her face gently between his hands, and lowered his lips to hers. Sweet, tender passion flowed between them. Anne's heart raced, and her knees felt as weak as water. She was always shaken to her toes by Lucien's kisses, but tonight she felt a difference. There was a sort of reverence about the way he was holding her. She felt treasured, adored . . . loved?

They pulled apart. Lucien's gaze roamed her face, her hair, the substantial amount of white bosom showing above her torn gown. With his thumb he wiped away a tear that had fallen from Anne's eyes when she'd squeezed them shut for his kiss. Finally his gaze lifted to meet hers. "Sweet Anne, my naughty angel ... how I love you."

Anne's heart soared like a bird just freed from a gilded cage. She had wanted to hear those words for so long! Now she knew. He loved her. He loved her! She pressed her face against his chest and smiled, the rest of her happy tears spilling out. Lucien simply held her, rocking her back and forth.

That was how Armande found them, the angel and the outlaw, hugging each other in the midst of the cypress woods. He was leading Lucien's horse. Lucien looked up, surprised.

"Armande, I thought we were meeting at the split willow tree. Is something wrong?"

"*Oui, mon ami.*" His eyes shifted to Anne. "There is word from Katherine. Anne must not go home."

She stiffened in Lucien's arms. "What is it, Armande? Is it Uncle Reggie? Is he worse?"

Armand nodded gravely. "*Oui.* He has the yellow fever."

Anne pressed her hand against her mouth, too stunned, too upset to speak. Reggie with yellow fever? She knew how bad it could be. She knew how many people died of that dreaded disease. She started shaking. It was too much to bear! Just when she thought all the people she loved were safe, this had to happen! Lucien tightened his arms around her, steadying her.

"You'll go, Armande?" said Lucien.

"Of course. Katherine has specifically asked me to come. What will you do with Anne? Where will you take her?"

"To the cabin tonight. Tomorrow, to Bocage."

Armande hesitated. A dozen obstacles to

course were probably tumbling through his brain. He mentioned the first one that came to mind. "Will your parents be there?"

"Yes," said Lucien. "And I want them to be there. Early tomorrow, they are returning to Bocage for a few days to plan a betrothal party for Renee."

Even in her present state of shock, Anne wondered at Lucien's reasoning. How would Lucien explain her to his parents?

"Good luck, Armande," said Lucien. "Send Katherine my love."

"And mine," said Anne weakly. "To both of them."

Armande nodded, then rode off. Lucien put his arm around Anne's waist and led her to the horse. It felt good to be able to lean on him, to draw comfort from his closeness. Her happiness had been dulled by the distressing news of Reggie's illness, but she would take solace in Lucien's arms tonight and pray for better news on the morrow.

When they got to the cabin, Anne was overwhelmed with memories of the night they'd spent together there two weeks before. So much had happened since then. She watched Lucien light candles, the room taking on a soft, seductive glow. He looked so handsome in his simple black clothes. Was it possible that this man—this incredible man—really loved her?

Lucien turned and saw Anne watching him. She looked vulnerable in her torn, dirty angel's costume, the wings twisted, the halo bent in two. But it was the question in her eyes that wrung his heart with compassion. He had withheld his confession of love from her for so long—long after 'd expressed her own devotion and commit-

ment to him. But he hadn't been completely sure
of his feelings till tonight. He hadn't been able to
make a commitment before tonight, either—before
Renard was put to rest forever. And now Anne
had to be convinced that she was not just a passing fancy.

"Come here, Anne," he said, opening his arms
to her. She came, nestling against his chest like a
lost kitten.

He took off her halo, smoothing her golden hair
with his hand. "You must be tired, *cher*."

"I am, a little," she admitted, not moving.

"But first you need a bath, eh?"

She lifted her head and looked at him inquir-
ingly. "Here?"

He chuckled. "But of course. Everything we
need is here." He took her hand and led her to a
chair. "Sit and rest while I prepare your water, mademoiselle," he teased, making a gallant bow.

Anne looked embarrassed. "But, Lucien—"

He lifted an admonishing finger. "No buts,
Anne. I want to do this."

She closed her mouth and sat back, a small
smile tilting her lips. Lucien dragged a large tin
tub out of the corner of the room, then lighted a
fire in the hearth and heated water he brought in
pails from a large barrel of rainwater outside. As
soon as he had enough hot water, he doused the
fire to keep the cabin cool. He produced a bar of
soap from the pantry cupboard and a squat, three-
inch candle. Anne wondered what he was going to
do with the small candle, especially when he went
outside and returned with a large magnolia blos-
som.

As Anne watched, Lucien nestled the candl
quite securely in the deep petals of the blosso
lighted the candle, then set the decoration afloa

the tub full of warm water. He tossed in the soap, too, and instantly a flowery scent drifted on the air in steamy wisps.

"Lucien," she whispered wonderingly. "This is so romantic."

"Another side to me you didn't know about, eh, *cher?*" he teased.

"It might take me a while to get to know who you really are," she admitted. "But I think I'll like the process."

Lucien caught the slight tentativeness in her voice. He enjoyed the idea of maintaining a little mystery in their relationship. Surprises could be very arousing. "I hope so," he returned, moving toward her. "Now let's get those clothes off, Anne."

Her eyes got as big as saucers. He was sure she was expecting a full-blown seduction, but she was in for another surprise. Slowly, carefully he undressed her. As each piece of clothing came off, he worshipped her with his eyes. He loved how her skin glowed with awareness of his nearness, the way goosebumps rose on her arms, and the way her nipples puckered and hardened with desire. But he didn't touch her.

He helped her into the tub, then lathered her back, massaging the tight muscles till she slumped in the tub like a drooping flower—relaxed and rosy. He soaped his hands and slid them over the long length of her smooth legs. He even bathed her feet, kneading the arch of her foot till her eyes drifted shut with pleasure.

After the bath, he toweled her off with a cool sheet of soft muslin and put her to bed. With a light blanket tucked under her arms to hide her nakedness, she sat up in bed and brushed the tans out of her long, beautiful hair. Through sultry, half-closed eyes, Anne watched while he undressed and quickly bathed, too. Striding completely naked to the bed, suppressing his own arousal with much difficulty, he slid in beside her. He drew her into his embrace, their warm, clean bodies fitting together as if they'd always belonged in each other's arms. Anne's head rested just under his chin.

Several minutes passed while neither spoke. Then Anne said, "Lucien? Are you awake?"

"Yes," he answered. How could he sleep with her delicious body so close to his? But, with the ordeal she'd been through that day and the news of Reggie's illness, Lucien didn't want to press her into lovemaking.

"Can we talk a little? I can't sleep."

"If you want to. I thought we should perhaps postpone talking till the morning, when you're more rested."

She sat up, propping herself with a small, warm palm on his chest. Her breasts gleamed like alabaster in the candlelight. Despite his noble intentions, he felt himself tightening, hardening with arousal. Her eyes were luminous, glowing with love . . . for him. It was humbling. It was damned erotic.

"I'm not tired anymore," she said.

Hell, that was just what he didn't need to hear.

"I want you to tell me about yourself. I want you to tell me how you got started being Renard, and why. There's more to it than your abolitionist beliefs. I think there's a more personal reason why you embraced the cause with so much passion."

Lucien's ardor cooled—for the moment. But just knowing she already understood him so well knew so much about him intuitively, gave him an other reason to love her. His boyhood experier when he was forced to beat his friend Roy was a serious, painful subject, but he wanted Anne to know what had happened. He wanted to share another part of himself with her, a part he'd shared with few others. And certainly with no other woman.

He told her. She listened with grave, sad eyes. She felt his remembered pain and shared his continued sense of injustice.

Nestled against his chest again, she asked, "What will you do now, Lucien? I know you will still want to help the cause in some way."

He hadn't planned to speak so soon about the future. But he had plans, all right. Plans that included Anne. Was now the time? he wondered. Was now the time to ask her?

She rose again, propping an elbow on the bed, cupping her chin in her hand. She looked adorable, desirable. Her breasts pressed against his side, the hard nipples tantalizing his sensitized skin. She lifted a hand and languorously drifted her fingers through the soft swirls of hair on his chest.

"Anne, if you keep this up I'm going to have to stop being noble and make love to you."

She smiled tenderly. "Who asked you to be noble?"

"You aren't too tired, too upset . . . ?"

"You're the best medicine for anything that ails me," she said. "I love you."

Lucien sighed and caught her hand, lifting it to his lips. He kissed the palm and was thrilled to hear her gasp with pleasure. He looked up into her starry blue eyes. "Anne, may I have your hand—"

She grinned. "You have it already."

"—in marriage, *cher.* May I have your hand in marriage?"

Her smile fell away. "Marriage? Do ... do you mean it, Lucien?"

"More than anything I've ever said in my life," he assured her ardently. "But do you think you'll like Canada?"

She blinked. "Canada?"

He grinned. "Is there an echo in here?"

"You want to live in Canada? With me?"

"I want you for my wife, Anne, wherever we decide to live."

For a long, agonizing moment, she didn't reply. She simply looked at him as if she didn't believe him. She searched his eyes, and he felt her intense examination at the very core of his soul. His feelings were laid bare for her to see, to believe. Finally she did believe. But how could any mortal man hide a love so strong?

Vivid joy lighted her face like a hundred candles. "There is nothing I would rather be than your wife, Lucien," she said with sweet fervor. Then she kissed him, and everything was forgotten in the ecstasy of Anne's arms. Sweet, sweet Anne.

Katherine had never spent a worse night. She'd had grief in her life—she'd lost three husbands and a child—but she'd never watched someone go through the hideous stages of yellow fever firsthand. And because it was her beloved Reggie suffering so much, it was killing her, too.

By the time Armande arrived late that night, Reggie's skin was yellow. He twitched and moved fitfully under the single layer of sheeting with which Katherine had covered him, moaning and calling out two names: Anne and Katherine.

Katherine thought her heart would break. She spoke soothingly to him, bathing his forehead a wetting his parched lips with cool water. Armande mixed up some sleeping herbs that would help him rest. He was convinced that the most important thing they could do to help Reggie ride out the devastating disease was to conserve his strength through rest, and to keep his temperature down. Katherine believed him and trusted him implicitly.

Reggie had been resting more quietly that morning, though he was still burning up with fever. Armande was dozing in a wing chair by the window, his chin resting on his hand. Even before coming to the house, he'd had quite a night. Between ministering to Reggie, he'd told Katherine everything that had happened with Bodine and the police, and about Anne's appearance on the scene.

Katherine clucked her tongue over her niece's antics, but wasn't surprised. She looked forward to hearing the whole story later, in detail, when Reggie was well. Reggie would have to be told everything sooner or later, too, including Katherine's connection to Renard.

Katherine stood over Reggie, watching him sleep. She was encouraged by his continued restfulness after bouts of vomiting and bleeding had passed. Armande's sleeping herbs must have done the trick.

When Armande awoke and checked Reggie again, Katherine said, "I wish I could do something to stop this. Lord, I feel so helpless!"

Armande laid his hand on Katherine's shoulder. "You're doing everything humanly possible. He couldn't have a better nurse. I'm quite sure, too, that if he'd had a choice, he would have chosen you to take care of him. And he'd have done the same for you."

"Yes, I know he would have." Katherine's vision blurred with tears. "I just want him to live, Armande."

"And if he does, will you tell him?"

"Tell him what?"

"That you love him."

Katherine felt a tear roll down her cheek and drip off the end of her nose. She didn't care. "Yes, I'll tell him. I just pray he doesn't leave this earth before I get the chance."

Armande squeezed her hand, but said nothing. Then he moved to the dressing table where he'd neatly sorted out his herbs, and started mixing another potion.

Katherine appreciated Armande's compassion. Then she remembered, rather shamefully, that Armande had his own troubles, his own family worries. She looked over her shoulder at Armande's straight, broad back. No one would guess that he was suffering, but he had to be. They now knew for sure that Christian was the one who'd been leaking information to Jeffrey. Lucien had suspected the troubled young man of dealing with Jeffrey to get money to support his opium habit. He'd tested this theory by telling him, and only him, last night's rendezvous point.

The fact that Jeffrey knew exactly where to take the police was proof that Christian was the informant. Though he acted as if nothing was bothering him, Katherine knew that Armande had to be upset about this development. They'd trusted Christian and taken him into the organization to help the young man find a positive direction in life.

"Armande?" she said.

"*Oui?*" He turned and looked at her. Sensitive

his situation now, she could see the pain in Armande's hazel eyes.

"I'm sorry about Christian."

A flash of fresh anguish showed on his handsome face. For a minute she was sorry she'd expressed her sympathy, but then Armande said, "*Merci*, Katherine. I appreciate your interest. I'm grateful to you for not judging him."

"What can you do now to help him?"

Armande sighed and turned back to his work. "I would like to get him away from here, away from the caste system that belittles him in his own eyes, away from a society that makes him turn to pipe dreams for escape from prejudice."

Armande finished mixing and turned around, folding his long arms over his chest. "Lucien and I have been talking. We are thinking about going to Canada. He will talk to Anne about it first, of course, and see if she agrees to such a move. But I think she will see the potential of starting fresh somewhere. I hope to persuade Christian to go with us."

Katherine's tired face lighted up, her interest piqued. She laid one hand protectively on Reggie's chest, the rise and fall of his breathing reassuring to her. "Tell me about Canada, Armande. I've been all over the world, but never there. Tell me everything you know."

Chapter 22

Bocage meant "shady retreat." Now that Anne was seeing it for herself, she thought the name perfectly suited to the beautiful plantation. Behind a curving line of ancient oak trees, the house definitely appeared to be a place of quiet withdrawal.

She and Lucien rode up the front drive in his carriage, both of them dressed suitably for a formal visit to his family. He had ridden into town early that morning, inquired about Reggie, and returned to the cabin with clothes for them both. Anne was wearing a walking dress of plum-colored satin with fancy trimming.

Lucien had even brought Anne's abigail, Sarah, who sat with them now in the carriage. He seemed determined to keep up appearances for the sake of Anne's reputation. Her reputation was also the reason that they were staying at Bocage instead of his apartments at the St. Charles Hotel. Even though Anne had given up thinking of her reputation days ago, she thought his gallant concern was quite sweet. Reggie would appreciate it.

Despite the fine day, the bright sun, the chirping of birds, and the general tranquility of her surroundings, Anne's stomach churned with nervousness. She was meeting Lucien's family for the first time, and she had a pretty good idea what they thought of British people—which was much the same as they thought of Americans. They considered them as coming from an inferior genealogy.

Last night had been bliss, but today reality reared its ugly head. Anne had to face the fact that Reggie had the yellow fever and might die, that she was banned from the house, not even allowed to see him, and, finally, that she was going to have to stay at Bocage till it was considered safe to return to Prytania Street. These were all depressing facts.

The fact that Lucien had told her he loved her, however, made everything easier to bear. She was deliriously happy in the knowledge that they'd be sharing a future together. They had lain awake last night for hours after their lovemaking, discussing their move to Canada, his relationship with his family, and many other things they'd not had the time or freedom to discuss before. She knew he was dreading this final good-bye to Bocage, to his family, to his father in particular. There were painful things that needed to be said after years of silence.

The carriage stopped directly in front of the house, and Lucien stepped out first, turning and extending his hand to Anne with an encouraging smile. She tried to smile back, stepped out, then waited with downcast eyes while he helped Sarah alight, too. Their unexpected arrival must have made quite a stir inside, because several of Lucien's family were congregating at the front door. Perhaps they'd been sitting together eating a late lunch.

Because of Sarah's presence in the carriage, Lucien had kept their conversation general throughout the short journey to Bocage. Sarah was probably dumbfounded by her mistress's sudden intimacy with the likes of Dandy Delacroix, but Anne certainly couldn't explain.

Looking up at the long gallery as the Delacroixs filed out and lined up to stare, Anne could well imagine the astonishment of Lucien's family, too. She and Lucien had certainly shown no preference for each other, or even a particular friendship, in public.

Lucien took Anne's arm and carefully escorted her, in the Dandy's usual languishing pace, up the steps to the gallery, his cane swinging on his outside elbow. Standing at the forefront of this imposing group of raven-haired, dark-eyed, astonishingly attractive people, was the *paterfamilias*—Lucien's father.

Tall, slim, and silver-haired, Monsieur Delacroix was an older version of Lucien. He was very handsome, but his expression was grim and unyielding. He did not return Anne's tentative smile. "Père," greeted Lucien, tipping his hat.

His father's mouth turned down in a moue of distaste. "*Bonjour*, Lucien. To what do we owe this rare visit? What brings you to Bocage?"

"To introduce you to my fiancee, of course."

"This is so sudden, Lucien!" said his mother.

"*Oui*," said Lucien, his expression softening. He bent and kissed her cheek. "I know it is sudden. I just discovered myself that I was in love with Mademoiselle Weston." He turned to Anne with a charming, insouciant smile. "How do the Americans say it? It has been a whirlwind romance, *oui*?" Then he turned back to his mother. "Maman, I trust you will show Anne the meaning of a true Creole welcome."

"She's staying here?" She cast Anne a fleeting, uncertain smile. "It's not that I'm displeased, *tu comprend?* But, Lucien, this is not the customary way to conduct a betrothal!"

"There are unusual circumstances. Anne's uncle—her guardian—has come down with yellow fever."

Lucien's sisters gasped, looking fearful. His mother appeared concerned and sympathetic. Anne found herself warming to the pretty Creole woman. Lucien must have inherited his compassionate nature from her.

"Naturally Anne can't return to the house until he's quite recovered."

"Of course not," said his mother, taking Anne's hand and squeezing it. "This is difficult for you, *n'est-ce pas?* I think you love your uncle very much."

Anne felt her eyes smart with the beginning of tears. Sincere sympathy was always her undoing. "Yes, Madame Delacroix, I do."

She squeezed Anne's hand again. *"Pauvre fille."*

Monsieur Delacroix spoke up, the sudden insertion of his deep voice into the conversation startling Anne. "Who is your uncle, Miss Weston? Where does he live?"

"My uncle is Reginald Weston, sir, and we live at my aunt's house on Prytania Street."

She saw his brows rise at the mention of Prytania Street, part of the American District of town. In fact, his brows had begun to rise the minute she started speaking. Her accent was obviously British.

"Katherine Grimms is my aunt," she added. She liked Lucien's mother, but she had doubts about being able to rustle up some affection for his father. And if he was going to disapprove of her, he might as well have all the damaging details. Everyone knew Katherine was anti-slavery.

They were all staring at her, disbelief and confusion written on their faces. Lucien's brother, Etienne, looked especially incredulous and disapproving. Anne had no doubt Etienne would one day fill his father's shoes very well as master of Bocage. Much better than Lucien could ever do, or would ever want to do.

Standing there was becoming rather awkward. Finally Lucien spoke up. "*Mon Dieu*, are we going to remain on the porch all day?" he drawled, his eyelids drooping disdainfully. "Surely, Maman, we can offer my bride-to-be a little refreshment? Perhaps a mint julep"—he got a wicked gleam in his eye—"or a good strong cup of English tea?"

This comment recalled his mother to the duty of Southern hospitality. Anne was treated very nicely for the next hour, plied with refreshments. Lucien's mother and sisters admired her gown, and even Etienne spoke a polite though brief word to her. Then she was shown to her room and left to rest till dinner.

Sarah was downstairs in the kitchen, and Anne was alone in the beautifully furnished bedchamber. She immediately began to miss Lucien. Without his supportive presence, she worried herself sick over Reggie. She missed Reggie dreadfully, too, and Aunt Katherine. She missed her *family*.

Anne moved to the window and looked out over the closely scythed lawns, the lush foliage, and handsome buildings that were all part of Bocage. Despite its beauty, she understood Lucien's alienation from this place. He'd been raised here, but he'd never really belonged, never felt at home.

She could never feel at home here, either. She and Lucien were alike in this. They could never be part of a racist society. Someday slavery would be abolished, but racism would probably persist for decades. In the meantime Anne knew that she and Lucien would have to find a home somewhere else. In Canada. But first he must say good-bye.

Lucien paused outside the thick-paneled door of the library, his hand still on the cut-glass knob. The interview with his father had been just as painful as he'd anticipated. But it had been inevitable and necessary. His father must know exactly how he stood on important issues.

For Lucien, it had been a sort of purging, a cleansing. Actually making his father understand why he felt the way he did about certain things had been too much to hope for, of course, and not worth attempting. But by being totally honest with his father for the first time in his life, he could now start fresh—be his own man, make his own way.

He took a deep breath and strode down the hall. Taking the steps two at a time, he quickly ascended the stairs to the upper floor and Anne's temporary bedchamber. He didn't bother to knock but simply went inside, closing the door softly behind him.

Anne was standing at the window, looking out over the extensive grounds. She did not turn as he approached. He slid his arms around her waist, pulling her against his heart. Still she did not speak, only leaned her head against his chest and covered his hands with hers.

"I could have had all this someday, Anne, but I've told my father to bequeath it to Etienne. Do you think I should regret giving it up?"

"Do you regret it?"

"No. I have some wonderful childhood memories, but I can take them with me."

"Did you . . . settle things with your father?"

Lucien's voice became grim. "Yes. He's glad to see me go now that I've given him no hope of changing into the kind of man he admires."

"A man like himself, perhaps?"

He sighed. "Yes."

Anne turned in Lucien's arms, sliding her arms around his neck. "I'm sorry, Lucien. I'm sorry you have to leave your home like this. I'm sorry you and your father couldn't be closer. Your mother will be sad to see you go. She loves you very much."

Lucien smiled weakly. "That only makes it harder, Anne."

She reached up on tiptoe and kissed him. "I'll always be a support for you, Lucien. I'm your family now." She blushed prettily, averting her gaze to his vest, where she toyed with one of his buttons. "And there will be children."

He touched the underside of her chin with his finger, urging her to look up at him. He smiled down at her. "But first, *cher*, there must be lots of practicing." He lifted her and carried her to the bed.

"Good God, what's that stench?"

Half-dozing in the chair beside Reggie's bed, Katherine jumped up at the sound of that dear, querulous voice. Reggie's eyes were open, blinking against the small amount of sunshine peeking through the shuttered windows. After three days of uncertainty and fear, Katherine knew now that Reggie would live. She wanted to cry with happiness, but she laughed instead.

"It's either you or me, Reginald," she said.

He turned his face to her slowly, as if it still hurt a little. He squinted. "Where are my spectacles?"

Katherine picked up Reggie's spectacles from

the bedside table and carefully put them on him. He took a moment to focus, then said, "You look like hell, Katherine."

She laughed again. "I know. I finally combed my hair—I think it was yesterday—but I've had very little time to fuss over my appearance, you see. I've been taking care of you."

Reggie's brows lowered. He turned his head again, slowly, looking about the room as if he were trying to get his bearings. "This is my bedchamber, but where's James? And what are you doing in here? I recall I had a headache . . ." He glanced down, and Katherine would have given a hundred dollars to have his expression etched in ink to keep forever. "My God!" he croaked. "Where are my *clothes?*"

Katherine bit her lip to keep from laughing again and quickly covered him with a thin sheet. "Armande thought it best for you to remain uncovered. You were burning up with fever."

Mortified, his eyes averted, Reggie lifted a weak hand to tug distractedly on his mustache. "Who the hell is Armande?"

"Your doctor. And I've been your nurse. You've had the yellow fever. There's no need to be embarrassed by your nakedness—"

"My God!" he choked out again.

"—because I've only thought of you as a patient," she lied. "I tried to keep you as clean as possible—"

"May the saints preserve me!"

"—but I'm quite sure you'll want a bath. I know I do!"

At Reggie's startled look, Katherine stifled a giggle, saying, "Oh, don't worry. I don't plan to bathe you, or bathe *with* you. I'm convinced you don't have the strength just yet for either eventuality."

"B'gad!"

"Now that you're over the crisis, I'll call James to attend to your needs. Armande will be back shortly, too, and I know he'll want to examine you thoroughly. And I can send word to Anne that it's all right to come home. I know that will be good news to her. She's been worried sick about you."

"Where is Anne?" Reggie managed to bluster, still tugging rather violently on his mustache.

Katherine bustled about happily, tucking in his sheet, plumping his pillows. "She's at Bocage."

Reggie concentrated, still a little woozy. "That's Delacroix's plantation, isn't it?"

"The very same. You'll be happy to know she's going to marry him."

"Marry who, for heaven's sake?"

"Why, Delacroix, of course. You always liked him. But I daresay there are a few things we'll have to tell you before the wedding."

"The wedding? It's already planned? How long have I been sick, Katherine?"

"Three horrible days and nights." Katherine stopped bustling and stood over Reggie, pushing a long, lank strand of hair out of her eyes. She couldn't help it. She smiled like an idiot. "Oh, Reggie," she gushed, "I'm so glad you're alive!"

Reggie looked up at a disheveled woman with dark circles under eyes that were bright with tears. He'd never seen anyone more beautiful or desirable in his life. And there he lay, naked, weak, as little able to make love as a eunuch. But he had to tell her something, and he had to tell her now. "Katherine," he said. "I suspect that I owe you my life."

She shook her head, disclaiming any credit. *It was just like her,* he thought.

"And despite all you've done for me already, I have to ask you for one more favor."

"What, Reggie? Do you want a drink? Are you hungry?"

"No, my dear. I'm not hungry, I'm in love. With you, of all people."

"Reggie!"

"And the favor I'm asking is this . . . Will you do me the honor of making me husband number four?"

"You're still delirious!"

"No, I've never been more lucid in my life."

"Reggie!"

Reggie now seemed in grave danger of being mauled. Mauling and being mauled was something he looked forward to once he got his strength back, and once he was properly bathed and scented. But not now. He held up his hands, and with a loving look warned his bride-to-be, "Not without my bath first, Katherine. Please send for James."

With much enthusiasm, Katherine left the room to look for James. The sooner Reggie bathed, the sooner she could kiss that dear old face of his.

Epilogue

Anne sat in the tiny cabin on the top deck of the *River Belle* waiting for her husband. It was the best cabin on the boat, according to the captain. But even for the best, it was small and the furnishings simple. They were traveling economically, saving their money to build a house and start a logging business in Hamilton, a booming little town in southeast Ontario.

Anne loved the cabin because it was where she and Lucien would begin their honeymoon. At the last stop, Lucien had had the room filled with flowers picked from the local Tunica Hills: wild azalea, Indian pipe, cinnamon fern, and sunflowers. Anne was touched and thrilled by this romantic gesture and couldn't wait to show her husband just how much she loved him.

As she brushed her hair, she remembered the wedding. Or, she should say, the double wedding. Katherine and Reggie had tied the nuptial knot, too. It had been a simple affair in Aunt Katherine's drawing room, attended by a select few.

Lucien's mother and sisters had come to the wedding, but his father and Etienne had chosen not to attend. This had not surprised Lucien, and he had refused to let it spoil his happiness. He had said fond farewells to his mother and sisters, phil-

371

osophically resigned to the fact that he might never see them again.

Their special day was not marred by concern over Jeffrey, either. He had taken Lucien's threats seriously and left town the day after Bodine's arrest.

Katherine's house had been sold practically overnight to a rich American who had coveted the elegant mansion for years. He bought everything Katherine would sell, including most of the furniture and artwork. Many of the servants stayed on, too. The things Katherine took with her were the treasures she'd collected in her travels, family paintings, and mementoes of her three previous marriages.

Somehow in the shuffle, she'd left her cane behind. When Reggie had commented on this, she'd simply said, "Oh, I don't need it. I never did, you know."

Katherine and Reggie planned to open a school in Hamilton. Lucien intended to hire for his logging establishment many former slaves who had escaped to Canada, and Katherine knew a school in the area would be needed to educate their children. It would be open to the French, the Indians, the blacks, and whoever else showed up.

Armande was going to be the first physician in the primitive area, and Christian, recovering from the opium addiction and glad for a fresh start and the forgiveness of his friends, was going to assist him.

Having brushed her hair to glossy softness, Anne changed into the nightgown Aunt Katherine had given her as a wedding present. The nightgown was beautiful, made of white silk with puffed sleeves and a low decolletage. In fact, it was very similar to the angel costume she'd worn to the Bouviers' masquerade ball. As giddy as a schoolgirl, she arranged herself in an alluring pose on the bed and waited for Lucien.

When he returned, he had in one large, beautiful hand a bottle of wine and two goblets, and in the other hand a half-dozen candles. His eyes lighted up when he saw her. "My naughty angel," he said with satisfaction.

She eyed him complacently. Lucien Delacroix was a presence to be reckoned with. He was very handsome, very masculine in a finely tailored black suit, with an ivory brocade vest and white shirt. "My dashing outlaw," she replied.

"Not anymore, Anne," he said wryly, setting down the bottle and goblets, then filling a candelabra with the half-dozen candles. "Just plain Lucien."

"Just plain Lucien," she repeated, smiling. "What a contrast in terms. There's nothing plain about you, my dear husband."

He laughed, took off his neckcloth, then undid the first several buttons of his shirt, right down to the vee of his vest. Anne itched to thread her fingers through the dark swirls of hair that peeked from the open shirt. "I saw your aunt and uncle."

"Were they quarreling?"

"No. They were headed for their cabin." He waggled a brow. "The expressions on their faces suggested they were about to do some serious honeymooning."

"I'm so glad," said Anne. "I wish everyone as much happiness as we have, Lucien."

He began lighting the candles, making the room as bright as day. "That's a hard order to fill, Anne."

He turned to her, his dark, sultry eyes reflecting her own desire, then shrugged out of his jacket and unbuttoned his vest. Anne watched with avid interest. "Are you sure you won't miss the outlaw, Anne?" he taunted her.

She held out her arms and he came, sitting on the bed and pulling her against his chest. They kissed, the flame of passion flaring between them just as hotly as it always did. As their lips separated for an instant, she said breathlessly, "I won't miss him, but I was wondering, Lucien . . ."

"What were you wondering?"

She dropped her eyes, a sly smile curving her lips, a brazen finger tracing a line down his bare chest. "Sometimes when we're making love . . ."

"Yes?"

"And we've got nothing on but our smiles . . ."

He chuckled. "Yes?"

Her eyes lifted to his, playful sensuality reflected in their blue depths. "Could you . . . wear the mask?"